CODENAME LAZARUS

A. P. MARTIN

Copyright © 2017, 2021 A.P.Martin

The moral right of the author has been asserted.

Apart from any fair dealing for the purposes of research or private study, or criticism or review, as permitted under the Copyright, Designs and Patents Act 1988, this publication may only be reproduced, stored or transmitted, in any form or by any means, with the prior permission in writing of the publishers, or in the case of reprographic reproduction in accordance with the terms of licences issued by the Copyright Licensing Agency. Enquiries concerning reproduction outside those terms should be sent to the publishers.

This is a work of fiction. Names, characters, businesses, places, events and incidents are either the products of the author's imagination or used in a fictitious manner. Any resemblance to actual persons, living or dead, or actual events is purely coincidental.

This is an edited edition of Codename Lazarus: The Spy Who Came Back From The Dead published in 2017.

Cover design by Michael Moden (mickey19830@gmail.com.) Cover images courtesy of Shutterstock.

Publisher A.P.Martin 2017, 2021

Books by A.P.Martin

Spymaster Pym Series

Codename Lazarus
Spy Trap
Sacrifice of Spies (forthcoming)

Clavel and Snow Series

Sentence of Death
Death of an Asylum Seeker

Glossary

Abwehr – German Military Intelligence
Anschluss – the annexation of Austria into Nazi Germany 12th March 1938
Jüdische Kulturbund – the Jewish Cultural Federation, active 1933-1941. Closed by order of the Gestapo 11th September 1941.
Jüdische Nachrichtenblatt – Jewish Newsletter.
Landesgruppe Großbritannien – Nazi organisation in Britain.
Informationsheft – GB – Nazi manual to assist in the planned invasion of Britain in 1940.
Lebensraum – literally 'living space' – a concept which justified the Nazi's territorial expansion into Central and Eastern Europe.
Oberleutnant – First Lieutenant
Reichsmark – currency of Nazi Germany.
Reichsmarschall – the highest military rank in the German empire.
SA – Sturmabteilung – the original paramilitary arm of the Nazi party. Of little significance after 1939, by which time it had been overshadowed by the SS.
Schabzige Knöpfli – a kind of Swiss pasta or spätzle with spinach and cheese.
SD – Sicherheitsdienst – literally Security Service – led by Heydrich to monitor and act against any perceived threat to the Nazi party.

SS – Schutzstaffel – dominant Nazi paramilitary organisation during World War Two.
Torah – holy scriptures of the Jewish people.
Völkischer Beobachter – the daily newspaper of the Nazi Party.
Wehrmacht – the German Army.

SS Ranks and their equivalent.

Gruppenführer equivalent of Major General.
Hauptsturmführer equivalent of Captain.
Obersturmführer equivalent of Lieutenant.
Standartenführer equivalent of Colonel.
Sturmbannführer equivalent of Major.
Unterscharführer equivalent of Corporal.
Untersturmführer equivalent of Second Lieutenant.

CHAPTER ONE

CHAPTER TWO

CHAPTER THREE

CHAPTER FOUR

CHAPTER FIVE

CHAPTER SIX

CHAPTER SEVEN

CHAPTER EIGHT

CHAPTER NINE

CHAPTER TEN

CHAPTER ELEVEN

CHAPTER TWELVE

CHAPTER THIRTEEN

CHAPTER FOURTEEN

CHAPTER FIFTEEN

CHAPTER SIXTEEN

CHAPTER SEVENTEEN

CHAPTER EIGHTEEN

CHAPTER NINETEEN

CHAPTER TWENTY

CHAPTER TWENTY ONE

CHAPTER TWENTY TWO

CHAPTER TWENTY THREE

CHAPTER TWENTY FOUR

CHAPTER TWENTY FIVE

CHAPTER TWENTY SIX

CHAPTER TWENTY SEVEN

CHAPTER TWENTY EIGHT

CHAPTER TWENTY NINE

CHAPTER THIRTY

CHAPTER THIRTY ONE

CHAPTER THIRTY TWO

CHAPTER THIRTY THREE

CHAPTER THIRTY FOUR

CHAPTER THIRTY FIVE

CHAPTER THIRTY SIX

AUTHOR`S NOTE

CHAPTER ONE

Wednesday 1st February, 1939, Tunstall Chapel, Durham Castle, England.

The sound of the ancient Tunstall Organ's rendering of 'Jerusalem' almost drowned out the voices of the choir and sizeable congregation in Castle Chapel, the largest place of worship within Durham Castle. The dismal weather outside matched the sombre mood of those who had gathered to mark the loss of Dr John King in a hiking accident in Switzerland. Loss was indeed the correct term, for his body had yet to be recovered from its frozen resting place, high in the snow-covered Alps. King had been a successful and popular young History don at the University of Durham and many of the young faces in the congregation, deathly pale even in the warm glow of candlelight, belonged to those he had taught.

The Swiss authorities had determined that King had been the victim of an unfortunate accident while walking in the Bernese Oberland. The evidence afforded no room for doubt. A rock and snow fall, in a notoriously dangerous spot on the mountain path from the Gemmi Pass to Leukerbad, had swept King away down a deep and inaccessible ravine. Several of his possessions had been found scattered in the snow, close to where the avalanche had broken the safety fence. Analysis had proven that this bore traces of human blood of the same type as King.

Expert evidence had been submitted to the Swiss enquiry by Gerhardt Rösti, an experienced local mountain guide and Inspector Peter Graf of the Swiss National Security Service, both of whom had stated that the balance of probability was overwhelming that King had been the victim of a terrible misadventure. Further testimony had also confirmed that the Englishman, though young and fit, was relatively inexperienced in mountain conditions. Moreover, on the day of his death a freak snow storm had engulfed the area in which he was walking. Such conditions, Rösti had told the enquiry, would have challenged even the most capable of Alpinists.

As the music faded, King's father, a straight-backed veteran of the First World War, came forward to deliver the reading. His shoe heels clicked in perfect time as he walked briskly over the black and white tiles, laid out on the chapel floor like an oblique chess board. Perhaps it was fitting that, for the few seconds before he commenced, the only sound was the rain beating relentlessly against the stained-glass windows. As he began, in a confident voice conditioned by countless amateur dramatic performances, many in the congregation sensed something unusual about his tone. It seemed to reflect a defiant optimism, rather than the expected sense of loss and sorrow.

Positioned a little behind the family members, in one of the sixteenth century misericord seats, sat an alert looking, grey haired man in his mid-fifties. Without doubt, this mourner had been King's most important tutor and mentor during his curtailed academic career. Professor Bernard Pym's bright, intelligent eyes observed closely the two generations of the British-German Bernstein family who were sitting just in front of him. He was fully aware that John King had been instrumental in organising their escape from the anti-Semitic maw of Hitler's Third Reich. The parents, prematurely aged by the stress of their recent experience, and their son, David, longer established in Britain and proudly wearing the dress uniform of a serving police officer, sat erect and silent.

The Service of Remembrance was conducted in an understated way, of which Pym was certain King would have approved. As soon as the principal mourners had left the Chapel, the Professor discreetly viewed the floral tributes which had been placed on a large table to the side of the altar. These included a pretty bunch of snowdrops, collected by David Bernstein from some northern woods and accompanied by a hand written card from his sister, Rachel, who now lived and worked in America. Reading the signature on the card, the Professor smiled as he recalled how, back in 1933, John King's passion and persuasiveness had convinced him to accept his half Welsh, half German friend as a postgraduate student at Oxford University. Rachel had proved to be an excellent scholar and had gone on to obtain tenure at one of the universities in New York.

Looking further among the flowers, Pym was not surprised to see a number of bouquets with messages written in German. King had spent the last few months of his life participating in an academic exchange in Berlin, where he had made many new friends. The various floral tributes reflected both these and his longer standing friends in Heidelberg, where he had studied for eighteen months in the early 1930s. The Professor paused longer to look carefully at two individual arrangements which stood out from the rest. The first was a single red rose with the heartfelt message written in German: '*Goodbye my darling John. I will never forget you. All my love. Greta.*' The second, and perhaps the most unexpected message of all, read: *'Rest in Peace, John. You will always be my good and honourable friend. Erwin Kalz.'* Pym nodded in acknowledgement of the writer's discretion in not mentioning his rank. Arguably, for King to have received a message of condolence from a serving Major in the German *Abwehr* would have been in poor taste.

Moving out of the Chapel and into the grey half-light of a North East afternoon, Pym concluded that attending this service would not be the most difficult part of the business. *That will undoubtedly come tomorrow afternoon*, he reflected, *when I describe to John his own memorial service.*

CHAPTER TWO

Ten Months Earlier,

Wednesday 16th March, 1938, St John's Wood, London.

Despite the ever-lengthening shadows, the early evening sun still managed to shine gently across one corner of the green outfield of Lord's Cricket Ground. Professor Bernard Pym, wearing the off-duty don's classic uniform of tweed jacket and corduroy trousers, gazed thoughtfully through the window into the fading light. He had never regretted keeping the mansion flat in St John's Wood, inherited from an uncle who had died while on colonial service in India in 1921. It had served well, both as his preferred home during the cricket season and as a perfect pied à terre during his frequent study trips from Oxford, where he held a chair in German History.

As he responded to the telephone's insistent ring, fond visions of Hutton, Bradman and Hammond were displaced by the concierge's announcement that his guest had arrived. 'Show him right up, if you please, Mason,' Pym replied politely. The most discreet of knocks announced that Sir Hugh Sinclair, Chief of the British Secret Intelligence Service, with whom he had served for two years of the Great War on HMS *Renown*, had arrived. The Professor opened the door with a broad smile and both men shook hands with genuine affection. 'Quex,' Pym said, addressing the older man by his strange designation, 'it's good to see you. Come in and sit down.'

During their service together, Sinclair had been greatly impressed by the younger academic's grasp, both of naval strategy and of man management on-board a battle cruiser in wartime. They had remained close friends and colleagues and had together watched Hitler's rise to power with appalled fascination.

'Our latest intelligence says that Hitler has definitely made up his mind to annexe Austria, possibly as soon as this month,' advised Sinclair as he gratefully accepted both his first glass of a fine *Lafite* and a large slice of game pie.

'And, as a consequence, the devil's popularity at home is likely to soar,' added Pym with a heavy sigh. 'The reoccupation of the Rhineland was bad enough, but this is likely to whet his appetite for even more. Just how far will Chamberlain allow himself to be pushed? I'm increasingly concerned that if we want to make sure that Britain's interests are fully protected, we're going to have to act on our plan sooner rather than later.'

'Well,' Sinclair replied carefully, 'given the PM's obsession with sound finance, we certainly won't be able to rely on him to expand the SIS adequately. Even with Hitler on the march. Also, let's not forget my suspicion that the Service is not altogether watertight. I'm doing what I can to root out any bad apples, but it's a deuced slow and sensitive business. All things considered, if we wish to proceed with our plan, I think we have to give some serious thought to that 'under the counter' concept we discussed last month. Do you agree, Bernard?'

After a pause for thought, Pym replied decisively, 'We both know that Chamberlain is likely to deepen the policy of appeasement to Hitler. Also, we are agreed that this is based on a total misreading of the Führer's intentions and character. And we must not forget that the PM is desperate to avoid the cost of full rearmament, which a more realistic appraisal of Hitler must inevitably involve. So, yes, I think maybe we have to take our idea a stage further, otherwise it may soon be too late.'

Sinclair sat upright in his chair to emphasise his next point, 'The information MI5 is receiving regularly from Putlitz at the German Embassy is unequivocal – we must stand up to Hitler, otherwise we will face a Europe dominated by Fascism. I really don't understand the Government's reluctance to recognise the value of the information which our agents are continuing to supply.' Shaking his head in sad bewilderment, he asked, 'Do they really believe that these people simply make something up out of self-interest, if there's nothing genuine to report?'

'I'm afraid you're right,' agreed Pym sourly, 'Chamberlain has always been more prepared to take risks with defence than with finances. So, we develop our plan and I attempt to recruit a principal for our mission?'

'Yes. But remember, this is emphatically not an official operation. Your man must be made aware of that before he commits. How long do you think you'll need?'

'It's early days, Quex,' replied the ever-cautious Pym. 'But I do have a few initial ideas and, all being well, I think I could be ready to approach my target in a month or two.'

'That suggests you already have someone in mind, Bernard.'

Pym's face creased into a wistful smile, 'Indeed. You know, in many ways I wish I didn't, but I think I may have the perfect man for the job.'

CHAPTER THREE

Tuesday 17th May, 1938, The Universities Club, London.

The bas-relief of Sir Isaac Newton gazed down on John King as he bounded down the steps from the front door and across the entrance hall of the Oxford and Cambridge Universities Club. An Oxford man who had previously taken advantage of the club's facilities, King had a reasonable idea of its layout. Once past the doorman, he crossed the Staircase Hall and from there, took the main dogleg stairs two at a time towards the Committee Room and his scheduled appointment.

Since receiving the Professor's intriguing message, King had tried to guess the purpose of the meeting. After all, the world of academic history was sufficiently small to ensure that he and Pym met regularly at conferences. Moreover, the Professor, a long-standing member of the MCC, had already invited him to attend a day of that year's Lord's Test Match in five weeks' time. *But it wasn't just the urgency of the request that was odd*, King reflected. *That instruction not to mention it to any of my family, friends or colleagues was quite extraordinary.*

King's knock on the door was answered immediately by a warm invitation to 'Come in,' and he briskly entered the room. Having carefully placed his favourite pipe on the table, Pym rose to his feet, smiling broadly and with his hand outstretched in greeting. 'John! It's very good to see you again. How are you? Thanks for coming.' King immediately felt his hand taken in the still familiar paw-like grasp of the Professor, whose eyes twinkled with joy at the sight of one of his star students.

'I'm fine, sir. Thank you. And I must say you look in the pink. It was a bit of a surprise to receive your summons last week. I expected to see you again for our annual day at the cricket – we'd agreed the Saturday of the Second Test, hadn't we?'

A smile of regret passed briefly over the Professor's face, as if in his mind's eye he could see England taking on Australia, Bradman and all, at his beloved Lord's. 'That's right, John. But something rather urgent has come up. Anyway, do tell me how things are up in Durham. What are you working on at the moment?'

'All is good in Durham, thank you, sir. But I must say that I was intrigued by your instruction to keep our meeting under my hat.'

'Thank you for agreeing that, John,' replied Pym gravely. 'I know it may sound somewhat melodramatic, but it was an essential precaution. However, I interrupt…. Are you still interested in the Second Reich? I seem to remember an excellent piece you had on 'The Kaiser after Bismarck'; *The English Historical Review*, wasn't it?'

'Yes, it was and indeed I still have that major interest,' replied King with the undisguised enthusiasm of a committed scholar. 'But hang it all, sir, and with all respect, I doubt you've asked me here like this to offer me a cup of tea and discuss my research.' King had good reason to put things so bluntly. He had heard on the academic grapevine that a new post was being created in the History

Department at Oxford University and he had wondered whether Pym wanted to sound out his interest in it. The problem was that, unlike the certain response of almost all his contemporaries, he had no interest in the possibility of a position at Oxford. Over the past three years, he had settled very well into his life in Durham, where he was viewed as a hard-working and popular member of staff. Indeed, he was unusual in that he was a gifted academic, but totally without any sense of separateness from ordinary people. He was just as happy discussing Newcastle United with his college janitor, as he was debating some arcane academic point with a colleague. King's ease of manner and innate sociability, not to mention his tall, sporty physique and his pleasant, open face also ensured that he was very popular with the ladies. This was not, however, to suggest that he was a ladies' man. It was precisely his complete lack of awareness of his attractiveness to women which served to draw them to him even more. In certain circles in Durham he was regarded as something of a catch, but while he did not lack female company, he was very content with his current status as single and a member of Durham University.

Pym smiled enigmatically at his protégé, 'Yes, I do have a specific reason for asking you to meet me here.' As he busied himself pouring the tea, the Professor realised that this could be his last opportunity to consider the fairness of seeking to involve King in the proposed mission. A lifelong bachelor, Pym had never had the pleasure of being a father. He did, however, permit himself to take an almost paternal interest in the progress of some of his ex-students. *In some ways*, he had debated endlessly with himself, *John hasn't changed since he came up as a callow eighteen-year-old a decade ago. For a bright fellow, he can still be unnervingly naïve and, arguably, his spirit is far too Corinthian for the modern world of the Thirties. But he is very perceptive, a rational thinker and analyst and not without courage.* It was his recognition of King as perhaps too generous of spirit that led Pym to begin the conversation in a rather oblique way. 'I wonder, John, if you'd share with me your general views on the rise of Fascism in general and Hitler in particular?

King was momentarily confused, *Why the heck is the old man asking me about that?* he pondered, before relaxing as he realised, *at least it looks like I was wrong about the Oxford post. Good! I won't have to turn him down.* 'Actually, that's a very interesting question for me, sir,' King began enthusiastically. 'The Second Empire remains my principal area of study, but I am becoming more interested in the contemporary history of Germany. I've been thinking a lot about my experience in Heidelberg in '32-'33, the recent *Anschluss* and the situation in Czechoslovakia. I've concluded that Fascism in general and Nazism in particular are the greatest extant threats to the maintenance of peace. I'd also argue that the democracies need fully to understand them in order to be able to resist and ultimately to defeat them.'

'I think I agree with every word of that, John. So, what do you think of the political prospects for Europe over the next couple of years?'

'Well, sir, it's very hard to believe that Hitler will be satisfied by his reoccupation of the Rhineland in '36 and his more recent gobbling up of Austria. It beggars belief that the British and French didn't send him packing when his troops crossed the Rhine. Neither was I surprised at the invasion of Austria. My friends over there had been telling me for some time that the Austro-German Agreement was specifically designed to effect both the release of Nazis from Austrian jails and the inclusion of National Socialists in Schuschnigg's Cabinet. In return, of course, Hitler was to have supported Austrian sovereignty. But the events of the past few weeks have shown what value the assurances of the Führer are worth. Anyone with even the vaguest appreciation of Hitler's writing would know that it's eventually to the East that he'll turn to seize the *Lebensraum* he requires for his Third Reich.'

'So, you don't think that Herr Hitler will be satisfied by his latest conquests, John?'

'I'm afraid not, sir. We already know that the Czechs are fortifying their borders with Germany and that the opposing Sudeten Germans who, let's not forget are part funded from Berlin, are getting stronger by the month. In my view, it's highly likely that Hitler will want, as an absolute minimum, the incorporation of the Sudeten Germans into his Reich. Of course, he might also want the total destruction of Czechoslovakia as a sovereign state to provide space, resources and manpower for his expanding empire. From there, anything's possible. Poland is ripe for conquest and the Germans are clearly building up army, naval and air-force strength. To believe these are solely for defensive purposes is ludicrous.'

'You paint a very gloomy picture, John,' observed Pym archly. 'Do you really believe this will happen?'

'Not *will*, sir. But most definitely *could*,' responded King with eager emphasis. 'A key factor, of course, will be the attitude adopted by ourselves and the French. If Britain and France stand firm and call his bluff when he next moves to acquire territory, we could yet face Hitler down. Sadly, I fear that this is not at all likely. Now, were Churchill to become PM....' King left this thought hanging between them, before reaching his conclusion. 'Neither France, nor Britain seems in any way ready to oppose Hitler; America is clearly uninterested and while Stalin is waiting to advance westwards, there is sufficient territory to be shared with Germany to prevent immediate conflict between the two dictators. If we also recognise that the League of Nations is wholly ineffectual, it leaves us with a very bleak picture. A picture which suggests to me the inevitability either of war with Germany, or of a morally base peace.'

'You say a 'morally base peace', John,' probed Pym. 'Surely the people of Britain and France wouldn't wish to revisit The Great War, or something likely to be even worse? Is peace not the most desirable outcome?'

'Of course it is! But at any cost? Things were already deteriorating when I left Heidelberg in '33. But consider more recent events. Look at Hitler's introduction of conscription and massive rearmament. Look at the Nuremberg Race Laws and the tightening of his racist policies. Look at the so-called labour camps, into which anyone who disagrees with him is consigned, many to a painful existence, or even death. Can we really have an honourable peace with such a madman?' King looked deep into the eyes of his mentor and was pleased to see a fire burning there, every bit as determined as that in his own.

'I can't disagree with any of your analysis, John,' conceded Pym. 'Indeed, I would go further and say that, undoubtedly, war is coming.' Fiddling with his pipe, Pym finally added, 'I think, my boy, that it's high time I told you a little bit about my, how shall I put it…. non-academic work.'

***

Grey cloud was covering the sun when King emerged from the Universities Club and meandered towards Trafalgar Square. He had planned to go straight to the nearest underground station after the meeting, get to Kings Cross and catch the first train back to Durham. However, what Pym had said to him in the previous two hours had left him reeling. He needed time and peace to think through the extraordinary proposal that his old mentor had made. King decided that the calm and anonymity of a church would offer the best possibility to gather his thoughts. As he made his way along the edge of Trafalgar Square, he passed in front of the National Gallery and recognised St Martin-in-the-Fields. Thanks to its Georgian design, the interior of the church was bright and welcoming and, King noted with relief, almost empty.

Pym had taken nearly an hour to explain to King the 'little bit' about his 'non-academic work.' He had begun by stressing that anything further that was said that afternoon should be regarded as falling under The Official Secrets Act. King having accepted this condition, Pym had outlined how he had served as a consultant to the Secret Intelligence Service on German issues since 1918. 'Well, John,' he had summarised, 'I think we're both agreed that war with Germany is inevitable. Given that this is the case, I'm sure that you'd also agree that we must take every step to hinder German activities, insofar as they threaten Britain and her security.'

'Of course,' King had replied. 'That goes without saying.'

'What I'm going to propose speaks exactly to that goal,' Pym had said with an enigmatic smile. 'Tell me, John, do you know anything about Nazi sympathisers in Britain?'

King had met his mentor's gaze as he had replied, 'Well, of course I'm aware of the British Union of Fascists. They had a pretty respectable vote in the London County Council Elections last month, around 8000 votes, if I remember rightly.'

'Yes,' Pym had interjected, 'but thankfully none of their candidates was elected to office.'

'Then there are surely whole sections of the British aristocracy, from the Duke of Windsor down, which are sympathetic to Hitler. Let's not forget that he and Wallace Simpson left Britain for Germany on a Nazi ship last December – a great propaganda coup for Goebbels. Then there are sections of the press which are supportive of both British and German Fascism. Rothermere fawned over Hitler in '34 and his *Daily Mail* has supported the BUF ever since.'

King had by no means finished his answer when Pym had interrupted with a question. 'Would it surprise you, John, that we estimate the number of active sympathisers - not pacifist appeasers you understand, but those who are positively enthusiastic about Hitler and Fascism - runs into tens of thousands in Britain today?'

King had recoiled in shock. 'Surely that can't be true, sir. That must be an exaggeration.'

'Not at all,' Pym had replied gravely. 'In fact, I'm afraid that the real number could be far higher than that.'

'But in the event of war, which we both feel is inevitable, that could be absolutely catastrophic,' King had protested.

'Yes, it could, John. Unless we do something to neutralise, or better still, actually to make use of such people. Of course, plans have been drawn up in the event of war to interview and classify foreign nationals, especially Germans and Austrians. Those deemed a risk would be interned… but what about those Fascist sympathisers who are British?'

King had studied the older man thoughtfully, before arguing, 'Then, surely, we'd have to do the same thing with them.'

'Well,' Pym had countered quickly, 'consider this argument, John. If we round up significant numbers of Nazi sympathisers and intern them, then in all likelihood those remaining would be driven further underground to maintain the flow of help or information to Germany. They'd then be even harder to track down. What if, instead, we decided to leave them in place and run them ourselves?' *This is the crunch*, Pym had thought to himself, *either he'll see it, or he'll miss the point.*

It hadn't taken long before the Professor had been able to afford himself a smile as his protégé, almost thinking aloud, had said, 'You mean they think they're sending sensitive and valuable information to Germany, but all the time they're simply giving it back to us?' King had rubbed his chin, while evaluating the proposed plan. 'It's elegant, enables us to control and direct the flow of information and perhaps even identify the sources of sensitive leaks. But the Nazi sympathisers would believe that they're doing their bit for the Third Reich. It's a brilliant scheme, sir. But what's it got to do with me?'

'Before I answer that, John, consider also that if our man wins the trust and obedience of the people he is running, we may actually get leads to authentic German agents who are operating in Britain. This could be a key element of our counter espionage strategy, both in the run up to the war and after war is declared.' Pym had sat back in his chair and watched King's face as it had revealed his dawning realisation of the potential scope and value of this operation. Finally, after having filled his pipe again and enjoyed the first puffs of his favourite tobacco, Pym had put the crucial question, up to which this whole discussion had been leading. 'How would you like to be the person, both to run these Nazi sympathisers for us and perhaps even to root out enemy agents?'

Having seen the look of total disbelief on King's face, the older man had hastily continued. 'Before you say anything, John, just hear me out, please. You will agree that we need someone who can present himself to potential informants as, to all intents and purposes, German? Our man must be bilingual and someone who fully understands German culture and mores, especially those of the Nazis. You most assuredly fit perfectly this part of the bill. At the same time, as a native Englishman, you'd raise no suspicions among more loyal sections of the population - a great advantage for any German agent, real or fictitious. Finally, we need someone who is not emotionally or privately involved.

Someone who can go undercover without causing too much of a stir. I hope you will forgive me John, but I did commission a full review of your private life before approaching you.'

'Hang on a minute, sir,' King had interrupted, his hand raised in emphasis. 'I haven't spent any significant time in Germany since '33 and a lot has changed since then. Yes, I have a few academic colleagues and friends there, but getting periodic letters from them and following the news is by no means the same thing as witnessing Nazism at first hand.'

'You make a good point, John. What, then, would you suggest?'

'Well, that really depends on your projected timescale, sir. I believe that, ideally, the person you select must have recent experience of living and working in Germany.'

'Hmm. Yes, I can see how that might be necessary and also how it might work well,' Pym had replied carefully. 'As an academic, you could easily take a sabbatical in Germany for 'research purposes,' without causing suspicion or raising questions among your colleagues, neighbours or friends. You could use this time to try to find out as much as possible about how the German security services operate. I'll give some thought as to how this might be facilitated. But, John, if you do take this on, you must recognise fully that, once your mission begins for real, back in Britain, you would be operating under an assumed name and, as far as all your friends and family are concerned, John King would be dead.'

Pym had noted with concern the shock this had brought to his erstwhile student's face. 'Are you really sure that's necessary, sir? Surely parents could be told.'

'It's absolutely necessary!' Pym had insisted harshly. 'There can be no exceptions at all. But, please, allow me to finish. You're young and fit and we could easily teach you all other aspects of your tradecraft. Surely you can see, John, how you are the perfect match for our requirements?'

King had shifted uneasily in his chair. He had disagreed with his mentor, but had struggled to explain his reasoning. 'I can accept the logic of your argument, sir. But, dash it all, what I don't understand is that there surely must be a professional SIS operative who fits the bill every bit as well as I. And who would have the advantage of being fully trained in such operations already.'

'I agree, John,' Pym replied dourly. 'But there is one final fact that I haven't told you, which I'm sure will alter your view. You see, we strongly suspect that SIS has been penetrated by the Abwehr. We don't know for certain, but in these circumstances, we have no option but to operate on the assumption that it has. So, you see, this operation will have to be 'off the books' and not part of the general work of SIS.'

'What would that mean, exactly, sir?'

'It will mean that, apart from myself, only one other person, a retired SIS chap, will be involved fully in the operation. He will be responsible for your training in tradecraft and when that's complete, he will initially act as contact between the two of us.' Pym had been studying King's reactions to these revelations, especially for any signs of fear. While he had noticed evidence of concern that he was up to such a task, he had not seen any indication that the younger man was scared to take on the mission. Taking heart from this, the Professor had continued, 'You'll be alone, my boy. Your family will believe you to be dead. You'll be working closely with enemies of Britain, but as far as the forces of law and order and the secret services in Britain are concerned, you, too, would be an enemy of the state. If things were to go badly wrong, you could find yourself being pursued both by the British and by authentic German agents. However, in discussing this with you I'm speaking with the full authority of Sir Hugh Sinclair, Head of SIS. I know it's a heavy burden that I'm asking you to take up. But I honestly believe that it's vital to keep a very close eye on the enemy within, in order that we may be able to neutralise any threat, both before and after war comes.'

***

King was jolted from his reflections on his conversation with Pym by the busy preparations being made all around him for the regular 5PM evensong. He politely declined the order of service and hymn book which were offered to him and, with an apologetic smile at the young curate, slid out of the pew and made his way to the main entrance of the church. After experiencing such a summersault in his own life, King was somehow shocked that the world seemed to be carrying on exactly as normal. The rush hour traffic was clearly building up around Trafalgar Square and, putting his hand into his jacket pocket, he felt the piece of paper with the address of the hotel arranged by Pym. The older man had insisted that King should take the evening in order to think things over and that they meet again the following day.

***

King did not enjoy the most restful of nights in the far from luxurious hotel. Time after time he turned over the arguments which the Professor had deployed to convince him that he was the right man for this particular task. He had also laughed at his own notion that Pym had wanted to test the waters with regard to a post at Oxford. In truth, King was unconvinced, either that he was up to the job, or that he was actually prepared for the sacrifices that it would entail. It was not, he instinctively knew, because he was frightened of the degree of risk involved. Like most men in their late twenties, he tended to see himself as indestructible and any associated danger constituted more of an attraction than a reason to decline the proposal. Neither was he unprepared to give up his life at the University in Durham. He was very happy there, enjoyed teaching his students and had a wide circle of interesting and committed friends. But he was also sufficiently aware that, in times of crisis, people had to make sacrifices.

As he lay in bed, analysing the situation, he came to the conclusion that his concerns were partly about his suitability for the job. Most important of all, however, were the possible effects on his parents. He was fairly certain that, in his shoes, his father would understand the call of duty and would put the interests of the nation before his own or even his family's. On the other hand, the effect on his mother of faking his own death was not something that he cared to have on his conscience and he resolved to discuss this more fully with Pym at their meeting the next day.

***

Unsurprisingly, given his state of agitation, King arrived early for his appointment with Pym in St James's Park. He sat with his back to the bandstand, gazing over the Blue Bridge and watching the succession of office workers and government bureaucrats making their way towards the Treasury and Foreign Office buildings. On such a glorious Spring morning, with the sun reflecting on the water and the ducks making their noisy circuits of the lake, King half believed that the events of the previous twenty-four hours were but a dream. However, the purposeful approach of Pym from the direction of Buckingham Palace served as sufficient reminder of the reality of the situation in which he now found himself.

'Good morning, John,' Pym greeted the younger man warmly, before asking sympathetically, 'I don't suppose you slept so well last night, my boy?'

King smiled thinly, 'Not really, sir. I must admit that I've had more restful nights.'

Pym went on to reassure King that such a reaction was perfectly normal. 'In fact,' he said decisively, 'had you said yes to this proposal yesterday, I would've had serious doubts as to whether you were the right chap for the job.'

'But that's exactly my concern, sir,' the younger man said miserably. 'It's not that I'm in a funk about it, though of course I recognise the potential dangers. It's more that I'm worried that I don't have what it takes to succeed in the mission and I'm very concerned about the effect that faking my death might have on my family, especially my mother.'

Pym shuffled uncomfortably on the bench and gazed silently towards the Royal residence. Eventually he turned to the younger man and spoke with great sincerity. 'I understand your position, John. For myself, I debated long and hard the fairness of asking you to carry this burden. You know that I've always taken a keen interest in your career and your welfare. Believe me, I wouldn't be asking you to consider this proposal unless I was certain that you could carry it out successfully. And that you're by far the best man for a job which is essential to the interests of Great Britain. As to the issue with your family, that unfortunately is part of the deal. We couldn't compromise on that at all. I'm sorry, John. But there it is.'

Deep in thought, King nodded his head slowly before turning to his old mentor and asking quietly, 'How soon do you need a decision, sir? How long do I have to think about it?'

Pym looked even more pained as he replied sadly, 'Not long at all, John. We need a decision pretty quickly, because if you turn us down, we'll have to start our search for a likely candidate all over again.'

'I see,' replied King gravely. 'Then I'd better give you my answer now, sir. No point in prevaricating.'

Pym tensed as he waited for the younger man's decision, all kinds of thoughts swirling through his mind. Part of him would certainly be relieved, should the invitation be declined. But he despaired of having to find someone as suitable and who he would trust as implicitly as he trusted this man. Eventually King continued, 'I've given this sufficient consideration, sir, and I'm keen to accept your proposal. I'm aware of the certain, likely and possible consequences of this decision, but my mind is quite made up. I can make myself available at your convenience.'

Pym's face flushed with pride and gratitude and his eyes had a certain moisture about them as he shook King's hand. 'I'm delighted, my boy. Your country is grateful to you, even though it may not yet realise it.'

CHAPTER FOUR

Monday 12th September, 1938, The English Channel.

It was a beautiful September day as SS *Canterbury* steamed sedately out of Dover harbour. Having experienced a constant stream of meetings and briefings following the decisive meeting at the Pall Mall club, it was only now, onboard ship, that King felt able to reflect on the process by which his old life had been sloughed off like a dead skin.

Once the plan for King to spend an academic year in Berlin had been agreed, Pym had efficiently ensured that the necessary pieces fell perfectly into place. He was provided with a grant which would cover both his costs and that of a replacement for his hardly onerous teaching duties at Durham University. His request for a year's study leave in Germany had, therefore, been immediately approved by his Head of Department. Pym had then engineered King's position at the top of a list of British nominations for an academic exchange with Germany. As the scheme had been devised specifically to promote better mutual understanding between the two nations, King's proposal to analyse 'Mutual Security and How to Achieve It' was very much welcomed by the German officials. Their enthusiasm was such that King had even been offered Visiting Research Fellow status at Berlin University and could, therefore, look forward to some official support in his work. When he had met with King to discuss the cover story for his presence in Germany, Pym had enthused, 'This has worked out extremely well. Indeed, your project and your status in Berlin may well afford you some opportunity to find out at first-hand how their security and espionage organisations are structured and operated.'

As he leaned on the ship's rail and looked back on the white cliffs, fading and then finally disappearing into the fine sea haze, King felt a genuine pang of homesickness. The ferry was busy, with a mixture of various European nationalities en-route home and British couples off to France for a late holiday, buoyed no doubt by the Prime Minister's recent promise of 'peace in our time.'

King thought it scarcely possible that barely a week had passed since he'd been enjoying several days at home with his parents at their fine home in the Gloucestershire countryside. After a distinguished military career, Henry King had succeeded in reinventing himself as a country solicitor and pillar of the local amateur dramatic society, while Amanda still taught part time at the local primary school. King was immensely proud of his parents, whom he loved and respected deeply as fundamentally good and decent people. They had been undemanding and essentially tolerant in raising both him and his sister, encouraging them both, without favour, in their respective life and career choices. Indeed, King often reflected that he undoubtedly owed his love of study, of history and of ideas to both his parents, who, in equal measure, had encouraged him first to go up to Oxford and later to choose an academic career.

On his first evening at home, over a fine dinner of roast beef, King's mother had enjoyed relaying the latest family news. 'Cordelia is blissfully happy,' she had gushed, 'and George simply dotes on his sons.' King had immediately felt a brief stab of guilt that he had not made more effort to see his sister and her husband before he would leave for Germany. Especially as Portsmouth was not so far away and George had been enjoying a couple of weeks leave, while his command was enjoying a minor refit in the naval dockyards there.

'Oh, and we had a lovely letter from Rachel. She says she's very settled in New York and still loves her apartment and her teaching post at Columbia.' King had remembered with great pride and love how his parents had, without hesitation, taken in siblings Rachel and David Bernstein after they had fled Germany in the winter of 1933-4. 'And young David is in the last year of his police training in Lancashire. Such a lovely and gentle young man, I do wonder sometimes if police work is quite right for him.'

'I don't know about that, my dear,' King's father had disagreed gently. 'It's one of my greatest pleasures that, in some small way, I could help him achieve his career goal. He's just the sort of sensible and intelligent chap that we need in the forces of law and order.'

King had not discussed the European political situation with his father until his final evening at home. Then, over brandy and cigars on the terrace, King had asked his views on the Prime Minister's recent visit to Hitler's Berghof mountain retreat in Berchtesgaden. In response, Henry had simply snorted with derision. 'Chamberlain's a disgrace to his office. If the French and we abandon the Czechs, we'll hand Hitler an enormous propaganda coup. If we don't stand up to him now, he'll demand more and more concessions until he has hegemony over all of continental Europe.'

In many ways, after dinner was King's favourite time of day. He loved listening to all the nocturnal shuffling and hooting which replaced the merry birdsong of the day and he enjoyed the various garden scents which became more pronounced as the dew settled. Gazing out over the garden, as dusk finally gave way to darkness, King had tried to imagine the inner battle his father must have fought to come to the same conclusion as he himself had reached. For, in common with the overwhelming majority of his contemporaries who had survived the horrors of four years on the Western Front, his father had always been adamant that no generation should be sacrificed in the same way as his own.

In the end, he had simply agreed, 'You're absolutely right, Pa. Chamberlain is only postponing the inevitable and giving Hitler more time to strengthen himself. We should tackle him now, not let him decide when he's ready to take us on.'

King's father had then shifted uneasily, as if unwilling to ask the obvious question that had been troubling him since he had learned of his son's plans to stay in Berlin. At last, he had been unable to hold back any longer and asked with real exasperation, 'Then why on earth are you about to take part in this 'academic exchange' of yours? You must surely realise that the Nazis will simply want to use you as a propaganda tool?'

As the two men had stood in the increasing gloom, enjoying their cigars and one another's company for what

King had feared might be the last time in years, he had felt a desperate urge to tell his father the truth about his business in Germany. He had had no direct intention to disobey Pym's strict instruction to say nothing about his mission, but, having held his father's gaze for a full minute, he had finally replied. 'I know that's a real danger, Pa. And you're not the first person to have pointed that out to me. Believe me, a couple of my friends have been rather blunter in their comments. But on this question, I must ask you to trust me. I do believe that my visit there may serve those causes and interests that we both hold most dear.'

There had been something in his son's expression and tone that had dissuaded Henry from pursuing the matter further. Indeed, the briefest of nods from the older man had been all the confirmation King had required that some important message had passed between them.

The formalities at Calais took longer than King had envisaged and it was with relief that he finally found himself comfortably seated by a picture window in a quiet compartment of the fast train to Paris. The fields and villages of the Pas de Calais hurtled by in a hypnotic whirl and, exhausted by the tensions of the previous days, he soon fell into a deep sleep. A little more than an hour after the train had left the coast the call for the first sitting in the dining car was issued. King, roused from his sleep, made his way to the dining car, where a waiter in starched white jacket showed him to a small table for two on the left side of the carriage. The silver cutlery and crystal glassware glinted invitingly in the light of the small chandeliers which were hanging from the carriage ceiling. The crisp white linen of the tablecloths and the rich velvet curtains at each window completed the impression of a long narrow drawing room, incongruously moving at speed through northern France.

***

After spending a quiet evening and night in Paris, King arrived early the next morning at the impressive Gare de L'Est. The station had experienced a doubling in size in the early 1930s and now boasted an airy and light entrance foyer with a superbly curved glass roof. The first part of the journey to Berlin was uneventful and King took the opportunity to catch up on a little reading, from which he was distracted only by the border police as the express entered Belgium. Later, as the train waited in Brussels, he gratefully took the chance to stretch his legs on the platform. When he returned to his compartment, he was a little disappointed to see that he was no longer alone. He had been joined by a tall, slightly built, fair-haired man in his late thirties who was dressed in civilian clothes and, King noted with distaste, a small swastika lapel badge on his suit jacket.

The two men nodded politely but, to King's relief, they did not exchange words as the train steamed grandly out of the Belgian capital. The nearer he came to entering Hitler's Reich, the more King began to feel a mixture of excitement and tension. On the one hand, he was repulsed by everything that the Nazis believed and practised, especially the cynical racism, casual violence and overbearing militarism. On the other hand, in some ways he was looking forward to experiencing Berlin at first hand and felt a grim determination to use his time there productively.

'What is the purpose of your visit to the Reich?' demanded the officious-looking German border guard, as he peered suspiciously through his thick glasses at King's passport.

'I'm here by invitation to participate in an academic exchange,' replied the Englishman politely and in perfect German. 'Here are my official invitation and my credentials from the appropriate ministry.' King smiled as the official, having read his papers, stiffened and saluted.

'Thank you, sir. I hope that you have an interesting and educational time in Germany. Heil Hitler!' The guard took the briefest of glimpses at the identification documents which were proffered by King's travel companion, before handing them back and exiting the compartment with such speed, that it seemed he feared contamination.

'So, Herr....?' asked the German, making it clear that he wanted to know King's name. 'You are a visiting academic, come to observe and learn from us Germans?'

Not wishing to give offence, the Englishman smiled and replied noncommittally, 'It's Dr King and I'm certainly hoping to learn much about Germans and Germany while I am here.'

'Well, Herr Doktor, there is much to admire about the new German Reich. By the way, my name is Erwin Kalz and I would be pleased to offer you any assistance during your stay in Berlin. But, please, could you explain what is the precise nature of your exchange visit?'

As soon as King explained the purpose of his work in Germany, Kalz demonstrated an even keener interest. He listened patiently as the German argued that, 'Of course, there is no reason for disagreement between Great Britain and the Reich. It is in Britain's interests to have a strong Germany and Germany has no territorial interest in the British Empire. We two great and related nations can coexist in peace, as your Herr Chamberlain clearly believes. The real threat, of course, comes from the East and Stalin's barbaric hordes. Surely you would agree with me, Herr Doktor?'

'I can see some merit in what you say, Herr Kalz,' replied King evenly. 'However, I must also caution you that there are many in Great Britain who are concerned with your country's policy towards Czechoslovakia.'

'Pah!' snorted the German dismissively, 'you mean Churchill and the rest of his equally marginalised followers? They surely count for next to nothing in the great scheme of things. The Munich Agreement has settled this question of the German minority. But come, my friend, let us not argue. Let me give you some advice for your stay in Berlin.'

King was happy to allow Kalz to spend the greater part of the next hour offering advice on where to eat, what to see and what to do in Hitler's capital city. The German was also keen to learn where it was that King lived in Britain. In conversation, it emerged that Kalz had spent some years in England and they happily exchanged stories and memories, both of London and of Oxford. The time went by unexpectedly pleasantly with his urbane fellow traveller and King was surprised to see that the train was slowing down to enter the main station at Köln.

Kalz also seemed to have been taken aback by the train's arrival and he quickly reached into his briefcase for paper and pen on which he hastily wrote his name and telephone number. As he handed the note to King, he smiled and said, 'I should have liked to continue our very interesting conversation, Herr Doktor. Regrettably, duty takes me to Köln for a few days. However, I should be back in Berlin by the week after next and it would please me very much if you would get in touch with me then. I would be very happy to offer you any assistance with your work that is in my power.' The German offered his hand and King immediately reciprocated, pondering whether a contact who had signed his name as Major Erwin Kalz would be potentially useful to his mission in Berlin, or extremely dangerous to his security there.

***

King had a late afternoon meeting with the Administrator of the History Department at the Humboldt University of Berlin, at which he would collect the keys to the flat which had been arranged for his stay in the city. As he had time to spare and it was a pleasant afternoon, he decided to deposit his cases in the left luggage office at the station and walk to the university. His journey took him over the river Spree and down towards Königsplatz, where he saw the Siegessäule, with the glittering bronze sculpture of Victoria atop its stone column. King wondered with a pang of nostalgia whether he would ever be able to return to his academic life and his interest in the military victories and their consequences which were celebrated by this rather garish monument. Shortly after leaving the square, he took a left turn and the unmistakable Brandenburger Tor came into view. As he approached his destination, he realised that he was impressed with the grandeur of the city and the happy mood of the people who were thronging the pavements and streets. Once inside the university buildings, which occupied a central position on the fine boulevard Unter den Linden, he was appalled by their evident Nazification. Party posters, swastikas, and photographs of the Führer adorned almost every available surface. Having introduced himself at the reception desk, King waited a few minutes until an attractive woman in her mid-forties came down the stairs into the reception hall and approached him. 'Heil Hitler!' she began perfunctorily. 'Welcome to Berlin Herr Doktor King. I am Fräulein Müller, Administrator of the Department of History.'

The woman led him to a large, airy office on the third floor of the building, where he was immediately greeted by two men, both of whom offered what he now feared was the obligatory Nazi salute. The first, a dapper man of medium height and build, with a shock of silver hair and furtive, weasel-like features, introduced himself as Professor Brunner. The second man was much taller and younger and, King noted, a less enthusiastic performer of the Hitler salute. Smiling shyly, he offered his hand and said in very good but accented English, 'Hello, I am Dr Schwarz. I'm delighted to meet you.'

Fräulein Müller quickly gave King the keys of the centrally located, fully-furnished flat, informing him that she had provided an initial supply of basic household essentials. 'I hope you find them useful, Herr Doktor,' she said shyly. King immediately thanked her, joking that he had brought few clothes, but a great deal of tea in his luggage.

'Ah, you English,' chided Professor Brunner, with a not particularly pleasant smile. 'Where would you be without your tea?'

'Your flat is on Ludendorffstraße,' Frau Müller explained anxiously. 'It's just over half an hour's walk from here. I do hope you will find it to your satisfaction. Dr Schwarz has kindly agreed to show you where it is and to help you settle in.' King smiled at Schwarz, before admitting that he was very tired and would be pleased to set off for the flat as soon as possible.

Schwarz seemed preoccupied during the walk to the flat and restricted himself to pointing out the most obvious and famous landmarks. After just over thirty minutes of steady walking, the two academics arrived at the entrance to number 66 Ludendorffstraße. King could clearly sense the discomfort of his young colleague and confessed that he was happy to let himself into the flat and to find his own way around. Schwarz seemed relieved and, with a nervous smile said, 'Professor Brunner instructed me to ensure that you're settled in the flat. As it happens, I've an urgent engagement, so I'm very happy that you don't need me to do this. But please, you'll not tell the Professor of this?'

King laughed and reassured his colleague. 'Of course not. You're simply letting me do things my way. But, look, I can't go on calling you Dr Schwarz. I'm John and I hope we'll be friends.'

The younger academic seemed pleased and replied warmly, 'That's my hope too, John. And I'm Andreas. I look forward to seeing you tomorrow. But now, I really must go.' With a final smile of apology, he turned and walked quickly down the street.

Some thirty minutes later, a mentally and physically exhausted King finally managed to close the door on Berlin and, especially, on Frau Bauer, the indomitable caretaker of the block. He had been intercepted by the elderly, yet supremely observant woman as soon as he had gently closed the front door and turned towards the stairs. After providing his older interrogator with a detailed autobiography, King had been relieved to see her eyes glaze over as soon as he responded to her question about the purpose of his stay in Berlin. He had begun to outline his role at the university only for her to cut short his explanation with an imperious wave of her short, plump arm and to insist that he follow her into her 'office.' To the old woman, this may have been a desirable administrative hub. In fact, it was merely a tiny, flimsily constructed cupboard which had been placed across a corner of the spacious hallway. However, King could hardly fault Frau Bauer's hospitality, as no sooner had he squeezed himself into her office than he was offered a glass of schnapps by way of welcome. Moreover, she had insisted that a couple of the younger residents would bring his suitcases from the station, 'if you would be so kind as to give me the receipts for them.' As he settled into his new home, King reflected that his first impression of Berliners was that they were unexpectedly pleasant, generous and engaging company.

CHAPTER FIVE

Autumn 1938, Berlin.

King's first weeks in Berlin passed quietly, as Pym had advised would be appropriate. 'Don't rush your fences, my boy,' he had said, in his quiet yet authoritative way, during one of their last meetings in London. 'Let your information come to you. If I know anything of the Nazi mentality, they'll be unable to stop themselves boasting to you of their organisation and achievements.' King had genuinely enjoyed finding his way around the city, establishing his office at the university and gradually getting to know his colleagues. Both Schwarz and Brunner were the staff with whom he had most contact and his first impressions of each had been confirmed. Brunner seemed a slippery, possibly untrustworthy character, whereas Schwarz was a genuinely liberal and free-thinking academic. Unsurprisingly, King had spent more of his leisure time with the younger man and his Bohemian circle of friends than with any other group.

One Thursday morning, when the late October sky had taken on a steely grey colour which hinted at the winter to come, an unusually flustered Fräulein Müller approached King as he sauntered into the department. 'Excuse me, Herr Doktor, but there is a letter for you. It was left here earlier today by a man in uniform. I do hope that you are not in any kind of trouble.'

As soon as he let himself into his small corner office, King threw down his briefcase and coat onto one of the two worn armchairs and flopped contentedly down into the other, studying the envelope with interest. Intriguingly, the initials 'OKW' and '76-78 Tirpitzufer, Berlin,' were neatly printed on the envelope. *The address of the High Command of Germany's Armed Forces, if I'm not mistaken. Now I wonder what they want with me?* To his further surprise, the contents of the envelope comprised a short, handwritten note and an invitation card.

'*My dear Herr Dr King,*' began the note written in perfect Gothic lettering. '*It was a great pleasure to converse with you on the Berlin train and to learn of the purpose of your visit to Germany. It would give me great pleasure to invite you, as my guest, to a Reception which is being held in order to celebrate the Munich Agreement and the reincorporation of Sudetenland into the Reich. The Reception will take place in the Columned Hall of the OKW, Bendlerblock on November 2nd at 7.30PM. I do hope that you will be able to attend and I look forward very much to further discussions with you. Heil Hitler!*' The note was signed '*Major Erwin Kalz, OKW, Berlin*', and the gilt-edged invitation card informed King, both that he should confirm his attendance and that formal dress or uniform was obligatory.

On the day of the reception, King was touched to learn that Fräulein Müller had arranged for him to be picked up at home in one of the university's cars and chauffeur driven to Tirpitzufer. 'It's a proud day for the department and for the university, Herr Doktor,' she cooed as she brushed away an imaginary speck of dust from his tweed jacket. 'Now, are you sure that you have your formal dress organised?'

'Yes, Anna, don't worry,' replied King, as he reflected sadly that so many Jewish professionals, no longer permitted to practise, had been reduced to selling their possessions in order to survive. To his discomfort, it had proved much easier and cheaper to buy rather than to hire a full dinner suit.

Frau Bauer was beside herself with excitement, as the uniformed chauffeur pulled up in a perfectly polished, gleaming black Horch, with its huge front wheel arches and characteristic bug-eyed headlights. 'Now you behave yourself, Herr Doktor. This could be the making of you!' she exhorted King as she ushered him out of the house and into the waiting car. As the car drove smoothly away from the kerb, he smiled as he noticed that she was surrounded by her fellow caretakers from the neighbouring houses. The crowds on the pavement stopped to stare as the Horch cruised down Hermann Göringstraße, past the Reich Chancellery and on across Potsdamerplatz. The traffic was building up as they turned into Tirpitzufer, the cold grey waters of the Landwehr Canal on their left and the huge stone frontage of the Bendlerblock, looming in the distance on the right. It was clear that this was a major event and King began seriously to consider who might also be in attendance. The Wehrmacht Chiefs of Staff would be there for sure, but perhaps also more political figures, such as Himmler, Goebbels, Hess or even Hitler himself. For one mad moment, King wished he had brought a grenade which, with luck, could wipe out the whole foul lot of them in one redeeming blast.

The Horch took its turn in the parade of meticulously polished cars, queuing to disgorge their invited guests. As they drew nearer, King could see both a phalanx of uniformed officers, saluting each new arrival, and the huge red, black and white swastika flags fluttering in the arc light beams above the main entrance. Finally, it was his turn to step out of the warmth of the car and into the cold autumn air and the dazzling artificial light. He was vaguely aware of the cheers of the crowd and the light marching music which was being played by an immaculately uniformed military band. He kept his eyes firmly forward and, having shown his invitation, was able to pass inside the door and be directed towards the cloakroom.

'Herr Dr King?' asked a fresh-faced officer with an expression that changed from concern to obvious relief at the Englishman's nod of the head. 'I'm pleased that I've found you at last. There are so many people here in dinner suits. It's quite overwhelming. Please follow me. Major Kalz is awaiting you in the Columned Hall.'

The adjutant led the way through the throng of men, all in uniform or formal dress, and their partners in their glittering finery. They crossed the large reception area and made their way through a huge doorway into a rectangular hall which boasted, at first floor level, a gallery supported by huge stone columns. Massive flags were hanging from fixtures which were positioned just underneath the magnificent glass ceiling and, at the far end of the gallery level, a podium with a microphone had already been set up. White-jacketed waiters, carrying trays of champagne and canapés, made elegant pirouettes between the crowds of excited guests. Over the shoulder of the young officer, King caught sight of the tall, fair haired figure of Kalz, in the full dress uniform of a Wehrmacht Major, deep in conversation with a Colonel. At the first suitable pause in the conversation, his guide coughed discreetly in order to attract Kalz's attention. 'Excuse me Herr Colonel, Herr Major. May I present Herr Dr King.'

Kalz turned to face the Englishman, a beaming smile on his face, 'My dear Herr Dr King. How good it is to see you again. Please, allow me to introduce you to my commanding officer, and Weber, another round of champagne, if you please.'

'Yes sir,' responded Weber with a salute, before rushing off to find the nearest waiter. Kalz placed a proprietorial arm on King's elbow as he announced 'Herr Colonel, may I introduce Herr Dr John King from the University of Durham in England. The Herr Doktor is here as part of an academic exchange between Great Britain and the Reich. His particular interest concerns issues of mutual security for our respective nations. An admirable subject, I am sure you will agree.'

King could scarcely believe his ears as the older German murmured his agreement and introduced himself as Colonel Hans Oster. As soon as he heard the name, King was transported back to one of his many briefing sessions in Pym's St John's Wood flat. 'We really could do with you picking up as much information as you can about the Abwehr, John.' His old mentor had gone on to explain that, while SIS knew relatively little of its workings, it was confident that this organisation would run most, if not all agents sent from Germany to Britain. 'Military Intelligence is commanded by Admiral Wilhelm Canaris and his deputy is Colonel Hans Oster, so do listen carefully to any gossip or opinions about these men that come your way. Almost anything you can bring back would be useful. But don't, for heaven's sake, jeopardise your mission by seeming to be too interested.'

Suddenly, it all fitted into place for King; Kalz in plain clothes returning from some sort of assignment in Brussels; the fear of him shown by the German border guard; his genuine interest in his reasons for travelling to Germany and the invitation to an event such as this. It was now crystal clear to King that he had enjoyed an incredible stroke of luck in meeting an Abwehr Major. *And now I'm meeting its Second in Command!*

Every inch the career officer, around fifty and with astute, penetrative eyes, Oster addressed King directly. 'Well, Herr Doktor, you certainly have an interesting topic of study. I'm sure that you have found many in Germany who are prepared to expound on this subject.' King immediately recalled the advice offered by Pym that, with German officers and officials, flattery is often the most effective strategy to get them to talk. 'Indeed, I have, Herr Colonel,' he replied, 'but none in such a senior position as yourself.'

Oster gave a brief, self-satisfied nod, before continuing in a tone which stated loud and clear that he was a man who was used to being listened to. 'What Europe needs is a strong Germany. We live in a very different world to that of 1918 when the Fatherland was crippled by the terms of the Versailles Treaty. The real threat to a civilised and peaceful Europe now comes from Stalin. A strong Germany which is able to withstand the Soviet Union and a strong Great Britain which can continue to maintain order throughout its Empire; these are surely in the interests of both our great nations.'

'I said much the same to Herr Dr King when we met on the train, Herr Colonel,' interjected Kalz, with a challenging look in the direction of the Englishman. 'But I had the feeling then that our guest was not in full agreement with our views.'

King chose his words carefully lest he alienate the Germans, or appear wholly implausible. 'Well Herr Colonel, like you I have little positive to say about Stalin, with his total disregard for humanity and his routine use of terror. And I'm certainly not one of those naïve intellectuals who see developments in the Soviet Union as representing an advance for mankind.' Both Oster and Kalz nodded vigorously, but before King could continue an orderly approached the Major, saluted and said something discreetly into his ear.

'I'm afraid that we shall have to postpone this most interesting conversation, gentlemen, as the *Reichsmarschall* will be arriving shortly. We should make our way to the reception area Herr Colonel,' suggested Kalz with little enthusiasm. The Colonel nodded curtly, as if irritated to be taken from an engaging conversation in order to carry out a distasteful duty. 'I hope we have the chance to continue this discussion another time Herr Dr King,' said Colonel Oster suavely. 'In the meantime, enjoy the rest of your evening with us in OKW.'

King barely had time to take his second glass of champagne and a couple of canapés from a passing waiter, when a burgeoning gaggle of chattering guests streamed into the hall. Feeling very much an unbeliever among the zealots, King moved towards a quiet corner, sure that his height would afford him as good a view as he would want of the Nazi star in action. Nothing could have prepared him for his first view of Reichsmarschall Hermann Göring. A dazzling white uniform braided with gold, whose look was rather spoiled by the double-breasted jacket having to strain over his sizeable girth, here was a man who had clearly gone to seed. His face resembled a round, soft pudding and showed obvious signs of his well-known predilection for narcotics. Indeed, it was only the sight of the Iron Cross decorating his left breast pocket that reminded King that he was looking at what remained of an authentic German First World War hero. After waiting for the applause to die down, Göring began to speak.

As the leading Nazi warmed to his theme of the successful annexation of the Sudetenland, King noticed Oster and a dapper-looking man, in the uniform of an admiral, standing immediately behind the corpulent Reichsmarschall. *That must be Canaris,* King reasoned, *and neither he nor Oster look enthusiastic audience members.* In contrast, those in the crowd wearing the jet black of the SS and, to his surprise, most of the women present, displayed the light-in-the-eyes-look of the true believer. King grudgingly had to admit that, for all his grotesque appearance, the Reichsmarschall knew how to manipulate an audience. In particular, he was a master of the planned pause, which offered just the right number of opportunities for the audience to join in with their ritual outbursts of 'Heil Hitler!' and 'Sieg Heil!' Turning to 'the fearless and astute statesmanship of the Führer,' Göring was working himself into such a frenzy that he gratefully used the opportunity, created by a particularly enthusiastic round of Nazi salutes, to quickly produce a bright yellow, silk handkerchief from his jacket pocket. Having dabbed his sweating brow, at the same time exercising considerable care not to smudge his all too obvious facial make-up, he raised an arm to silence his audience before continuing. 'Our grateful thanks must also go to the organised and efficient military, which carried out its duty with exemplary skill and bravery.' At this compliment, the hall echoed to dozens of military boots being stamped on the floor. 'However, as the Führer has stated, we will never step away from a fight, if it is in the interests of Germany. So, I give warning to all those powers which may be tempted to stand in the way of the legitimate claims of the Reich. With the unfailing support of the Fatherland, I say to these... do so at your own peril!'

By this time, King had heard enough and was considerably relieved to hear Göring say that his address was almost at an end. 'Today, fellow Germans and members of the glorious Nazi Party, is not about speeches. It is about celebrating a great triumph in the succession of victories masterminded by the Führer. But it is also vital that we all recognise that we must retain our perfect state of preparedness for the many battles ahead. These will no doubt be necessary to ensure that the destiny of our Thousand Year Reich is properly fulfilled. Sieg Heil! Heil Deutschland! Heil Hitler!'

After a brief wave and smile for the press cameras, Göring left the platform to a rapturous reception from the body of the hall and made his way along the first floor gallery to the stairs which descended to the ground floor just to the right of King's position. With a mounting sense of horror, mixed with a morbid fascination, King realised that, unless he moved quickly, the Reichsmarschall was going to walk right past him. Once again King found himself struggling against the tide, as he attempted to move towards the centre of the hall just as most of the crowd was pushing for a closer look at Göring. When he finally emerged from the frenzied mass, King caught sight of Kalz's back, no more than a few metres away. The major was in animated conversation with two officers in SS uniform and King blinked with shock as he realised that he actually recognised one of them.

Joachim Brandt.

Suddenly King was transported back to a warm, sunny evening in June 1933, the last day of his stay as a visiting student at Heidelberg University. He had enjoyed a farewell stroll along the Philosophenweg with several of his close friends, including Rachel Bernstein. But his closest friend of all, the man who had given him a love of Wagner and in whom he had instilled a near obsession with cricket, had not shown his face. He remembered how, during a discussion with Rachel about the increasingly precarious situation of Jews in Hitler's Germany, he had realised that he must do everything he could to help her and her family emigrate to England. But his most painful and vivid memory of that day concerned the man who was now standing less than five metres away.

The group had met King's tutor and mentor Professor Daniel Berg in Universitätsplatz and had just begun the short walk to the Weisser Bock restaurant. To their surprise, their path had been blocked by an SS *Untersturmführer*, accompanied by a platoon of men.

Joachim Brandt.

King had been shocked to see his friend, for the first time dressed in the sinister black of Himmler's feared organisation. Admittedly, he hadn't seen him for some weeks, but this had been totally unexpected. As he had approached his friend with outstretched hand, King had assumed that Brandt would join the group for his farewell meal. However, as soon as he had noticed Professor Berg and Rachel Bernstein, Brandt's smile had been instantly replaced by an expression of outrage and disgust. Incredulously, he had demanded, 'Surely, John, you do not mean to socialise with types such as these?'

When King had replied that a farewell meal without such close friends was unthinkable, Brandt, perhaps conscious of the sharp looks being exchanged by his platoon of soldiers, had begun to shake his head, as if having to instruct a rather slow-witted student in the basics of his subject. 'John, John. That is not a good idea. You surely realise how Germany is changing. And changing very much for the better. I think it is important that you respect this process and what it means. And,' he concluded in a more menacing tone, 'you should respect my uniform.'

Before King had been able to answer, Professor Berg and Rachel had moved away from the group, saying, 'We've no desire to cause difficulties for you, John. Perhaps it would be better if we say our goodbyes now.' Keen to establish his command of the situation, Brandt had moved quickly towards Berg, pushing the old man roughly away, 'That's right, old Jew! Get out of here. You have no place in the new Fatherland!'

King had never been able to recollect clearly what had happened next. He had merely noticed the graze on the knuckles of his right hand and then Brandt, struggling back to his feet and wiping away the blood from his lip. Half a dozen jack-booted SS soldiers had immediately surrounded the group, two of whom had seized King by the arms. 'Shall we arrest them all Untersturmführer?' one particularly brutish type had asked with evident relish.

As Brandt had picked himself up from the floor, trying in vain to maintain what dignity he could, he had quickly glanced at King. The eyes of both friends had been full of sadness and incomprehension, for they both knew instinctively that this had changed everything.

'No,' Brandt had barked loudly as he had blinked away his shock, 'That will not be necessary.' Moving close to look King directly in the eye, he had hissed, 'You know that I could have you and all your friends arrested? With one word from me, you would all be on your way to one of our special camps for the antisocial elements in our society.'

Looking at his friend, a feeling of great sorrow had come over King as he had realised what he had done. 'You gave me no choice, Joachim. Surely you must see that?'

A hardness and fury had come into Brandt's eyes as he had replied, 'I had hoped that you would respect my choice to act for my country in the best way that I see fit. I can see now that I was mistaken. Our friendship is over. But one last thing I can and I will give you is my solemn promise that you will live to regret what you have done today.' Before King had been able to reply, Brandt had turned his back on his former friend and, with an icy 'Release him!' had obviously hugely disappointed his squad. The soldiers holding King had reluctantly shoved him back towards his friends, but only after each had delivered a hefty blow to the Englishman's upper body. They had then followed Brandt as he marched quickly out of the square, pushing interested bystanders roughly aside as they went.

'We know you feeble Junkers army-types were terrified that the Czech crisis would lead to war and that you've breathed a great sigh of relief that it didn't,' crowed Brandt's SS *Sturmbannführer* comrade, instantly returning King to the Bendlerblok from his focus on the past. 'But it would be a mistake to get too comfortable in your barracks, Kalz. The Führer sees war with the decadent western powers and the inferior eastern people as both inevitable and desirable. And, as for you amateurs in the Abwehr, we in the SS await only the order to show you how best to protect the interests of the Reich. Believe me Kalz, not many weeks will pass before you and your aristocratic cronies will see the power of the SS.'

'Be that as it may, gentlemen, for the moment I suggest that we enjoy the evening and the peace, long may it last. And my dear Schröder,' Kalz added suavely before turning his back on them, 'do calm down and try to enjoy this rather fine champagne.'

King wanted at all costs to avoid a confrontation with Brandt, but just as he was turning to walk away, the German looked straight at him. An unreadable expression on his face, Brandt quickly approached as King held out his hand, saying amiably, 'Joachim. I hardly expected to see you here tonight. What a coincidence.'

'Indeed, John,' began Brandt, studiously ignoring the proffered hand. 'I thought it was you when I caught sight of you earlier. I imagine,' he added sarcastically, 'you recognised me too, but after our last meeting, I suppose you were keen to avoid me.'

'Not at all, Joachim,' countered King pleasantly, while deliberately looking at his still outstretched hand. 'In fact, it seems to me that it is you who takes little pleasure in our meeting.'

Brandt immediately bridled at what he saw as the smug superiority of the Englishman and fumed as he recalled how it had taken all his self-control not to have King and the rest of them arrested after their confrontation in Heidelberg. Indeed, as a direct consequence of the reporting of his perceived lenience by one of his platoon, he had had to work assiduously to alter his reputation in the SS as too soft on opponents of the Party. Since then, he had frequently proved his worth as a cunning and astute officer and his ongoing posting in America had finally caused his fury at his friend's perceived rejection of him to dissipate. However, while part of him may have been prepared to try to rebuild some sort of relationship with King, his recently developed self-confidence insisted that the Englishman must first make some gesture of penitence for his previous behaviour. Believing that he was acting with perfect reasonableness, Brandt suggested, 'I trust that you have learned since our last unfortunate meeting and that this time you will show me the respect that my status warrants.'

King gazed into the eyes of his former friend and reflected bitterly, *He's asking me for something I just can't give him.* Despite knowing that his refusal would almost certainly destroy any remaining opportunity to avoid a final breach, King deliberately looked down his nose as he answered. 'Indeed, I have learned a great deal since we last met, Joachim. Believe me, I know exactly how much respect to pay to that uniform.'

As intended, this response stung Brandt like a slap across the face and he reacted furiously, 'Be very careful. You are in my territory now and I could destroy you with a click of my fingers.'

King burst out laughing at the threat, responding confidently, 'Really, Joachim? You must do your worst; you don't scare me in the slightest.'

His face burning with embarrassment, Brandt instinctively opened his holster, only to find his hand gripped by his superior officer. 'Brandt!' the man whispered urgently. 'What the hell's going on here? This is not the place...' The sound of Schröder's voice brought Brandt to his senses and, aware of several intrigued faces turning towards the incident, he immediately nodded. 'What on earth are you playing at?' demanded Schröder as he stared with undisguised hostility at King. 'And who is this, that he disturbs you so much?'

Before Brandt could respond, the Englishman introduced himself with a frosty smile. 'My name is Dr John King and I am here at the invitation of your Government to take part in an academic exchange with Great Britain.' Pleased to note both a look of confusion appearing on the Sturmbannführer's face and one of consternation on that of Brandt, he continued icily. 'Joachim and I are old acquaintances from Heidelberg, where, I'm afraid, we parted on unfriendly terms. It appears that, in the intervening five years or so, the poor chap hasn't been able to get over it.'

Brandt, his face a strange combination of fury and disappointment, came nose to nose with King, shaking his head slowly, 'You have just repeated the same mistake you made in 1933. Sadly, you are still incapable of recognising the new reality. So, I will repeat my promise to you. I will enjoy teaching you the error of your ways. Take very great care while you are here in my country. Unfortunate accidents can always happen.'

'That's enough, Brandt,' ordered Schröder urgently, as he pulled him away from King and out of the hall. 'He evidently enjoys a certain protection here and remember, you're only here on leave from America. Don't do anything stupid. He's not worth it.'

All appetite for the event now thoroughly spoiled, King decided to leave the Bendlerblok. Outside, the evening was crisp and dry and, despite the long line of taxis, King decided to walk home. As he strode out, he reflected on the bellicose attitude of Göring. *The Reichsmarschall's comments were obviously directed at the senior officers of the Wehrmacht and Abwehr*, he concluded. *And just how disengaged did they look? They can't be entirely happy with Hitler's aggression towards Czechoslovakia.* As he walked through the cold night, he pondered the significance of the exchange between Kalz and Sturmbannführer Schröder. *Does it suggest a power struggle between the army and Himmler's SS? It certainly implies that the SS holds a pretty dismissive view of the Abwehr.* Approaching Ludendorffstraße, he shivered involuntarily as he remembered Schröder's menacing boast that the power of the SS, and its view of how to protect the interests of the Reich, would soon be demonstrated for all to see. *It seemed almost that some plan was already in place. A plan that's just waiting for the order to proceed.*

King, along with Kalz, Germany and the rest of Europe did not have long to wait for the shocking fulfilment of Schröder's prediction.

CHAPTER SIX

Wednesday 9th November, 1938, Berlin.

On alternate Wednesday evenings since his arrival in Germany, King had enjoyed supper and conversation with Schwarz, his brother and a couple of university colleagues. The members of this loose grouping took it in turns to choose the location and King proposed that they meet at Café Kranzler on the Kufürstendamm. In reply, Schwarz groaned, 'You must be joking, John. I know you're still a bit of a tourist here, but just think of the ghastly types who'll probably be there. And think of the cost for Sebastian and some of the others. They're not lucky academics with tenure, you know.'

'Point taken, Andreas,' replied King quickly. 'Look, I've got a decent allowance on top of my university salary, so how about if tonight's on me?' Seeing the dubious expression on his friend's face, he hurriedly went on. 'I insist. I've really enjoyed your company over these last weeks and I think it's the least I can do. I'm sure they'll all want to hear what I made of 'Fat Hermann' and besides, I've been to the Kranzler many times. It's no more frequented by Nazis than anywhere else in the city centre. Come on, we'll have fun and I've a very special treat in store that I hope you'll all enjoy.'

King had managed to obtain tickets for the Café Leon, where he and his friends would enjoy a review, hosted by the legendary Max Erlich. He really hoped that an entertaining evening at the Kranzler and the Leon would cheer them all up. *We could all certainly use it*, he thought sadly, as he reflected on the dreadful news from Paris, regarding the attempted assassination of German Embassy official vom Rath by the Jew Grynszpan.

It was a pleasant, calm evening with a full moon and clear sky as, shortly after 8.15PM, King approached the Kurfürstendamm. He even thought that he could hear the plaintive calls of some unknown animals, echoing into the night sky from the nearby Berlin zoo. *Perhaps*, he was to think later, *they could sense the imminence of some awful event.* Most of the buildings on either side of the wide boulevard were draped with Nazi flags and the windows of even exclusive shops were adorned with crude propaganda posters. Consciously trying to 'unsee' them, he finally reached Café Kranzler and made his way to the first-floor salon, where he had arranged to meet his friends. The room was about half full and King had no difficulty in selecting a round table for six, perfectly situated in the front window overlooking the Kurfürstendamm. He ordered a coffee from a passing waiter and instructed him that everything consumed on the table should be charged to him.

Schwarz arrived some five minutes later, accompanied by Hans Breitner, one of his doctoral students and Elaine Duval, a Professor of French from the Department of Foreign Languages. Hans was a serious young man who invariably dressed from head to toe in black, whereas Elaine was a typically gamin Frenchwoman. The waiter had just arrived to take the drinks order when Schwarz's younger brother Sebastian entered the salon with his girlfriend Sophie. Sebastian was a slightly smaller and fresher looking version of Andreas and Sophie was a very delicate, fine featured and nervous girl. Jokes about 'Fat

Hermann' were forgotten, as the talk around the table glumly focused on the shooting in Paris and its possible consequences, especially for Germany's remaining Jewish population. King reasoned that, on any reading, this must be seen as the action of a single deranged individual which, therefore, should have no broader ramifications.

'You've got to be kidding,' disagreed Andreas with uncharacteristic hostility. 'Grynszpan's timing could hardly have been worse. He chose the exact date when the Nazis think the 'November Criminals' and Jews stabbed the army in the back in 1918. To make matters worse, it's also when Hitler's 'Bierkeller Putsch' was attempted in '23. The Führer made his usual speech yesterday and they all marched through Munich. Goebbels must have been rubbing his hands with delight that this shooting should happen on such a significant day in the Nazi calendar. We're in for trouble, no doubt about it. The forced removal of the Jews of Polish descent a couple of weeks ago will be nothing compared to what will happen now. I don't even know what it might mean for Sebastian and me. Our mother is Danish after all.'

Sophie looked terrified, as Andreas finished by shaking his head in desperation. 'Don't worry. You know he always exaggerates,' Sebastian said comfortingly, as he placed a protective arm around his girlfriend's shoulders. 'And besides, I'll look after you, I promise.'

'On the way here, I did see quite a lot of SA types hanging around the streets,' said Elaine, so nervously that King decided it was time to attempt to lighten the mood.

'Relax, Elaine. They were probably all out drinking themselves stupid and boasting that they were at Hitler's side in '23. Look, I suggest that we all try to put this stuff out of our minds for one night. I've tickets for us all at Café Leon. It's Max Erlich's latest review, *Mixed Fruit Salad.*

'How on earth did you wangle tickets for that?' exclaimed Hans in excitement. 'I've heard the demand is so great that they're having to move to a bigger venue.'

King was absolutely delighted at the sight of a circle of broad smiles, his friends all nodding in agreement to his suggestion that they 'have another round of drinks here and then push off for the start of the show.' Thankfully, they saw no evidence of any Nazi gangs as they made their way along the Kurfürstendamm to the popular performance venue.

The review comprised a series of excellent musical numbers, composed by Willy Rosen and arranged scenically by Erlich, the theatrical and comedic genius. King was hugely impressed by the spirit, bravery and talent of those members of the *Jüdische Kulturbund,* who performed regularly in the face of hatred and violence from the Nazis. He was also heartened by the level of support offered by an audience which evidently cared little for the race or religion of the person sitting in the next seat or performing on the stage. The drinks and the laughter had flowed freely for almost three hours, when the ecstatic audience finally allowed Erlich and his fellow performers to retreat offstage for the final time that evening. As it cascaded haphazardly onto the pavement, the audience was still excitedly exchanging recollections of the performance and rehearsing their favourite extracts. However, even with their generous level of intoxication, as soon as they set foot outside the Café Leon, it was obvious to the vast majority of the audience that something was very badly wrong.

The stillness of the night was constantly disturbed by strange shouts, screams and loud crashes and the air smelled of smoke and burning. To King, it brought back childhood memories of the bonfire parties which people back in England would have enjoyed just four nights previously. He quickly realised, however, that what was happening on this night in Berlin was not such innocent and harmless fun, but rather something altogether more sinister and brutish. As the friends stood together on the pavement, preparing to set off for their various homes, a group of men in the black breeches and boots of the SS, but wearing civilian overcoats and hats, bustled past and headed directly for the nearby shop, café and restaurant fronts. Each was carrying what appeared to be a long metal stick, which they then used to smash the large front windows of many of the commercial premises. It was obvious from the start that the vandalism was directed exclusively towards property owned by Jewish people. Far from the random actions of some Nazi hotheads, to King this looked much more like a calculated and targeted assault on any Jewish owned business. A second wave of thugs followed the window smashers, using white paint to daub what remained of the damaged shop frontages with crude representations of the Star of David and racist slogans. The first looters soon appeared, their cars and vans screeching to a halt in front of the broken windows of the shops. Shamelessly, and without intervention by the on-looking police, they grabbed what they could and made their getaway. King could see the shock on the faces of his companions and said urgently, 'Let's get ourselves off to our homes. Sebastian, Hans and Andreas, you all live near one another. Now, Elaine and Sophie, where do you live?' The former replied immediately that she could go almost to her apartment block with the three others and it was quickly agreed that King would ensure that Sophie arrived home safely.

Sophie was obviously very distressed, but before King could reassure her, she pointed ahead and her hand flew to her mouth in horror. 'I can smell smoke and see flames over there on Fasanenstraße,' she cried. 'A fire must have broken out. I know people who live there. Let's see if we can help.' Against his better judgement, King followed the running woman in the direction of the smoke and flames. The smell of petrol was very strong and he was sure that the fire was no accident. As they approached the synagogue, with its Moorish design and three large cupolas, they were both shocked at the thick column of smoke which was billowing out from the central dome. King was grateful for the police barricades which restrained the crowds to the opposite side of the street. He was sure that, had these not been present, Sophie would have rushed across the street, with no care for her own safety, to prevent a pile of *Torahs* from burning.

He was sickened to witness the fire brigade hose down the buildings on either side of the synagogue, but leave the beautiful building to the uncontrolled flames. Just as appalling for King was the realisation that many in the crowd were actually enjoying the spectacle of the burning synagogue. Anti-Semitic chants and slogans began to roar through the night air, as increasing numbers of people surrendered to their basest instincts. It did not take long for violence against property to transform into that against people. The catalyst was an unpleasant looking, small man shouting to the mob with shameful relish that a Jewish family lived in the ground floor of the building immediately behind them. No more encouragement was needed than an anonymous 'Let's get them!' to cause several hot heads to begin to break down the door. A roar of triumph went up as a middle-aged man was dragged out of his home and cruelly beaten by members of the baying crowd. The sight of such senseless and indiscriminate violence caused King to recall Sturmbannführer Schröder's sinister boast. *So, this is what the bastard meant.*

King had been briefly distracted by the physical violence and when he turned to speak with Sophie, he realised to his horror that she had vanished. Desperately pushing his way through the laughing people, he called out her name, but when he finally reached the edge of the crowd there was no sign of her. Despondency overwhelmed him, as he realised that he had let both her and his friends down. He had undertaken to get her home safely and he had failed. Just as he was beginning to fear that he would not find her safe and well, he heard a terrified scream coming from a dark alley between two large apartment blocks. The attention of the crowd was still firmly on the burning synagogue, which was now well ablaze, and the beating up of more Jewish residents of the nearby house. King plunged into the darkness of the alley and, as soon as his eyes had adjusted to the poor light, he could clearly make out the shape of a young woman, pushed back against the wall by a much larger and more powerful man in SA uniform. She was whimpering and pleading with him to allow her to go, while he merely shrugged and began to unbutton his coat. 'You have seen how we treat your churches and your holy scriptures... now you will discover how we will treat you, Jew,' he spat with pure malice.

King recognised Sophie and, moving further into the alley, he shouted at the man to leave her alone and let her go. 'Relax, friend,' the man replied irritably. 'We can both take our pleasure here...Just wait your turn.' Outraged, King grabbed him by the shoulder as he turned back towards Sophie, spun him round and hit him hard in the face. His fist felt a satisfying crunch as it broke the man's nose and sent him careering into the wall of the alley, where he slumped, unconscious, to the floor.

'Come on Sophie, let's get out of here,' King urged his terrified and shaking friend. However, he had failed to notice the shadow which had appeared further down the alley and which now blocked their escape route.

'Stay where you are.... both of you,' the figure growled in a thick Berlin accent. 'What's going on here then?' As the man advanced, King was able to make out the upturned plant-pot helmet and thick overcoat of the Berlin police force. The Englishman groaned inwardly, expecting little sympathy, given that a man in SA uniform was spread-eagled and unconscious at his feet.

'I ... er.... that is to say. .. er.' He never got to attempt his explanation of the situation because Sophie, leaning heavily against the wall of the alley, sobbed quietly, 'He was going to rape me. Just because I'm a Jew. My friend saved me.'

A look of distaste crossed the policeman's grizzled face as he weighed up what the distraught young woman had just said and the evidence before his eyes. He gave an almost imperceptible nod of the head before replying in a kindly voice, 'Then you'd better let your friend take you home straight away, Fräulein. There's all kinds of riff- raff on the streets tonight.' Kicking the prone body of the SA man, he continued, 'I'll stay with him until he wakes up. And don't worry your head, if any similar types show up, I'll tell them you ran off in the opposite direction. I'm sorry that you had to endure this tonight, Fräulein. Please be careful and good luck to you both.'

Sophie was crying tears of relief as King, with a nod of gratitude to the old policeman, ushered her out of the alley and towards her home.

CHAPTER SEVEN

Wednesday 16th November, 1938, Berlin.

Two weeks after the reception at the Bendlerblock another message from Major Kalz was delivered straight to King's flat in Ludendorffstraße. Having recognised the familiar handwriting of the German, he eagerly began to read:

Dear Herr Dr King,

I regret very much that I had to cut short our conversation at the recent Reception, but I am sure that you recognised the call of duty. It would give me great pleasure to be able to continue our conversation, both on the very interesting topic of your research project here in Germany and on other possible areas of mutual benefit. I am sure we would have a fascinating exchange of views on these subjects. I would therefore like to invite you to have dinner with me at the Adlon Hotel at 8pm tomorrow evening.

I am aware that this is very short notice. Nevertheless, I do hope that this suggestion meets with your approval and I look forward to seeing you tomorrow evening.

RSVP to the Bendlerblock.
Erwin Kalz

King was eager to experience the Adlon, with its reputation, both as one of Hitler's favourite hotels and as the 'Little Switzerland of Germany'. This, Schwarz had told him, was a sarcastic reference to its status as a playground for diplomats and spies. The scale and grandeur of its frontage was undoubtedly impressive, but even this did not prepare King for the splendour inside the hotel. Saluted crisply by two liveried doormen, he passed through the main entrance and into the opulent lobby, with its vaulted ceiling, grand staircase, rich rugs and high-quality furniture. It brought to his mind a heady cocktail of castle, palace and cathedral, perhaps with a dash of country house. He was totally captivated and did not initially hear the bellboy who was urgently paging him by name. 'Herr Major Kalz is waiting for you, sir, in the dining room,' the functionary explained when he'd secured King's attention. Please permit me to show you the way.' He confidently led King down a long corridor which boasted a parquet floor, covered at various points with beautifully coloured Persian rugs. The arches which connected the columns on either side of the corridor and the ceiling itself were all gently curved, adding to its Middle Eastern feel. Finally, they arrived at the large dining room with its many French windows, some of which looked out onto the deserted dining terrace. Unsurprisingly, all save one of the tables were occupied by men in evening dress or military uniform and their female companions.

    Kalz was seated at one of the smaller tables by the windows. The nearest adjoining table was some distance away and King wondered whether he had chosen this particular position in order to enjoy a degree of privacy. The Major rose with a broad smile, offering a warm handshake to greet his guest. 'John, may I call you that? It's a great pleasure to see you again. Come, please, take a seat. And do call me Erwin.'

'Thank you for the invitation, Erwin. It's most kind of you, although I fear that, as a mere academic, I'll be dull company.'

'Nonsense my dear fellow,' responded Kalz with evident sincerity. 'But first things first. Would you like champagne?' Indicating the bottle which was chilling in a silver ice bucket on a stand by the window, he continued disarmingly. 'I make no pretence of being a great connoisseur, but I am told that this 1928 'Salon' is a very fine vintage.' King gladly accepted the offer and the wine waiter served a flute of the wine to both men.

King was impressed that the German began their conversation by making direct reference to *Kristallnacht*, expressing the hope that he had not been caught up in any of 'that unfortunate unpleasantness.' The look of distaste on Kalz's face, as they discussed the previous week, convinced King that he had no sympathy with the widespread violence to people and property. Clearly no rabid anti-Semite, Kalz nevertheless attempted to pass the whole thing off as the actions of the lunatic fringe of the Third Reich.

'You can't be serious, Erwin,' countered King, determined not to let his host get away with such obvious nonsense. 'I saw enough on Wednesday to convince me that this was neither a disorganised rabble, nor some spontaneous expression of public feeling.'

'You may well be right,' sighed Kalz. 'But I would like to reassure you that such behaviour and attitudes are not shared by everyone in Germany. You must believe that. Hopefully, such excesses will be discouraged and ironed out in time and we can concentrate on building on our more noble achievements.'

'Well, I'm sure that we can both agree with such sentiments,' responded King cautiously. 'But I fear that may well be a forlorn hope. It very much seems to me that the anti-Jewish policies are becoming more central to Hitler's strategy and I, for one, can see no immediate prospect of that changing.'

Kalz used the return of the waiter to refill their glasses and take their order to defuse what could have become a significant argument between them and to turn the conversation toward his guest's ideas on issues of mutual security for Great Britain and Germany. King was also happy to maintain a generally convivial atmosphere in order to encourage Kalz to remain in an expansive mood. Picking up and twirling his champagne flute, King eventually replied diplomatically. 'Well, Erwin, let's consider the proposition that neither the British nor the German people want war. What evidence is there to support this? In the case of Great Britain, the generally relieved reaction to the Munich Agreement, despite some feelings of unease at leaving Czechoslovakia in the lurch, suggests that there exists little appetite for war in my country. But what about Germany? When I arrived in Berlin, it seemed to me as if the population was solidly behind their Führer and his expansionist policies. The feeling of celebration and excitement was palpable.'

'But the feelings here are actually little different from those you described in Britain,' protested Kalz without hesitation. 'It was precisely because Britain and France had accepted the Führer's territorial claims, which in turn meant that a war was not necessary, that the people celebrated. Again, it was relief, not triumphalism.'

King evidently looked sceptical because the German continued in a much lower voice. 'Did you know, for example, that before the Munich Agreement, when war was a distinct possibility, the Führer attempted to generate public support for military action by staging a large parade through Berlin? And what do you think happened, John?' King looked suitably nonplussed. 'I'll tell you. No one bothered to turn up and watch, let alone cheer. Hitler, apparently, was furious. It was also a disaster for those who want war because it showed clearly that the German people have no appetite for it. So, I believe that we can safely begin from the position that neither people wants war.' The German went on to develop the standard argument that many of the recent political and military actions of Germany did not reflect expansionist tendencies at all, but had their roots in a desire to undo some of the most hated elements of the Versailles Treaty.

'It's certainly possible to make that case from a German perspective,' King conceded. 'Equally, there are those at home who believe that Britain should revert to the nineteenth century policy of 'Splendid Isolation.' That we should avoid all continental entanglements and focus solely on our Empire. There are still strong memories of how the Great Powers sleepwalked into war in August 1914 and many are resolute that such a thing should not happen again. But, of course, there are also many who see Germany's rising strength bringing it into inevitable conflict, both with France over leadership of Europe and with Great Britain over colonial influence.'

'Many John, really?' asked Kalz doubtfully. 'Is it not just Churchill and his ragbag band of camp followers who say this? And in any case, surely any possibility of conflict would depend on the point at which Germany's ambitions are satisfied? Remember that the Führer is on record as stating that he hopes that Britain and Germany can together, in equal strength, guarantee long term peace and security. There is simply no argument with your country.'

As King was about to reply, the waiter appeared with the first course of chicken consommé with anchovy biscuits, served with a bottle of chilled Mosel wine. The silver service was excellent and he congratulated Kalz on the choice of starter. 'Let's leave the serious part of our conversation until later, John,' suggested the Major with a twinkle in his eye. 'For now, I'd like to know a little bit more about you, if that's not too impertinent.'

For all Kalz's evident urbanity, King was fully aware that his host was a senior Abwehr officer and thus a potential enemy. Nevertheless, he warmed to the German and happily offered a concise version of his life story, up to and including his appointment at Durham University. Kalz explained that, before embarking on a military career, he had also studied history and, through much of the main course of medallions of lobster à la favorite, the two men chatted happily about the Second German Empire. The waiter had just cleared the empty plates and shared the last of a wonderful Montrachet, when a commotion among the waiting staff caught the attention of both men. Clearly, the entrance of some dignitary was imminent and King could not help but notice the distaste on his host's face as he watched *Gruppenführer* Reinhardt Heydrich sweep into the room with his entourage. Tall and blond, Heydrich looked the epitome of the Aryan ideal and was obviously used to being the focus of attention wherever he went. Gazing intently at the spectacle, King noticed that Sturmbannführer Schröder was among Heydrich's group and that he was staring with undisguised hostility in his direction. Kalz seemed disturbed by the arrival of the Gruppenführer and rapidly suggested that they forgo dessert and make for the lounge, where they could enjoy cognac and cigars.

'Of course, Erwin,' replied King graciously. 'I've eaten far too much already and I'm happy to skip the pudding.' The major laughed at the use of the English term and, with a quick signal to the waiter, indicated that they would take coffee and cognac in the lounge. Their plan to slip unobtrusively out of the dining room was ruined, however, when Heydrich's odd, high-pitched voice called out. 'Herr Dr King, I believe. And Herr Major Kalz. What an interesting pair of diners.'

King and his host had little alternative but to divert towards the large circular table at which Heydrich was seated, smiling icily towards them. Kalz scarcely looked happy as he saluted briskly. 'Herr Gruppenführer. A pleasure, I'm sure.' Heydrich ignored the Abwehr officer and turned the full malevolence of his gaze onto King. 'I understand that at the recent reception at the Bendlerblock you had a disagreement with one of my most valued officers.' Sturmbannführer Schröder, seated at Heydrich's side, grinned at what he imagined was King's discomfort.

Perhaps he had not been in Berlin long enough to be cowed by Hitler's favourite, for King responded with affable charm and confidence. 'With all due respect, Herr Gruppenführer, it was Joachim Brandt who had a disagreement with me. Poor man, I fear he has a disagreement with life itself.'

'That's as may be,' spat the leading Nazi through gritted teeth, his fury at King's response all too evident. 'In any case, that officer is now back in the USA. But you would do well to watch your step here in Berlin, Herr Doktor. It may not be in your best interests to be so unconcerned about the people you irritate.' Content at having had the last word, Heydrich ostentatiously dismissed both King and Kalz by turning away from them and engaging his fellow table guests in conversation.

As Kalz and his guest approached a small table in a far corner of the lounge, their waiter appeared, carrying a tray with a beautiful porcelain coffee service, a bottle of fine old champagne cognac with two enormous balloon glasses and a box of fine hand-rolled Hoyo cigars. Having placed the contents of the tray on the table, the waiter was immediately dismissed by Kalz. 'I had thought that this would suit us admirably,' the German said diffidently as he invited his guest to take a seat. 'But I fear that I may have just lost some of my appetite. What on earth was that all about?'

While King did not possess a Gothic imagination, he was also happy to be out of the presence of Heydrich who, in some inexplicable way, radiated an aura of pure evil. Sensing that the evening might end fairly quickly and unsuccessfully, King decided to play down the whole episode. 'Oh, it's nothing, Erwin,' he began lightly. 'I had the misfortune to run into an old acquaintance of mine from Heidelberg at the reception the other week. We had not parted on happy terms and, unfortunately, he still bears a grudge. And it seems that one of Heydrich's dinner guests could not resist telling tales out of school.'

'And this friend, is he in the SS now?' asked Kalz with evident concern.

'Since 1933,' King nodded, 'He'd just joined up when we last met. In fact, that was one of the issues, over which we disagreed. It looks like he might be some kind of protégé of Heydrich now. But there's no problem. You heard him say that Brandt was back in America.'

'That's true, John,' said Kalz gravely, 'but I must counsel you to be very, very careful not to make an enemy of the Gruppenführer. That could be very bad for you indeed.'

Having poured the cognac and smiling as he held open the box for his guest, Kalz insisted, 'You really must try one of these Hoyos. They are hand rolled in Cuba. To my mind, their flavour is a little sweeter than normal and I like them very much.' King settled himself into the comfortable armchair and gratefully accepted a cup of coffee, a good measure of cognac and one of the cigars.

'You now know that I am an officer of the Abwehr,' began Kalz through a cloud of fragrant cigar smoke. 'Indeed, I have made little attempt to conceal that fact from you. And, of course, you are aware that I take a strong personal interest in the topic of your academic exchange with the Reich as, may I say, do both Colonel Oster and Admiral Canaris.' Smiling suavely, he asked, 'But surely, if we are to talk of mutual security, a key question is what kind of Europe, perhaps even what kind of world, do we desire? I have already this evening mentioned the Versailles Treaty. I'm not surprised that you, as a student of German history, have already acknowledged that it is possible to hold the view that this was a foolish and vindictive act against my country. The economic terms have undoubtedly contributed directly to the current political status quo here and there are many forces pushing us towards barbarity. Do you not agree that, in such circumstances, it is incumbent on all men of civilised standards and goodwill to seek to keep these forces at bay?'

'I have to say, in all candour, Erwin, that I saw little evidence of civilised behaviour a week ago in Berlin,' retorted King sharply. Kalz grimaced before replying with evident sincerity, 'Neither my organisation, nor the Wehrmacht had any knowledge of, or participation in, what can only be described as those atrocities.' In a clear reference to Heydrich, he added softly, 'I believe we have just left the company of one of those responsible. No, the real issue is that civilisation is at the present moment surrounded by threats, and the major one clearly comes from the East. Surely you would agree that a strong Germany, which can hold Stalin at bay, would be in the interests of your country. A civilised bulwark against the tide of Bolshevism, which is, of course the real enemy of both our countries.'

'Well as you know, Stalinism holds absolutely no attraction for me,' declared King firmly.

Recognising the moment for which he had been working, Kalz pounced, 'Then I wonder, John, what would you be prepared to do to help the process of creating a stronger European barrier to such barbarism?' Kalz immediately saw his guest's frown and attempted to reassure him. 'Oh, don't worry, my friend. I know that you are an honourable and patriotic man. As am I. I would never ask you to do anything which is obviously against the interests of your own country or which, in your position, I would not be prepared to do myself. I am merely asking if you would consider sharing with me any information that you acquire during your stay in Germany which you feel is in the joint interest of our two countries. I am, of course aware that you, how shall I put it, have a varied circle of contacts here and that you may well hear things that are of interest to us both.'

'So, you have had me followed then, Erwin. That's not very friendly, is it?' snapped King, before taking another pull at his cigar.

'Of course not, John,' replied Kalz reassuringly. 'But don't be naïve. You must know that there are many informers, most of whom are concentrated in areas where we might expect to find activity which is counter to the interests of the Reich. You have been noticed, that's all. We don't object to your activities in the slightest. But we would, subject to the conditions I have already stated, like to benefit from them.'

King immediately thought of Brunner and his suspicions that he was some kind of informer. *I'll have to be a bit more careful around him in future*, King resolved. *But Kalz looks like he wants an answer.* 'Well, Erwin,' King replied disingenuously, 'you've taken me by surprise tonight and given me much food for thought.'

Kalz deftly concealed any disappointment, conceding, 'Of course you must think about my proposition. There's no rush. Maybe we could meet again in a few days' time, when you've had time to consider things fully. I'll contact you then, and in the meantime, I suggest that we give our full attention to this wonderful cognac and the excellent cigars.'

The evening wound down quickly and King politely declined Kalz's offer to drop him at his flat. As he walked home, he reflected on how, in some ways, his mission was going better than he could have hoped. His growing relationship with Kalz and the attempt to involve him in the work of the Abwehr was more than he could have expected. On the other hand, the uncertain ramifications of his confrontation with Joachim Brandt and now the involvement of someone as powerful and evil as Heydrich could be disastrous for him. *I'll look forward to discussing it all with the Professor. But there's something very important that I have to do first.*

CHAPTER EIGHT

Monday 21st November, 1938, Berlin.

On a cold, grey morning King jumped off the tram as it slowly passed Anhalter Station. A classic railway terminus in the centre of Berlin, with its huge curved roof and tall windows, it embodied the promise and adventure of travel. Shortly before leaving for Germany, King had told Rachel and David Bernstein that he would visit their parents at Christmas, when he would also spend some time with his old mentor Professor David Berg. However, the dreadful events of Kristallnacht had compelled him to bring forward his long trip to Heidelberg. He calculated that the almost twelve-hour journey would give him plenty of time to map out his initial ideas for a paper which the Head of the History Department had asked him to present before the end of the semester. While his attention was fully occupied in contemplation of his academic work, King failed to notice the small, dark-haired man in a grey overcoat, who hastily bought a copy of the *Völkischer Beobachter,* before following him out towards Platform Three and the waiting train.

King passed through the ticket inspection and looked back towards the magnificently curved archway, through which the train would shortly pass, before jumping athletically into a second-class carriage. He easily found a window seat and settled down with his books and notepads. Ever since his time as a student at Oxford University, King had been able to shut out any distractions and get on with even the most challenging of reading. On this occasion, he was so absorbed in the development of the argument which he was looking forward to presenting in his lecture, that he didn't even notice that the old man who had been sitting facing him had been replaced at Erfurt by a much more attractive travelling companion. Indeed, King didn't look up from his papers until the train had left Würzburg and the attendant had passed through the carriage announcing the first sitting in the dining car. He was very pleasantly surprised to find the large, green eyes of a young nurse, with a pretty, open face and bright red hair, looking at him with amusement. 'It seems that you have a very interesting topic of study,' she suggested, a playful twinkle in her eye. 'But you know, all work and no play make Hans a dull boy.' She had spoken the last phrase in accented English and King spontaneously burst out laughing. Of course, she had managed to read the English title of one of the many books which he had formed into a barrier on the table between them. Consciously registering both her appearance and engaging manner, King berated himself for being so absorbed in his work. *At least try to make a good first impression on her, you dolt.*

'Actually, it's John,' he replied brightly, 'and yes, I think you're right. Now, what can we do about that? Was that the call for the dining car that I just heard? Maybe something to eat would be in order?'

'That would be very pleasant,' agreed the nurse willingly. 'I may even be able to practice my English.'

'It just so happens that I am a teacher,' replied King as she looked at him evenly. 'But a teacher of History, I'm afraid.'

'No matter,' came the immediate reply. 'I'm sure that with your excellent German and my basic English, we'll manage. Let's go, while there's still a chance of a free table.' As King followed his dining companion, the sight of her swaying hips and shapely figure promptly sent all thoughts of academic lectures flying out of his mind. A discreetly offered *Reichsmark* note, suavely pocketed by the head waiter, found them quickly seated at a table for two in the rapidly filling dining car.

'You know, I don't even know....' King asked tentatively.

'It's Margaretha... Margaretha Maier. But that's a bit of a mouthful, so all my friends call me Greta,' interrupted the nurse with a beaming smile.

'So, may I call you....' suggested King.

'Greta? Of course, you must,' she replied instantly, before adding mischievously, 'if you'd like to be my friend, that is.'

Unused to being wrong-footed in conversation with a young woman, King felt his heartbeat race in excitement. 'That's a deal, Greta,' he said happily. 'But do you think I'll ever be able to..'

'...finish a sentence?' suggested Greta, with an impish grin. 'I don't know, John. I really don't know.' Their laughter attracted the waiter's attention and they placed their orders before Greta asked with arched eyebrows, 'So, John, what brings you to Germany?'

The conversation and laughter flowed for the next hour, as King briefly explained his part in the academic exchange programme. He then regaled his guest with accounts of his time at Oxford and some of the antics of his students back in Durham, while Greta reciprocated with a series of hilarious stories from her time working in various hospitals throughout Germany. King was very attracted by an ability she shared with him. While she could effortlessly tell amusing stories about those she worked with and for, her concern and commitment was always evident. For once disregarding Pym's instructions to be extremely cautious when socialising in Germany, he relaxed into the simple pleasure of enjoying the company of a very attractive and interesting woman.

The time, both during and after their meal, passed so enjoyably that the waiter was left with no alternative but to suggest that they vacate the table in favour of one of the waiting couples. As they swayed out of the dining car, partly because of the movement of the train and partly due to the effect of the wine they had shared, Greta put her hand on King's arm. At her first touch, an unforgettable pulse of electricity ran through his whole body and his senses shot to red alert. Greta, however, was looking intently through the glass of the door between the dining car and their carriage. 'Did you see that man?' she whispered, 'I'm sure he was looking through your things.'

King was conscious only of his proximity to Greta and by the time he looked up, he simply saw a man walking down the carriage towards his own seat. 'I'm sure you're mistaken,' he replied reassuringly. 'He probably just stumbled into our table as he was walking past.'

As soon as they were seated, Greta replied doubtfully, 'Really, John? I'm not so sure. It looked like he had one of your books in his hand.'

'It had probably fallen on the floor and he just picked it up,' replied King with a relaxed smile. 'A simple kindness. Forget it,'

Greta, however, was far from convinced. 'Be careful, John, please. You must promise me. Germany can be a dangerous place.'

'Of course, I'll take care, Greta,' King hastily reassured her. 'Please don't worry about me.' *She doesn't seem the neurotic type*, he reasoned, *so maybe I should be extra careful when I visit Rachel's parents and Professor Berg. And, I'll make sure I'm not followed when I arrive in Heidelberg.*

King thought it wise to change the subject and asked why Greta was on the train. 'Oh,' she replied, 'that's easy. I work in Heidelberg, but I'm from Erfurt. I've been to see my parents for the weekend and I'm on my way home.'

King explained that he was looking up one of his old teachers at the university and the parents of friends who no longer lived in Germany. He felt a huge surge of frustration as he told her that, unfortunately, he would have to return to Berlin after only two nights in Heidelberg. Although never short of female company, King was by no means adept at reading those signs of immediate chemistry between people. But even he could not fail to recognise the mutual attraction between himself and Greta. The train was only minutes away from their destination, when he began hesitantly, 'Er.... Greta.... er.... I er ... don't suppose......'

'That I'd have dinner with you tomorrow evening?' interrupted Greta, 'I'd be delighted to.' As the train slowed down on its approach to Heidelberg, she quickly suggested that they meet at the Hotel Hirschgasse at 8.30 the following evening. They gathered their belongings and emerged together into the freezing air. A chaste kiss on the cheek and Greta was gone, waving from the rear window of her tram as it disappeared into a light snowfall. *Never mind,* King consoled himself, *I'll be seeing her again tomorrow. And I'm sure that was another kiss she just blew from the tram!*

The chill of the night focused his mind and he discreetly looked at the few people waiting outside the station. The man suspected by Greta was no more than twenty metres away, lighting a cigarette, as if waiting for someone. King quickly put into action his plan to lose any unwanted shadow. He had noticed that the queue of taxis was dwindling rapidly as passengers took them. *Now, if I just wait until there's no one queueing and there's only one taxi left...* Without warning, he seized his chance to jump quickly into the last available cab, taking the man completely by surprise. It was a good end to the day for King, as he smiled triumphantly at the sight of him, unable to follow and reduced to staring angrily at the back of the car as it sped away through the thickening snow.

CHAPTER NINE

Tuesday 22nd November 1938, Heidelberg.

From his hotel window, King saw immediately that several inches of snow had fallen overnight. This afforded the old town a peaceful, charming appearance that not even the few, visible Nazi posters and sagging flags could altogether dispel. He could just make out the twin towers of the gate on the Old Bridge and he immediately thought back to his last day in Heidelberg in 1933. Then, the mere thought of returning to the city as some kind of British secret agent would have sent him into gales of laughter. *But I am,* he reminded himself, *and I'm even being propositioned to spy for the Abwehr!* Smiling at the unexpected turns that life can take, he shook his head and made his way downstairs to the breakfast room.

No one was loitering outside the hotel as, fortified by a generous German breakfast, King set off down the Steingasse. His route took him through the gate and across the river Neckar by means of the Old Bridge. Despite harbouring some concerns over what the day might bring, he felt like an excited schoolboy at the prospect of seeing Greta again. *She really is something special; I can't wait to see her tonight.* Relieved that his trusty old hiking boots were still waterproof, he turned right towards the Hotel Hirschgasse, where he reserved a table for dinner. He then retraced his steps across the Neckar and on into the old town, where he hoped to find Professor Berg still in his quaint old flat on the Seminarstraße. Conveniently close to the university library, this was an area which, during King's time in Heidelberg, had been Bohemian and inexpensive and had, therefore, been popular among the less status conscious faculty staff. The twice weekly market was in full swing as he crossed the Marktplatz, the city's grand town hall which dominated one side of the square. Had he not just enjoyed a good breakfast, he would have been sorely tempted by the roasted chestnuts or the spiced sausages which were sizzling over glowing charcoals. The various smells of food, spices and wooden articles from the various stalls, combined with the clear sky and bright snow gave the square a very seasonal air. This was spoiled only by the inevitable groups of uniformed Nazi activists, busily distributing propaganda material, whose headlines shrieked outrage at the latest 'atrocities' being committed by Poles on peaceful Germans in the Danzig Corridor.

Enjoying his return to the city, King took an indirect route to Berg's flat, turning down Dreikönigsstraße and making his way back towards the river. While Heidelberg looked every inch the prosperous, ancient university city, he despaired about the extent to which it had almost certainly been changed by several years of Fascism. As if to underline the point, as he turned away from the riverbank up Große Mantelgasse, he was immediately confronted by the burned-out shell of one of the city's finest synagogues. More worried about his Jewish friends, King hurried directly to Seminarstraße and as soon as he arrived at the familiar old building, he rang the Professor's doorbell. He was not unduly concerned that there was no immediate answer; *after all, he didn't know I was coming. He's probably just gone out. I'll come back later.* Just as he was about to leave, the door was opened by Frau Ziegler, the caretaker. As a student, King had been a frequent visitor to this building and he remembered her as a powerful and indomitable woman, the wrong side of whom, it was wise not to find oneself. He was now faced by an old lady, squinting anxiously at him, as if trying to recall some long-forgotten face.

'I know you, don't I?' she whispered uncertainly. As King began to answer, she interrupted, more sharply this time. 'No! Don't tell me. It'll come back to me. I may be getting on a bit, but I pride myself in never forgetting a name.' King waited patiently for a couple of minutes, before seeing the warmth of recognition in Frau Ziegler's eyes, closely followed by what he could only describe as terror. 'You shouldn't have come here, Herr King,' she whispered in a tiny, terrified voice. 'I can't tell you anything. Please go away quickly.'

'What's the matter, Frau Ziegler?' King asked gently. 'I've just come to say hello to the Professor.' Holding out a fine leather bound volume, he added, 'Look, I've brought him a present from England. It's an 1843 edition of Shakespeare's poems. I know Professor Berg has a large collection of works by the Bard, so I thought he might like it. Is he at home?'

Prompted by this innocent question, an infinitely sad look came into the caretaker's eyes and she fainted, falling heavily into King's arms. Thankfully, he managed to open the door sufficiently to enable him to struggle through and help the old lady into her ground-floor flat. He carefully lowered her down onto a threadbare sofa and fetched a glass of water which he offered to her lips. Gradually, she recovered her senses and, with them, her look of terror.

'You must go now, Herr King. It isn't safe. What if they were to find out that I was talking to you about the poor

Professor?' she sobbed. 'I have heard that they send people to terrible places.'

'Don't worry Frau Ziegler,' King replied soothingly, 'I'll leave through the back. No one will see me. I know the way and I'll be very careful. But, please, I've come a long way to see Professor Berg. You know what he means to me. What's happened here? Is it something to do with Kristallnacht?'

The mere mention of this word opened the floodgates, as if she was desperate to rid herself of some dreadful knowledge. He could barely keep up with her emotional outburst as she gabbled, 'He was such a good and brave man. Even after he was so unfairly dismissed from the university all those years ago, he was so accepting. Many of his ex-colleagues helped him financially, but he was a proud man. Most of his beautiful books, ornaments, paintings and furniture had to be sold.' Frau Ziegler suddenly stopped talking and stared at King who steeled himself for the worst. 'You know me, Herr King, I'm just an ordinary German, as proud of my country as the next person. But what they've been doing to the Jews, it's just plain wrong. It sickens me, as it sickens all good people. I begged the Professor not to go out when we heard the noise from the street. But when his friend came to tell him that the synagogue had been set on fire and the holy scriptures were being desecrated, he wouldn't listen to me. He went straight down to Lauerstraße to try to save what he could. I was told later that the crowd laughed and cheered as he was beaten to death by those thugs. Such a civilised and good man, Herr King. To meet such an end. How can we continue to believe in God?' She shook her head in total incomprehension, tears flowing down her sunken cheeks.

Almost as quickly as the tears began, however, they stopped, as if she had finally let go of Professor Berg and was now focused only on King. 'Now, please, you must go' she insisted. 'For some days, I've had the feeling that the house is being watched. I don't worry so much for myself these days, but you are so young.'

For the first time in his life, King simply had no words; of hope, of consolation, or even of promised retribution. He simply hugged Frau Ziegler tightly, kissed the top of her grey head, whispered 'Look after yourself' and was gone. He followed the familiar back route out of the building, certain that no one had seen him leave. For an hour, King wandered around in a complete daze. He had feared for Berg, but never expected him to have suffered such a brutal and unwarranted death. He experienced periodic surges of almost uncontrollable anger, during which he had to struggle hard to stop himself taking out his urgent need for revenge on the first uniformed Nazi to cross his path. Eventually, without having any idea how he had got there, he found himself sitting on a bench overlooking the river. The timeless, sedate motion of the water calmed him and he regained control of himself. *The Professor's gone. I've got to focus on those I hope are still alive.*

The Bernstein family lived in a pleasant, though unassuming garden flat in Obere Neckarstraße, overlooked by the famous old castle. King took a slow and circuitous route through the snowy streets and arrived just before 1PM. As he rang the doorbell, he hoped desperately that the news would be better here. No one came to answer the door, but he was sure that someone was inside the flat. *Those net curtains definitely moved and I'm sure I just saw a shadow cross the living room.* He rang three more times, but was forced to conclude that the person inside was, understandably, as frightened as Frau Ziegler. Unwilling to give up and leave, he decided that his only option was to tap gently at the window. 'Dr Bernstein,' he whispered to the glass, 'It's John King here, sir. I'm a friend of Rachel and David. They asked me to come to see you while I'm in Germany. I have a message for you from them.' He saw the curtain move slightly and continued, 'Do you remember me, Dr Bernstein? I was at the university with Rachel in 1933 and I helped her and David to emigrate to England? They both stayed with my parents for a few months.'

Slowly, the door to the flat opened just enough for King to see a small, grey and frightened face peering out at him. 'John, is it really you? I thought you were in England?'

'Yes, Frau Bernstein, it's me,' he confirmed softly. 'Are you and Dr Bernstein all right?' Wordlessly, the old lady turned back into the flat, where she slumped, sobbing into a chair. King immediately noted that many of the family's prized possessions and fine furniture were gone. *Sacrificed to the need to survive*, he realised angrily.

Finally, Frau Bernstein broke her silence. 'They took him just over a week ago. After all the trouble,' she explained in a flat voice. 'They said it was because of all the bad things we've done. But John, my Erich and I, what bad things did we ever do? He's a doctor. He helps people.' King looked on with pity as she trailed off into sobbing incomprehension.

'Of course, you have done nothing bad, Frau Bernstein. You must never think that. But do you know where they have taken your husband?'

'They talked about a place near Munich. A camp where he will have to work in order to make up for the bad things they say he did. They took a hundred and fifty others with my Erich. They said they have all done bad things.... Dachau they called it, I think.'

King's blood froze. He had heard rumours of such concentration camps during his time in Berlin and he was sure that unless Dr Bernstein could be granted a quick release, he would never leave that place alive. Over the next two hours, he tried to comfort his friends' mother as best he could, with news both of Rachel and David. She smiled proudly on learning that her son was a serving police officer in Britain and for a fleeting moment King was able to see a glimpse of the refined and happy woman he once knew. A native of Wales, she seemed particularly pleased to hear that her son was now more British than German. She even managed a weak laugh, as King told her that her son absolutely adored tea with milk and fish and chips.

'We should have gone with them, when we had the chance,' she whispered sadly. 'But it's too late for that now.... far too late.'

King took both her hands in his and said earnestly, 'No it isn't Frau Bernstein. I'll try to arrange for you to go to England as soon as possible. Would you like that? And I promise that I'll do all I can to get Dr Bernstein home, so that he can come too.' As soon as he had said the words, he knew that he had made a promise that he had no certain way of keeping. But, looking now at the hope dawning in the eyes of his friends' mother, he also knew that it had been the right thing to say. He would worry about the practicalities and how Pym might react another time. For now, he simply wanted to offer what little hope he could to this frail lady, who had treated him with such kindness in the past.

'Do you really think we could go to England, John? Would it be possible? Can you help bring Erich home? I'm sure he will be worrying about me and his patients. Of course, officially now he can only treat Jews, but some of his old patients still came to him in secret. They like him you see. My Erich has such a lovely manner.' Listening to her and seeing the faraway look in her eyes, King had some concerns that, without the strength of her husband beside her, she might collapse psychologically.

'Do you see anyone, Frau Bernstein?' he asked gently. 'Is there anyone who can help you?'

King was surprised when she replied with something of her old spirit. 'Don't worry about me, John. I can look after myself. Just do your best for my poor Erich, I beg of you.'

'I'll do my best,' promised King again. 'But you must say nothing of going to England. Not to anyone at all. That must remain our secret. Do you understand, Frau Bernstein? That's very important.'

'Of course, John. I understand fully. You can rely on me.'

The air was noticeably colder, as King walked by the riverbank towards the Old Bridge. He had no clear idea of how he might be able to effect the release of Dr Bernstein from Dachau and help them both to escape Nazi Germany. But, as he trudged through the freezing snow, he was determined that he would succeed in both aims.

***

It was dark when he returned to the welcoming light and warmth of the Grüner Baum. Hurrying through the hotel lounge, he headed straight up to his room, where he quickly removed his boots and overcoat and promptly collapsed on the bed. The rumblings in his stomach reminded him that he had not eaten since breakfast, but the warmth of the room, combined with the nervous energy he had expended during the day, made him drowsy. Before long, and forgetting totally about his planned dinner date with Greta, he was fast asleep.

Some hours later, King was turning restlessly, disturbed by a strange tapping noise and a whispered voice, of which his half sleeping brain could make no sense. Waking up, he could hear more clearly now the insistent knocking at his door and the urgent call 'John! John! Are you in there? It's Greta!'

In an instant King looked at his watch and saw to his consternation that it was nearly ten o'clock. *Oh God,* he thought, as the realisation dawned that he was supposed to have been at the Hotel Hirschgasse for dinner an hour ago. 'Hang on, Greta. I'll be there in a second,' he called, as he scrambled off the bed and moved groggily to the door. There, he was greeted by a sardonic smile.

'So, this is the way you treat a lady on her first date, is it, John? And I thought Englishmen were supposed to be such gentlemen. I can't say that I'm overly impressed...'

'I don't know what to say, Greta. I'm so sorry,' he gabbled. 'I've no idea what came over me. I must have been exhausted. Are we too late for dinner? How can I make it up to you?'

The undiluted amusement in her dazzlingly green eyes simply nonplussed King. He could only gape idiotically, as she mock scolded him. 'You must be joking, John! This is provincial Germany, not the metropolis of London. At this time, we'll be lucky to find a sandwich.'

King had always felt himself to be a man of reason, not prone to flights of fancy or over emotionality. Certainly, he believed that the concept of love at first sight belonged firmly in Hollywood. However, he was totally unprepared for the joke that Cupid seemed intent on playing on him. Standing there in his hotel room, the rationalist knew that he was very much in danger of falling for this woman, whom he had known only a matter of hours.

Instinctively, King began to explain, 'It's important to me that you understand, Greta.' Immediately the red-headed German recognised that something terrible must have happened. She led King back to the bed, took off her coat and sat down next to him, holding his right hand between both of hers. And he told her about Professor Berg and his dreadful end; about the courageous Frau Ziegler and finally about the Bernsteins and his promise to help them in any way he could. He finished by saying that he felt almost guilty because of his happiness, amid such abject misery.

'Oh John, of course you believe that everyone should have a good life, like you. But here, now, in Germany, it's not always that simple. You must never feel guilty for feeling happy. It's surely the fact that some of us are lucky enough to experience good and normal things, even in times like this, that helps keep alive some sense of belief in the human spirit. Do you honestly think Professor Berg would be glad, or sad at your happiness? Be happy in his memory, as well as for yourself.'

King felt humbled by the absolute sense of her conviction, 'You're right, of course, darling Greta. Thank you for helping me to see that. Now,' he smiled boyishly, leaping to his feet, 'what was it you said about a sandwich?'

King had to use all his powers of persuasion, combined with the promise of a hefty tip, to persuade the hotel to provide a range of cold meats, cheese, bread and wine. They enjoyed the meal, and one another's company, all alone in the dining room which was illuminated only by flickering candlelight. Much later and after the final candles had guttered into darkness, they made their way slowly back to King's room. As if to confirm their joint commitment to love and humanity, King and Greta spent the night locked in one another's arms, gently making love and waiting for the dawn to herald a new day.

***

As King awoke, he instantly he knew that Greta was not beside him. The side of the bed on which she had lain was cold to his touch and he quickly realised that she must have been gone for some time. As he moved his hand in the forlorn hope that, somehow, he might again touch her warm skin, his fingers brushed against a piece of paper. He quickly sat up and read:

My darling John,

You looked so peaceful and happy this morning that I didn't have the heart to wake you up - even though I yearned for your caress!

Today, I have an early shift at the hospital and I suppose that I'll be almost half way through it before you read this.

I find this difficult to explain, but life for me seems to have taken on a whole new and a much better meaning since we met on the train, what.... less than two days ago.

But now, I really must go. I'm not sure what the Matron would say if I turned up for work in my best evening dress, so I have to rush home to change.

Take care, my love.

Greta

***

With mixed feelings, King checked out of the Grüner Baum and walked through the bright sunshine and cold dry air towards the railway station. He once more chose an indirect route with several exposed sections, ensuring that, by the time he reached the railway station, he was certain that no one had followed him. On the journey back to Berlin, King couldn't believe that it had been barely forty-eight hours since he had been on the train travelling to Heidelberg. *It seems like a lifetime ago. Or maybe it belongs to a different life to the one I can see now. Greta! I don't care that our countries look like going to war. I want her to be part of my life. The biggest part, too.* He enjoyed only a few minutes to savour his time with Greta, before problems wormed their way into his mind. *I must keep my promise to Frau Bernstein. But how? And what will Pym say? The old man's sure to be furious.* As his eyes fell to the books and notes which he'd ignored since spreading them out chaotically on the table in front of him, he remembered both that this work was crucial to his credibility at the university and that he still had a deep commitment to Pym and his mission. *But other things are also important to me now.*

CHAPTER TEN

Tuesday 29th November, 1938, Berlin.

A Siberian wind was blowing from the east as King walked along Wilhelmstraße towards the British embassy and his appointment with Pym. Bizarrely, the NSDAP headquarters were situated on the same street and, as he approached the flag-festooned building, a car drew up. It was immediately surrounded by a platoon of SS guards forming a cordon that blocked the pavement to pedestrians. With sinking heart, King realised that some star of the Third Reich was just arriving. Ragged cries of 'Heil Hitler' were raised as Rudolf Hess, characteristically dressed only in shirt sleeves despite the cold, climbed out of the car and rushed up the steps of the main entrance. King could not help but notice that his saturnine features were even more pronounced in the flesh than in the many photographs that were published regularly in the media. Moving on quickly, he gratefully left the small crowd gaping at the retreating back of the Deputy Führer and approached the elegant building which housed the British Embassy. There, he was surprised to see another crowd swarming around its four columned neo-classical entrance. The steps leading up to the door had been hastily blocked with trestle tables, behind which stood officials who were monitoring those who sought entrance. Most of those in front of the embassy were Jewish, dressed in decent quality, but very worn coats and all had the hunted look which King was finding increasingly familiar.

'But you must let me in!' one of the women was crying desperately. 'They're only babies.... seven and five. You must find room for them. We've read about the plans in the *'Jüdische Nachrichtenblatt'*.' King never heard the official's response as he was approached by a British soldier. 'Excuse me sir, do you have business at the embassy?'

'Yes,' replied King evenly, as he handed over the letter requesting his attendance. 'But what on earth's going on here?'

'Oh, it's the kiddies, sir,' replied the sergeant sadly as he reviewed King's documentation. 'You know, sir. The plan to allow Jewish children to leave Germany. It looks like Britain's going to take some. Not many, mind. Bloody shame, if you ask me, sir. We should take as many as wants to come. Help them get away from these barbarians here. But I suppose that's too simple a view, eh sir?' The soldier then saluted and returned the letter before confirming, 'That's all in order, sir. Thank you. I'll take you through the barrier, then it's up the stairs, through the door and the reception desk on the left will sort you out.'

King took a final glimpse at the increasingly desperate-looking crowd, before thanking the sergeant and making his way into the embassy. The young woman at the reception desk was evidently expecting him and immediately led him to the lift which took them to the top floor. After she knocked at a door marked 'Meeting Room 12', he heard the unmistakable voice of Pym bid him enter. 'John! It's good to see you again,' the Professor said warmly, his hand outstretched in greeting. 'As you can see, they've laid on tea and sandwiches for us. It looks like they think we've a lot to talk about.'

The room had ten chairs, placed evenly around a boardroom table and its large windows offered both natural light and a splendid view along Wilhelmstraße and its many important buildings. Pym sat at the table and pulled out the chair next to him so that both men could enjoy the warmth of the blazing coal fire. A portrait of a rather stern looking King George VI, dressed in full naval uniform, stared down at them from the wall above the fireplace as if he also had things to say in the meeting.

'I hope you didn't have too much trouble getting into the building, John', began Pym with a faint smile. 'I'm afraid we're coming more under siege as each day passes.'

'What exactly's going on out there? They all looked Jewish to me and a sergeant tried to explain, but I didn't quite catch his drift,' replied a frowning King. Pym explained briefly about the *'Kindertransport'* plans which had been developed to allow the rapid emigration of Jewish children from Germany to Britain. 'Damned disgrace that some back home don't seem to want to take any of them,' he grumbled. 'Have they no idea what's going on here? Or do they simply not care?'

'I imagine it's more that they want to bury their heads in the sand and pretend it doesn't concern them,' said King sadly. 'It's much easier to justify that kind of position to oneself when one has no direct experience of the Nazis and what they're capable of.'

'You may be right,' conceded Pym, 'I just wish we could do more to protect these people.' King seized this unexpected opportunity to remark that he wanted to discuss a similar issue later in the meeting. Immediately on guard, Pym stared at him and murmured noncommittally, 'Very well, John. But first, tell me how things have developed since your arrival here.'

King gave a full account of his experiences at the university, in which Pym showed little obvious interest. However, his ears pricked up noticeably when King told him of his chance meeting with Kalz on the train to Berlin. And when he went on to offer an account of the evening at the Bendlerblock and his subsequent attempted recruitment, Pym was beside himself with agitation.

'Good Lord!' he exploded. 'This is splendid. Absolutely splendid. I never dreamed that such a thing might happen. But now the opportunity has presented itself, we must use it to the maximum.' The two men discussed how King's involvement with Kalz might provide a valuable insight into German Military Intelligence and agreed that he should make a sympathetic response to the German. King was surprised, however, when Pym insisted that no time should be lost in exploiting the unexpected opportunity. Noting this reaction, the Professor raised a hand, 'I'll make clear my reasons for saying that when you've finished your report.'

King then offered a brief description of his encounter with Joachim Brandt, 'Do you remember him, sir? He was a very good friend at Heidelberg until he joined the SS in '33. We didn't part on the best of terms.' Recognition began to dawn for the older man and he slapped his thigh in irritation. 'Of course. Brandt. Now I remember. I'm not sure I ever met him, but I remember you telling me all about how he went over to the 'dark side'. God, what rotten luck!' King then outlined the thinly veiled threat from Heydrich and the information that he had given about Brandt's return to America.

'Well, John,' the Professor responded, 'I won't insult you by pretending that all that's good for you. But, accepting that Heydrich is a very powerful man, I think we can hope that neither you, nor Brandt will occupy his mind for long. Just keep your eyes open even more now for any threat. How did Kalz react to Heydrich?'

'He was obviously repulsed by and terrified of him in equal measure,' replied King. 'However, other than making our meetings more discreet, I don't think it will affect things significantly. I'd say he thinks that I could be a useful source for the Abwehr.'

'That's clear,' agreed Pym with a firm nod, 'but he's going to have to hurry up. You see, John, your faked death and secret return to England is likely to take place some months earlier than had been anticipated.' Responding to King's shocked expression, the Professor explained, 'The way Hitler has broken Czechoslovakia and is now circling Poland makes it highly likely that we'll be at war with Germany within six to nine months. Naturally, you'll need to come back to Britain before hostilities start in order to establish yourself among the pro- German communities. That means that we should meet in January to finalise details of your return.'

January? reflected King in horror. *Christ, I expected to be in Berlin until the summer at least. And what does this mean for Greta and me?* He had thought a great deal about her since his stay in Heidelberg and his initial attraction showed no sign of fading. However, the distance between

Heidelberg and Berlin and their respective jobs meant that seeing her again would be possible only when Greta could take a few days' holiday, possibly at Christmas. *What a bloody mess!* King moaned inwardly.

Is there a problem, my boy?' asked Pym astutely. 'Only you look a bit off.'

'No, Professor,' replied King flatly. 'I was just surprised at the suddenness of the new plans. I suppose I'll get used to it.'

'Very well. But now John,' asked Pym unenthusiastically, 'you mentioned earlier that you had something else to discuss with me.... something of a personal nature perhaps?'

King explained concisely what he had found when he had gone to Heidelberg, what he had been told about Dr Bernstein and Professor Berg and what he had promised the Doctor's wife. 'I want you, or rather I want Britain to do whatever it can to help these people, sir,' said King firmly. 'I would regard it as a personal favour to me.'

Pym seemed genuinely taken aback by the younger man's account and sat with his head in his hands for a full minute before whispering. 'My God, John. That's terrible news. I knew Berg, of course. When we were both much younger. He was a gentle and kind man and an excellent scholar.'

'Yes, sir,' interjected King, determined to press Pym. 'It is appallingly sad. But these last few weeks here in Germany have taught me that we should, above all else, do what we can for the living. A dear friend of mine helped me to understand that that's exactly what the Professor would have wanted.'

At his mention of 'a dear friend', Pym gave King a penetrating look, but didn't broach the matter, preferring to dead-bat the younger man's plea. 'I'm not at all sure that we can do anything. I'm fully aware of what I said about all those poor people outside, but that's quite different. You must realise that your mission is by far the most important consideration and I will not do anything that may compromise it.'

'Then frankly sir, I have to ask myself whether the mission is worth continuing,' asserted King forcefully. 'After all, surely it's precisely what we're fighting for... the value of the individual and the rights we all should be able to enjoy.'

'It isn't as simple as that, and you know it,' retorted the older man angrily. 'We can't afford such luxuries in our line of work. Damn it all! I really thought you understood that.'

Pym's disappointed sigh deeply irritated King and he pulled no punches in clarifying his position. 'Then let me make myself clear, sir. If you wish me to carry on with this assignment, then you must promise me that you will do all you can to help Dr and Frau Bernstein.'

'All right,' Pym conceded half-heartedly. 'You leave me little option. I promise I'll do what I can to help your friends. I should have some news for you when we meet in January. But, until then, I insist that you do nothing that might compromise your position.'

CHAPTER ELEVEN

Christmas 1938, Berlin.

With only a few hours to wait before Greta arrived in Berlin, a relaxed King was savouring a cup of strong coffee and congratulating himself on the success of his recent end of semester lecture at the university. His mellow mood was shattered, however, when Frau Bauer bustled into his flat, dusters in hand. 'My God!' she gasped, 'I didn't expect you to still be here. But it's good that you are.'

'Why?' asked King, 'Can I do something for you?'

'Not exactly,' she responded carefully, 'It's just that I know that you two young people won't have that much time together. So, if your lady friend wants to stay here well, after all, there's plenty of room in your flat.'

'Thank you very much Frau Bauer,' King replied gratefully, 'But Greta has already arranged to stay with an old friend of hers. They studied nursing together.' Smiling at the old lady he promised, 'I'm sure you'll get to meet her though. Never fear.'

The caretaker's crestfallen face immediately lit up, 'I should think so too. After all, I am in the place of your dear mother here. It's my duty to meet her and besides,' squeezing King's arm as she spoke, 'I do love a bit of romance in life, even if it's not in mine.' With a cackling laugh, she finally allowed King to get on his way, adding as an afterthought, 'Oh, and don't you forget to buy her something nice for Christmas.'

Greta's final night shift at work had finished very early that morning and she was scheduled to arrive in Berlin late in the evening. King had arranged to meet her at Anhalter Station, from where they would go to her friend's flat in Charlottenburg. He had thought he had plenty of time, but Frau Bauer's words sent him into a panic. *A present. Of course! How could I have forgotten?* He suddenly leapt up, grabbed his coat, gloves and hat and rushed out of the door, Frau Bauer's knowing laughter echoing in his ears.

Never an enthusiastic shopper, King nevertheless ventured in vain into several stores and had ended up in the 'last chance saloon' of the enormous *Kaufhaus des Westens.* Perplexed, he stood gazing at the floor directory and marvelled at the sheer scale of the store. Fortunately, there was a temporary section dedicated to assisting men in search of a suitable last-minute present for wife or girl-friend. 'You should try this, sir,' the pretty young assistant said, while holding out a plain cylindrical bottle, containing a bright orange-red liquid. 'It's called Tigress and it's the very latest from Fabergé. It only came out this year. Just try it,' she urged him hopefully.

King had to admit that the scent was very exotic, in a spicy-oriental way. 'OK. Sold', he smiled at the delighted assistant, 'Now would you gift wrap it for me, please?' As he left the shop, he felt pleased with his present of the perfume together with some tickets for the recently released Errol Flynn film, *The Adventures of Robin Hood.*

An excited King arrived to meet Greta's train far too early and killed time slowly drinking a coffee and a glass of schnapps in the station buffet. *Should calm any nerves*, he told himself. Finally, the train moved slowly into the station and began to disgorge its passengers, mainly business travellers, those coming home for Christmas and military personnel. At last he caught a glimpse of bright red hair and then he could see her, struggling along the platform with the most enormous suitcase. He waved and shouted for her to put the case down before running into her warm embrace, asking himself happily, *Is this what falling in love feels like?*

'Welcome to Berlin,' King said, a cheesy grin on his face. 'It's wonderful to see you again.'

Greta smiled, but replied wearily, 'It's super to be here John. But I've had a very tiring day. I wonder, would you mind too much if we went straight to Anna's flat?'

King had noticed her pale face and the dark shadows under her eyes and agreed immediately, 'Of course not. Come on, let's find a taxi.' Anna's flat was on the first floor of a small block, situated on a pleasant, tree-lined road and King observed jokingly, 'Very nice. Nursing must pay pretty well in Berlin.'

'Oh, Anna inherited money from a maiden aunt who died some years ago,' replied Greta, while ringing the doorbell. 'She definitely couldn't afford a place like this on nurse's pay.'

A dark-haired woman opened the door and immediately exclaimed joyfully, 'Greta! It's lovely to see you. Come in please.' Once inside Anna's flat, they walked through a generous hallway and into a well-proportioned living room. Greta introduced King to her friend as 'my English professor' before going to change out of her nurse's uniform. After showing Greta to the guest bedroom, Anna offered King a glass of wine and asked about his impressions of Germany. After almost fifteen minutes, they realised that Greta had been away far longer than a change of clothes would require. 'I'll go and see what's keeping her,' Anna proposed, only to return alone with a shrug and a smile. 'She's fast asleep, I'm afraid, John.'

'Oh,' replied King, hiding his disappointment. 'Not to worry. I remember doing something similar myself in Heidelberg. I know what it's like sitting in a packed train for twelve hours. Look, tell Greta I'll be in the Café Kranzler at 11AM. And if that's too early for her, I'll just come on here.'

As he entered the dark hallway of his flat, King was suddenly struck by the contrast between his own home and the warmth and conviviality he had just left. Wide awake deep into the night, he wondered, *why do I have to leave Berlin so soon? Should I tell her what I have to do? I know she's no Nazi lover, but she is German and I'm British. And we'll be at war very soon. What would she think of me? A spy? A brave anti- Fascist? Would it be fair to her to put her in such a position? Would it,'* suggested his last thought before he subsided into a restless sleep, *actually be fairer to leave her thinking I'm dead? At least then she could draw a line under me.*

***

At Café Kranzler, King managed to grab a window table for two which looked out over the busy Christmas shoppers thronging the Kurfürstendamm. He didn't wait long before Greta arrived, looking refreshed and turning heads as she made her way to his table. He rose and they instinctively entered a lovers' embrace, during which King murmured into her ear, 'Greta, you look absolutely stunning!' Having ordered coffee cognac for two, King asked how long it had been since she last visited Berlin. To his surprise, she explained that she had not been in the city for several years and they spent some time deciding how to spend their day.

First, they enjoyed a happy hour at the Christmas market in the Lustgarten, followed by visits to several of Berlin's famous department stores. Being with Greta, and surrounded by the bustling crowds, immunised King against his dislike of shopping and he realised that he was really having fun. When they stopped to take a cup of glühwein from a gaudily coloured stall, Greta asked suddenly, 'I know we had planned to go out for dinner tonight, but will you come to Anna's instead? Her partner and her brother and his wife will be there and she particularly asked if we'd make up the party. You must have made quite an impression on her. She's usually quite a private person, but it seems that she's really taken a shine to you. Do say you'll come, please.'

'Of course I will,' he replied without hesitation. 'I can easily cancel the restaurant.'

'And don't forget your toothbrush, darling,' she said with an inviting twinkle in her eye. 'You never know when you may need it.'

King swept her off her feet in a fierce embrace, before asking doubtfully, 'It's not black tie is it? That area where she lives looks terribly posh to me.'

'Of course it is,' she laughed. 'The butler and servants will be there too!' As she said this, she quickly picked up some snow from the window frame of the stall and threw it at King, before running off into the crowd.

The rest of the afternoon was spent, mingling with the crowds and really entering into the Christmas spirit. As the light was beginning to fade, Greta explained that she'd promised to help with the meal, 'And, of course, I'll need to get ready for you.' King felt an unmistakable thrill of anticipation as they parted with a long lingering kiss at the Charlottenburg tram stop. It was a somewhat light headed King who walked happily through the slush back to Ludendorffstraße, pausing only to buy a couple of bottles of red wine for the party and a box of chocolates for Anna.

On arriving home, King gave Frau Bauer a bottle of sherry and half a dozen sweet mince pies for Christmas. "I couldn't believe it when I saw them in the English section of the KDW food hall,' he explained as she studied them dubiously. In return, she insisted that he toast the season with a few of her friends in her ground floor flat. The middle- aged ladies were unexpectedly lively company and they certainly relished having a younger man in their midst. When he thought to check the time, King was shocked to see that it was almost seven thirty and he hastily made his excuses. A quick shower and, having decided that he may as well go the whole hog, a rapid change into his dinner suit, saw King rushing out of the flat barely half an hour after he had left the caretaker's party.

Christmas spirit was much in evidence on the tram, as an obviously intoxicated conductor announced to everyone that, 'In the seasonal spirit of goodwill to all men, I'm not taking any fares this evening. Merry Christmas everybody!' A loud cheer went up from the passengers as bottles of schnapps and other fiery spirits were passed around the car. It was, therefore, a very mellow King who arrived at Anna's flat. A smiling Greta opened the door, causing him to stagger backwards. 'Gosh, you look sensational. You almost bowled me over.'

She giggled girlishly in response, 'Are you sure that it's not the effect of the schnapps I believe I can smell on your breath?'

'Well, maybe I did toast the season en-route here,' he acknowledged sheepishly, 'but seriously, you look like a million dollars.'

Greta smoothed the full skirt of her long black dress and, much to King's pleasure, did a quick twirl. 'It's silk and satin, embroidered with black sequins,' she announced proudly to him. 'A neighbour of mine in Heidelberg is a wonderful seamstress and she made it from a photograph in a fashion magazine that I gave her. It's a copy of an original by the French designer Madeleine Vionnet. I'm so pleased you like it. And,' she whispered, 'I'm really happy to see you in your dinner suit... your tweed jacket wouldn't have matched half so well! Anyway, come on in and I'll introduce you. The others are already here.'

Anna and the other guests were lighting the candles on the large Christmas tree and Greta introduced him first to a man in his early thirties with an improbably handsome face and dark wavy hair. 'This is Guido. Anna's friend. He works at UFA, the film studios. We all think that must be terribly glamourous.'

The man shook King's hand vigorously and remarked with a smile and a self- deprecating shrug, 'It's not so glamourous being up before dawn and having to put up with the histrionics of some of the actors.'

The other couple comprised Anna's brother, Carsten, and his wife, Ilse, who were both several years older. 'Hello, John,' Carsten said warmly, 'I'm sure I speak for everyone here, when I say that I'm delighted to meet you, especially as you are an English guest in Berlin.'

King felt immediately at home and, over the pre-dinner *sekt,* the conversation settled into reminiscences of Christmases past. As their glasses were being refilled, King asked eagerly, 'Mmmm. What's that divine smell?'

Anna laughed with delight, 'It's our traditional Christmas meal and you'll just have to wait to find out what it is. But now, ladies, we have work to do in the kitchen.'

King only had time briefly to explain the reason for his stay in Berlin, before the first course of thick vegetable soup was served. To King's satisfaction, the conversation centred on Guido, who regaled the table with hilarious accounts of his experiences at UFA. King was interested to hear Guido explain that, during the previous year, he had been involved in helping Karl Hartl direct a mystery comedy, *The Man Who Was Sherlock Holmes*, and that he had spent most of the current year working on the musical *Carmen - de la Tirana*, which was based loosely on Bizet's opera. Carsten declared himself to be an avid reader of Conan Doyle's stories and, of course, Guido had had to read many of them in preparation for his work on the film. It was, therefore, little surprise that the three men spent some time debating which was their favourite Holmes tale. In the end, they had to agree that they couldn't separate *The Sign of Four, The Hound of the Baskervilles* and King's choice, much to the amusement of Greta, *The Red-Headed League*. 'You're clearly a terrible charmer, John,' teased Anna, to which he protested in vain that it was, indeed, his favourite story.

The main course of roast duck with vegetables was served with the rich Chateau-neuf-du-Pape, brought by King. For several minutes the conversation faltered as the six people seated round the table gave their full attention to the delicious food. 'Well, Anna,' Guido said, as he finished his plate, 'I'm sure I speak for us all. That was absolutely superb. Our compliments to the chef.'

'But now, it's time for the presents!' declared Anna as she held up an improbably large parcel for Guido. Greta was delighted with her perfume, but it was the film tickets which caused the most interest.

'It's in Technicolor, isn't it?' asked Guido keenly. 'At UFA the boffins tell me that system is absolutely incredible.'

'And I've heard that it's a pretty thinly veiled attack on Fascism,' added Carsten approvingly.

Not wishing to encourage a political discussion, King replied, 'It's a traditional English tale which has been given the full Hollywood treatment. Green tights obligatory. I think it'll be a fun thing to do over Christmas.'

'I agree. Thank you, darling,' said Greta enthusiastically, before planting a lingering kiss on King's eager lips. The dining table was then pushed to one side, the rug rolled up to reveal the polished wood beneath and the gramophone player set up. 'I'm a dedicated jitterbug,' declared a tipsy Anna. 'Now, which of you will join me?' She immediately put a new copy of the recently released *Benny Goodman Live at Carnegie Hall* on the turntable and pulled Guido up from his chair to join her. King had been to many student jazz parties in the last decade and he invited Greta onto the impromptu dance floor.

After a good half hour of frenetic swing, Carsten found copies of 'Smoke Gets In Your Eyes' and 'I've Got You Under My Skin.' Moving closer to Greta as the music slowed, King felt her respond to his touch and before long they were both lost in their own world, totally oblivious to the others in the room. The warm and relaxed feeling from the food and wine, combined with the music and, of course, the feel of Greta in his arms, overwhelmed him. He was absolutely certain that he had never been happier in his whole life and things became even better for him some hour or so later as the party broke up with many 'Merry Christmases' and promises to meet again soon. Carsten and Ilse set off for their flat and the four remaining guests enjoyed a final glass of cognac, before a smiling Greta led King to their room.

***

King awoke to the merry peal of church bells and, somewhat dimly after the excesses of the previous evening, he remembered that it was Christmas Day. Greta's luxuriant hair was spread across his chest and, as he looked at her peaceful and contented face, he felt totally at one with the world. He smiled as he recalled their love making which by turn had been fierce and urgent, then gentle and mellow. A particularly loud peal of bells caused Greta to stir from her slumber and King's 'Happy Christmas, darling,' accompanied by a hungry kiss brought her into full wakefulness. They decided to take advantage of the bright sunny weather and the covering of new snow, by having a quick breakfast and going for a long walk to Wannsee. 'We might even be able to skate there,' suggested an excited Greta.

In common with most people falling in love, they found joy in the simplest of things; a snowball fight as they passed the lurking monstrosity of Hitler's Olympic Stadium; looking at the snow-covered trees of the Grünewald and finally reaching the Wannsee itself. Although snow covered, few people were walking or skating on the lake's harmless looking surface. Neither King nor Greta were keen to risk a dip in the freezing water and, by mid-afternoon the sun was fading fast, so they decided to head back to Charlottenburg. The four other people from the Christmas Eve party had been invited to a traditional family meal with Anna's parents in Dahlem and she had, therefore, offered Greta the use of her flat for the evening.

They spent a much quieter evening alone in what was a tantalising taste of what life could be like with Greta, were circumstances different. After the feasting of the last twenty-four hours, they enjoyed a simple meal of bread and cheese and soon had the crockery and cutlery washed, dried and put away. Until Anna and Guido returned, they listened to music, discussed its merits and, of course danced, opting more for the slow, romantic tunes, which encouraged him to hold Greta tight. It was in the middle of one of these slow dances that King suddenly held Greta away and declared, 'You do know, that I've fallen in love with you?'

His determined look told Greta that he was absolutely serious and she hugged him tight. Tears forming in her eyes, she began to whisper in his ear, desperately hoping that he would understand. 'I like you, John.... I like you a lot.... a very great deal, in fact.... and I love making love with you. And if it could always stay like that..... But I know that with you, it would become much more. And I really don't think that that would be a good idea, do you?' The last words were said as a sad and realistic acknowledgement of what they both knew to be true.

King desperately fought to reject her logic. 'Why not?' he challenged. 'Why couldn't we just live together. Anywhere. You could get a transfer to Berlin or I could move to the university in Heidelberg. I'm sure they'd be pleased to be associated directly with the exchange programme. And when that's over, you could come back with me to Durham.' As soon as he had said the words, he knew that they were both ridiculous and impractical, especially given the reason he was in Germany. He blinked and looked down at the floor between them, a desolate expression on his face. Greta led him to a chair and kneeled on the floor beside him, 'Oh John. You're such a dreamer. Can't you see, it could never work. We're not children who can pretend that we can change everything. We can't. But we can live for the moment. We can enjoy our time together and, when the time comes as we both know it must, we can part as good friends.'

King was not prepared to give up so easily, 'But I think we can have a future together. I think it would be great.'

Greta seemed even more saddened by this. 'Would it?' she asked, 'Would it really, John? You know as well as I do that next summer you must go back to England and I must stay in Germany. It's also not impossible that our two countries will soon be shooting at one another. Let's not fool ourselves. War with Britain is a very real possibility... it nearly happened last year. And I know that you think that too. I really don't think that I could survive letting myself fall in love with you and then losing you straight away.'

'You're not going to lose me,' King replied, more in an effort to persuade himself, just as Anna and Guido returned from their family party. After a quick cognac with the returning couple, Greta and King retired to their room where they lay, exhausted after making love, each in some ways alone with their own thoughts and concerns.

Their tickets to see *The Adventures of Robin Hood* were for the evening of Boxing Day and they spent the hours before they left for the cinema eagerly anticipating some genuine swashbuckling from Errol Flynn. By some unspoken mutual agreement, neither of them had mentioned their conversation of the previous evening and, much as it gnawed at him inside, King had to admit that silence was now probably the best policy. They both said their farewells and thanks to Anna, as they were moving for this last night of Greta's stay in Berlin to King's own flat on Ludendorffstraße. Frau Bauer, of course, just happened to be in the hallway as they arrived. She happily gave Greta a resounding seal of approval, by welcoming her and expressing the view that, 'I'm very pleased that my charming English gentleman has found himself such a lovely German girl. It's a real pleasure to see such a handsome couple as you. After all,' she added with a mischievous glint in her eye, 'so many of those we see most frequently in the newspapers are hardly oil paintings, are they, my loves?' With a final knowing nod, she confided in Greta, 'I can see that you'll be the making of him, my dear,' before she bustled off into her own flat humming happily.

Given the film's brand-new colour system and superb action sequences, King was easily able to overlook its questionable history and join in the audience's huge enjoyment. Greta was due at work on the early shift on December 28th and planned to leave Berlin the next morning. They decided, therefore, to enjoy a late supper on the Kurfürstendamm, before returning to spend their final night together at King's flat. They were both up early the next morning, aware that this escape from real-life was rapidly coming to an end. Holding to their unspoken agreement not to raise the issue of where their relationship could go, they both agreed to rule out any last-minute declarations of undying love as too painful to bear. After King loaded Greta's suitcase onto the train, they simply kissed one another goodbye. As he watched her train disappearing from view, a miserable King wondered when he would see her again.

***

Climbing up the stairs towards his flat, King was moodily pondering how on the one hand, chance had introduced him to Greta while, on the other, fate seemed determined to take her away from him. Frau Bauer waddled out from her office and commiserated with him. 'Poor dear. You look terrible. Has your sweetheart gone home? Never mind, she's keen on you, there's no question of that and you'll have plenty of chances to see her again.... After all,' she continued with her playful cynicism, 'it's not as if you do a full day's work at that university, is it love? Now my poor Gottfried, he certainly knew what a day's work was and no mistake.'

'Yes, I'm sure, Frau Bauer and thanks for your concern,' interrupted King impatiently. 'But if you'll excuse me, I actually do have a lot of work to do.'

'Of course, dear. I just wanted to give you this. A smart young man delivered it just after you and your lady friend had left for the station. I do hope you don't mind me taking it in for you. I thought it might be important and I didn't want to leave it in the hallway. Might it be another invitation to one of those big political events? You might even see the Führer...'

'Thanks Frau Bauer, I'm sure it's nothing so important,' King lied, as he took the handwritten envelope from the caretaker. 'It's probably a message of some kind from the university... they did say something about an emergency staff meeting being called for just after New Year.' As soon as he was comfortably seated in his favourite armchair, schnapps warming the back of his throat, he opened the brief note from Pym. It informed him that he would be leaving Germany at the end of the first week in January and asked him to visit the British embassy on New Year's Eve, in order to receive a full briefing and to make firm plans for his departure.

King was appalled that these orders outlined an even earlier departure than he had expected. In a strange way, this unanticipated change in the time remaining to him in Germany helped to crystallise his thoughts. *It's obvious that I must do my duty. And that means I'll just have to try to clear my mind of Greta and what might have been. At least if she thinks I'm dead, she'll be able to forget me and move on with her life.*

CHAPTER TWELVE

Friday 6th January, 1939, Switzerland.

As King sat in the dining car of the train, taking his second café cognac in an attempt to dull the emotional pain he felt, he began to reflect on the rush of events that had taken place in the week since New Year's Eve.

King had expected that the plans for his unfortunate 'death' in Switzerland, and speedy reincarnation in Britain as James Kemp, would be the first priority at his last meeting with Pym. However, as soon as the Professor had learned of it, he had insisted on a full report on King's most recent meeting with Kalz. 'You played him perfectly, my boy,' Pym had declared exuberantly. 'Getting him to give you up to date information about the restructure of the Abwehr, while offering nothing in return was excellent work.'

King had been in no mood to listen to the Professor's praise and had interrupted urgently, 'I realise why we are here, sir, and I have no wish to seem difficult. But we do have an agreement. Can we deal with that before we discuss anything else?'

Pym had replied with a frosty smile, 'Of course, John. Well, it took quite a bit of string pulling, but I'm pleased to confirm that Dr Bernstein will be released from Dachau as part of a New Year amnesty and that both he and his wife will be leaving for Britain within the week. I didn't like the way in which you forced the issue,' he added gravely, 'and I must insist that you never try such a stunt again, but you do have what you wanted.'

King heaved a sigh of relief, 'Thank you very much, sir. I do appreciate that I am involved in work, in which sentiment really has no place and I promise that there will be no repetition. Let's agree to call it John King's final act before he becomes James Kemp.'

Pym smiled more warmly and nodded in agreement before explaining that King should arrange to take a week's leave from the university before the start of the new semester. 'Maybe say that you've arranged a winter snow walking holiday in the Bernese Oberland in Switzerland. I need hardly remind you that it's vital that you leave the flat in Ludendorffstraße with only those items you would reasonably be expected to take on such a holiday.' Pym had quickly assured him that his other possessions, including his academic papers, would be returned safely to Britain. 'You must not, emphatically not bid any special farewell to anyone, John. However much you may feel that you should,' Pym had stressed. 'Do you understand? This is crucial to the whole deception and the whole mission. No one can be an exception to this rule. Absolutely no one. Is that clear?'

King had been surprised by the vehemence of Pym's approach to what seemed an obvious precaution and had wondered whether or not his mentor had some knowledge of his relationship with Greta. *I don't care anyway*, King had resolved, *I'm not mentioning her and that's that.*

***

'Welcome to Switzerland. I hope you have an enjoyable stay,' said the smiling guard as King's train crossed the border at Basel. Those banal words drove a dagger into King's heart as he realised that he had left Germany and Greta, possibly forever. He broke his journey with an overnight stay in Thun, a pretty lakeside 'City of the Alps' which offered a total contrast to the bustle and menacing air of Berlin. As he approached the solid looking hotel building, with its huge curved arches and romantic round tower, he could smell the appetizing aromas emanating from the kitchen. After dropping off his rucksack in a wonderfully warm and well-appointed room, he shook off his tiredness with his first local *Rugenbräu* beer and eagerly anticipated his meal.

King noted appreciatively the manner in which the other hotel residents demonstrated the classic Swiss virtues of friendliness and openness, combined with a natural discretion and respect for another's privacy. The wall adjacent to his table was covered with a large tourist map of the area and he realised with pleasure that he was not far from Meiringen and the famous Reichenbach Falls, from which Sherlock Holmes plunged to his death, locked in a mutually fatal embrace with his arch-enemy Professor Moriarty. *Well, neither Watson nor Moriarty will be around,* King reflected, *and it will be an avalanche rather than a tumble down a waterfall. But I suppose I could say I'm about to follow in the footsteps of the greatest detective ever. There are certainly worse role models.*

King awoke the next morning to clear blue skies and a wonderful panorama of the Eiger, Mönch and Jungfrau mountains which towered across the lake from Thun. He breakfasted heartily on typical Swiss fare and, after settling his bill, he strolled at a leisurely pace back towards the railway station and his connection to Kandersteg. He stopped to buy a copy of *Die Neue Berne Zeitung* before boarding his train which, of course, left punctually. The journey took him the short distance along the lake of Thun to Spiez, where they branched off up the dramatic Kander valley towards Kandersteg, a relatively undeveloped village, although one known to climbers, hikers and cross-country skiers.

As the train moved effortlessly further up the valley, King noticed with some amusement that the Bernese dialect of the passengers boarding became more difficult for him to comprehend. Turning to his newspaper's sports pages, he saw that these were eagerly anticipating something called the 'Lauberhornrennen', which was to take place in the next few days at nearby Wengen. King didn't have to read much to realise that the excitement surrounding this particular downhill ski race concerned the chances of the Swiss, Karl Molitor beating the German, Josef Jennewein and repeating the triumph of another Swiss over a different German the year before. *Here's to you, Karl! The best of British luck to you,* toasted King silently as he contemplated Hitler's likely fury at another sporting defeat for the supermen of Nazi Germany.

As the train curved around and doubled back on itself, in order to negotiate the considerable altitude difference between the small town of Frutigen and Kandersteg, he marvelled at the alternating mountain and valley views. It was also obvious that the snow was now much deeper and he silently gave thanks for the efficiency and resilience of the largely electrified Swiss railway system. Just after noon on what had become a grey day, full of low clouds which completely hid the soaring mountain peaks surrounding Kandersteg, King emerged from the station into swirling snow. As the train glided off towards the Lötschberg Tunnel and the Rhône Valley beyond, he turned his collar up and trudged off towards the Hotel zur Post, a basic pension which would provide for his one night's stay in the village.

Even as he walked slowly towards the hotel, he recognised immediately that the little village lacked the drama of the more famous Alpine ski resorts with their famous peaks and downhill pistes for all levels of ability and courage. It was also true, however, that many hotels had been built since the opening in 1913 of the railway tunnel which brought excellent connections to the cities of Switzerland and beyond.

As he plodded past the local food and general store, he was approached from behind by a thick-set man with a luxuriant beard and piercing blue eyes who whispered urgently. 'Herr King? Please just listen. I am Gerhardt Rösti, a friend of Professor Pym. I am to help with the arrangements here in Switzerland. Please meet me at the bench on the curve in the river just before the Scout Centre at three-thirty. We can sort out the details then.' Rösti then casually overtook King and quickly disappeared into the thickening snow.

King's inn was in the centre of the village and he had plenty of time to lunch and to study the maps of the area which Pym had provided. Later, on the way to his meeting, he bought a couple of postcards before taking the path along the many curves and bends of the river Kander. The secluded location was ideal for a discreet meeting and

Rösti was waiting on the bench when King arrived. A typical mountain man, he spoke only when necessary, though thankfully in high German rather than the extremely challenging local dialect. Having confirmed a fine weather forecast for the next day, followed by possible snow showers later, Rösti outlined the plan for King's disappearance. 'You should leave the hotel early and take the path at the head of the valley up to Sunnbüel. From there, it's a much gentler two hour walk across the Spittalmatte to your overnight stay at the Schwarenbach mountain inn. A room is already reserved for you there.'

Seeing King's dubious expression, he added reassuringly, 'The walk up to Sunnbüel will be the hardest, but you look in reasonable shape, so I'm sure it will be no problem. You should arrive at the Schwarenbach well before dusk.' King felt unaccountably pleased with Rösti's positive evaluation of his physical fitness and replied eagerly, 'That's fine. Where will you be?'

His guide explained that he would meet King at a predetermined point on the path down from the Gemmipass to Leukerbad. 'This is a notoriously dangerous place, where many accidents have occurred,' he said, crossing himself. 'There will be lots of snow and the rocks there are loose, so they can be moved easily by even a small avalanche. It will be relatively easy to make it look as if you have fallen into one of the deep ravines and been buried under a rock fall. It's a remote place; there will be no one around and it's not at all uncommon for people to be lost in winter. It should be easy to create this deception.'

He went on to advise that King should hint at his relative inexperience in mountain walking and make sure people know his plan to walk to Leukerbad. 'It shouldn't be too difficult to do that at the zur Post. It's the place where all the locals go to gossip.' King noticed the Swiss man's eyebrows rise in a sardonic expression as he added, 'Someone as exotic as you is bound to pique their interest.'

'Thanks for the advice and for the reference,' King smiled. 'But what are you likely to need to fake the accident?'

'Good question. We'll leave one of your gloves, your hat and maybe one of your poles and some things which could have fallen from your rucksack. Afterwards, we will return quickly to the Kander valley by a different route which no one else will be using. A car will be waiting to take you immediately to Thun, from where a Lysander will fly you back to England. You will be home by evening the day after tomorrow.'

King was impressed by the organisation that Pym had put in place, but one question concerned him. 'And what kind of investigation will take place?'

'That need not concern you Herr King. You can rest assured that the authorities will make an appropriate investigation and reach the correct conclusion; that the unfortunate death by accident of a pleasant, but sadly inexperienced British walker has taken place.'

The two men shook hands and parted as the light was fading. 'Good luck, Herr King. Until the day after tomorrow,' Rösti said, as he turned towards the village and walked off in a cloud of smoke which billowed from his huge cigar. King, following Rösti's directions, walked on past the Scout Centre before turning left on the valley road and back towards the village.

Shortly after six thirty, King entered the bar and immediately placed his order for a hearty Swiss meal of beetroot salad to be followed by *Schabziger Knöpfli.* Having received his first cool beer, he settled down at an ancient wooden table to wait for his food. Looking around the busy, smoke filled bar, he recognised that Rösti had not been exaggerating. He had barely started his first drink when a wizened old man came to sit at his table. 'You're not local,' he stated baldly. 'So, you'll be here for the winter sport then.'

King was relieved that, after barely a day in the Canton of Bern, he was able to understand at least some of the local's speech. 'Yes, that's correct,' he replied brightly. 'I'm told the walking around here is excellent. I intend to walk the Gemmi pass over the next couple of days and spend a night or two in Leukerbad.'

The man merely snorted derisively, 'Well, the walk's certainly lovely. But, of course, it's much better when you're walking towards Bern, rather than away from it.' The old man's face cracked into a laugh at his own joke as he continued the interrogation. 'Where are you from then? I just heard you order your food. You sound, and even look, German, but you don't behave like them.' King replied that he was English, but currently on an academic exchange in Berlin.

'Berlin you say.... hey, Urs! Hans! come here you two. We have a guest who lives in Berlin. He's English though.' At this command, two even older men picked up their half-filled beer glasses and shuffled over to the table, eager anticipation in their faces.

'Berlin is it?' asked Urs, almost before he had seated himself. 'We've had climbers here from Germany, practising on the rock face up to the Allmenalp. Didn't like any of them. Arrogant, nasty types they were. Are they all like that in Berlin? Put a fancy uniform on them and they think they're supermen.' His friends burst out in raucous coughing and laughter, making numerous ribald comments and gestures, which barely required translation.

'I've certainly come across many like that, sir. And yes, a lot were in uniform,' King replied seriously. 'But there are also kind and peaceful Germans who are as bemused at what is going on there as you and I.'

'Aye young man, I'm sure you're right,' pondered Hans, his brow knitted in concentration. 'But tell me, do you think Hitler will be satisfied without a war? None of us think so.'

'I'm afraid I agree with you, sir. As long as Hitler and his Nazis are in control, they'll not be satisfied until they've created their Lebensraum in the East and that means Poland must go the way of Czechoslovakia. I can't see either Britain or France accepting that.'

Just then the owner's wife came into the bar to tell King his starter had been served in the dining room. 'I see you've been entertained by the three wise men of the village Herr King,' she said, nodding affectionately at the three old timers. 'Now, come on you three. Give the young man some peace to eat his dinner.'

'I have indeed,' replied King with a broad smile, 'and, please, be so kind as to bring these gentlemen whatever they would like to drink and put it on my bill.' As he stood up and moved towards the dining room, Urs touched King briefly on the sleeve, saying with obvious sincerity, 'Thanks, son. And if it comes to it, take good care of yourself and give those Germans a bloody good thrashing. Can't abide that Hitler and all his strutting minions.'

King enjoyed his meal in silence and, shortly after nine-thirty, retired to his room to ponder his imminent 'demise' and to write appropriately banal postcards to his parents and to Greta.

After consuming another wonderful Swiss breakfast and provisioned with a picnic from the hotel, King set off early for the Schwarenbach mountain inn, pausing only to post the two cards at the nearby post office. It was a cloudless morning and despite the valley still being in shadow, the snow's reflection was bright. King felt in his pocket for the sunglasses, given to him by Pym at their last meeting in Berlin. At the time, he had thought that the older man's insistence that he did not leave these in Germany was a little fussy. Now he realised that the Professor had been perfectly right. He made good time up the valley and was soon tackling the uphill trail which led to Sunnbüel. Despite Rösti's positive assessment of his fitness, King found the initial going tough and his heartbeat quickly accelerated. A fundamentally sociable person, he had, nevertheless, always enjoyed periodic solitude. And here, on this narrow mountain path, his snow shoes ploughing on through the crisp snow, alternately in the shade of the fir trees then in surprisingly warm sunshine, he felt in his element. Part way up the head of the valley, he had a splendid view into the hidden Gasterntal, which runs off to the left, and at a higher altitude than the Kander valley. The extreme dryness of the snow, in contrast to the wet and slushy stuff he was used to in Durham, was a pleasant surprise to him and, after ninety minutes of measured walking, he emerged from the trees to reach Sunnbüel. He rested on a conveniently shaped rock and enjoyed the spectacular view back down the valley. Appreciating the perfect location of Kandersteg at the top of the valley, just where it broadens out to offer both more light and more grazing land for cattle, he could see the dark, glistening Kander river snaking its way down through the village and the much straighter railway line disappearing beneath him into the ornate mouth of the Lötschberg Tunnel. An audible rumble from his stomach persuaded him that it was time to consume his packed lunch of cold cervelat sausage, bread and a bottle of beer.

Feeling suitably rested and replenished, King set off over the much easier terrain of the Spittalmatte, a wide, relatively flat landscape with the magnificent Altels peak to his left and the somewhat smaller Gällihorn behind him and to the right. After traversing the snow-covered meadows, King began the short, steep climb and descent to the Schwarenbach inn. Rösti had advised that this may take him a couple of hours, but he took a little longer, making frequent pauses in order to enjoy the landscape of pure, untrodden snow. King nevertheless arrived at the inn well before dusk and was able to enjoy the final rays of the sun with a celebratory beer on the terrace. He was bewitched by the constantly shifting shadows on the mountains and the way in which the sun's rays turned from gold to pink and then, finally, to a deep red. 'Herr King,' the young waitress pleaded with him, 'please, you must come inside now. It is much colder.' With no little regret, he left the terrace and followed her into the warmth of the inn.

The only guest at the Schwarenbach, King was able to ensure, during dinner, that his hosts knew both his plan to walk to Leukerbad and that he was of rather limited experience. He also heard much about the proud history of the inn, especially its many notable guests such as Mark Twain, Alexandre Dumas and, to his delight, Sir Arthur Conan Doyle. That really did seem appropriate to King as he made his way to an early bed. He had been warned by his hosts that, while the next day might begin bright and sunny, there was a possibility that the weather could deteriorate and, in the nicest possible way, he was encouraged to be on his way as quickly as possible.

The next morning, King demolished his final Swiss breakfast, packed his things and bade an early farewell to his hosts. His path took him, again in bright sunshine, up a steady incline which, when peaked, offered an uninspiring view of what he knew was the Daubensee, but what in effect looked like a massive snow-covered field. As he skirted the frozen lake, he became aware of a significant picking up of the wind, shortly followed by the appearance of the first clouds. As he finally traversed the Gemmi pass the snow began; the odd flake initially, but within minutes visibility had all but vanished and he was caught in a mountain blizzard. King had studied the maps which showed the steep route down towards his planned rendezvous. *But in weather like this*, he cursed, *it's not going to be easy*. Rösti had told him that, in good weather, it would be possible to see the Matterhorn from his current position. *Bloody hell,* he thought grimly, *I can hardly see my nose in front of my face.*

He was just about to set off in what his compass told him was the right direction when he heard a familiar voice. 'I wouldn't go that way, if I were you, Herr King. Ten metres further on and there really would be no need to fake your death. Come quickly, this way is better.'

King could now see Rösti's smiling face and shouted over the howling mountain wind, 'My God! You're better than a St Bernard!' The Swiss quickly led King to the path downwards, the first section of which permitted them to walk side by side and exchange some words.

'The weather is perfect,' exclaimed Rösti with what for King was inexplicable pleasure. 'An avalanche today will be all too believable and for sure we will see no one else up here. Come on, it's only fifteen minutes down to the place we have chosen for your fall.' An extremely relieved King felt totally safe with his Swiss guide and even managed to improve his snow walking style by observing the other's technique. Rösti indicated when they had reached the spot and King could see immediately how appropriate it was. The path hugged the steep slope of the mountain on one side and, with only a rickety wooden fence for protection, on the other gave onto a dramatic drop which the Swiss said was at least a hundred and fifty metres down to a rocky ravine.

'Please rip off a piece of your rucksack and place it with one of your snow shoes, one glove and one pole just here.

Then make sure that your wallet and passport are in your jacket pocket, take it off and put this one on. Good. Now, please tear off one sleeve of your old jacket and put it with the rest of the stuff on the ground. Then go thirty metres back up the path. I'm going to set a small explosion to start the avalanche. You shouldn't hear much noise over this howling wind. Here are some more gloves, snow shoes and poles for you.' King was unhappy with the instruction to leave his wallet, as it contained his only photograph of Greta, but he recognised that it made absolute sense. 'It's very common for avalanches to cause people to lose part of their equipment or even their clothing,' Rösti explained sympathetically. 'I'm very sorry about your wallet and personal things, but they'll be valuable in identifying you with this accident.'

The mountain guide then scrambled twenty metres above the path, where the terrain was particularly steep and the snow seemed quite loose. Expertly, he set the charges for a small explosion and moved fifteen metres away from its planned seat. After a quick wave to King to ensure that he was safe, he detonated his small charge and the avalanche began. King heard a soft 'crump', but was completely stunned by the sheer power and weight of the moving snow, as it levered a rock from its resting place and pushed it down onto the path. The effect was dramatic, as more snow, together with many smaller rocks started to slide down across the path, taking with them a section of the wooden fence and the items King had left in the snow. Once the snow and rocks had ceased moving and having removed any remaining evidence of the use of a charge, Rösti descended to the path and retrieved the material left by King. Having carefully placed these items around the scene, he finally smeared some of King's blood onto the nearest standing fence post. 'Now you know why I asked you to bring me that small sample of your blood,' he smiled, before continuing his explanation. 'The snow will soon cover these things and hide all our footsteps. When you don't appear at your hotel in Leukerbad, they'll contact Kandersteg and eventually send out a search party. They'll soon find this broken fence with its blood marks and one or two of these items and hopefully reach the intended conclusion. It'll be weeks or even months before any thorough search for your body will be possible and anything could have happened to it in that time.'

Rösti took a final look at the orchestrated scene, before nodding in satisfaction and saying with an enigmatic smile, 'Now, you must complete your disappearance from Switzerland.' Recognising King's sacrifice in giving up his very identity, Rösti patted him encouragingly on the back and urged, 'Come on, my friend. It's time we were away from this spot. We have a hard walk ahead of us, at a much higher level than the one you took this morning and yesterday. We'd see spectacular sights, if only this cloud would clear. It should only take us around three hours, if we walk steadily.'

The weather began slowly to improve, as the two men took a route, high above the Daubensee, the Schwarenbach inn and the Spittalmatte and back towards Sunnbüel and Kandersteg. They didn't take the direct route down to the Kander Valley from Sunnbüel, but used the narrow Gurnigel down into the Gasterntal and from there to the Kander valley. King made better progress with the modern snow-shoes and sticks provided by Rösti and they reached the valley floor in good time. A car was already waiting, hidden from the narrow road behind a disused farm building. The driver merely said, 'Please hurry, we have a good forty minutes to drive and the conditions aren't so good.'

King was about to get into the car, when he saw Rösti's outstretched hand, 'Goodbye, it has been a pleasure to meet you. God go with you, and if you're ever back in Switzerland, please look me up.' With a final smile, he added, 'There are many more challenging walks that we could perhaps take together.'

King had time only to say a quick 'thanks for everything' before he was bustled into the rear of the car which then raced off as quickly as conditions would permit towards Thun.

An hour and a half later, King was looking down at the snow-covered landscape of Switzerland, as the Lysander battled its way across the darkening skies towards England.

CHAPTER THIRTEEN

Thursday 2nd February, 1939, London.

It was a cold, sunny day when King took the mid-morning train from Canterbury into central London. The clouds, however, were already beginning to build up as he approached the capital for the first time since the previous September when he had left for Berlin.

From the moment of his clandestine arrival at RAF Biggin Hill in January, King had been staying with George McNair, a retired SIS officer, in his Georgian terraced house in the centre of Canterbury. McNair was an untypical highland Scot, fiercely proud of his Celtic roots, yet with a love of England and all things English. With thick, dark hair and surprisingly gentle, brown eyes, he was not much above average height, broad shouldered and, for his age, supremely fit. He shared his home with Polly, his forty-something housekeeper, an authentic Cockney and, in his words 'the best damned cook in the whole of this blessed United Kingdom of ours.' During his first day in Kent, King's appearance had been changed dramatically. 'Prof's orders, I'm afraid,' McNair had said with a mischievous grin. His longish, fair hair had been cut short and dyed almost black, as had his newly grown moustache but, by some miracle of hairdressing known only to Polly, she had managed to accentuate what were the beginnings of grey hairs at his temples. When this was combined with the clear glass, horn-rimmed spectacles which disguised his twenty-twenty vision, the overall effect had been to make King look a good ten years older than his actual age and quite unlike himself. Polly, having wrought this amazing transformation in his appearance, had simply nodded and said, 'That'll do nicely,' before happily returning to her kitchen.

Both McNair and Polly had wisely given King, who they knew as James Kemp, the space to recover from his swift departure from Germany. He had spent the first couple of weeks in England resting and enjoying Polly's excellent cooking, but had gradually begun to relish being so close to the centre of the city and had spent many happy hours exploring its historic locations.

On arrival in London, King took the tube to Baker Street, along which he walked towards Lord's Cricket Ground. Some minutes later, he was introducing himself to Mason, the long serving concierge at Pym's mansion block apartment. 'Just wait there, please, Mr Kemp. I'll ring up to the Professor right away.' After the briefest of exchanges over the telephone, King was escorted to the lift and the button for the top floor pressed. 'Straight out of the lift, sir, and the Professor is third on the left,' advised Mason superfluously, as King had visited Pym at his flat many times in the past. *Well,* King reflected happily, *at least the disguise seems to work.*

The door to Pym's flat opened before King could ring the doorbell and he was faced once again by the beaming face of his mentor. 'Come in, my dear chap. It's good to see you, although I must say, looking quite unlike yourself.' King laughed as he shook hands vigorously with the older man, who continued, 'I can see that the inestimable Polly has been working her magic again. But for God's sake, get rid of those spectacles while we're indoors.'

'With pleasure, sir,' replied King. 'I don't think I'll ever get used to the damned things. Never mind Mason not having a clue who I am, I scarcely know myself.'

'Oh,' countered Pym lightly, 'he's pretty discreet, you know. He'd never let on, even if he did recognise you, which incidentally I very much doubt. And, if the spectacles cause you so much grief, I daresay you could ditch them.' The last words were spoken with a twinkle in his eye and an arm clapping his guest amiably on the back. King felt immediately at home and willingly allowed himself to be led into the spacious living room, with its view of the deserted cricket ground. The host immediately insisted that they both help themselves to a cup of tea and a plate of the excellent sandwiches, prepared by his housekeeper, before they sat down to talk.

'Rösti sends his regards from Switzerland, John,' began Pym, as he added milk to their cups of tea. 'He's a rather reserved fellow of course, like many of his countrymen, but when they take a liking to you, there are no more loyal chaps on this earth. And he seems to have taken a liking to you.'

'I liked him too, sir,' replied King readily, 'but did the investigation into my 'death' go as expected?'

'Oh, yes, there were no problems on that score,' replied Pym with an emphatic nod. 'Graf and Rösti between them prepared the ground excellently. And it appears that you also did a good job convincing the locals that you were a little naïve for those conditions. The conclusion was, as expected, 'accidental death'.'

'And how did yesterday go, sir? It was one aspect of this whole thing that I really didn't feel comfortable with,' said King heavily. 'How did my parents seem?'

'Yes, John, I know that was a most unsatisfactory part of the deception and I feel wretched about requiring it of you,' said Pym sincerely. 'But you must see that there was absolutely no alternative, if all the hard work done so far was not to be jeopardised. Anyway, your mother and sister were, of course, distraught, but it's a funny thing about your father. If I didn't trust you implicitly not to have revealed anything about your mission, I could've sworn that he didn't believe in the accident at all.'

The statement was left hanging between them for a full half minute before King replied. 'Yes. I know what you mean, sir. On my last visit to see them in Gloucestershire, I had the feeling that he thought there was much more to my trip to Berlin than a simple academic exchange.'

'Well, your father's no fool,' confirmed Pym. 'It's entirely possible that he suspects something not a million miles away from the truth. That you're working incognito somewhere for the good of the country. But he also knows and accepts the meaning of duty and discretion. I'm certain that he'll say and do nothing to put your mission at risk.'

The two men spent the next couple of minutes enjoying their lunch and refilling their cups of tea, before King asked in a tentative way, 'I don't suppose....' Pym instinctively knew what the younger man was about to ask and quickly replied. 'Yes, John. There were flowers from Germany. The ones that interested me were those from a woman called Greta and Major Kalz. The tone of the message from the woman suggested to me that there was an aspect of your time in Berlin that you did not divulge to me.'

King nodded, his face for a moment a picture of misery and loss. This prompted the older man to conclude, 'Well, I suppose that's not really relevant now. I'm sorry John, but it's for the best, believe me. But, on a happier note, Dr and Frau Bernstein were there and, despite their recent ordeal, I'm sure they'll recover fully.'

King smiled vaguely and replied, 'That's good to hear, sir. Thank you for organising things.'

Eager to change the subject, Pym asked lightly, 'How are you getting on with McNair and the delightful Polly?' Meaningfully patting his stomach, and grinning in a boyish manner, he added, 'I imagine that if you stay there much longer, it'll not only be your hair's appearance that'll be altered.'

'You can say that again, sir,' replied King, his expression lightening. 'After two weeks there the old waistbands were feeling a bit tight, so I had to get out and exercise with McNair. He's a fine fellow. I'd be delighted if he's going to be involved in my training.'

'Then you'll be pleased, John,' confirmed Pym. 'McNair is going to be your principal trainer and I know of no finer man for the job. Of course, he's retired from the Service now, but what he can't teach you about field craft is simply not worth knowing. He's the best tail I've ever worked with and if you can pick up a half of what he has to offer, that'll serve you in very good stead in the months to come.'

'That's all very well, sir,' interrupted King, a frown creasing his unnaturally old looking face, 'but no one has yet fully explained to me why the date for me to leave Germany had to be brought forward so much. I wasn't really happy about that. I couldn't say much about it in Berlin, but now I'd like some answers.

'A fair point and a good question, John,' conceded the Professor. 'And if anyone is to be held accountable for that decision, it's undoubtedly myself. Call it a gut feeling or intuition, but I felt that things might begin to happen more quickly than we originally thought. As it turns out, I think I was right.'

'I take it that you're referring to Hitler's speech on the 30th?' King asked sharply.

'Yes,' replied Pym seriously. 'It spells out two things; first that Hitler is bent on war, whatever the other powers may think and second, that given half the chance, he'll use the cover of war to destroy European Jewry.'

'I agree about Hitler and his intentions,' countered King. 'But if Britain and France continue their wretched policy of appeasement, how is war any closer?'

'Well, there's the interesting thing, John,' said Pym gravely. 'Chamberlain genuinely thought Hitler was interested only in incorporating native Germans from Austria and the Sudetenland into the greater Reich. But the Führer's policy towards Czechoslovakia has, in the PM's own words, shaken his confidence in that belief. He's coming rapidly to the conclusion that Hitler's drive for Lebensraum in the East must lead inevitably, and possibly very quickly, to war.' Pym face was a model of concentration and focus as he added, 'There's a great deal of intelligence and corroborating evidence which suggests that Germany is preparing to occupy the remainder of Czechoslovakia as soon as spring comes. The Poles are very worried about the Danzig Corridor and Chamberlain is minded to guarantee Poland against Nazi aggression. The economy here at home is gearing up much more realistically to the likelihood of war, with increased production of armaments. In summary,' Pym shrugged, 'it all begins to look...'

'Somewhat inevitable,' suggested King, with a reflective smile.

'Yes, John, I believe so,' said Pym firmly. 'Hopefully you can now understand the urgency to get you out of Berlin as soon as possible. Of course, your connection with Kalz would undoubtedly have remained extremely useful to us, but getting you prepared and established among Nazi sympathisers here in Britain became the greater priority.'

Pym went on to offer an account of the latest intelligence on Nazi sympathisers and right wing and other extremist groups in Britain. He explained that the actual or potential threats could come from a range of sources; Germans and other aliens, Fascist groups, communists and even the IRA. 'Of course, your focus is on Fascist sympathisers and, possibly aliens. There are many sources that might be interesting. The British Union of Fascists, for example, and other rank anti-Semites such as Archibald Ramsey.'

'The MP, you mean?' cut in King. 'That's right,' continued Pym, in his unhurried, professorial way. 'He's gathering like-minded friends around him, such as the Duke of Westminster and the Duke of Wellington. There's also a retired admiral, Sir Barry Domvile, who founded a pro-Nazi propaganda organisation called The Link. It has its own organ called *The Anglo-German Review*. There are many possibilities for infiltration,' Pym reasoned, 'but that work isn't for you.'

'Really, sir,' King replied in some confusion. 'I rather thought that was exactly what you wanted me to do.' Pym took his time before answering, filling his pipe, lighting it and taking a deep satisfying draw before explaining. 'You're right. That was originally the plan. But there are others in SIS who are involved in that work and I'm sorry to say that we still suspect that there may be a German agent working within that organisation.'

King had hoped that this issue would have been cleared up before he established himself in Britain, so that he could work in concert with other agents. He nodded his head slowly, 'I see, sir. So, I am still going to be operating in isolation from SIS?'

'I'm afraid so, John,' Pym confirmed. 'We have a chance to establish something with you that we are certain isn't being fed back to Germany. I must stress that we don't know whether SIS has been infiltrated, nor, if it has, at what level. But the bottom line is that we can't afford to take the risk. Unfortunately, it'll make your life more difficult, as you'll be a German agent as far as the British authorities are concerned.'

'But an English imposter as far as any genuine Nazi agent is concerned,' cut in King sharply.

'Yes,' Pym said regretfully, 'that about sums it up. But for the time being you need to concentrate on your training with McNair. I have some ideas on how we can get you into the field which we'll discuss in due course.'

Pym explained further that it was likely that he would begin to operate fully in the field by May or June. The two men parted after agreeing that Pym would visit King in Canterbury in early March. The main target for the next weeks, emphasised by Pym over a parting glass of single malt, was for King to learn as much tradecraft as possible from McNair.

CHAPTER FOURTEEN

Monday 6th February to Wednesday 22nd March, 1939, Canterbury.

Throughout February and into March, King diligently practised those skills of deception, disguise and observation that he learned from McNair. He was such an adept student and practitioner that, by mid-March, the Scot was sure that King was ready for the next stage of the operation. Events made this positive assessment extremely timely as, late on March 20th, Pym turned up unexpectedly at the Canterbury house.

Descending the stairs to greet his mentor, King's cheery smile faded as soon as he registered the determined expression on the face of the older man. With a curt nod of acknowledgement, Pym began urgently, 'I have news which greatly affects our plans. Let's adjourn to the sitting room and I can explain how the operation's going to develop.' The Professor ushered King into the comfortable room, before calling out, 'McNair! Come and join us in the sitting room, and be good enough to bring one of your special bottles of whisky.' Pym was clearly in business-like mood and, having found three appropriate glasses in the sideboard, waved them meaningfully towards the Scot, as he approached carrying a bottle of single malt Laphroaig. 'Come on, man, hurry up! The war'll be over before I get the chance to wet my whistle.'

As soon as the three men were seated comfortably, Pym explained to King, 'It looks like your graduation is going to have to be brought forward. Hitler, having more or less made Czechoslovakia part of his *Ostmark*, is now about to rattle his sabre in the direction of Poland by making demands relating to Danzig.' King and McNair exchanged glances as they each took a sip of whisky. 'The PM has definitely learned his lesson at Munich and is disposed towards guaranteeing Polish sovereignty. We're led to believe that this will also be the French strategy.'

'Then it all hinges on the 'Austrian corporal's' reaction. Will he cut and run or is he now too drunk on his own invincibility?' mused McNair.

'I doubt Hitler will back down,' argued King. 'The time to challenge him was three years ago.'

'I agree,' replied Pym dourly. 'War is coming. My best guess is towards the end of the summer, or early autumn at the latest. In these circumstances, it's imperative to get you into the field as quickly as possible. And this is how I propose to do it.'

McNair suddenly jumped up. 'Then, begging your pardon Professor, I should leave you to it. Best I don't know too much, after all.'

Pym responded immediately and with some force, 'Sit down please, George. I want you to stay because I want you to be his day to day contact, at least at the start of the mission. You're the obvious choice, as I hope you'll both agree when I outline the plan.'

Pym began by explaining briefly the purpose of the mission to McNair, who commented thoughtfully, 'Aye, it's a neat plan alright. But how will he infiltrate these groups quickly without causing suspicion?'

King looked up to see Pym beaming at him. 'Precisely! How on earth can this be achieved in a relatively short space of time? I think I have a very neat solution. What would you say, if we thought we could get you to take over an existing network of Nazi sympathisers?'

'I'd say 'lead me to them and let me get to work,' replied King enthusiastically.

'Then I'll explain,' said the Professor excitedly. 'As you're both no doubt aware, relations between our country and Germany have deteriorated sharply since the fiasco at Munich and Hitler's takeover of Czechoslovakia. We've been keeping an eye on one or two Nazi officials, believed to be engaged in espionage. It's inevitable that some will be expelled from the country. Indeed, we already have characters by the name of Otto Karlowa, Edmund Himmelmann and Johanna Wolf in our sights. Now, let's suppose that we give these Nazis the heave-ho, what d'you suppose Jerry's going to do about it?'

'Retaliate, at a guess,' offered King immediately. 'Of course he will,' responded Pym. 'Nothing would be more certain and here's the clever bit. We can definitely use such a response to disguise our real purpose. We've already identified half a dozen Germans to kick out. They're all small fry, but we can use this group expulsion to add another name to the list. He's currently of no special interest to SIS, but some of my 'off the books' informers, people who keep their eyes and ears open, but who are not officially part of SIS, tell me he is definitely an interesting type.'

'So,' King continued, understanding the drift of the Professor's argument, 'we mix our chap up with a few others, so neither the Germans nor SIS are alerted to his importance to our mission.'

Pym nodded, 'Exactly. Now, he's called Rudolf Gottfried Rösel, a slippery character who has been responsible since 1936 for 'Education', or more accurately indoctrination for the Nazi organization *Landesgruppe Großbritannien*. Basically, he's a propagandist for the Nazis and runs a pretty rabid German information service. Now, frankly, we couldn't care tuppence about his propaganda rag, but one of my people is certain that Rösel is running some very interesting Nazi sympathisers across London and the south of England. The plan is that sometime within the next month or so we kick Rösel out, hidden in plain sight among a group of low-level undesirables and, after a certain interlude, you pop up as his replacement. It could also be that Rösel's informers may give you entry to other like-minded pro-German sympathisers, but they may well be interesting enough in their own right. So, my friends, that's the plan. What d'you think should be our next step?'

King responded immediately, 'Well sir, I need to familiarise myself with my back story and establish myself in London. And, of course, I need to shadow this Rösel while he is still here in order to get some idea of who his Nazi sympathiser friends may be.'

Before the Professor was able to agree, McNair interrupted, puncturing the increasingly euphoric mood .

'There's one potentially serious problem here, Professor. What happens if the Jerries send someone to replace Rösel? Our young friend's life may be in very great danger.'

'You're right, of course, George. But I'm afraid that's a risk he has to take. We'd do our best to intercept such a replacement, and our record is pretty good, but there are no guarantees.'

'And nor would any be expected,' replied King immediately.

'Well, that's agreed,' concluded a satisfied Pym. 'I suggest we all have a nightcap and turn in. We'll have a great deal to do tomorrow.'

***

'There you are at last, laddie. It's already gone ten. What happened? A little too much of the whisky was it?' McNair asked with an innocent smile, as he briefly interrupted his huge, fried breakfast. King grimaced and sat down to pour a cup of strong tea, saying, 'I see the Professor's already hard at it.'

'Indeed, he is,' replied the Scot. 'I'm surprised you didn't hear them ringing up for him. It must be nearly forty-five minutes ago now. I hope he'll be able to join us before too long.'

As he tentatively poked around his own smaller breakfast, King heard the tinkle as the telephone was replaced on its cradle. A thoughtful looking Pym entered the kitchen and sat down. 'Well, my friends, it looks as if my information about Hitler and Danzig was spot on. He has demanded it be ceded to Germany. We've no time to lose. You have to be operational as soon as possible. I'll fill you in on the details after breakfast.'

Pym explained that King would pose as the nephew of Paul Kemp, a second-hand book store owner in Charing Cross Road. 'He's a good man, served with me in the last war and has helped me out at various times since then. You'll be staying in his spare flat on the premises and working for him. This role will allow you to travel extensively and keep unconventional hours.'

'That sounds perfect, sir. But how much does this fellow know of my mission?'

'He knows you're working for me. Other than that, he doesn't need, or want to know any more,' explained Pym. 'Unless it's a dire emergency, we'll initially contact one another via weekly meetings with McNair. He'll send you a card with a time and place and you can pass on messages to me in this way. If you need urgent help a coded phone call to McNair in Canterbury will result in him being in the Lyons Coffee House near the bookshop at 10AM the next day.' The Professor then passed over a thin file with the advice 'Study this well. It'll give you all the information we have on Rösel. It's vital that you begin to shadow him as soon as possible. I've no idea how long it will be before he's expelled, but it'll be weeks rather than months. So, get familiar with his routines and start to shadow some of his informers. If necessary, we can talk about other potential leads when you're settled in at Charing Cross Road. Finally, and most important of all, your codename for use with your informers will be Lazarus.'

'How will I go on for funds, sir? Will Mr Kemp be paying me?' King asked, as Pym started to pack up his things. 'And when is he expecting me to arrive?'

'There'll be a small stipend passed through Kemp's books, but that will be bogus. No money will pass from him to you. Rather you should open an account at the local branch of Williams Deacons Bank and you'll receive a sizeable allowance of £30 per week. That's more than a Civil Service Principal receives, so it should cover all contingencies. Of course, you'll have to account in writing for your expenses, but feel free to use the money creatively. And Kemp is expecting you around lunchtime tomorrow. That should give you plenty of time to study the file on your assumed identity as his nephew, in case anyone other than Kemp should show an interest in you. And of course,' Pym suggested with a smile, 'you'll also have time to bid farewell for now to McNair and Polly. Good luck, my boy, and remember all that you've been taught. Now, if you'll forgive me, I have one or two things to say in private to McNair.'

King couldn't wait to get stuck in to memorising the details of his new identity and bounded up the stairs two at a time. *At last I might feel like a new person, instead of John King with a different name.* In the early evening, McNair knocked briskly and poked his head round the door, 'Sorry to bother you laddie, but I've something to give you.'

Immediately recognising the case which contained the Scot's collection of revolvers, King said dubiously, 'Oh, I don't know.....'

McNair quickly cut him off. 'Look, son, the boss was quite insistent. Whether you like it or not, you're going to London with one of these and a reasonable supply of ammo. Now, you were pretty good with all of these, but if you'll take my advice, you should have the Walther P38. It has the advantage of being semi-automatic, it's extremely reliable and, of course,' he added with a sardonic smile, 'it's German.'

King returned McNair's smile and raised his hands in surrender. 'OK, Mac. You win. The Walther it is.'

'Good lad,' replied the older man. 'I'll sort out an arm holster and an initial supply of ammo for you. Now, before I forget, get on with your packing and make sure you're down for dinner by 7.30 prompt. Polly is planning to see you off in style.'

CHAPTER FIFTEEN

Thursday 23rd March, 1939, London.

King felt an unmistakable rush of excitement as he approached the frontage of Paul Kemp: Second Hand, Rare and Antiquarian Book Dealer on Charing Cross Road. Situated several doors away from Collets Russian Bookshop, Kemp's premises were double-fronted and equipped with moveable book shelves on the pavement, which were evidently brought out on dry days. King's heart was racing as he went into the shop, whose front windows offered sufficient light and sunshine to make it feel positively bright. The walls held an unlikely number of shelves, neatly labelled into various sections, but, King noticed to his pleasure, with a distinct emphasis on History. A middle-aged man, perhaps an inch shorter than King and of slim build, emerged from a doorway behind the counter. His warm, open smile and grey eyes immediately made a favourable impression. 'Hello there,' he began, 'Can I help you? Are you looking for something in particular?' As he spoke, his eyes fell on King's two suitcases and he strode out from behind the counter, hand outstretched in greeting. 'Ah! You must be James,' he said with genuine pleasure. 'Welcome to your new home. Delighted you found it, as London can be confusing.' He moved past King, went outside and covered the pavement shelves with woollen blankets and placed a sign in the door, which informed potential customers that he would be back in thirty minutes. 'Come along. Let me take one of your bags.'

'Thank you very much sir,' King replied nervously. 'That would be most welcome.'

'Call me Uncle Paul please,' said Kemp. 'Best to do that all the time, so that it becomes second nature.' Feeling a little foolish at such an elementary mistake, King followed his 'uncle' through a narrow internal door and into a spacious hallway which was cluttered with boxes. He counted three doors, one obviously a very secure external door, probably leading to a yard which would give out onto the back alleyway running parallel to Charing Cross Road. The other two were slightly ajar and King could see that they led to a toilet and a small kitchenette. He followed Kemp upstairs, where the bookseller explained, 'Righto, James, this is the door to my flat. We'll nip in there now and have a cup of tea and a sandwich. You'll be staying in the flat on the next floor up. It's not so large but it has everything you need to be pretty independent. Professor Pym said that you may have to keep unconventional hours, so it's best you have your own place, rather than share with me. I try to keep the shop open as much as possible, so I'll show you round properly later on.'

'That's fine, si.... Uncle Paul,' said King, smiling bashfully as he caught sight of Kemp's amused expression.

'Come on,' said the older man, clapping King on the back. 'You'll soon get used to it. Let's get a cuppa.' Kemp moved gracefully around his kitchen, making the tea in a measured and fluid way which suggested that he was a man who neither rushed things, nor panicked. 'So, James, do you know much about book selling?'

'I'd have little idea of values and such like, but I think I'll be able to find my way around the stock fairly quickly,' replied King, as he picked up his cup of steaming tea. 'Tell me Uncle, have you known Professor Pym for a long time?'

Kemp set down his cup and burst out laughing. 'More years than I care to remember! We served together during the last war on HMS *Renown* and we kept in touch after the Armistice. I've helped him on several occasions with his more, how shall I put this?... secretive work.' When they had finished their tea, they went up to King's flat. 'I hope everything will suit you James,' said Kemp genially. 'There should be sufficient towels and bedlinen. Anyway, you get yourself settled in. Here's your keys for the flat, the shop door and the rear door. Come down when you're ready. I'd better get back to the book-buying public.'

King quickly unpacked and placed the files on Rösel, his new identity, the revolver, ammunition and holster in a lockable drawer. He then went down to the shop, where he found Kemp busy with a customer. The afternoon, spent familiarising himself with the layout of the shop and its stock, went surprisingly quickly. King had planned to be outside the premises of Rösel's Anglo-German Information Service by 5.30PM and was shocked to see that it was already after 4.30PM. Silently cursing himself for becoming too engrossed in the contents of the shop, King bade a hasty farewell to Kemp and rushed to the nearby underground station at Leicester Square. He was relieved to find a small tea room on the opposite side of the road to Rösel's workplace, which would serve as a perfect observation post. Having taken a table one row in from the window, he settled down with a drink and the *London Evening Standard,* which was full of Hitler's annexation of Czechoslovakia and his ultimatum to the Poles over Danzig. He had been nursing his drink for almost half an hour when the instantly recognisable figure of Rösel emerged from the front entrance of the building opposite. He was about five feet four inches tall, with dark hair and a narrow moustache, well dressed in a smart suit and carrying a mackintosh and brief case. King casually finished his cup of tea, stood up from the table and unhurriedly left the tea room. The number of pedestrians had declined from peak rush-hour levels, so King could easily keep his quarry in sight. Rösel led him up Whitefriars Street towards its junction with Fleet Street, where he turned towards St Paul's Cathedral, its magnificent dome given a golden hue by the early evening sunshine. Fleet Street was busier and, having decided to move closer to his mark, King was surprised when Rösel suddenly darted across the road in front of a red London Transport double decker bus. King had no choice but to wait until the bus had passed, by which time the German had disappeared. *Surely he didn't spot me so quickly,* King reassured himself, while trying to remain calm and follow McNair's advice. 'Don't panic and rush about. Give him time to reappear,' had been the Scot's instruction and, sure enough, within a couple of minutes the German reappeared from the doorway of a tobacconist. There, he paused on the pavement to light a cigarette before hastily re-crossing the road and making his way to the Punch Tavern.

    King waited two or three minutes before following him and found Rösel ordering some food at the bar. He decided to follow suit and, feeling fortified by the food and beer, he carefully followed the German, as he left the tavern, turned into Bride Lane and strode purposefully towards St Bride's Passage. He dropped back a little as Rösel entered the St Bride Foundation, where a poster promoting a meeting read:

Mayfair Book Club
Public Meeting March 23rd 1939 at 8.00PM.

**Bridewell Hall, St Bride Foundation, Bride Lane, Fleet St
'The Future of Europe'
ALL WELCOME**

The risk of being seen at such a public meeting was too great, so King returned to the bookshop, where he decided that he would work in the bookshop in the mornings and follow the German from lunchtime on.

The next few days passed uneventfully, with King getting to know his way around the bookshop in the mornings and shadowing Rösel in the afternoons and evenings. During these days, the German seemed to be engaged in the normal business of the Anglo-German Information Service and had no obvious encounters involving his circle of informants. One week after King's arrival in London, however, that was to change.

CHAPTER SIXTEEN

Thursday 30th March, 1939, London.

   Having spent his usual morning in the bookshop, followed by an observation of Rösel's office building in the afternoon, King was surprised to see the German leaving work much earlier than normal. He initially returned to his flat in a fine four storey building, with classical porches and large windows overlooking the tree lined Colville Terrace in Kensington. After spending two hours there, Rösel emerged and, as King expected, headed towards the nearest underground station at Ladbroke Grove. Unexpectedly, however, the German took the first left down Portobello Road and began to walk away from the underground station. After a few minutes, he quickly unlocked and passed through a door to the side of an antiques shop which was closed for the night. Sensing a possible breakthrough in his surveillance, King moved into the shadowed recess of the doorway of a nearby shop. He then saw a light go on in the front room of the first-floor flat, followed almost immediately by Rösel drawing the curtains.

   At 8.10PM, a masculine looking, middle-aged woman approached the door and rang the bell. By the street lighting, King caught a flash of grey hair as the door opened, before quickly closing again. Ten minutes later, an older man, dressed like a City gent, strode confidently to the door and patiently awaited his admission. The final people who arrived at regular, ten-minute intervals were younger men, one dressed as a manual worker and the other wearing the uniform of a railway official.

Having committed to memory a basic description of each of the group members, King settled down to wait until the meeting broke up, when he would follow one of the group home. As he stood in the shadows, he wondered whether the order of arrival was significant. *The first to arrive and last to leave will spend time alone with Rösel*, he reasoned, *so I'll follow the last to leave*.

When the railway official was the last to leave the meeting, King followed him to a cottage on Roupell Street, near Waterloo Station. *Maybe he works there*, mused King on his way back to the bookshop, *I'll tail him from home tomorrow morning.* Having scribbled a brief apology to Paul Kemp, King ensured that he was ready to follow the target as he left his house at 6.45AM and walked briskly towards Waterloo Station. There, he confounded King's expectations by catching a bus to Victoria Station, where he headed towards a row of offices next to Platform One. These were clearly identified as 'Private: Official Railway Personnel Only' and King saw the man enter the fourth door of the six which stretched along the length of the platform. He quickly bought a platform ticket and told the guard that he had forgotten to give a crucial message to his wife who was on the train which was standing, hissing and primed ready for departure. He dashed down the platform and pretended to speak to someone through the open door of the carriage adjacent to the office which the man had entered. When the guard blew his whistle, King smartly closed the carriage door and quickly examined the sign on the office door. Intrigued to read 'Timetable Planning: Non-Passenger Services,' he made a mental note of the three names: L. Smith, P. Jenkins and J. Watkins. *But which of these blighters is my man?* he wondered. As he was walking back through the ticket barrier at the entrance to the platform, King spontaneously said to the ticket inspector, 'By the way, I thought I saw a neighbour of mine from Roupell Street go into one of those offices just now...'

The man was happy to chat and immediately responded, 'Ah. You must mean Joe Watkins. He lives down there, I believe...'

'That's right,' agreed King. 'Mr Watkins. We live quite a way further down from him, so we don't really know one another.'

'He's quite an important man here, you know,' confided the inspector. 'He controls all the scheduling of freight and other non-passenger services out of this station. What he doesn't know about what's being moved, where and when, simply isn't worth bothering with.'

***

Exactly a week after the first group meeting, Rösel once more led King to the flat in Portobello Road. There, he observed five different people arrive for a meeting. *Obviously, the kernel of a second circle of informants,* King realised and noted the middle-aged couple, the two manual workers in their twenties or thirties and the young, smartly dressed woman. Once again, he followed the last to leave and trailed the woman to her flat in Maida Vale. The following morning, King followed her to work and was astonished to see her go into the Foreign Office.

Over the following weeks, King continued to track Rösel and found that the meetings at the flat over the antiques shop followed no obvious pattern. However, by the last week of April he had the addresses and names of all Rösel's informants, including the owners of a small hotel in Folkestone, a man working in an arms factory, one in an airplane manufacturer, a GPO Telecommunications worker, a middle aged lady and a retired professional man.

At his scheduled meeting with McNair at the end of the month, King attempted to take stock of his progress. 'I now know the names, addresses and jobs of all of Rösel's informants,' he told the Scot, 'and I also know where they meet. However, I don't yet know how he arranges meetings and, given that these happen on an irregular basis and sometimes don't include all group members, it's essential that I discover this. Also, it's not clear how, or even if group members can communicate with him. To request a meeting, for example. I watched him like a hawk and I'd swear that there's no sign of a drop box.' King struck the pub table with such frustration that their two pints of beer almost spilled.

'You need to calm down a bit, laddie. No point getting yourself all het up,' advised McNair. 'I agree that if, as the Professor says, Rösel's going to get his marching orders soon, we've very little time. But all's not lost yet. We need to think this through rationally.

'Well,' reasoned King, 'communication must either be by telephone or by post. Telephone is not very likely, as we know that at least three of his informants don't have one at home and using public phones or ones at work would be far too risky.'

'So, it must be by post,' concluded a smiling McNair. 'And don't forget. the Professor's always got a trick or two up his sleeve.'

'What do you mean?' asked King excitedly. 'Tell me his plan.'

'As you know, he has a small army of his irregular, 'off the books' informers. Well, one of these has good contacts in the sorting office, from which three of our 'friends' receive their post. Best of all, they also have contacts in the offices which deliver Rösel's home and office mail. They've been discreetly intercepting post for about a week now, and we had our first breakthrough yesterday. Would you believe that we found a coded letter, written in invisible ink, from Rösel to one of his informants? The code was real schoolboy stuff and our boys cracked it in minutes,' he added dismissively, 'so, I'll bet you a pint of this best bitter that there'll be a meeting of Rösel's second group tomorrow.' McNair took a long draft of his beer and sat back contentedly, beaming at his younger friend.

'But that's splendid, Mac,' enthused King. 'We've got more or less everything we need. And when the news breaks that Rösel's to be expelled, one of these people is bound to try to get in touch with him. I'd stake my life on it.'

CHAPTER SEVENTEEN

Thursday 4th May 1939 , The House Of Commons, London.

The sun was shining wanly through the leaded windows of the 'Mother of Parliaments' as Geoffrey Mander, the veteran Member of Parliament for Wolverhampton East, rose to his feet to put a question to His Majesty's Secretary of State for Home Affairs. Sir Samuel Hoare knew exactly what was coming, for Mander had been one of the first Members of the House to take a strong stand against the appeasement of Fascist dictators and, for several months, had been posing awkward questions about pro-Nazi organisations and Nazi sympathisers in Britain. After clearing his throat, the MP asked whether, in addition to the three recently expelled from the country, any further German individuals had been asked to leave Britain.

The Home Secretary replied courteously that, while there was no truth in the rumours that up to fifty more foreign nationals were to be expelled, such people and their organisations were kept under constant observation. As a result of this activity, he advised that a further nine people, three of whom had already been named in The House, were to be asked to leave British shores. The remaining six were listed as:

Richard Hans Curt Frauendorf
Captain Adolf Eduard Julius Jäger
Ernst Lahrmann
Rudolf Gottfried Rösel
Gunther Schallies

Friedrich Wilhelm Scharpf.

***

Friday 5th May 1939, The Athenaeum Club, London.

'So, you see John, our friend Herr Rösel is very much on borrowed time now,' said Professor Pym with a contented smile as he sat back in his favourite armchair in the otherwise empty smoking room of his Pall Mall Club. 'I'm delighted with your progress over the last couple of months. You've achieved more than it was reasonable to expect. We've almost all the information we need to enable you to step into the German's shoes and begin to run his networks.'

'How long before he has to leave, do you think, sir?' asked King keenly.

'I expect it to be a matter of days, John. But there'll be a short delay before we can put you in place. It would be unrealistic if you appeared and tried openly to contact the members of his networks on the day after Rösel is expelled. So, we need to wait and see if any of his contacts panics about not hearing from him. In that case, they may well try to get in touch and reveal their method of contact. As you know, we're pretty sure that would be by post and I have all bases covered to intercept any message.'

'What about the flat on Portobello Road?' King asked sharply. 'Do you think I'll still be able to use it after he's expelled?'

Pym rubbed his chin thoughtfully before replying with conviction, 'Oh, yes. I'm sure that won't be a problem. At least initially. The landlord has confirmed that the rent has been paid for the next year and it might look suspicious, if a new man appeared and insisted on meeting in a different location right away. So, we'll keep things as they are for the time being at least.'

'That's fine, sir. But what happens if the Germans try to replace Rösel themselves? That might be a little tricky.'

'Of course, you're right,' agreed Pym calmly,' but I think that we just have to play that one by ear. It's most likely that any replacement for him will take some time to organise and you should have your feet well under the table with his circle of informants by then. I'll do what I can to ensure any replacement is intercepted before he can contact the group. But I can't guarantee that and, in such an eventuality, you might have to deal with the problem yourself. Are you happy with that? McNair sorted you out with a weapon, I believe?' The Professor looked keenly at King, searching for any evidence of uncertainty or unwillingness to take such potentially drastic action.

'It's yes on both counts, sir,' replied King firmly, 'I'm sure I can look after myself.'

'Well, you make sure you keep in touch with McNair and call on him whenever you feel the need. Don't forget that he's a good man to have on your side in a scrape because, from now on, things could well become much more dangerous.'

Pym ended the meeting by passing a thin folder to King. 'This summarises the personal details of all Rösel's, or should I now say your informants. Of course, you already know them from your observations of the meetings. But this report is pretty comprehensive and contains some information that you may not have.'

***

Some twenty-four hours after Geoffrey Mander's question in the House of Commons, Rudolf Gottfried Rösel climbed aboard a Junkers passenger plane at Croydon Airport on his way to Tempelhof Airport in the centre of Berlin.

***

Friday 12th May 1939, Sevenoaks.

Martha Perrygo stood impatiently by her occasional table and gazed out of the lounge window. 'Where on earth is the postman?' she fumed. 'It's typical of the sloppy way Britain is degenerating.' Wolfgang, her almost blind tortoiseshell cat, had heard it all before and, sensing the possibility of a full-scale rant, pulled himself up from the carpet and stalked off towards the kitchen and his bowl of milk.

Perrygo stepped back from the window when she saw the postman walking jauntily up the path and heard him tunelessly whistling 'Heaven Can Wait.' *At last*, thought the woman triumphantly, *surely there'll be details of our next meeting. I've such a lot to tell him.* As soon as she went out of the front parlour of her neat semi-detached house in the High Street, her expression changed from eager anticipation to crushing disappointment. She could see immediately that the eagerly anticipated, hand-addressed envelope had not arrived. Only a bill lay staring up at her from the mat. 'This can't be right', she mumbled, before going to the kitchen and filling up the kettle. As she searched for a match to ignite the gas ring, suddenly she remembered. *Of course! He gave us details of how we could contact him urgently. Should I send him a note requesting a meeting?* For the next thirty minutes Perrygo argued with herself the pros and cons of making contact. On the one hand, they had all been told that this was to be done only in extreme circumstances; for things that simply could not wait. Moreover, to her knowledge this means of communication had never been used by anyone in the group. On the other hand, it was now much longer than normal since they had met and it was worrying her. *Surely, anyone would agree that it would be quite in order to invoke this procedure. After all, I do have interesting things to tell him. There*, she decided finally, *I've made up my mind. I'll write to him today*. She sat back in her chair, pleased with her decisiveness and ready to enjoy her tea. She could have little inkling that soon several other people would be equally pleased with her decision.

***

Tuesday 16th May 1939, Charing Cross Road, London.

'It's for you,' said Paul Kemp with a smile, as he held the telephone receiver for King. 'I think it's the Professor. I'll just put the 'closed' sign up and get the kettle on... let's take a break; it's been a busy morning.'

'It's happened my boy,' declared an ecstatic Pym, 'a big piece of the jigsaw fell into place this morning. We've intercepted a letter from one of your 'friends' to the recently departed German. It's in invisible ink again and pretty basic code. We even know the codename, by which he was known to them - Parsifal - and it looks like they identify themselves by their first name also in code.'

***

Just two weeks after Rösel's expulsion from Britain, McNair and King met to draft an invitation to be sent to the first of the groups of informants.

CHAPTER EIGHTEEN

Tuesday 30th May 1939 , Portobello Road, London.

The two men met at the junction of Elgin Crescent and Portobello Road and, with a brief nod of recognition, fell in step towards the flat. 'You have your stuff? Time will be tight as we'll only have about half an hour before the first member arrives,' King explained nervously.

'Don't worry your head, laddie,' replied the Scot. 'I've checked and it's a Yale. You'll be in there in thirty seconds.' McNair crossed the road, casually approached the door to the flat and tried to open it. Shaking his head as if in surprised disappointment, he then retraced his steps back up Portobello Road. King waited a couple of minutes then crossed the road himself and pretended to unlock the flat door, which McNair had left slightly ajar. His heart pounding in his chest, King pushed open the door and entered Rösel's meeting place.

It had been decided that King's first meetings with the informants should take place at the usual flat. However, he would explain to them that, for security reasons, they would soon be meeting elsewhere. 'This tactic', Pym had explained, 'will offer the benefit of some continuity and give plausibility to your status as the replacement from Germany. It will also give an excellent reason for us to move the group meetings to another place, where we needn't fear the appearance of any authentic German agent.'

Once inside, King quickly spotted a Yale key, which fitted the front door, hanging by the doorframe in the kitchen. He then familiarised himself with the layout of the flat, which comprised a living and dining area, a small kitchen, a bathroom and one bedroom. The furniture had that unmistakably shabby look found in many furnished rentals and there was no evidence that the flat had been used since Rösel's last meeting. King paced nervously as the appointed time for the arrival of Mrs Perrygo approached. He was all too aware that these could be the most crucial minutes of the mission to date. *If I can't convince them that I'm Rösel's replacement*, he fretted, *the whole damn project may collapse.*

On hearing the doorbell's insistent buzz, King descended the stairs to be confronted by an unmistakable look of suspicion and fear clouding the hard face of Martha Perrygo. 'Thank you for being so punctual, Martha. Parsifal always said that he could set his watch by you.' The mention of both her name and Rösel's codename reassured her and she willingly preceded him up the stairs. Over the next half hour, King greeted the three remaining informants who became noticeably less suspicious as soon as they realised that other group members were present. Firstly, the older Gervaise Cromwell, known to be retired from a senior position at the Bank of England; next Fred Beach, a younger, wiry and nervous man who worked at the Supermarine Aviation Works in Southampton and finally Joe Watkins, the burly railway controller from Victoria Station.

'Thank you for coming,' King began. 'I'm sure you will all agree that it's essential that we carry on the work begun so well by Parsifal.'

'Yes, that's all very well,' interrupted Beach, his eyes darting around like a frightened bird which could find nowhere to land. 'But what's happened to Parsifal? And who are you?' A murmur of agreement passed through the other informants and, emboldened by this apparent support, the young man continued. 'And, more to the point, why should we trust you?'

'I'm sorry to have to inform you that the British authorities have expelled Parsifal from the country,' King explained. 'He returned to Berlin on May 5th.'

Beach was now beside himself with anxiety. 'But if they've expelled him, they must also know about us! That must be the reason for his expulsion. Why have you brought us here? It's too dangerous! We'll all be arrested.' Wild with panic, he leapt up from his seat and rushed towards the stairs.

Perrygo's deep voice immediately boomed, 'For God's sake, pull yourself together, young man!' Startled, Beach stopped in his tracks and turned around. 'Let's just calm down,' she added more reasonably, 'and at least allow the man to explain himself.' The other group members mumbled their agreement and a shamefaced Beach resumed his seat.

'Thank you,' King began, gesturing to Perrygo, 'I'm grateful for your sensible words. But I understand fully the concerns you will all have. However, I am absolutely certain that these will be put to rest when I explain the new situation. Parsifal's real name is Rudolf Gottfried Rösel and there is no evidence that the British are aware of his activities with you. He was expelled in retaliation for the entirely justified removal from Germany of several agitating British journalists. Because of his excellent work leading the German Information Service in London, he was an easy target. This flat has been kept under surveillance since his expulsion and the British have shown no knowledge of, or interest in it. Nevertheless, we should all be cautious, suspicious even.'

King then produced four pieces of paper, on which he wrote each group member's full name and place of work. Having passed these to the confused looking informants, he was gratified to see each nod as they read the information. His credentials and authority established, he asserted, 'I am your new controller and you are to refer to me as Lazarus. I have been sent from Germany to continue Parsifal's work. In fact, I had the pleasure of several long conversations with him, after his return to the Fatherland. How else would I know all your names, where you work and how and where to call meetings with you? In case any of you are still unsure, I have one further conclusive proof. Here is a copy of *The Times* newspaper, dated May 6th 1940. If you look on the bottom right side of the front page, you will see the list of names of those expelled by the British and even a photograph of some of them walking towards a plane at Croydon Aerodrome. The list includes the name Rösel and I am sure that you will all recognise Parsifal on the tarmac. He's on the left side of the group in shot.' Sitting back confidently, King saw that the faces of the group members were far less anxious and Cromwell summed up the change of mood saying, 'Well, I for one, believe Lazarus is who he says he is. After all, if he were some kind of British plant, why would he not have already arrested us? Why would he have invited us here, just like Parsifal?'

'And we certainly can't argue with *The Times* added Watkins with a smile.

King reassured the group that there was no need to change the code for communications, but that they would be given details of a new meeting place soon. He also provided details of a new Post Office Box, which they could use in emergencies to contact him. There followed a series of brief oral reports from each member and, as he made detailed notes, King quickly realised that Rösel had done an excellent job in selecting his informants.

The meeting finished around 10PM and King left half an hour later. Just as he was shutting the door, he noticed, in a shop doorway on the other side of the street, a man strike a match to light a cigarette. This was the prearranged sign, by which McNair would let him know that all of the group members had left the area and that he could assume that none were suspicious enough to try to follow him.

***

Tuesday 6th June 1939, Portobello Road, London.

The sun was still shining strongly as King arrived for his first meeting with the second group of informants. Jane and Peter Lambton were the first to arrive. The owners of a mid-sized hotel in Dover, they had connections with several senior members of the Anglo-German Fellowship and had a wide circle of pro-Nazi friends in Kent and Sussex. The next two members of the group were Paul O'Grady, an Irish telecommunications worker, who was sympathetic to Nazi Germany on the principle that 'my enemy's enemy is my friend' and Albert Shaw, a foreman at the Royal Small Arms Factory in Enfield. 'These may well prove to be significant sources to control,' Pym had said to King, during their briefing. 'But I would wager a pound to a penny that the final member, Abigail Stevenson, is by far the most important in the group. Try to keep a special eye on her.'

The meeting followed a very similar pattern of initial suspicion allayed by King's knowledge of the personal details of the group and the arrangements for their meetings with Parsifal. Each member had made a brief report and King had again instructed them to await a summons to the next meeting. He had been careful to arrange for Stevenson to be the last to arrive, so that she would be the last to leave and would have some private time with him. As he returned from showing Shaw out of the flat, King noted that she was tall and slim with long, blond hair and a pretty face. *A classic 'English Rose,'* he reflected as she reached into her handbag to extract a packet of cigarettes and an exquisite silver lighter. 'Do you have anything you wish to say to me in private?' he enquired gently.

'Well, maybe it's not so significant right now, but I think that may well change,' she began anxiously. 'You see, I'm on very friendly terms with a couple of the senior private secretaries at work. In fact, on fine days we often go to eat our lunch together in St James's Park. It's so peaceful and pretty there.' Stevenson paused to take another draw on her cigarette and to push her hair behind her ears, before continuing, 'I don't have clearance for the most secret work. But they do. And one day last week they were talking about how they didn't think Britain should form an alliance with Russia.'

King's ears pricked up, as he could imagine that a real German agent would be desperate to discover more information on this theme. 'That's very interesting. Did they say anything else?'

'Not really…. Just that neither of them was keen on this, and that many senior officers in the Foreign Office felt the same.' As soon as she had finished speaking, she looked up at King as he offered enthusiastic praise. 'You were right to keep this topic back for me alone, Abigail. Don't talk about it with anyone else. I want you to keep your eyes and ears open, but above all, don't arouse suspicion. Time is on our side and we don't have to rush things. Use what opportunities arise, but be wary of taking too many risks.'

CHAPTER NINETEEN

Summer 1939, London.

Despite a rapidly deteriorating political situation and increasing evidence of preparations for war, the summer months were a relatively quiet time for King. Nevertheless, his deepening experience with his informants had promoted a genuine interest in the psychology of treason. 'They clearly have differing definitions of what they are doing, their motivations and their preparedness to discuss them,' he explained eagerly to Pym at one of their regular meetings in late June. 'Take Cromwell, for example, the retired Bank of England executive. He's always very keen to justify himself, invariably arguing that his actions are actually helping to save the country from the defeated politics of democracy and its evident capitulation to socialism.'

'And what of the Stevenson woman, the Foreign Office secretary?' Pym asked sharply, 'has she revealed anything of her rationale for treason?'

'I can't say that she has,' replied King, 'which suggests to me a motivation rooted deep in her very private past. It'll take time and patience to dig it out. But she has, as you suggested, provided by far the most sensitive information.'

'Good, well keep her close, John. I doubt the Germans will be content to leave such a source untapped.'

'I will sir, in fact she's just requested an urgent, private meeting. I'll let you know what she says.'

King and Stevenson agreed to meet at 7PM on Tuesday July 4th, on a wooden bench overlooking the Serpentine in Hyde Park. King arrived early to enjoy a stroll through the park on a lovely, warm afternoon, before he took a table at one of the park's tea rooms and enjoyed a lemonade in the sun's comfortable embrace. Surrounded by happy people, he began to reflect on how he had lost any connection with the normal things in life. Walking hand in hand with a sweetheart, happy family picnics in the park or garden, energetically good-natured discussion and argument with colleagues. These were all things of the past for him now. *At least for now. But,* he promised himself, *not forever.*

The bench King had chosen for the meeting was situated directly in front of the Serpentine, enjoying forty metres of open, straight path on both sides and a rather rough and steep rise immediately to its rear. As he approached it, he almost didn't recognise Abigail Stevenson, as she was dressed in a bright, summery frock, rather than her habitual uniform of smart office wear. King sat down and, having nodded a polite stranger's greeting, he unfolded his *Evening Standard* and pretended to read it.

'I'm sorry to call you to a meeting like this, but I have useful information on the topic we discussed the last time we met,' Stevenson began quickly.

'That's fine,' replied King in a steady voice. 'Take your time. It's a beautiful evening and I'm in no hurry.'

The young woman flickered a brief smile in his direction and continued, 'One of my friends, a Senior Private Secretary, has been ill and I had to replace her as minute taker in a meeting between senior civil servants. This was called to discuss Britain's attitude to a possible alliance with France and Russia against Germany. It appears that the Soviets are very serious about this possibility. There is even the suggestion that they have offered an army of one million men to help defeat Germany.'

'That could be very serious, if it forced Germany to fight a two front war...' King acknowledged. 'Was anything said about the likelihood of this alliance being realised?'

'That's the point I want you to understand,' Stevenson emphasised. 'All the civil servants present stressed that the British Government is very lukewarm about the proposal. Basically, they are suspicious of communism and believe that, after Stalin's systematic purges of the military leadership, the Red Army is probably not fit for purpose anyway.'

'Have you any definite information about the formal British response to the Russian overtures?' King demanded sharply.

'Well, I didn't understand everything that was said, but yes, the most senior person there said that Lord Halifax doesn't want a meeting with the Soviets and intends to play for time by sending a low-level official to Moscow to delay things.'

A week later, King visited Pym in his flat to update him on the meeting with Stevenson and the progress of the operation generally. The Professor was genuinely astonished by the information offered by Abigail Stevenson, but was also keen to know what intelligence the other group members had provided.

'Well, of course, I've only met these in group meetings, but I'd say that Joe Watkins, the goods train controller from Victoria Station and Fred Beach, the worker at the Supermarine Aviation Works, may be crucial sources to keep an eye on. The first could give full details of train movements, which may well be useful to the Luftwaffe or to German saboteurs. The latter could provide vital intelligence concerning production levels and technical data on fighters such as the Spitfire.'

Pym heaved a heavy sigh as he rubbed his chin thoughtfully. 'It hardly bears thinking about, does it, John? If just the intelligence from these few sources were to find its way back to Berlin, who knows what might be the consequences?'

'You're right, of course,' replied King, 'but as to O'Grady, the Irish telecommunications worker, his loyalties are definitely not to Germany. I've the distinct impression that he takes his orders from some Republican cell or other and may well have connections to those who would commit acts of sabotage. For the time being, however, he and Shaw, who works in the Royal Small Arms Factory, may be rather lower priorities. But we definitely shouldn't forget that Martha Perrygo has a wide group of Nazi sympathisers who clearly provide her with all sorts of information about what's going on in the South East and on the South coast.'

***

During the dog days of summer King contented himself with working in the bookshop and holding periodic meetings with his informants in the new flat, above a tailor's shop in Tottenham Court Road. A week after their last group meeting, on a drizzly, unseasonably cool morning in mid-August, King received another request for an individual meeting from Stevenson, which he scheduled in the flat. The rain was still pouring down out of a leaden evening sky when she arrived, her stylish trench-coat and small umbrella having prevented a thorough soaking. Nevertheless, her long blond hair looked damp and the shoulders and bottom edges of her coat were very wet. She grimaced as she came through the open front door of the flat to King's cheery greeting. 'A typical English summer day, if I am not mistaken.'

'You can say that again,' she replied miserably. 'As usual I'm cold and wet.'

King turned on the small gas fire and urged her to sit closer to it before saying, 'From the tone of your message, something urgent must have come up.'

'Yes, I think it has,' she replied seriously, 'though it's not to do with that alliance issue.' Recognising the look of disappointment on her handler's face, she hastily continued. 'Nothing much has happened on that front that I'm aware of. However, last week I was given some meeting minutes to file. As you'll imagine, at the moment the Foreign Office is very busy. It has, however, felt obliged to honour requests for summer leave from many secretarial and administrative staff. We've brought in a few temps to do the low-level work, but the permanent staff like me have been given the more…. shall we say sensitive tasks.'

'I see,' interrupted King, using the pause in her story to pick up his notepad and pencil.

'Of course,' continued the young woman confidentially, 'I had to be very careful. There was very little opportunity for me to have a good look at them, but I was allowed into the filing room just before lunch one day. As I was searching for the correct drawer in which to place the file, one of the staff from the outer office shouted that they were all going for lunch and could I please make sure that door to their office was locked when I left. It was just lucky timing really. I would've finished and left before they went to lunch, had I been a minute or two earlier,'

'And are they supposed to leave the filing room unattended and with someone still in it?' asked King incredulously.

'Oh no. Of course not. The office managers are quite strict about that kind of thing,' she replied. 'But, as I said, we're very short staffed and they know me as a permanent member of staff. So, I imagine that they could see no harm in leaving me to shut and lock the door. It's a Yale lock, you see.'

'Well,' encouraged King with a smile, 'you may have been lucky. But that isn't everything. You used your luck to the fullest.'

Stevenson hardly seemed to notice the compliment, merely continuing, 'The minutes, which I had the opportunity to study, were from a meeting involving senior civil servants from the Foreign Office and the Treasury.'

'Really? That sounds very interesting. Please tell me more.'

'Well, it appears that at the end of April, Poland approached Britain for help with the financial cost of rearming. Specifically, in May the Polish Foreign Minister Beck asked for a loan of £60million to purchase weapons and crucial raw materials.' King was once more astonished at the sensitivity of the information that his informant was imparting. 'The Treasury civil servant is minuted as saying that the Chancellor of the Exchequer, Sir John David, had advised Mr. Chamberlain that the idea of Britain bailing out Polish rearmament in such a fashion was 'really impossible.' His reason was that the financial position of Britain herself had been greatly affected by the costs of her own rearmament. The minutes also noted that a decision had been made on 24th July, that Britain could possibly offer some £8million, which would, however, have to be spent by the Poles on British materiel. There is no record of whether or not this offer was either made, or accepted.'

***

Sunday 3rd September, 1939, Charing Cross Road, London.

'James! James! Come down here quickly and listen to this!' Paul Kemp's voice carried an urgency that brooked no contradiction and King immediately dropped what he was doing and hastened downstairs. He was just in time to be shushed by the bookseller and shown to a battered armchair by the fireplace… 'Just listen to this.' the older man hissed 'For God's sake… here we go again…'

King was transfixed as, crackling out of the ancient radio set, came the unmistakable voice of the Prime Minister:

'I am speaking from the cabinet room of 10 Downing Street. This morning the British ambassador in Berlin handed the German government a final note stating that unless we heard from them by 11 o'clock that they were prepared at once to withdraw their troops from Poland, a state of war would exist between us. I have to tell you that no such undertaking has been received and that consequently this country is at war with Germany.'

CHAPTER TWENTY

Wednesday 15th November 1939, London.

War may have been declared in September, but the last months of 1939 and the first three months of 1940 saw very little military or naval action. Indeed, this period was dubbed 'The Twilight War' by the Prime Minister, Neville Chamberlain, and 'The Phoney War' by the British press and people. Nevertheless, war had brought noticeable changes. Many theatres, public buildings and shops had their entrances protected by thick walls of sandbags and their windows taped in criss-cross patterns to inhibit flying glass. And most people had got used to carrying the Government issue square cardboard box containing a gas mask.

As soon as Britain was officially at war, King suspended group meetings, preferring to meet his informants individually and on this particular evening he had an appointment with Albert Shaw, a foreman at the Royal Small Arms Factory. He easily recognised the medium build and thinning, fair hair of Shaw, as he casually entered the Horatia pub, bought a pint of pale ale and sat at King's table. They spent the first few minutes discussing the banalities of the weather, fictitious family matters and the increasing effects of rationing. Shaw was an unattractive, furtive man, with darting, narrow eyes and restless hands which were forever clasping and unclasping one another. 'For goodness sake, calm down, man,' King warned him. 'You'll arouse suspicion carrying on like that.' Shaw smiled, revealing his misshapen and nicotine stained teeth, 'Sorry, but you know, since September I've become much more anxious. They could hang me for what I'm doing.'

'If we exercise a modicum of caution, it won't come to that. We're just two old friends having a catch up in a pub,' King said smoothly, 'So, what have you got for me?'

'Well,' Shaw replied, 'since the Nazi-Soviet Pact, it seems that some of the more hard-line, pro-Soviet trade unionists are secretly encouraging industrial sabotage in the factory. It's only small scale and uncoordinated stuff for now and it's only caused minor disruption. But who knows? With organisation and planning, it could have quite an effect. A mate of mine is involved and he knows my views about Churchill and his policies.'

'You've not said anything about me, have you?' King asked sharply. 'The British are no fools, whatever we may think. They'll have counter espionage agents deployed in factories now.'

'Of course I haven't. But I might be able to get us both an invitation to their next meeting. I'd tell them you were a friend and sympathiser. You could see how the land lies. What do you think? Are you already working with Bolshevik agents? Should I organise it?' Shaw's face glistened with beads of sweat as he waited for a response.

King had already discussed with Pym the possibility that pro-Soviet sympathies among trade unionists could, in light of the Molotov-Ribbentrop pact, metamorphose into a willingness to sabotage the British war effort. For all they knew, Moscow might already have been organising Communist workers to undertake such work. 'It's vital that we get a good idea of the implications of that foul agreement,' Pym had insisted. 'So, if you have the opportunity to find out what the Soviets are up to, take it with both hands. Try to get an idea of numbers and the names of the organisers.'

Despite his excitement at Shaw's suggestion, King replied cautiously, 'Of course the Reds have their own network of agents here and, though collaboration has been discussed at the highest levels, nothing has been decided. So, you shouldn't say anything about our relationship. But to attend such a meeting is a good idea. Let me know if this can be arranged. In the meantime, keep your eyes and ears open and try to get me a list of names of these Soviet sympathisers. The sooner we all start to work together for the defeat of Britain, the better.'

Barely a week later, Shaw confirmed details of a meeting of the Enfield factory's communist cell, due to take place in a function room above The Goose public house in Wood Green, at which a regional organiser was to make the key address. They agreed to meet in the tap room of the pub at 7.45PM, some fifteen minutes before the meeting was due to start.

***

Shaw, looking typically shifty and unhealthy as he nursed a pint of ale, looked up and nodded quickly to King as he bought a glass of bitter before joining him. The room was a thick fug of tobacco, beer and the stale sweat of the working class clientele. Several hostile faces glared at King as he ordered his beer, but noticeably relaxed when he went to sit with Shaw. 'Friendly natives around these parts,' said King sarcastically. 'Now, Albert, what's the score for tonight?'

'I've told them that you're an old friend of mine, down visiting from the Midlands, and they're OK with that,' replied Shaw. 'But we mustn't speak during the meeting and I need a name I can give them. I can hardly use Lazarus.'

'Just call me Fred or Freddie,' instructed King, 'and leave the rest to me. Did you get me the list of the local Reds?'

After a careful look to make sure he was not being observed, Shaw offered King his newspaper to read. Clipped to the bottom of page five was a small piece of paper which King extracted, before he threw the paper on the table, declaring with exasperation, 'All the same old rubbish in that!'

After taking another pull of his beer, Shaw stammered 'All the names I could get are there. But you must realise how dangerous this is... I don't like it at all. They'd hurt me badly if they as much as suspected.'

'They won't', I'll see to that,' said King reassuringly as he expertly pocketed the paper and took a sip of his beer.

'A fellow shop steward, Nixon, has arranged to take us into the meeting,' continued Shaw. 'He'll be here in a couple of minutes.'

'Then I'd better pay a quick visit. Back in a jiffy,' said King as he rose to his feet and made his way through the thickening crowd of drinking men. Once inside the appallingly dingy, but thankfully deserted Gents lavatory, King made for the nearest cubicle. Holding his nose against the smell and trying not to pay too much attention to the dreadful state of the facilities, he quickly took out the piece of paper which Shaw had given him, folded it until it was about the size of a cigarette card and then slipped it into a secret compartment in his glasses case. King smiled to himself at this piece of theatrically spy-like behaviour, flushed the lavatory for the sake of appearances, though it did seem to him that few did so even when they should, and made his way back to the tap room.

As he entered, King saw that Shaw had been joined by a huge, brutish man who was perched on the edge of the seat that he himself had occupied. On seeing King, Shaw rose rather stiffly and began to make the introductions. 'This is Freddie,' he began edgily, his nervous eyes flicking from King to the man-mountain and back again. 'He's a good friend of mine. Freddie, meet....'

'If it'd been left to me,' Nixon interrupted as he eyed King with undisguised suspicion, 'you two wouldn't be here. But we're a disciplined lot in the workers' army. We do as we're told,' he grumbled with a harsh laugh which indicated his obvious contempt for these particular orders. With an angry jerk of his bullet like head in the direction of a narrow door to the right of the packed bar, he indicated that Shaw and King should follow him. King realised, as he made his way up the dark stairway, that this must be some kind of service route to the upper floors. At the top of the stairs, another narrow door opened onto the corner of a broad, well-lit landing which was crowded with men. *They must all have come up the main staircase,* King reasoned.

'Follow this lot in and take the seats immediately to your left, up against the rear wall,' barked Nixon as he carefully closed the door to the back stairs. 'I'll join you before the meeting starts.' King noticed that the door was so well disguised that, once closed, it could easily be mistaken for one of the simple wooden panels which lined the walls of the landing. *That might be useful,* he thought.

The meeting itself was extremely lively, with many heated points being made about the ethics of actively supporting Soviet Russia, in view of the Molotov-Ribbentrop Pact. 'Hitlerism is the exact antithesis of Socialism. How can we positively help towards the possible victory of Fascism?' asked one of the more articulate members of the audience. The main speaker was just about to offer his solution to this dilemma, when the rear doors of the room burst open and two men rushed in shouting, 'Special Branch! Special Branch's here! It's a raid... get out while you can!'

After a second's stunned silence, the room filled with the sound of chairs being pushed hastily back onto the floor and incoherent shouting as members of the audience desperately tried to flee. Nixon immediately grabbed Shaw by the arm and hissed, 'Come with me, you two.' King's mind was racing. *Special Branch must have received a tip off and that oaf made no secret of his suspicions about us.* Not relishing the idea of being left to the tender mercies of the likes of Nixon, King decided to get away from him as quickly as possible. *The raid must have come through the pub's main entrance,* he reasoned, *so if I can get to those rear stairs, I might just escape.*

To his frustration, the flow of panicked communists was towards the main staircase and he found himself being dragged in that direction. Ahead he could see Nixon, holding Shaw firmly by the arm. His sheer size meant that he was able to forge his way through the crowd and King used the movement of the crowd in his wake to fall further and further behind. Eventually, feigning injury to his leg, he made his way to the side of the landing just in time to see Shaw's terrified face as he was dragged down the return staircase by the huge shop steward. As all the other men were totally focused on getting down the stairs, King managed to edge his way towards the door to the rear stairs and, when no one was looking, he quickly slipped through. Taking the dark stairs dangerously quickly, he emerged into the deserted tap room and escaped through the back door of the pub. Shouts and curses filled the air as King ran across the back yard of the pub and climbed over its six-foot wall. *The commies must have gone down the stairs and straight into the arms of the waiting Special Branch,* King guessed. *Christ! It sounds like a battle in there.* Crouching down in the pitch-black alley, King gave silent thanks for the blackout which made it almost impossible for the police or Special Branch to find and apprehend any escapees. Nevertheless, he could hear police whistles and barked orders echoing all around as he moved cautiously down the alley. Eventually, it intersected with another passage, but, in the total darkness, he had no idea which way to go. He thought he heard some traffic noise to the right and so, aiming to reach a less deserted road which would disguise his escape, he moved in that direction. After staggering about fifty metres down the uneven, pitch dark passage, he came to Station Road. Without hesitation, he turned left and began to walk briskly away from the pub. He had just begun seriously to entertain the hope that he might have got away with it, when he was pinned by the strong beam of a police torch and heard the inevitable, 'Stop where you are! Do not move! You're under arrest!'

King immediately began to run away from the police officer who was struggling to follow in the darkness. He was at least maintaining his lead until he tripped over a loose pavement slab and hit the ground hard. As he lay winded and in pain, the wild movement of the torch beam indicated that the police officer was almost on him. Just as he thought it was all up, a darkened car screeched past the policeman, stopped right by him and, through the open passenger door, he heard a familiar voice hiss, 'Get in quick, laddie, or we're both done for.' King struggled to his feet and collapsed rather than jumped into the car, which sped off, even as he was struggling to close the door. 'There's a bottle of single malt in the glove compartment. You look like you could use some. Oh, and pass it over to me when you've had a wee dram.'

'How on earth do you come to be here, Mac?' King asked incredulously, but McNair simply waved an arm expansively. 'Oh, leave all that until later, son. Suffice to say that you, the Professor and me, we're a team are we not? And team members look out for one another. Now let's get out of here while we still have the chance.'

***

Bolton, England.

'Thank God that's over for another day,' sighed the young police constable. 'These night shifts don't half take it out of you.'

'You can say that again, David,' replied an older officer as he sat down with a heartfelt groan on one of the wooden benches scattered about the station locker room. 'You just wait 'til you're as old and clapped out as me, my lad. Then you'll have reason to moan.'

Sergeant Holmes bustled into the room and looked directly at the older man, 'Joe, you'll have to complete the report this morning. David's wanted upstairs by the 'Guv'nor' asap.'

Joe Atherton saw the anxious look on his young colleague's face and taunted, 'What've you been up to now, young fella? I told you that the Inspector's daughter is off limits.'

'What does he want with me, Sarge?' Bernstein asked nervously. 'Have I done something wrong?'

'We've all done that plenty of times son,' replied the Sergeant kindly. 'But this time, no, you've done nothing wrong. He just wants to speak to you, that's all. Now get along as quickly as you can.'

David Bernstein had only ever wanted to be a police officer and, having been helped to leave Nazi Germany by John King, he had applied as soon as he was old enough. However, his application to join the police force had been complicated by his dual nationality, at a time when Britons were becoming more and more anti-German. The intervention of the respected Mr and Mrs King, with whom he'd been living, had finally been decisive in tilting the balance in favour of his acceptance. Determined to make the most of his opportunity, he had finished top of the class at the Police Training School near Warrington and had jumped at the chance of a permanent posting in Bolton, where he had done part of his 'on the beat', practical training. He had found his newly adopted hometown to be a poor, but extremely welcoming place with its fair share of villains and crime. But it also had a heart of gold and, despite his routine moans about the cold, wet and exhausting night shifts, he loved his job and couldn't think of anything that he would prefer to do. It was, therefore, with some trepidation that he mounted the stairs to the station commander's office. Inspector Haslam was a jovial, pudding of a man in his early fifties, who looked as if he had eaten a few too many of the meat and potato pasties, which were the local delicacy. 'Sit down, Bernstein,' Haslam barked at the young constable. 'And for God's sake don't look so worried. I'm not going to eat you, lad.'

'Yes, sir. Thank you, sir. Sorry, sir,' stammered Bernstein in hopeless confusion.

'It's like this,' continued the Inspector, 'some weeks ago, all police forces in the country were asked for the names of officers who understand German. Your name was, to my knowledge, the only one sent by the Lancashire Constabulary. Now you don't need me to tell you that the war will be fought in lots of ways and in lots of locations. And by no means all of them will involve facing the enemy on the field of battle. There are hidden and secret wars going on and you could well make a significant contribution to that kind of effort. How would you feel about being transferred to the Metropolitan Police's Special Branch? It would mean moving to London, of course. Would that be a problem?'

'Problem, sir?' whispered Bernstein. 'Oh... no, no, of course that would be no problem.'

'Good lad. You've made an excellent start as a policeman here in Bolton and we'll be extremely sorry to lose you. But I think that you can do far more for the war effort with Special Branch than here plodding the beat. You're to report to Inspector Renton at Scotland Yard in two weeks' time. You go and make all your friends up here in Bolton proud of you, son,' said a beaming Haslam as he vigorously shook the hand of his stunned constable.

***

London.

'He's just over here, sir. The doc's with him now. But it doesn't look good.' Inspector Renton of Scotland Yard's Special Branch was barely paying attention to the young constable. He was enjoying their success in getting the prize catch of the District Organiser for the Soviets safely in the bag. A lean man, light on his feet and with the intelligent air of a hunting dog, Renton followed the constable around the corner of a back alley behind The Goose pub. There he was confronted by a grisly tableau. A man's body, pushed up against the wall, had been severely beaten and the fact that he was still alive bore strong testimony to the will of some to survive.

'Do we know who he is?' Renton asked the constable.

'Yes, sir. His papers identify him as Albert Shaw of Enfield,' replied the officer after consulting his notebook.

Perhaps the damned Reds thought this poor sod was the informant, Renton surmised before shrugging his shoulders. Wholly unembarrassed by his cynicism, he smiled as he realised that the heat would be off the actual informer. Renton rubbed his chin and asked the doctor sharply, 'Is he conscious? Has he said anything?'

The doctor looked up from the mangled shape on the floor and replied wearily, 'He's been battered to within an inch of his life, man. His face hardly exists anymore. God knows what was used... wooden or metal implements, I imagine. He's said nothing, but is just barely conscious.'

'Look, sir!' said the young constable, 'I think he's trying to say something.' Renton looked quickly down at the ruins of Albert Shaw and saw that the officer was right. He overcame his distaste for such close proximity to the consequences of extreme violence and bent down to hear Shaw whisper, through bubbles of blood frothing from his mouth. 'Did they get Lazarus? Warn him. For God's sake warn Lazarus.' Suddenly Shaw's eyes opened and swivelled in panic as he saw Renton peering down at him. Evidently mistaking the Inspector for someone he knew, the mortally injured man continued deliriously. 'Tell him to go back to Berlin. Tell him to get out while he can. Tell him....' A surprisingly quiet gurgle later and Shaw was dead, leaving Inspector Renton to contemplate what he might have meant by his dying words.

***

Aachen, Germany.

At just about the same time as Shaw was breathing his last, *Oberleutnant* Adolf Beyer was enjoying the traditional pre-mission meal at a Luftwaffe training base in north west Germany. Admiral Canaris had always insisted that officers about to embark on a field mission should enjoy the best hospitality that the Abwehr could offer. Perhaps this was the reason that pilots queued up to undertake the relatively tedious 'taxi driving' involved in making clandestine drops into enemy territory. The improbably young pilot of his Heinkel He46 was certainly tucking in with relish to the filet of beef which had been prepared exactly to Beyer's taste. 'The weather's perfect for the journey, Oberleutnant,' announced the pilot between mouthfuls of the succulent meat. 'The weather boys say that there should be a scattered covering of cloud, no wind and a less than half moon.' Noticing that Beyer's appetite seemed to be waning, he added with a boyish grin, 'I'd eat as much of that as you're able, sir. From what we hear, you'll not get such quality on that accursed island.' Beyer was not really in the mood for such inane banter and made no response to the pilot who shrugged his shoulders and continued to help himself to the delicious food.

Beyer's silence reflected his genuine concern that he was not adequately prepared for the mission. He knew that the agent initially selected had almost killed himself just over a week earlier in a drunken car chase through a Bavarian forest. *That makes me very much the second choice*, he fretted. *At least that's how the bastards made me feel during what passed for my preparation.* Dreadfully brief though that had been, at least he had been able to spend a little time with Rösel, whose networks he was to take over. He had gleaned some idea of what to expect of his informers and he had the key to the Portobello Road flat, engraved with '77PR', carefully tucked away in his left trouser pocket. It had been Canaris who had given his personal approval for Beyer to take over the mission, mainly because he had been impressed by the Oberleutnant's fluency in English and deep knowledge of the island race's culture and mores. Despite the obvious reservations of other officers, the Admiral had felt that Beyer was exactly the type, both to cope in what was now enemy territory and to manage networks, of which the Abwehr had such high hopes. Rösel had been clear that, while each of his informants was capable of offering useful intelligence, it was the woman Stevenson who frequently provided acute insights and very accurate information from the heart of the British Foreign Office.

Shortly after midnight, the Heinkel took off on its flight towards the drop zone just outside Ipswich. From there, Beyer was to make his way by train via Colchester and Chelmsford to London in time for his scheduled meeting with his contact.

It should have been routine. He bailed out in perfect conditions, exactly over the drop zone and was able to guide his parachute down towards an excellent landing spot in a field next to the main road into Ipswich. No one will ever know quite what happened next. Did Beyer simply fail to see the tree as he fell towards it? Or did some freak gust of wind, rising from the fens, take him at the last moment off his chosen path? Or was it simply the dangerously small number of practice jumps he had made that finally caught up with him? Whatever the cause, Beyer crashed heavily into the thick branches of a British oak, snapping his neck and ending his mission to England before it had even begun. The speed of his descent caused his body to plunge through the branches, until it came to rest with its parachute tangled up in the tree only metres from the main road.

CHAPTER TWENTY ONE

Winter 1939-1940 , London.

King quickly recovered from the physical injuries suffered during his escape from the Special Branch raid. Psychologically, however, he struggled with a sense of guilt over Shaw's death. While he accepted Pym's argument that he could not possibly have helped the man on the night, he did believe strongly that he should have contacted the police. 'I could give them the name and a good description of the likely killer,' he asserted, 'I'm certain that it must have been that oaf who sat with us at the meeting. Shaw called him Nixon. If you'd seen the poor devil's face as he was dragged down that flight of stairs, you'd have no doubt that the police would do well to find and interview that brute.'

'Good God, John,' Pym shot back with genuine exasperation. 'Have you learned nothing about the business in which you're engaged? Do you really think that you could go to the police and give evidence? How would you explain your presence at the meeting? Not to mention your relationship with Shaw?' Pym heaved a huge sigh as he removed his spectacles and rubbed his eyes. 'There's something else, John. A rotten stroke of luck. Rösel's replacement was recently parachuted into Suffolk. He was found with a broken neck, still strapped into his parachute. Evidently, something went wrong and he hit a tree and probably died instantaneously. He was identified as the replacement by a key, engraved with the letters 77PR, in one of his pockets. I managed to get hold of this key and McNair tried it at the Portobello Road flat… it fitted perfectly. There's no doubt that his death was a pure accident, but it's bad luck for us.'

King looked doubtfully at the older man who quickly explained, 'Had he lived, we would've picked him up as soon as he turned up at his contact. The one chosen for him, you see, is our double agent and that's what we would've tried to do with this new man. Turn him and get him to feed trivial information back to Abwehr headquarters, so that they would think all was working well with the networks.'

'But surely we could send messages and pretend that he's still alive,' suggested King hopefully.

The older man smiled sadly before replying, 'I'm afraid that's not possible. We don't know his codename, or when, how and to whom he was to communicate. Also, each agent has his own 'signature' style when he sends radio messages. We can try to copy these when we have examples on which to base our attempts. But with this man, we've nothing to go on. So, you see….'

'They're bound to send another agent when they realise this man's dead. And he may be allocated a different contact…' said King dully, 'so we might not catch him.'

The two men agreed that, in the circumstances, King should continue to liaise with his informers, but otherwise maintain a low profile. 'We'll not be greedy again,' said Pym with surprising feeling. 'I should never have let you go to that meeting. I would never have forgiven myself, had that been you instead of Shaw.'

***

Over the last months of 1939 King's personal war matched that of the regular armed forces which were largely frozen into inactivity. While he kept in touch with his remaining informants, there was little to report and, in common with them, he had the feeling that everyone was waiting for the real conflict to begin.

Paul Kemp had decided to travel north for the Christmas holidays to spend some time with his younger son and his family. King, in contrast, not only felt the loss of his family most keenly at this time of the year, but he also looked back wistfully on the previous Christmas which he had spent in Berlin with Greta and her friends. He was, therefore, very pleased to accept McNair's invitation to spend a few days in Canterbury and left London a couple of days before Christmas Eve.

After a very quiet and pleasant Christmas Day, King was surprised that Professor Pym paid a visit on Boxing Day. He was delighted, if also a little saddened, when his mentor informed him that he had recently visited his parents and had found them both well and happily surrounded by their daughter's young family. 'Of course,' Pym explained, 'they still grieve your loss, but you definitely don't need to worry about them.' Towards the end of the evening, and perhaps influenced by McNair's seasonal generosity with his single malt whisky, Pym had taken King to one side and said, 'I really am in two minds whether or not I should tell you this, my boy. But, given the season, perhaps it's fitting that I let my heart rule my head.' King was intrigued by what the Professor had just said, but was stunned by his next words. 'I have news of Greta.'

'What?' spluttered King, 'How? How is that possible?'

'Never mind that,' replied Pym, brushing away what he saw as possible further pointless questions. 'The fact is, I have news. She is well, still working as a nurse in Heidelberg and, it seems, misses you very much. Also, she is, I am reliably informed, active among those honourable German opponents of Nazism. It seems your lady friend is made of fine stuff.'

As Pym related his news, King could almost feel Greta's presence and he had to excuse himself rapidly, pleading the need to get some air in the garden. A few minutes later, the French windows opened and Pym appeared, carrying another two tumblers of whisky. 'I thought I'd find you out here', he began with concern. 'Here, take this, it'll warm you up. Polly insists...' King turned to face his old mentor and could see the emotion flooding his face. 'I wanted you to know about Greta, John, because I don't want you ever to forget exactly what you're fighting for. In the shadow world which you now occupy, it's all too easy to lose one's moral compass. Hold on to the idea of your family and of Greta. God willing, you'll enjoy a long and happy life with them all, once our job is done.'

King took a sizeable swig of the whisky before replying. 'Thank you. I understand that by telling me these things you've broken many of your cardinal rules.' Pym made to speak, but the younger man raised his hand to stop him. 'I know that, on occasion my scruples have been a cause of concern to you and for that, I am deeply sorry. What you've just told me about Greta has really heartened me to return refreshed to the fray in the new year.'

Feeling desperately wretched, Pym nodded his head, gave King a firm embrace and, without another word, went back into the house. He could no longer bear the sight of King's eager, yet stricken face, in the full knowledge that his protégé must never know the biggest secret of all. In September, Greta had given birth to a healthy daughter who, he understood, bore a striking resemblance to the man he had just left in the garden.

***

Once the Christmas season was over, King returned to London and his life took up a similar pattern to that of December. Over the next three months, he kept in regular postal contact with his informers, but the extreme weather continued to prevent frequent face-to-face meetings, especially outside London. It was with some relief, therefore, that King, in company with many of his countrymen, welcomed the first stirrings of spring. Little were they to know what was to lie ahead.

***

New Scotland Yard, London.

'I simply can't understand it, David,' declared Inspector Renton, throwing his pen down in frustration. 'It's more than two months since we got the lead on Lazarus and we're no further forward. We've not had a decent sniff at all. It's as if he doesn't exist.'

David Bernstein nodded sympathetically, though since his transfer to Special Branch, he had come to regard Renton as somewhat obsessed with the agent Lazarus. Despite this tic, the younger man had generally found the Inspector an interesting and sympathetic boss and he felt proud every time he went to work at New Scotland Yard. Conscious of his Inspector's frustration, Bernstein tried to respond positively, 'The weather's been terrible, sir. With that and the phoney-ness of the war, maybe there's not much for him to do and he's just laying low.'

Renton shifted uneasily in his chair, 'You could be right, son. But let's just go over what we do know and any progress we've made since Shaw's death. Something might suggest itself.' As Bernstein opened a dispiritingly thin folder, Renton slumped deeper into his chair, closed his eyes, folded his hands behind his head and wearily began. 'First, we have Shaw's dying words. He mentions Lazarus and that he should be warned to go back to Berlin. Now, what are we to make of that?'

'The most likely explanations,' Bernstein began thoughtfully, 'are that Shaw was delirious and it meant nothing, or that Lazarus is a German, possibly a spy, and he should escape while he can.'

'Agreed,' declared Renton, his eyes beginning to twinkle with the thrill of the chase. 'So, which interpretation is the more likely?'

Bernstein recalled that a search of the dead man's flat had revealed a large collection of pro-German and Fascist pamphlets and newspapers. 'But that's not, in itself, particularly unusual,' he readily admitted. 'Many British people sympathised with Nazism in the years up to the outbreak of war. What was altogether more significant, however, was the discovery of a series of note pads, in which Shaw had written a lot of information about his place of work at the Royal Small Arms Factory in Enfield. This was divided into sections, each of which was headed by a date. The dates were usually two to three weeks apart.'

'Exactly!' enthused Renton. 'And we took this as pretty clear evidence that he was collecting information to pass on to a Nazi agent at regular meetings. But,' Renton asked keenly, 'wasn't there another book? One in which he'd written much sketchier lists of other information under these same dates?'

'That's right, sir,' replied Bernstein. 'Our best guess is that Shaw met with his contact as part of a group of informants and that this was what he recalled of the information the other informants brought to the meetings. But nothing was written in this book after war was declared.'

'So how do you explain that?' prompted the Inspector with raised eyebrows.

'Well, it could be that group meetings were considered too risky. It looks like one to one contact from then on.'

'In other words,' summarised Renton eagerly, 'Shaw was part of a cell of informants which, in all probability, was pro-Nazi rather than Red. So, let's deal now with the question of what the hell Shaw was doing at that communist meeting in the first place.' The Inspector argued that since the Nazi-Soviet Pact, it was by no means uncommon for Nazi sympathisers to attend communist meetings and vice versa. 'However, in this case, Shaw's brutal death suggests that the Reds blamed him for the raid on their meeting. We know, of course, that he was not the informer, so it was a case of him being in the wrong place at the wrong time. Taking all that into account, the strong probability is that Shaw was part of a group reporting to a Nazi agent, Lazarus, based in London. Now, what else was there from his notebooks?'

'Well sir,' Bernstein replied firmly, 'I believe that the letter next to each of the pieces of information in Shaw's second book could be an identifier for each individual informant.'

Renton smiled at the optimism of his junior officer, but nevertheless questioned this assumption. 'Hang on, David. You know my enthusiasm for catching this Lazarus, but a lot of that last bit is pure conjecture. We don't know if the letters refer to a name and even if they do, whether they are actual first or family names, or even some sort of code.'

Bernstein was not dissuaded by this and, much to Renton's pleasure, went on to argue, 'That may be so. But this is one of the best leads we have. I'm going through this information and trying to deduce anything which may help us to identify the informants. For example, we may be able to gather some idea of where they work. We could then ask for lists of employees and look at those with the appropriate initial. It is very long and painstaking work and I've only just begun, but who knows where it may lead?'

'Excellent, David,' said Renton encouragingly. 'Keep up the good work. And you're right, it may well lead us closer to this nest of vipers and to Lazarus himself. Now, what else was there?'

Bernstein reminded his Inspector that, in examining Shaw's address book, they had found one address that was different to the rest. 'All the entries bar this particular one had a precise name and address, including the appropriate door number,' said the young Special Branch officer excitedly. 'Of course, all of these were checked out, but they proved to be family, work colleagues and a couple of friends who have all been cleared of any involvement in the case. However, the unique address simply said 'Portobello Road.' Working on the assumption that this might refer to the meeting place of this group of informants, we checked on all possible addresses on that road. We finally found one flat on a long pre-paid lease. According to the owner who runs the shop below the flat, this had been used relatively infrequently and almost always in the evenings for a couple of hours. However, he also suspected that it had not been used at all for several months now.'

'Ah yes,' recalled Renton with a wide grin, which transformed his normally taciturn features into something altogether more friendly. 'This is where your skills of detection came to the fore, if I'm not mistaken.'

'If you say so, sir,' spluttered the junior officer, 'though in truth it was just luck. It could've happened to anyone in my place.'

'Nonsense' replied Renton dismissively. 'You had the very good sense and patience to give the place your own thorough search. As a result of this you found, in the bottom of an umbrella stand, a note which had clearly fallen there by accident. The note said, 'Lazarus, can we have a short chat after everyone else has gone. It's important. A.'

'This discovery was the first definite corroboration that we were on the right track, with our assumption that Lazarus is the codename of a German spy operating in Britain,' continued Renton, gazing thoughtfully at his steepled hands. After a brief pause, he continued in a surprisingly relieved tone, 'You shouldn't underestimate the importance of that to me, David. Many colleagues had said that I was 'spy crazy', and, to be perfectly frank, I'd begun to wonder the same thing. But that's over now and we're on his trail. For now, just concentrate on checking those names. It may be tedious, but it's probably our best lead.'

'I'm focusing more on 'A',' explained Bernstein, 'as this is the firmest link with Lazarus. From Shaw's notes on the information provided by 'A', my guess is that this person is a civil servant of some kind. Could be in the Home Office, Foreign Office, Ministry for War, or even the Cabinet Office. I've requested lists of employees who have a first or surname beginning with 'A' from all of these government departments. But they're deuced slow to respond. I imagine that there must be hundreds, if not thousands of such employees. And I have to give some thought as to how these individuals can be checked discreetly. After all, I wouldn't want to alert our 'A' to Special Branch's interest.'

Renton sighed in sympathy, 'Yes, it's galling how uncooperative some people are, but keep at it. To date, it's really the only clear way forward for us. If you get nothing back in the next two weeks, let me know and I'll try to bring some pressure to bear on them. In the meantime, let's keep our eyes and ears open too. We don't want him to slip through the net, if he resurfaces.'

'That won't happen, sir,' replied Bernstein confidently. 'We're gearing up our networks of informants in London and the South East. If Lazarus sticks his head over the parapet again and arranges meetings with his Nazi sympathisers, there's every chance that one of our people will get a whisper. Maybe then we'll have him without even having to identify 'A.''

CHAPTER TWENTY TWO

Thursday 11th April 1940, New York.

Joachim Brandt read the coded telegram from Berlin with very mixed emotions. During the months since Great Britain had declared war on Germany, he had envied those involved in the real fighting against the enemies of the Reich. The prospect that he now might be given the chance to do the same excited him. He had, however, also relished his four year posting in the USA.

When he'd received the order to move to America, he had initially been very disappointed. Having joined the SS in 1933, while still a student in Heidelberg, he was ambitious to progress and had been reluctant to move so far away from the centre of power in Berlin. How wrong he had been. His official status as a diplomat had concealed his true appointment as a *Hauptsturmführer* in the SS and, during his time in America, Brandt had made himself the key link between Germany and pro-Nazi organisations such as the German American Bund. He had been intimately involved in organising pro-German propaganda, like the Bund parade which had marched in its thousands through New York City on October 30th 1939. However, he regarded his greatest achievement as the coordination of the huge Madison Square Garden Rally which attracted a febrile crowd of twenty thousand on February 20th 1939. His suggestion that Bund leader Kuhn should sarcastically refer to the US President as 'Frank D Rosenfeld' had earned him admiring comments at the very highest levels of the Nazi hierarchy back in Berlin. To the power brokers in the SS, he was proving to be a devious and successful advocate for Germany and had become one of Reinhardt Heydrich's favourites. Tall, athletic and having deep set eyes and high cheek bones that could give his face either a charming or a positively devilish appearance, he had also made the most of his opportunities to mix among extremely rich, ardently pro-Nazi American families. He had even found the time to be seduced by one of their daughters, Emma de Jongh, with whom he had been relishing a sado-masochistic relationship for eighteen months and from whom he had learned how best to express his own increasingly violent sexuality.

Contrary to his expectations, therefore, Brandt had thoroughly enjoyed his time in the USA which he saw as an extremely divided society. The Jews, to his disgust, clearly influenced many city areas such as New York, but he had come to understand that this contrasted sharply with what he saw as the much more sympathetic and traditional farming areas of the Mid West. In common with many ideologically committed Nazis, Brandt simultaneously hated and enjoyed his proximity to what he saw as the decadent aspects of New York culture. Indeed, thanks to a sympathetic millionaire, he had lived very comfortably in a spacious Upper East Side flat overlooking the Metropolitan Museum of Art and Central Park.

It was there, as he looked through the huge picture window of his living room towards the sunbathed green of the park, with its seasonal, bright pink cherry tree blossoms, that he opened the telegram which was to change his life. Sent to the German consulate in New York, it had been immediately despatched by courier to his apartment. As soon as he had it in his hands, Brandt hastily opened the small wall safe, concealed behind a thrillingly degenerate modern painting, took out his codes and eagerly translated the message.

'**MOST PRIVATE. To Hauptsturmführer Joachim Brandt. Your posting in America is at an end. You are to report to Room 311, Prinz Albrechtstraße, Berlin at 2PM on Thursday April 25th. You are to travel to Germany via Lisbon, where you will liaise with** *Obersturmführer* **Baumgartner who is taking over your role. I look forward to meeting you in Berlin. Heil Hitler! Gruppenführer Reinhard Heydrich.'**

He felt an immediate surge of pride at the personal order and, especially, the friendly salutation from Heydrich himself. Savouring the moment, he reached for his decanter of finest brandy - he had never come to like the taste of American bourbon whisky - poured himself a good measure into a fine, lead crystal tumbler and contemplated his future. *What's next for me?* he wondered. *It has to be Great Britain! My new posting must be related to the inevitable invasion and subjugation of that weak and exhausted nation.* With an almost physical sense of arousal, he assured himself, *This could be exactly what I've been waiting for. The chance to play a leading role in the defeat of Britain.* He couldn't wait to tell Emma at their dinner date that he must return to Berlin on Heydrich's personal order. *That should enthuse her,* he thought as his lascivious smile emphasised the devilish quality of his face.

***

Sunday 21st April 1940, Lisbon.

The huge Boeing 314 Clipper seaplane banked steeply over the rooftops of the capital city of Portugal, its twin engine wings and silver fuselage glinting in the early morning sunshine as it made its final approach to land on the calm waters of the river Tagus. Emma de Jongh looked excitedly out of the porthole and gasped at her first glimpse of the city. Of course, as the daughter of an extremely rich and politically ambitious father, she had frequently travelled to Europe, but always with one or both parents and invariably first class on one of the luxurious transatlantic liners. This had been both her and Brandt's first flight across the huge ocean and the comfort and quality of service on board had been impressive. The crossing had also been remarkably short and the possibility of converting their seats into beds for the overnight section of the flight had been unexpectedly relaxing. Moreover, that only thirty four other passengers were on board added to the sense of exclusivity and adventure that they both so relished.

During their dinner date at The Stork Club in Manhattan, when he had told her of his reassignment back to Europe, she had at first pouted like a spoiled child, deprived of her favourite plaything. It had taken much of the suave charm that Joachim had picked up during his time in America to persuade her that his transfer, while necessarily secret, was a huge boost both for himself and for his career. Later, after dancing until the early hours and during one of Emma's characteristically provocative sex games, he had found himself literally in a position where he had to agree to her proposal that she travel with him as far as Lisbon. She assured him that she would not be in his way as she would meet an old school friend who was returning from a sixth month study period at the Sorbonne University in Paris. Deep down he knew that he should have waved goodbye to her in New York, *but,* he had to admit, *she's a force of nature and, damn it all, it's great being with her.*

As soon as they had completed the necessary immigration formalities, a German embassy official drove them to the magnificent Monte Estoril Hotel. Emma smiled at the commanding manner in which Brandt ordered the driver to wait until he had completed their registration. 'The luggage will be delivered immediately to our room. You just wait here for me, darling,' he advised his girlfriend solicitously. 'I may be an hour or two, but I'll be back in time for dinner.'

Emma flung her arms round his neck and, in the busy reception area, kissed him hard and open mouthed. 'Hurry back, darling. I'll be waiting for you,' she breathed into his ear, before giving him a playful bite. Brandt reluctantly detached himself from her tight embrace and, blowing a kiss, hastened out of the hotel and back into the embassy Mercedes.

***

'Brandt, my dear fellow,' beamed *Standartenführer* Horst Grünewald as he ushered his guest into his top floor office in the splendid palacio which served as the German embassy in Lisbon. 'Welcome to 'spy city'. Ambassador von Hoyningen-Huene sends his regards and his apologies that he is not able to greet you in person.' Brandt was invited to take an armchair, placed perfectly in front of a huge window offering wonderful views of parkland and the city beyond.

'Thank you, sir,' he replied, looking the Standartenführer confidently in the eye. Unlike the majority of deskbound officers and despite approaching fifty, Grünewald was still in good shape, carrying only a few pounds over the ideal weight for his large frame. He had the face of a street fighter which, of course, he was, having been both one of the first to have joined the Party and selected personally by Himmler as a rising star for his new SS movement. His career had been somewhat derailed, however, by an unfortunate indiscretion with a fellow officer's impressionable daughter and he was now trying to rebuild his reputation and career in Lisbon. 'It's a real pleasure to meet you and to be able to speak German again, sir, after all the years in America.'

'Well, from what little I've been able to glean from my sources in Prinz-Albrechtstraße, I wouldn't get too used to that,' Grünewald said enigmatically. 'It seems that your ability in English is crucial to your next posting. But first, please tell me all the news from our supporters in the States and then, after lunch, you can brief your replacement.'

Despite his sense of excitement and anticipation, Brandt focused on selecting sufficient juicy pieces of information to keep Grünewald happy. As he sat impatiently conversing and sipping his host's admittedly excellent Dao wine, his mind was racing ahead to speculate on his first visit to wartime Berlin. Lunch was a pleasant affair and his replacement, Baumgartner, proved to be such an assiduous listener and student that, by late afternoon, he was able to excuse himself and return to the hotel and the unique demands of Emma.

In some ways, the two days in Lisbon could not pass quickly enough for Brandt, eager as he was to meet

Heydrich, whereas Emma would have liked them to stretch to several weeks. Indeed, he happily conceded that the romantically Latin atmosphere of Lisbon had inspired her creativity and abandon in the bedroom to ever greater heights. It was, therefore, a contemplative Brandt who bade a tearful Emma 'auf wiedersehen,' as he boarded the Luftwaffe Focke Wulf Condor, which was to fly him direct to Tempelhof aerodrome in the centre of Berlin.

***

The next afternoon, seated in the rear of an open-topped, SS staff car which had picked him up from the Hotel Kaiserhof, Brandt reflected that he had rarely felt so vital. In minutes, he had arrived at the universally feared headquarters of the SS and, after striding confidently through the main entrance, he grinned with pleasure as his announcement that he had an appointment with Gruppenführer Heydrich roused a bored looking receptionist into grovelling solicitousness. He had already met the high ranking Nazi several times, but always in the presence of more senior officers than himself. This was to be their first private meeting and he saw it as a huge compliment that he would have the sole attention of such a powerful and feared man.

As he was shown into the huge office, Brandt was surprised that it was furnished in a somewhat Spartan manner. Heydrich had few, if any of the physical trappings of high office which were so beloved of many of the most senior Nazi officials. Rather, he was content with a plain wooden desk, a few bookcases and filing cabinets and two easy chairs, positioned to face one another across a small coffee table in a corner of the room. Heydrich rose from his uncluttered desk as Brandt entered and responded enthusiastically to the younger man's salute. 'Come in Hauptsturmführer,' he began in his unusually high pitched voice. 'I have taken a real interest in your excellent work for the Reich in America.'

   Swelling with pride, Brandt spent several minutes briefing Heydrich about his work and was, in turn, impressed by the senior officer's deep grasp of attitudes in America. While he was determined to use this opportunity to enhance the positive impression his commanding officer had of him, Brandt felt the omnipresent threat from his piercing eyes. He was, therefore, in some ways grateful when Heydrich turned away from him and reached to press a concealed button underneath his desk. As soon as an orderly appeared at the door, Heydrich dismissed the younger man, saying enthusiastically, 'I've enjoyed this opportunity to meet you in private, Brandt. And I can tell you that I'm very impressed by what I've seen and heard this afternoon. You must now report to Sturmbannführer Schellenberg who is waiting to brief you on the reasons for your withdrawal from New York.' Brandt stood briskly to attention and offered the perfect 'Heil Hitler', before marching smartly out of the room.

   Schellenberg was about the same age as Brandt, but had obviously progressed rather more quickly through the SS ranks. A flicker of envy flashed through Brandt's mind as he saluted the superior officer. 'What I'm about to say to you is top secret,' began Schellenberg crisply. 'While I'm sure that you'll not be disappointed with the reason for your transfer from America, I would also like to say that you were doing an excellent job there. You are no doubt well aware that Gruppenführer Heydrich has very high hopes for you. I'd even go so far as to say that this assignment could be the making of you.'

'Thank you, sir,' replied Brandt, suppressing another surge of irritation at his contemporary's rather patronising manner.

'You are obviously aware that our forces have successfully invaded Denmark and Norway and humiliated the British at Narvick,' Schellenberg continued. 'I can tell you now that this was only the beginning. Within days, German forces will overrun Belgium and sweep into France. The French have no stomach for a fight and the British Expeditionary Force is no match for our Panzers . We are, therefore, already planning for the period after the defeat of France. I'm very proud to say that I've been entrusted with the responsibility to compile *Informationsheft GB*. Responding to Brandt's blank expression, he explained smugly. 'Essentially, it's a blueprint for the successful invasion and, particularly, the occupation of Great Britain. I need hardly tell you that this work will depend to a great extent on the quality of the information we receive from our agents in Britain.' Schellenberg went on to reveal that, while agents do provide information to their controllers in Hamburg, much of this is of an extremely low level. 'The Abwehr remains convinced that their networks in Britain are working effectively, but we in the SS have a different opinion. We think that there's something not quite right over there and we want someone very special to go and find out what has been happening, but also to provide us with the information we need.'

'And you believe, sir, that I have the qualities for such a job?'

'We certainly do, Hauptsturmführer. Of that, we have no doubt. You will operate in England, posing as an American journalist. But first things first. Because of our, how shall we say, uncertainty about many of the Abwehr agents in Britain, we don't want you to make contact with them when you arrive across the Channel. In fact, the Abwehr will know nothing about you, your cover or your mission.'

'Then how am I to proceed? Am I expected to build up my own networks? Surely that would take time?' asked Brandt cautiously.

'Good question,' conceded Schellenberg, 'but we have one agent whose informants we know have not been compromised by those incompetents from the Bendlerblock. According to their previous controller, these networks have the potential to offer us a great deal of useful information. So, you will start with them. I have arranged for you to be briefed by this man immediately.' The Sturmbannführer pressed a button on his desk and the door opened to a dapper, middle aged man, dressed in a smart suit and tie. 'May I introduce Herr Rösel, one of the most successful German agents in Britain until his unfortunate expulsion last year. Please, Herr Rösel, would you be so kind as to explain how you think your connections may be useful.'

Rösel gave a detailed account of his espionage activities, before Schellenberg interrupted, 'Extraordinarily, it was not until November last year, that the Abwehr sent a replacement. However, some time after this agent's arrival in Britain, we received notification, from a very reliable source, that he had been killed in a failed parachute drop. It was quite by chance that this source was given this information and we believe it to be true because nothing has been heard from Herr Rösel's informers.'

Rösel then offered a pen picture of each of his informants, stressing that Abigail Stevenson and Martha Perrygo were the most significant members of his networks. 'Stevenson is very lacking in self-confidence and is easily manipulated by the right sort of man. Perrygo is the spider at the centre of a large web of informants who live all along the south coast of Britain. I believe that the intelligence you will receive from those two people could be decisive to Germany's plans. 'I suggest that you initially try to gain Miss Abigail's confidence and trust and take it from there.'

'Thank you very much Herr Rösel,' said Schellenberg in dismissal and as soon as the SS officers were alone, Brandt asked sharply, 'How certain are you that Rösel's networks have not been compromised by the British? I might be walking into a trap.'

'There is an element of risk, of course,' conceded Schellenberg. 'We can't be absolutely certain. But, because the replacement agent died before he could make contact, these networks have had no direct connection with the Abwehr at all. There is the possibility that they have been rolled up by the British, but we believe that if the British had somehow managed to penetrate the networks, they would have been sending us trivial information to keep us happy. The fact that we have heard nothing supports the view that the networks have simply remained dormant.'

'But what about the Abwehr? Asked Brandt apprehensively. 'What role will they play in all this?'

'None at all,' confirmed Schellenberg. 'Rest assured, Brandt. They have been told at the highest level possible that this is a wholly SS operation. How you present yourself to your informants, of course, is up to you.' Brandt nodded his head thoughtfully as Schellenberg advised, 'There's no doubt that you will have to tread carefully and I agree with Rösel that you should use your cover to get close to the Stevenson woman. She should give you a good idea whether or not the networks have been turned by the British. But we have real hopes that they can still be made operational, especially now that the demand for information from Britain is a much greater strategic priority. It could also be that Perrygo becomes more significant as your mission proceeds. Regardless of what Rösel just said, on no account must you reveal your identity as a German agent to anyone, least of all to the people in his networks, until you are absolutely certain of their loyalty. Let them continue to think that you are American. Don't rush things too much, but remember the information is urgently needed. Keep the informants that will be useful in producing the *Informationsheft GB* and get rid of the rest.'

Brandt nodded before asking the obvious question. 'How soon is it likely that I'll be going to England and what, exactly, will be my cover and my other duties there?'

'As I said, you will present as an American journalist. We've made arrangements for you to pick up your accreditation once you're safely in London and we have also organised a small office for you in a building, rented by a sympathetic American news bureau. No one will bother you there. You will, however, have to put in some time to maintain your cover. We've even arranged for you to be able to wire stories to America from this building, just to add to the authenticity of your cover.' He could see the momentary alarm in Brandt's expression and, uncharacteristically, he laughed warmly. 'Don't worry Brandt, my dear fellow. They'll just go to a sympathiser in New York. The quality doesn't need to be high. They're simply to justify your presence in Britain. Anyway, I'd advise you not to make any contact with any of Rösel's people for at least two to three weeks after your arrival in Britain. If, by some chance, the British do tail you, you must be seen to be working normally. We understand that they are very stretched and will lose interest pretty quickly in yet one more American newsman. I must stress that your mission is of the utmost importance and the highest levels of secrecy must be maintained. Accordingly, you will work only through your contact at the Portuguese embassy in London. No one else is to know or contact you. Understood?'

Brandt had to admit that Schellenberg, for all his unpleasantly self-important manner, was an alert and competent officer and had expressed his orders clearly and succinctly. He had, however, one further key question. 'And when do I go, sir?'

'The precise timings are not yet fixed. They'll depend on the speed at which our armies are able to crush those of

France and Britain,' replied Schellenberg, his manner icily matter of fact. 'Our best guess is that you will leave towards the end of May. So, enjoy the time you have in Berlin.'

CHAPTER TWENTY THREE

Monday 27th May 1940, Hotel Kaiserhof, Berlin.

It was just after 5AM when the insistent noise of the telephone urged Brandt from his deep sleep. 'Report to SS Headquarters by 6AM. You will not be returning to your hotel and come in civilian clothes,' barked a commanding voice. Within forty five minutes, Brandt was in the office of Sturmbannführer Schellenberg who wasted no time in explaining to him that the German army had the British Expeditionary Force and some French units trapped in and around the port of Dunkirk. 'Luftwaffe reconnaissance suggests that the British are probably going to attempt to evacuate as many of their men as possible. Reports describe a chaotic situation, with literally tens of thousands of military personnel being evacuated in hundreds of ships. Some of them even appear to be privately owned pleasure craft.' Schellenberg's face creased into a wintry smile as he steepled his fingers in concentration. 'Where better to hide you, as you cross to England, than in plain sight among the remnants of the British army?'

He then let out a grotesque cackle at his own joke, while Brandt, evidently unconvinced by the scheme, asked sharply, 'Wouldn't it be easier simply to parachute me in, sir? I've done some training.'

'Yes, that would be an alternative, Brandt,' conceded Schellenberg with ill-disguised irritation. 'But our recent record of success in landing agents in this way is, as you are aware, rather poor. Moreover, we expect the British now to be on red alert. No, this is a perfect opportunity for you, disguised as a Canadian member of the RAF, to slip into England with the help of the Tommies. You have a wholly convincing American accent, so that'll help. Also, many British personnel have only the clothes they stand in. Few have any papers or identity documents, other than the normal discs. The British, you see Brandt, are effectively being routed.'

Schellenberg temporarily halted his narrative to light a cigarette. Without having had the courtesy to offer one to Brandt, he continued, 'We are taking this opportunity because one of our SS units, operating near the front line, has captured a downed pilot officer. This man's identity fits the bill perfectly. He's a Canadian Spitfire pilot who was shot down by one of our fighters. You'll have his uniform and identity tags, and our staff has pieced together a dossier on the plane he flew, where it was probably based and so on. This will be very useful to you in the unlikely event of you being questioned. Once in England, we imagine that everything will be in chaos, so it should be easy for you to slip away by train to London where you will go to one of our safe houses. There, you will be able to get out of your uniform and rendezvous with our agent from the Portuguese embassy. You'll be provided with identification papers as Joe Brand, an American journalist stationed in Britain, wallet, keys to a flat etc. All the details are in this file which you should read, memorise and then destroy. You leave for the front from Tempelhof in one hour. When you arrive in France, you'll be met at the airfield and driven to somewhere near Bethune. There, you should report immediately to Hauptsturmführer Knöchlein of the 14th Company SS Division Totenkopf. Good luck, Brandt. Heil Hitler.'

The formalities at Tempelhof were very brief and within half an hour of his arrival at the aerodrome, Brandt was squatting uncomfortably among boxes of medical supplies and looking down on Hitler's capital city. The airstrip on the outskirts of Lille proved to be a less than perfectly flat meadow. Having been hastily improvised by hard pressed engineers, in order to maintain the supply of essential medical and other military supplies as the army advanced rapidly towards the Channel coast, it offered a very uncomfortable landing. A physically shaken Brandt was unimpressed to see an SS *Unterscharführer* smoking by his small army vehicle. Obviously waiting to drive him towards the front line, he stunned Brandt by the tone of his first words. 'You must be pretty damned important that I've had to leave my unit at this time, just to offer you a ride.'

'Thank you for your assistance, Unterscharführer,' replied Brandt with a smile, before adding curtly, 'by the way, I may not be in uniform, but it's Hauptsturmführer to you. Get that cigarette out immediately and take me to Hauptsturmführer Knöchlein.' The corporal immediately jumped to attention before driving expertly, weaving among the flood of military vehicles and swarms of civilian refugees. Eventually, the corporal said rather shamefacedly, 'My apologies, Hauptsturmführer. I meant no offence. It's just that we've been battling the Tommies hard over the last couple of days and we've lost quite a lot of men. Things are building to a climax and I didn't want to leave my boys.'

Brandt looked carefully at the driver, a tough looking man in his mid- thirties, who bore the evidence of several days uninterrupted fighting. 'Forget it, Unterscharführer,' said Brandt, handing the man a cigarette by way of a peace offering. 'Let's see if you can get us back in time to join in.' Gratefully accepting the lit cigarette, the driver turned to Brandt, grinned broadly and shouted 'Yes, sir!' over the roar of the engine.

***

Monday 27th May1940, Thames Embankment, London.

King was staring out over the river Thames, his mind filled with hellish images of thousands of defenceless and desperate men trapped on the beaches of northern France as Stuka dive bombers ruthlessly attacked them from the sky. Pym had summoned him to a meeting on the Embankment and the older man looked extremely grave as he arrived. The Professor immediately outlined the true extent of the dire circumstances in which the BEF found itself across the Channel. 'The BBC may be painting a rather different picture of what's going on over there. But in the next couple of days everyone's going to find out what's really happening. The point is, John, that it's very likely that the Germans will mount an invasion of Britain as soon as practicable.' He reinforced this view, by emphasising that not only was the British army in serious disarray, but that it must of necessity leave all of its heavy equipment in France. 'The Chiefs of Staff think we'll be lucky to extract twenty thousand men out of a total complement of well over three hundred and fifty thousand still out there. In such circumstances, the retrieval of equipment is unthinkable'

King blinked hard at these bald statistics which outlined what was likely to become one of the worst disasters in British military history. 'Then, sir,' he answered resolutely,

'I will contact my key informants immediately. Now, more than ever, it's vital that I keep them under close control.'

***

Monday 27th May 1940, Near Lille, Belgium.

Progress was frustratingly slow on roads crowded, both with military vehicles making for the front line and with bedraggled civilians who were heading in all directions. 'If you think this looks chaotic,' said the corporal with grim satisfaction, 'just think what it must be like on the other side of the line. Those Tommies are running out of land… they'll get their feet wet in the Channel soon.' There was much evidence of the recent fighting; a great deal of burnt out British armour, tilted at crazy angles where it had been pushed off the road and the terrible number of fresh, tell-tale mounds, barely covering the hastily buried casualties. Increasingly irritated by their slow progress, the driver stopped abruptly on several occasions to peruse a worn map, desperately calculating their chances of making use of quieter side roads. On each occasion, however, his muttered 'Shit' indicated that they had no alternative but to remain on the overcrowded major roads.

Finally, after some hours of painfully slow driving, the last couple of which took place against the growing sound of both artillery and smaller arms fire, the corporal was flagged down near the Bois de Paqueaut woods. 'What's been happening since I left this morning, Hofmann?' he barked at the exhausted looking SS soldier.

'We got them cornered in a farmhouse, just the other side of the woods. It was tough going this morning and afternoon and we took a lot of casualties. I heard a few minutes ago that the Tommies have surrendered, so it's safe for you to go on towards Le Paradis. Hauptsturmführer Knöchlein is waiting for you there.'

The corporal looked shaken by the news and merely grunted 'Shit. I should've been there for my boys.' With little care, he ground the gears violently as he drove around and then through the woods. Eventually, he pulled up in front of what once must have been an attractive farmhouse. It was now a ruin, having taken considerable mortar fire and with walls that were heavily pock marked with bullet holes. Brandt looked about and saw soldiers running in all directions and that universal aftermath of any battle, a great many wounded being treated in makeshift field hospitals. He also noticed a bedraggled column of disarmed British soldiers being marched down the road away from the ruined farmhouse. 'Where will I find Hauptsturmführer Knöchlein?' Brandt asked a passing soldier. 'He's up there with the prisoners, sir,' replied the young man before rushing off.

Brandt marched quickly towards the column of prisoners which was shuffling slowly along the lane. He easily overtook them and presented himself to Knöchlein who was deep in conversation with one of his men. Brandt was struck by his cold eyes and thin, mean looking face which broke into a cold smile. 'Well, Hauptsturmführer, you've turned up at a very auspicious moment. You're about to see the fruits of victory and the consequences of defeat. Indeed, you may wish to apportion some of these consequences yourself.'

Brandt replied uncertainly, 'Naturally I will be happy to assist in any way I can.' Knöchlein gave him a bleak, sideways glance and indicated that Brandt should follow him. The prisoners had now been marched into a meadow and told to line up along the wall of a barn. Knöchlein seized a sub-machine gun from one of his soldiers and threw it to a perplexed Brandt, sneering, 'Join in, if you have the stomach.' The SS Commander then gave the order for two heavy machine guns, set up in the meadow facing the barn wall, to open fire on the prisoners. Rather than look at the slaughter of the defenceless men, he stared at Brandt, a challenging smile playing around his lips. It was clear to Brandt that these field soldiers held him in little regard; the attitude of the corporal and now this explicit questioning of his stomach for the fight. *Christ*, thought Brandt feverishly. *What the fuck do I do now?* He'd never been in such a situation before. *Beating up, even torturing unarmed prisoners in the cells, yes; but executing unarmed soldiers? And after they fought bravely and surrendered? That's something very different.* He knew he had only an instant to make up his mind and rapidly released the safety catch of the machine gun. He then swept those prisoners who were still standing with a deadly burst of fire. As his fingers pressed the trigger, he felt no disgust or shame at his actions. Rather, he experienced a burst of adrenalin so powerful that he almost felt that he was floating above the scene, looking down on the massacred prisoners and their executioners. Staring at the broken bodies of the slaughtered men, he was amazed to feel absolutely no remorse. Incredibly, he regretted only the shortness of its duration.

Afterwards, he felt different; he knew instinctively, both that he had crossed some kind of Rubicon in that French meadow and that there was no possibility of ever going back. For perhaps the first time in his life, he truly felt that he belonged somewhere; that he had a genuine cause and, above all, that he had been authentically empowered by his actions. In effect, he now felt himself to be a superman who could never be stopped by the weak British or the feckless French.

'Excellent work, Hauptsturmführer,' declared Knöchlein, at the same time clapping Brandt on the back like an old friend. 'See boys,' he shouted at the many young SS troops within earshot, 'even SS men in civvies have got guts. That's why we'll smash these British and French back into their damned Channel and let them drown there.' A few 'Sieg Heils' and 'Heil Hitlers' accompanied Knöchlein and Brandt as they walked back towards a waiting car. 'Oh, and don't waste too many bullets on any still alive. Bayonets are good enough for them, eh?' he ordered the Untersturmführers who were in charge of cleaning up after the massacre. 'And get those damned French peasants to bury the bodies or they'll get a dose of the same medicine.'

Once they were seated in the rear of the car, Knöchlein took off his gloves and offered his hand to Brandt. 'Welcome to the front line of the Reich, Hauptsturmführer. I hope you enjoyed your introduction to the real fight for Germany. Now, as soon as we get back to my headquarters, you'll have to explain what it is that we can do for you. I've only received the order to offer you every possible assistance, but I know nothing more of your purpose here.'

As the day was beginning to fade, the driver pulled off the road and into the yard of a less damaged farmhouse. 'Welcome to our company headquarters – at least for now,' Knöchlein quipped. 'With the speed of our advance, we're sure to be somewhere much nearer the sea tomorrow. So we don't have time to get too comfortable.' Brandt was led into a small office where he briefly outlined his requirements. 'I thought it might be something like that,' said Knöchlein with little interest. 'So, I've delegated this task to one of my corporals. He spent a lot of time in this area as a child and he knows it like the back of his hand. He's the best man to help you get through the British lines. I'll send him in now and leave you to it.'

After a few minutes, Brandt opened the door to the corporal who had driven him from Lille. 'Unterscharführer Kaube, at your command, sir,' he barked, demonstrating an entirely different attitude to that which he had on first meeting. Indeed, as Brandt looked him in the eye with a sardonic smile, he was pleased to notice a wariness, a suspicion, perhaps even a fear of him. Once Brandt had outlined the plan, Kaube took a map out of one of the cupboards and, with a nicotine stained finger, pointed out their current location.

'As you know, sir, over the last couple of days we have fallen a little behind the front line. We had to deal with very tough pockets of resistance in this area.' Indicating Ypres on the map, he continued, 'Our best guess is that the front line is around here, very close to the section on our right flank which faces the Belgian army. The Belgians are just about finished and have approached us to surrender. That means that tomorrow will be even more chaotic on the Tommies' front line. Tomorrow night, it should be fairly easy to get you across the line, find you a nice spot to wait for dawn and then you attach yourself to one of the lines of stragglers heading for Dunkirk. I'd definitely say that's the best way to do it. If you agree, I'll select a couple of my men to accompany us and we'll set out after breakfast tomorrow.'

'Perfect. Thank you,' replied Brandt. 'And send someone over straight away with my RAF uniform and identity tags. He can show me to the mess.'

***

Tuesday 28th May 1940, Northern France.

Brandt was awake the instant the door to the office clicked open. Through a gap between ragged curtains, he could see bright daylight. 'Time to get up, sir, if you want something to eat before we set off. Though I wouldn't have too much,' advised Kaube. 'You're supposed to be an RAF man who was downed three days ago. I doubt that he would've been fine dining.' Brandt quickly dressed in the RAF uniform which, though suitably damaged from the crash, was a remarkably good fit. Only the trousers were a little short, but that didn't matter as they were tightly tucked into the perfectly fitting flying boots. After breakfast the corporal took the wheel with Brandt sitting beside him and two troopers squatting in the rear of the vehicle. Because they were heading north east towards Ypres, rather than more directly north towards the Channel coast, they found that the military traffic on the minor roads was lighter than expected. To Brandt's fury, however, this advantage was eliminated by the crowds of refugees. He felt no pity for the shambling columns of dispossessed humanity. To him, they simply inhibited the essential movement of men and materiel. *If it were up to me*, he fumed, *I'd push them all off the damn roads.* By midday they had reached Armentières, about halfway to Ypres, when Kaube drew to a halt.

'Let's have a break for a few minutes while I find out what's going on up ahead,' he said before going over to an SS Panzer crew enjoying lunch in the sun by the roadside. Within five minutes, Kaube had returned and shared the news that, as predicted, the Belgian army had surrendered. This had created a huge gap in the eastern flank of the defence line of the enemy. He also reported that the front line was now at Ypres and would, by nightfall, be some kilometres beyond that. 'It's perfect, sir,' he said to Brandt, 'just what we hoped for and expected. The tank crew says that our progress will still be slow, but we're now on a main road and we should reach Ypres by late afternoon.'

As they came nearer to the town and to the front line, the detritus from the very recent fighting became ever more apparent. Many military vehicles were still ablaze and Brandt noticed with contempt the huge amount of equipment and weaponry that had simply been abandoned by the retreating British. They also saw many bodies of dead soldiers and civilians which had been pushed unceremoniously to the side of the road. Most had started to swell in the warm, late May temperature, despite the sun being blocked by the dark, oil filled smoke which billowed everywhere. As they entered Ypres, it was immediately obvious that this had been the scene of fierce fighting between the retreating British and the advancing Germans.

'It looks like the Tommies put up more of a fight here,' said Kaube. 'The town must only just have been taken by us.' After driving past buildings in the city centre which had suffered heavy shell fire, they reached the main square. It was, however, totally impassable, its centre comprising a massive crater, dug by the persistent shelling of the previous day. Many of the remaining buildings had holes punched into their front walls, which looked like the dark gaps where teeth have been knocked out. Brandt cursed as he realised that it would be impossible to drive across the square. His concern was short lived, however, for the corporal knew his way around Ypres, even in its current ruined state. 'I spent many summer holidays near here at my Belgian grandmother's,' he explained with a grin at Brandt's look of amazement, as the roaring vehicle darted down a succession of much narrower streets to emerge quickly on the northern side of the town.

'Halt!' shouted a military policeman, holding up his right hand in the universal sign of authority. 'You can't go any further up here.' Kaube immediately got out of the vehicle and produced the written orders brought by Brandt from Berlin. These seemed to impress the policeman, but he still insisted that they could go no further. 'As far as we know, the front line's about fifteen kilometres north of here. We've been told the road is impassable up ahead, so best to leave the vehicle here. It will only take you about three hours to walk.'

Brandt immediately confronted the policeman, 'That is not acceptable! We will drive as far as we can and then go on by foot. Unterscharführer Kaube, if this man makes any attempt to stop us, you have my full authority to shoot him where he stands.' Kaube nodded to the two soldiers, who jumped out of the vehicle and, grinning at the policeman, prepared their sub-machine guns to fire. 'Well, what's it to be?' asked Brandt matter of factly. 'These men are damned good shots.' The policeman's face had drained of all colour as he gaped suspiciously at this bully, dressed in an RAF uniform, who seemed to be in command of SS soldiers. Not wishing to die in such a futile cause, he sullenly raised his wooden barrier to let them drive through. As they sped past him, he contented himself by spitting on the ground and muttering, 'With luck, it'll be your funeral, you bastards! I hope a Tommy shell blows you all to hell.'

They soon discovered that the policeman had been correct; the road became increasingly clogged and airplanes of the Luftwaffe frequently roared overhead, on their way towards the sea on yet another mission to strafe the retreating British and French. Luckily for Brandt, a motorised column of Wehrmacht reinforcements was just ahead of them and their accompanying panzer tank made relatively light work of pushing most of the wreckage off the road. The four men fell silent as they approached the vast clouds of heavy, black smoke which hung over the current battle zone around the port of Dunkirk. Tapping one of his hands on the windscreen in the direction of the smoke, Kaube muttered, 'Some poor swine are really taking a pounding over there.'

One of the young soldiers asked nervously, 'Where is that, Unterscharführer. Are we heading there?'

Kaube laughed and turned around, even as he continued to drive forwards. 'That's Dunkirk over there, son. It's where the British are trapped. And, yes, God willing we will be going there and indeed across the Channel and all the way to London itself. But not today.'

They had just passed through what remained of the hamlet of Woesten, when the road ahead was totally blocked by the stationary vehicles of the infantry column.

The soldiers were jumping down from their trucks and lining up in the meadows at the side of the road. 'We must be very near the front now sir,' said Kaube to Brandt. Jerking his thumb back towards the soldier who had just asked the question about Dunkirk, he continued, 'I think this is where we get out. I'll leave the vehicle with him and we can proceed on foot. I know this area fairly well. But I'll just have a quick word with the officers of this lot. They may be aware of the current situation up ahead.'

When Kaube was away, Brandt addressed the one who had been told to stay behind. 'Forget what Kaube said,' he ordered with a vicious smirk. 'I think you need to get some stiffening in your backbone. So, you'll come with us across the lines. And you,' pointing at the other soldier, 'will stay here. Understood?' The two soldiers stood to attention and shouted 'Yes, sir!'

The warmth of the day was fading when Kaube returned. 'We'll carry on along this road for a little more than two kilometres and then strike out northwest across the meadows. We'll then lay low until midnight, just east of the village of Krombeke and get you into enemy territory there. The roads up ahead are full of Belgian troops who have thrown away their weapons and are running westwards, away from our advance. The fools don't realise we have this area totally surrounded. The British are trying to hold the line around here, but they're struggling. Unless we're very unlucky, we shouldn't encounter any enemy presence tonight.' Finally noticing the soldier waiting by the vehicle, Kaube rubbed his chin and asked, 'Something going on here?'

Brandt immediately responded, 'This fine young soldier volunteered to accompany us tonight, Unterscharführer. I hope you're happy with that.'

Kaube knew that Brandt was lying, but merely saluted and murmured 'Of course, sir.'

Once they had struck away from the road, Brandt was surprised that much of the countryside seemed completely untouched by war. Apart from the sounds of conflict and the smoke stained sky, the ground itself seemed perfectly normal. Finally, they approached a deep, dry ditch sheltered by a thick hedgerow and Kaube indicated that Brandt and the soldier should rest there. 'I'll have a quick look what's up ahead. Keep quiet and don't light up,' he whispered. 'We don't know how near we are to the Tommies.' Several minutes later, he returned with the information that the British had a string of defence positions just on the far side of a meadow which began on the other side of the hedge. 'Their positions are at least a hundred metres apart, so we'll slip through the lines at midnight, find you a good spot to hide and then we'll get back to our side before Tommy is any the wiser.'

To Brandt's relief, as evening gave way to night the sky became cloudier. Shortly before midnight, they set off in single file at a low crawl across the two hundred yard expanse of 'no man's land' meadow between the British and German controlled zones. Kaube was in the lead and only once indicated urgently that they should lie face down and make absolutely no noise. He was quickly embarrassed by a family of rabbits which was rummaging through the nearby grass, totally oblivious of the armed men all around. Once through the British lines, the three Germans moved quickly and silently until, about a hundred metres away from the edge of the meadow, they came to a dry ditch leading westward and slightly north.

'This is where we leave you, sir,' whispered Kaube. 'This ditch will take you in the direction of the French border. After a couple of kilometres, you'll come across a minor road. Keep heading in a generally north westerly direction and you'll intersect with the main road, running northwards towards Dunkirk. The less time you spend on that the better, as it's bound to be a target for the Luftwaffe. So, try to keep heading north-west, rather than west. We'll return the way we came. Good luck sir.'

'Thank you for your help Kaube,' replied Brandt, though the darkness concealed the insincerity in his eyes. 'Take care on your return journey.'

Brandt waited until the two soldiers were a good seventy metres away, before he very carefully began to follow them back towards the German lines. Kaube and his young comrade were too focused on possible dangers to the front and side to pay attention to the man who was now trailing them. When Brandt reached the edge of the meadow, he judged that the two Germans were about half way across. Without hesitation, he took out his revolver and fired three times into the sky, before immediately making haste back towards the ditch. His shots, however, had the desired effect. The British immediately focused all their attention in the direction of the German lines. Fearing the possibility of a night attack, they sent up flares which illuminated the whole of the meadow. Caught out in the open, the two Germans dropped to the ground and tried in vain to conceal themselves in the short grass. They were both dead before Brandt had reached the safety of the ditch. 'Leave alive as few people as possible, who know anything of your mission, Brandt,' Schellenberg had said before he left Berlin. *Well, it was a pleasure to rid the Reich of that coward and that insubordinate corporal,* he thought contentedly, as he moved stealthily towards the English Channel.

CHAPTER TWENTY FOUR

Wednesday 29th May 1940, Near Roesbrugge, Belgium.

After an hour's steady progress along the bottom of the dry ditch, Brandt came to an intersection with the dirt track which Kaube had mentioned. He hadn't heard or seen anyone since leaving the corporal to his fate in the meadow. When he reached the culvert, through which the ditch went underneath the track, Brandt dragged himself slowly and painfully up the bank where he lay motionless and alert. Having heard nothing, he started walking westwards towards Roesbrugge, a village about one kilometre from the French border. He hadn't expected to meet any British troops who were falling back to successively prepared defensive lines. However, he had been warned that these defensive positions would intensify at the concentric canals, which led the way to the coast. It was, therefore, essential that he join a retreating allied column before reaching this point.

The darkness continued to provide cover as, after about ninety minutes, he approached the main road from Lille to Dunkirk. Initially, he could hear British military vehicles about two hundred metres away, as they whined and rumbled their slow way northwards. Then he could see the glow of the flames from the besieged port of Dunkirk. The road was heavily congested, both with vehicles and horse drawn equipment and many soldiers and civilians on foot. As he squinted through the darkness, Brandt was just about able to make out a detachment of Military Police directing the traffic at the junction with the main road.

Shit! I'd better stay in the fields for now, he decided. *They'll not see me here. If I go parallel to the road for a bit, I should be able to join it well away from that damn checkpoint.*

He executed his plan perfectly, by simply waiting for a suitably large gap in the retreating column and slipping out of the shadows at the side of the road to begin his long trudge to the coast. By the time the first light of dawn was appearing in the sky to his right, Brandt had caught up with a platoon of Royal Engineers who were very happy to have been joined by a 'real life' Canadian. The first Luftwaffe strafing run occurred shortly before seven in the morning, at a time when Brandt and the Royal Engineers had left the road to rest. The German watched with morbid fascination as first the Stuka dive bombers attacked the column, closely followed by Messerschmidt fighters which raked the desperately fleeing soldiers and civilians with machine gun fire. It was all over in less than five minutes, yet the carnage created by the attack was unimaginable. The road was rendered impassable, burning vehicles littering its course for a length of some four hundred metres. But what struck Brandt most was the dozens of people, men, women and children, who were lying on the road, on its verges and in the immediately adjacent fields. Many were clearly dead, their broken bodies either left in the grotesque contortions created by bullet fire, or without limbs which had been blown off by the blast of the bombs. Despite the evident slaughter, Brandt was amazed at how many people began to emerge from their impromptu hiding places after the attack. The soldiers were quickly organised by officers and NCOs and ordered to begin the dreadful task of removing the dead from the roadway and clearing it of the irreparably damaged vehicles. Brandt, of course, had to help and was relieved when, after a half hour's hard work, both he and the Royal Engineers once more were able to begin their journey north.

Progress was invariably slow, but by turns it was also tedious, dangerous or horrific. During the day, the retreating column was subjected to a series of attacks by the Luftwaffe, each more deadly and effective than the one before. He had seen some poignant sights, including mothers weeping by their dead children and burned out shells of troop transporters, which had suffered direct hits while full of people. He had also come across members of the Royal Indian Army Service Corps Mule Company which, he discovered in conversation, had lost many of its men and animals during the retreat. Brandt was on the one hand disgusted that such inferior races should be part of the British armed forces. But he could not help but be impressed by their loyalty. As he was passing, he heard the order being issued to the mule handlers that, as they approached the coast, they must destroy their animals because nothing useful was to be left for the Germans. Brandt was astounded to hear the officer accept, after discussion with his men, that, should they be able to find a home for their animals on any of the French farms they were constantly passing, the animals could be permitted to live. *What kind of fighting army is this?* he wondered, *that it cares so much about dumb animals?* Towards the end of the day, Brandt approached the outskirts of Dunkirk, at which point many of the army personnel were extracted from the column to help boost the numbers in the lines of defence around the port. On more than one occasion he had been grateful for his RAF uniform which prohibited him being deployed in this way. Finally, he decided to settle down for the night in one of the roadside buildings that appeared still to have a roof and, having found a place among the dozens of military and civilian people with the same idea, he prayed that, for once, the Luftwaffe would not engage in too many night raids.

***

Wednesday 29th May 1940, Scotland Yard, London.

David Bernstein sat gazing out of his office window, reflecting on the irony that security and police forces were arguably among the greatest hotbeds of rumour and gossip. The general consensus of opinion among those 'in the know' at 'The Yard' was that the allied forces had been comprehensively outmanoeuvred and outfought and it was really only a question of how many men and how much materiel could be saved from the wreckage. He was roused from these glum thoughts by the loud ringing of his desk phone. Inspector Renton ordered him to report immediately to his office, adding with some irritation that he was being reallocated from his current duties. Bernstein found Renton crouched over a map of the English Channel which was spread over his unusually uncluttered desk. The grey pallor of the older man betrayed the effects, both of a chronic lack of sleep and the stress which he was clearly suffering. Renton nevertheless smiled weakly at his young subordinate. 'I'm afraid that there's a hell of a flap on,' he began with little enthusiasm. 'Anyway, if I know anything about how this place works, I'm sure you'll have heard the stories about what's happening in Belgium and France.'

'Yes, sir, I have. Is it as bad as they're saying?'

'I'm afraid not, David. It's actually far, far worse. Effectively, the BEF and the French have been surrounded by the Nazis. They're just managing to hold on to Dunkirk, but they won't be able to do that forever. They're continuing to take a fearful battering. It's a bloody mess, but the Navy, and anyone who can be prevailed upon to help, is trying to evacuate as many as possible from the beaches and the port before it falls. It's a very long shot and the top brass think we'll be lucky to get twenty thousand out.'

'My God, sir,' shouted Bernstein in horror. 'But there's over three hundred thousand of our blokes out there. What the hell will happen to the rest of them?'

Renton shrugged helplessly before acknowledging, 'Well, there's nothing we can do about that. But it is the reason that you're being involved. As I said, it's an absolute shambles, both over there and back in Blighty. Literally thousands of troops and others are being brought back on hundreds of ships. There's little organisation because many of the men were scattered from their units during the retreat. There are people purporting to be Dutch, Belgian, Polish and French, as well as some other nationalities, all mixed up with the remnants of the BEF. Many of the men can't be identified by their uniforms, as these have suffered during the march back to Dunkirk. To cut a long story short, the intelligence boys are very concerned that the Germans might try to slip some of their own agents into Britain, under cover of the evacuation. It wouldn't take much for them to pose as Dutch or Pole or whatever. I need hardly stress that such agents would most probably be tasked with organising the 'Fifth Column', in preparation for a likely Nazi invasion of Britain.' Having paused briefly to refill and relight his pipe, Renton went on, 'Basically, you'll have to leave the pursuit of Lazarus for the time being and get yourself down to Dover post-haste. There, you'll join a specialist screening team for all those returning from France who aren't obviously British. You'll focus initially on those claiming to be Dutch or East European and try to weed out any infiltrating Nazis hidden among them. You're to report to Major Brown at Dover Castle with immediate effect. Good luck, David. We'll miss you here but, for God's sake do your best down there.'

***

Thursday 30th May, Near Dunkirk, France.

Brandt awoke with a start just as dawn was breaking. As he stumbled out of his shelter for the night, he saw immediately that the road towards Dunkirk and the coast was already teeming with military personnel. The lucky ones were in vehicles, the rest of the desperate soldiers and civilians, like himself on foot. As he fell in on the march towards the sea, he noticed with great satisfaction that many of the retreating British could scarcely look the civilians in the eye. It was obvious to him that even this feeble rabble was ashamed of its rapid retreat in the face of the panzers. As they shuffled through each successive half destroyed town or village, where the stony-faced French stared at them with barely disguised hostility, one or two of the more cheerful types were loudly promising that, 'We'll be back to finish the job!'

Should have fought harder, rather than run away like scared children, thought Brandt contemptuously. As he moved slowly through the outskirts of Dunkirk, he noticed the first signs of a proper attempt by the French and

British to resist the German advance. Much better organised and well-equipped units were digging in on the seaward side of the various canals which surrounded the port. *So*, he reasoned, *it's here that they'll try to hold off our tanks to give as many as possible a chance to escape by sea.* He could almost taste his excitement as he began to see clearly how massive a victory this could be for Germany. *Even if some of them do escape the trap*, he gloated, *they'll have no equipment with which to fight off an invasion. And once they surrender here, hundreds of thousands will become prisoners of war.*

Buoyed by such thoughts, Brandt tried not to smile as he saw at first hand the enormous battering that Dunkirk had taken, both from the air and, as the Wehrmacht closed the noose around the port, from heavy shelling. The unmistakable stench of burning flesh hung over the town and craters of various sizes pockmarked the roads, many of which had tram tracks twisted upwards like crazy modern sculptures. The roar of collapsing buildings and the frequent surge of hot air, as walls fell to the ground, reminded him that he should make rapid progress while he could. His column was now close to the port itself, and one of the soldiers shouted, 'Come on lads! The docks are just over there. I can smell the sea and with it, our freedom!'

'Not so fast!' boomed the commanding voice of a small, wiry NCO who was directing the column to the right and away from the port. 'You have to go in a north easterly direction, parallel to the coast, until you reach the beach. It's a couple of miles or so. You'll have to take your turn up there with all the rest of the men. Good luck.'

Brandt was furious that he would have to spend more time at risk of being killed by his own side, but he recognised that he had little option but to retain his place in the column of tired and disappointed men as it shuffled away. It was late afternoon by the time they reached the beach, where they were greeted by the dreadful sight of a defeated army, surrounded by destroyed equipment and huddled down awaiting rescue by boat.

To a groan of protest from the British, another young officer revealed that there was no chance of their disembarkation that day. 'The ships will come in on the tide later and take off as many as possible. My guess is that you lot will be lucky to get out tomorrow. So, my advice is that you make good use of these sand dunes and dig yourselves in well … the Stukas are bound to be back soon.'

Brandt found a suitable spot, but before he started digging into the soft sand, he surveyed the cataclysmic scene. A little further along the beach, in the direction of the docks, he could see the burning wreckage of a destroyer, evidently the victim of a dive bomb attack. At the water's edge, several deserted ambulances stood motionless, seemingly abandoned after delivering their last cargo of wounded evacuees. Further in the distance, the pier of the harbour was visible through the smoke and he guessed that this would be where the larger ships would come to receive directly their human cargo. He was, however, most surprised by the lines of men, stretched out across the beach and right up to the shoreline. *What the hell are they doing?* he wondered. As night began to fall, he was amazed to see a motley flotilla of craft, from rowing boats to fishing vessels and even what looked like pleasure steamers come as close to the beach as possible. As soon as they appeared, the lines of men, drunk with exhaustion, began staggering into the shallow water. The first of the men, as they progressed away from the shore, were almost neck deep before they were finally hauled into the nearest small vessel. All of this activity, Brandt saw, was being directed by junior officers who were also in the water. Once full, the small vessels, many of which were listing dangerously under the weight of people, made their way out to sea where the larger ships were waiting to gather in their human harvest. Settling himself into his recently dug foxhole, as the ever-darkening sky caused the whole of the seafront of Dunkirk to stand out as one long, hellish line of burning buildings. For the first time since crossing into allied territory, Brandt began to feel truly afraid.

His silent prayer that the Luftwaffe remain grounded went unheeded, as less than an hour later the ominous drone of aircraft engines could clearly be heard. Parachute flares were dropped over the beach and dock areas to facilitate the air attacks which followed in short order. The dense smoke hanging over the beach and the need to hit larger targets meant that the bombers' main activity was centred on the ships lying just offshore or tying up on the harbour pier. Brandt was transfixed at the sight of the various Royal Navy ships, desperately firing their anti-aircraft guns into the night sky in a clumsy attempt to ward off the dive bomb attacks. Eventually the attack subsided and the beach became relatively still and calm until a huge noise came from the direction of the harbour. Brandt leapt up and saw that a troop ship which had been tied up to the pier and was just about to start embarking soldiers, had fallen victim to shell fire. The ship's boilers had suffered a direct hit, causing the vessel to explode and destroying it in seconds. Eventually, a sort of peace began to descend on the beach area and, shivering despite his flying jacket, Brandt settled into an uneasy sleep among the remnants of the British Expeditionary Force.

***

Friday 31st May 1940.

'Come on, Yank!' shouted the British infantryman as he shook the sleeping RAF officer by the shoulder. 'Time to wake up. It looks like we might be on our way.' Brandt woke with a start and instinctively reached down to his right flying boot which concealed a deadly knife. He quickly realised there was no danger and replied with a smile, 'I'm Canadian. How many times do I have to tell you that I'm not American. It would be like me calling you Scottish.'

The British cockney laughed and clapped Brandt on the back as he struggled to his feet in the sand. 'Listen, mate. You can call me a bleedin' Jerry, if it helps us get off this bloody beach... now come on!' Brandt clumsily followed the small Englishman through the sea mist and down the sand dunes where marshalling officers were organising the men into groups of around fifty. Each of these, in turn, snaked across the wide flat beach to the water's edge and the sea. There they would await rescue by one of the small craft which had made the perilous journey from the south coast of England.

As dawn broke to a grey and misty morning, a relieved Brandt realised the Luftwaffe would probably be grounded for much of the day. The British, it seemed to him, were preparing to make the most of this stroke of luck to save as many men as possible. As the murky morning wore on, Brandt and the other mixed bag of troops in his group edged, desperately slowly, nearer and nearer to the shoreline. He was surprised at the general orderliness and calm of the British as they moved in their turn, for all the world like some huge bus queue awaiting the arrival of the number 49 which would take them home from work. Only the odd shell, fired from inland, caused occasional alarm, but order was soon restored by the organising officers. There was little chatter to draw attention away from the continuous sound of small arms and artillery fire, clearly audible from the direction of Dunkirk town. To the great relief of those on the beach, however, this did not seem to be getting any closer. 'Those lads in the final defences are putting up a great fight,' murmured one wounded soldier. 'If we get out of this in one piece, we'll owe our lives to them.'

    Each run of the small boats to the larger craft offshore seemed to take an excruciatingly long time and, for a period in mid-morning, no pick-ups took place at all. Evidently, the larger ships had reached their quota and had set off back to England, to be replaced by other vessels with large, troop carrying capacity. By late afternoon, Brandt found himself, together with the other members of his group, edging into the cold water. The fires were still raging all along the front of Dunkirk, casting everyone in an infernal glow. After more than an hour in the water, the last minutes up to shoulder height, Brandt was beginning to realise that his soaked flying jacket was becoming more of a hindrance than a help. Just as he was contemplating jettisoning it into the sea, a large rowing boat emerged out of the mist and, to his great relief, he was dragged out of the sapping cold of the sea. 'Come on son,' said a burly, middle-aged man with arms like tree trunks. 'Let's get you on board and off back to Blighty'.

CHAPTER TWENTY FIVE

Saturday 1st June 1940, Dover, England.

Brandt certainly never imagined that his first approach to the famous white cliffs of Dover would take the form that it did. At least the steady sea breeze dispersed the worst of the smell of hundreds of men packed close together on the deck of HMS *Icarus*. Few had had the opportunity to wash for many days and most were wearing soiled and damaged uniforms. He had been transported by rowing boat from the beach at Dunkirk to the destroyer which had taken hours to embark as many men as were able to stand upright on the deck. Initially, he had been disappointed that he was not given a place below decks as this space had been reserved for the wounded. Now, he was hugely relieved to be in the open, as he frequently caught a whiff of the indescribably foetid air which wafted over him each time the nearby door to the lower decks was opened. There had been little or no conversation since the *Icarus* had finally steamed away from the catastrophe that was Dunkirk. Evidently each of the rescued soldiers remained locked in his own individual memories of the retreat and evacuation. Once the glowing fires of the French town had disappeared into the swirling sea mist and the sounds of explosions and gunfire had been replaced by the altogether more pleasant swish of seawater against the ship's hull, Brandt felt able at last to utter a silent, unconditional prayer that the Wehrmacht would sweep the remaining British and French forces into the sea.

In truth, he had found the whole experience of masquerading as an allied airman and leaving France with the remnants of this defeated rabble thoroughly unsatisfactory. His anger began to focus on Schellenberg and those intelligence people in their secure offices in Berlin who had massively underestimated the degree of danger he would face from German shells, bullets and bombs. As the first glimpses of the English coastline came into view through the early morning haze, he felt an absolute conviction that he would never again place any trust in his controllers in Berlin. *I'll run this damned mission by my own rules,* he promised himself, *not according to the whims of someone like Schellenberg.* Feeling at ease for the first time since his exhilarating participation in the shooting at Le Paradis, he prepared himself for the identity screening he would undoubtedly face in Dover.

As the *Icarus* entered between the breakwaters of the port, he saw an unlikely number of destroyers, cruisers and other large vessels, each absolutely packed with men. There were so many that they were berthed two or even three abreast along the jetties. As his ship pulled nearer to its designated docking position, he could see hundreds of men using dozens of gangplanks to leave the various ships moored at the dockside. Similar walkways had been placed between the inner and outer lying ships to allow men to cross, as space on the decks of the innermost ships was released by those who had finally reached the safety of land. He noticed several men who, on reaching land, dropped to their knees and ostentatiously kissed the ground. *They'd have been better fighting harder in Belgium and France than showing such womanly emotionalism* , he thought with disgust.

At last, the *Icarus* tied up on the outside of another destroyer and gangplanks were quickly put in place between the two ships. Officers were positioned at each exit and held the men back to allow the prior disembarkation of those on the innermost ship. Strangely, it was here, literally in touching distance of final safety that the first violence erupted. As Brandt waited in the impatient crush, several metres away from the gangplank, he felt a rough punch on his shoulder. Turning round in surprise, he was confronted by a red faced, overweight sergeant. The furious soldier ranted at him, 'You shouldn't be here, you swine!' For one terrible moment, Brandt thought that this ugly and abusive creature had somehow seen through his disguise. *Hell!,* he panicked, *how does he know I'm German?* To Brandt's relief, however, the sergeant spat out, 'You bloody cowards! Where was the damned RAF when we needed it? Me and my lads were shot to bits by the Luftwaffe all the way from Lille to Dunkirk, while you and your lot cowered at your safe airfields.' This intemperate outburst was followed by several shouts of encouragement and a few more pushes and attempted punches aimed at Brandt.

'Stop that immediately!' rang out the authoritative voice of the officer who was controlling movement across the gangplank. 'Just use your bloody head, man. How do you think this chap got here? By sitting on his arse at an airfield? He was one of the few who damned well did try to help and was shot down for his pains, you idiot. Now, any more of this nonsense and I swear by God that those responsible will face a court martial.'

This threat initially raised a muttering of objection, followed by loud cries of, 'He's right, sarge. You're shouting at the wrong man. He tried to help.' The sergeant and his supporters were not altogether appeased by this, but they grudgingly accepted the officer's reasoning and moved away somewhat shamefacedly. Brandt carefully wiped away the specks of spittle that had flown into his face during the sergeant's outburst and turned back to the gangplank. Men were already making their way between the ships and, when his turn came to leave, the officer suggested with a sad smile. 'You'd better stay with that group of Dutch and Polish flyers who've just left the ship. Safety in numbers, what?' Brandt nodded and pushed his way through the crowd until he was standing with the group of RAF personnel.

'You Dutch and Polish airmen, over there please!' instructed an officer with a clipboard, as he indicated a civilian, accompanied by a detachment of Military Police. Brandt had the uncomfortable feeling that there was something vaguely familiar about the civilian, *Do I know him? Does he remind me of somebody?* 'What's going on?' one of the airmen asked the officer. 'Why do we have to go with those Military Police?'

'Don't worry,' replied the officer soothingly. 'It's only routine screening for all Europeans. Detective Sergeant Bernstein will be finished with you in a jiffy.'

Bernstein? Where the hell have I heard that name before? After a few seconds of feverishly ransacking his memory, a dreadful possibility suggested itself to Brandt. *Surely it can't be? Is it possible that he's the younger brother of John King's Jewish friend back in Heidelberg? Now I think about it, he was always going on about wanting to be a policeman. And the cunning little brat did run away to England with his sister. Christ! I've got to keep out of his way. If he gets a really good look at me there's an outside chance it could jog his memory.* Brandt stood, frozen with indecision while the others had moved towards Bernstein. 'Stay with those men, please,' the officer commanded Brandt. 'Over there with the Military Police.'

'But I'm not European. I'm a Canadian member of the RAF,' Brandt protested in his best North American drawl. 'I should report directly back to my unit at Kenley. I somehow think that experienced fighter pilots are going to be needed now more than ever.'

For a moment the officer seemed undecided, talking to himself in his confusion. 'Well, our orders do only concern Europeans. There's no mention of Canadians….' After an excruciating wait, the harassed officer said, 'All right. You go with the Brits. Straight along the dockside, through the building at the end and collect your rail warrant.'

Brandt saluted and moved along the dockside, risking a sideways glance towards Bernstein. To his horror, their eyes met for a split second before one of the MPs distracted the policeman with a query. *With luck the damned Jew didn't recognise me,* Brandt hoped. *Just behave naturally and don't look at him again!* Tension still flooding through him, he walked briskly away, taking care not to be so fast as to arouse suspicion. Further along the dock, he was passing a building in which many men were changing out of their ragged uniforms into utility clothes which had been provided. He quickly decided to discard his RAF uniform and adopt this anonymous disguise.

***

When he had arrived in Dover the day before, David Bernstein had been appalled at the chaotic state of the screening operation. He was supposed to help with the checking of evacuees who claimed to be Dutch or East Europeans. The shortage of foreign language speakers, however, meant that he was ordered to screen any Europeans who arrived. He had found the work interesting, but tiring, as he spent several minutes with each man, trying to elicit an explanation of how he had reached Dunkirk. Sympathetic to their dreadful experience, where possible he avoided sending men for further questioning. Indeed, so far he had selected for further investigation only two of the hundreds he had seen. In both cases he'd felt that tell-tale prickling of the short hairs on the back of his neck. *It's odd,* he thought, *I felt the same bloody thing just now. I only caught sight of that airman for a second, but I'd swear there was something about him. Do I know him from somewhere or did he just remind me of someone?* When he looked for the man again, he'd disappeared. Working with Inspector Renton had taught Bernstein to trust the hairs on the back of his neck. 'With me, it's my fingertips,' Renton had confided in him. 'When they start to tingle, I know there's something not right. Trust your signs, David. Whatever they are, son, trust them.'

Even though it was purely a hunch, he sent a runner to the main dock exit points with the instruction that anyone in the uniform of an airman was to be detained, pending interview with Special Branch. There were after all, as the sergeant who had accosted Brandt on HMS *Icarus* had suggested, precious few of those passing through Dover.

***

As Brandt shuffled slowly through the crowded reception hall, he noticed a final guard point, before he could pass out towards the railway platforms and his escape to London. Just as he was approaching the gateway, a guard shouted, 'You there! You, in the RAF uniform. To one side, please.' In a moment of panic, Brandt thought that the order was directed at him, but then he remembered. *Thank God I got out of that uniform. That Jew's not so stupid after all.* A smirk crossed his face as he concluded, *Perhaps I owe my life to that oaf on the ship.*

No one gave Brandt a second glance as he passed through the control point and on into a large customs shed. In turn, the soldiers made their way to one of the many desks, positioned some fifty metres away on the far side of the shed. Brandt took his turn to be asked his name, before being issued with a rail warrant and advised where to go to catch an appropriate train. As no one at this checkpoint had been alerted to be on the lookout for an airman, he was able to identify himself as a pilot stationed at RAF Kenley and received his warrant to return to his base via London.

The trains operating from Dover to London were at full capacity, repatriated soldiers crowding into any available space, including corridors, luggage vans, dining cars and even toilets. The mood, it seemed to Brandt, was a mixture of happiness and relief to be back in Britain and shame and embarrassment at the scale of their defeat by the Wehrmacht. The German had managed to squeeze himself into a compartment designed to transport eight people, but which now carried twelve men. Uncomfortably sandwiched between two sweaty corporals who chain smoked their way through Kent and engaged in the most banal of chatter, he eventually nodded off, only to be awakened by the juddering of the train as it came to a halt.

Through the compartment's grimy window, he could see a sign for Maidstone and, to his amazement, dozens of people thronging the platform. The majority of these were waving Union Jacks and cheering at the top of their voices. 'Will you look at that?' said one of the corporals with a laugh. 'You'd think we'd won rather than been roundly thrashed by Jerry.' The soldiers' confusion was heightened as Women's Institute volunteers began to pass cups of tea and stamped envelopes through the train windows. 'Better if you seal the envelopes and use them as a kind of postcard, dearies,' said the middle aged, buxom lady, dressed in her classic English country tweeds. 'They're for you to let your nearest and dearest know that you're safely back home. Either post them yourself in London or write them quickly now and we'll post them for you.' The embarrassed soldiers enjoyed their first taste of 'proper British tea' and began to compose their postcards for home. The serious mood was finally broken when a corporal advised, 'Better not put anything too saucy, if you're writing to your missus or girl, lads. Remember they're postcards. Wouldn't want to embarrass the poor postie, now would we?'

Brandt passed the time until their arrival in Victoria Station repeatedly going over his plan. *Once there, find a public telephone and call my contact at the Portuguese Embassy. Use the pre-arranged code to request the safe house address.* There, he knew he would find all the information, clothes and documents he would need to start his life in Britain as Joe Brand - American newspaperman.

Everything went like clockwork as he easily found the safe house, situated just off Cannon Street. He waited until after nightfall and, having been told the back door would be unlocked, he approached the house from the rear. Once inside, Brandt was pleased to find a fine spread of food and drink and, perhaps most welcome of all, a bathtub in which he could wash away the grime and the memory of Dunkirk.

***

David Bernstein had at last reached the end of a long, demanding day. Exhausted, he consulted the sheaves of notes made during his interviews as he reviewed with the senior military policeman the cases he had processed. When they had finished, he fixed the man with a doubtful expression, 'You're absolutely sure that I interviewed all the RAF men to have come through Dover since my instruction?'

'I'm certain, Detective Sergeant,' he replied firmly. 'Your order was given immediately. Nobody could have avoided interception. You saw all twenty odd of them. There were no others.'

'But that one I saw wasn't among them,' sighed Bernstein heavily. 'He damn well wasn't.'

'Why is he so important?' asked the military policeman. 'Who on earth is he?'

'That's just it,' replied the Special Branch man with exasperation. 'I don't know. I wondered if I'd recognised him from somewhere and maybe that made me think it was important to intercept him. But... ah well... maybe my eyes were deceiving me.'

The military policeman noted the faint smile on Bernstein's face and, though he didn't believe a word of what he was about to say, nevertheless agreed. 'That's right, sir. So many faces. Mind playing tricks on you.'

'Yes, it must be,' replied Bernstein. But he, too, didn't believe what he had just said.

***

Wednesday 12th June 1940, Highgate, London.

As he basked in the sunshine which poured through the large bay window of his north London flat, Brandt reflected that life in the city was much better than he could possibly have imagined. Initially, he had been appalled, but later cynically amused that he should be living so close to the cemetery in which Karl Marx was buried. But there was no doubt about it, this bright and airy flat, located close to Archway underground station, was serving his interests perfectly. Especially as Highgate was not only a pleasant, leafy area, it also had discreet neighbours who kept themselves to themselves. In addition, the three suitcases of used American clothes, his genuine looking American passport, press identification card and permission to stay in Britain had all exceeded his expectations.

He had spent his time orientating himself in the city and familiarising himself with the means of communication with SS headquarters in Germany. Using a radio had been deemed too dangerous, so information was passed via a Post Office Box used by his Portuguese Embassy contact. He had already confirmed to Berlin that he had arrived on schedule and that he had started work at the office arranged for him. Schellenberg had insisted by return that he make Perrygo his priority and that, in the current circumstances, he should waste no time in contacting her. *He just wants the information to put in his damned invasion book*, Brandt thought bitterly. *And he doesn't care if it costs my life to get it.* To the obvious irritation of his controllers, Brandt had immediately advised that, as planned, he would act as a genuine American newspaperman for at least two weeks to enable him to check for a British 'tail'. He would not attempt to contact Rösel's informants until he was sure that he was 'clean'. However, he kept to himself his decision to make the first approach to Stevenson. He was acutely aware that any, or all of the network may have been blown and turned by the British. If that were the case, one false step and he could find himself in front of a firing squad. *I couldn't give a shit what that careerist Schellenberg says, I'll focus on Stevenson. Judging by her photo,* he reflected lasciviously, *she looks pretty and a romantic approach will seem natural and might be fun. If she's not been turned, chances are the British are still in the dark and I can risk seeing the others.*

***

Monday 17th June 1940, Dover.

'Yes sir. I agree, it's very annoying. But I'm afraid there's not much I can do about it,' David Bernstein repeated yet again. He had just broken the news to Inspector Renton that he was needed in Dover until the end of July. 'The screening is taking far longer than we anticipated. Plus,' he added wearily, 'there are so few good German speakers here that most of the 'high risk' candidates who say they are Poles or Dutch are sent to me.' He could have pointed out that he'd had precious little sleep since arriving in Dover, but he simply explained, 'The backlog's already huge because of the numbers who got away and my orders are to be very thorough, what with the heightened threat of invasion.'

'I understand, David,' sighed Renton. 'It's just that we, too, are short staffed. Anyway, keep up the good work and stay in touch.'

Bernstein also chose not to mention his strange experience with the disappearing RAF officer. *After the way I doubted the old man's obsession with Lazarus*, he reasoned, *I'd feel a right berk.* But that did not mean Bernstein had passed it off as a trick of perception or memory. *I still don't understand*, he worried. *Why the hell wasn't he intercepted by the Military Police? He couldn't possibly have reached the customs sheds before the guards were told to stop all RAF men.* Bernstein knew of the facility for men with badly damaged clothes to change into utility uniforms and deduced that the only possible explanation is that he changed out of his uniform. *But why would he do that? It looked in reasonably good shape.* Bernstein shook his head decisively before concluding, *Whoever he was, he must have recognised me and changed clothes to make himself more inconspicuous. I just wish there was a way to compare names of RAF officers who went through Dover that day with those who actually reported to the RAF. Maybe then I could find an anomaly and know for sure. But,* he cursed inwardly, *even that wouldn't help me figure out who the hell he is.*

CHAPTER TWENTY SIX

Saturday 13th July 1940, Central London.

'Is this seat free, ma'am?' the good-looking man asked in a strong American accent.

'Oh, er, yes. Yes, it is….' stammered the pretty young woman as she nervously flicked back her long blond hair.

'Then with your permission, I'll just sit myself down here and sample one of the coffees.'

'Oh, I'm not sure I would do that,' the young woman advised hesitantly. 'I'm afraid the quality here will be nothing like you're used to.'

'Well, it is true that I'm fairly new here in London,' the man said as he removed his expensive raincoat and hat and sat down in the crowded café. 'What would you recommend? Tea, perhaps?'

The young woman blushed as she looked self-consciously at her own pot of tea for one. *God!* she thought miserably, *I must look like some desiccated maiden aunt, sitting here with my tea.* The man stared at her with a quizzical expression, until she eventually raised her head from the table. He then burst out in a huge gale of laughter, 'Hey! That's fine. Tea'll be just great by me.' An inscrutable expression crossed his face as he saw the young woman's utter misery replaced by a relieved smile. *This may be easier than I'd dared hope,* thought Joachim

Brandt as he waited to give his order. *And she's a lot prettier too!*

For the past two weeks he had been following Abigail Stevenson from the Foreign Office to her flat in Maida Vale. She appeared to lead a solitary existence, usually making her way straight home from work, and it was particularly good that he'd seen no evidence of a man friend. *That could have meant real trouble*, he had told himself, *though I might have enjoyed dealing with him.* Brandt had seen her socialise in just two ways; the standard, quick drink with her fellow secretaries after work on Fridays and choir practice on Wednesday evenings at a nearby church. He had quickly ruled out both as acceptable opportunities to engineer a first meeting and had also decided that an approach, while she was eating her lunchtime sandwiches in St James's Park, was equally inadvisable. He hadn't seen any evidence of clandestine meetings and had concluded that, as an informer, she was almost certainly dormant.

Waiting for her to emerge from her flat that morning, Brandt had had no firm plan in mind. But when she had entered the crowded café and had sat at a table for two, he had waited outside for several minutes to make sure that she was not waiting for someone. Thrilled by the risk of extemporising, he had decided immediately to seize the opportunity to introduce himself.

When the waitress arrived at their table, he ordered tea and cake for two and politely overrode Miss Stevenson's attempted objection with a charming, 'You'll be doing me a great favour, ma'am. As I say, I'm new in this city and still trying to learn how you do things here.'

'You've only just arrived in Britain?' she asked, arching her eyebrows in a way that he found very stimulating.

'That's right, er … say, what can I call you? By the way,' he continued, smiling broadly and reaching his hand across the table in innocent greeting. 'The name's Brand, Joe Brand. Nice to meet you, I'm sure.'

'Oh', the young woman spluttered nervously, 'I'm Abigail, Abigail Stevenson.'

'Right then, Abigail. If I may presume to call you Abigail that is….' he continued with an old-world charm which she found most attractive. 'You asked how long I've been here.' Brandt went on to explain that he had arrived by ship from New York nearly two weeks before. 'I'm working as a reporter for one of the biggest East Coast news agencies. There's a lot of interest back home in how Britain will cope, especially now that it looks as if you're on your own against Hitler. But, say, that's not what I should be talking about. The first chance that I get to talk to such a pretty girl here in London and there I go with work stuff.' Her immediate blush told him that he should tread carefully and slowly, in order not to unduly scare her. They spent the next half hour talking about his first impressions of London and the British and where one could go to get a good meal and sophisticated entertainment. This confirmed his opinion that she was no expert on London's nightlife, but she did suggest a couple of restaurants. As Stevenson finally prepared to leave, Brandt used all his flattery and charm to extract her telephone number. Putting on his most naïve smile, he promised her that he would be in touch soon, 'if that would be okay with you.' She nodded and offered her hand before going out onto the Strand. As soon as she had gone, Brandt congratulated himself on a most satisfactory first engagement and allowed a predatory smile to cross his face.

***

Throughout the rest of July and the first half of August, Brandt ensured that he saw Abigail Stevenson regularly, although he was careful not to ask about her work. He simply maintained an affable acceptance of her description of it as 'a pretty boring office job where nothing much happens.' As a description of the Foreign Ministry of a nation fighting for its very survival, to him this seemed a singularly misleading description. On the other hand, his cover as a journalist did afford him considerable scope to discuss the latest events, rumours and public opinion as the war moved inexorably towards its first anniversary. Brandt was well aware that she was becoming more attracted to him, but he was equally conscious of her evident inexperience. He therefore kept things easy going, cementing their friendship with a series of unthreatening weekend lunch dates, walks in the park and the odd visit to the cinema. It was after such a visit to see Alfred Hitchcock's recently released film *Rebecca*, with its melodramatic emphasis on the secrets which surrounded the death of Max de Winter's first wife, that she suddenly posed a totally unexpected question. 'Tell me, Joe', she asked, her pretty face screwed up with concern. 'Do you believe that we all have our secrets? And do you think that having secrets inevitably stops us from getting really close to someone?'

While Brandt recognised that this offered the perfect opportunity to probe Stevenson for her secrets, he decided to treat the subject lightly. 'Heck, yes, Abby,' he answered with all the homespun sincerity he could muster and using the pet name to which she had not objected. 'Of course we do. But the point is, are these really important or not? Now you, for example, I simply can't imagine that you have any deep, dark secrets. You're much too pretty for that.'

Brandt was now absolutely certain that Stevenson had not been turned by the British. But he also had the strangest feeling that, somehow, she was still operating as an informer. He hadn't seen her meeting any possible controller and he was certain that such a person could not be another German agent. *It's a damned puzzle,* he frequently pondered, before promising himself that before long, *she'll be begging to tell me all her secrets.*

Brandt had sent several reports to Berlin stating how he intended to deal with Rösel's old networks. In return, he had received replies which expressed some satisfaction with his progress, but which consistently exhorted him to gather the information that was urgently required for the *Informationsheft GB.* Indeed, the last message from Schellenberg had hinted that planning for an imminent invasion was well under way. Given the cautious approach he was taking with Stevenson, he finally had to accept that he could no longer postpone meeting Martha Perrygo.

***

Monday 5th August 1940, Whitehall, London.

'How did the suggestion that they be given Abwehr identity cards go down with your informants, John?' asked a grinning Professor Pym. 'Bloody well, if I'm any judge.'

'I should say so, sir,' replied King, his eyes twinkling with amusement. 'They saw them as a kind of membership card for an exclusive club. They loved them and can't wait to show them to the first invading troops they meet.'

They were sitting in a quiet corner of The Red Lion, a pleasant and conveniently positioned London pub on Parliament Street, as King outlined how he had been given the names and contact details of over one hundred Nazi sympathisers across the south of England. 'Martha Perrygo had definitely not been exaggerating when she said that she had a large network of supporters,' King laughed while shaking his head in disbelief. 'She alone has given us over ninety names, many of whom are respectable members of various communities in Kent and Sussex. She's also given us lots of information about the operation and organisation of the LDVs, as well as detailed maps showing the positions of the coastal pillboxes and the shore defences. All in all, that stuff would've been deuced useful to the Germans in planning an invasion.'

'And what of the others?' asked Pym with interest.

Having listened intently to a brief account of intelligence provided by Fred Beech and Joe Watkins, Pym commented, 'But you've not mentioned our star pupil, Abigail Stevenson.'

'No sir, I haven't', the younger man began hesitantly. 'That's because, frankly, I'm not sure what to make of her.'

A frown spread across the Professor's face as he prompted an explanation, 'Really? Why's that?'

'Well, of course it may be nothing at all, but for the last couple of meetings, she seems different in a subtle, but quite definite way. She's a little more reserved, a little less cooperative. Perhaps even not as needy. I don't know sir, I can't put my finger on exactly what the issue is, but things have certainly changed.' The two men agreed that King should maintain contact with Stevenson, but withdraw immediately if he felt the situation was becoming dangerous or unpredictable. In such circumstances, she would be arrested by Military Intelligence.

***

Wednesday 7th August 1940, Scotland Yard, London.

Inspector Renton raised his eyes eagerly from the mountain of paperwork littering his desk, 'I thought I recognised the rhythm of that knock,' he said with a broad smile. 'It's very good to have you back, David. Very good indeed.'

'Thank you, sir,' Bernstein answered brightly. 'It's good to be back. Not that what we were doing down in Dover was a waste of time. It had to be done by someone, I imagine. But we more or less drew a total blank.'

'I'm not really surprised, David,' Renton replied while cleaning out the bowl of his pipe. 'I suppose that the speed of their advance to the coast caught the Germans out as well. I can't believe they were so organised that they were could use the evacuation as cover for infiltrating spies into Britain.' Seeing the doubt on Bernstein's face, he shrugged his shoulders. 'It looks like you don't agree.'

Bernstein argued that the Germans could well have used the chaos, both in France and back on the south coast of England, to try to slip some agents into Britain. 'After all, sir, what better way of getting them in, than letting us do the job for them?'

'Well, it's obvious that Hitler would be a total fool if he doesn't move quickly to invade and try to inflict a knock-out blow on us,' Renton said, while puffing his pipe contentedly. 'But, in order to protect his armies during the crossing, he'll need air superiority. Our intelligence boys are telling us that the next big battle to be fought will be for control of the skies over southern England and the Channel. Lose this, and things will be very, very hard for us.'

As if to take their minds off this pessimistic analysis, both men took a cup of steaming tea, before discussing Bernstein's priorities for the coming weeks. As the sergeant had expected, he was to return to his search for the agent Lazarus, initially by uncovering the contact known as 'A'. He had already eliminated all likely candidates from the Ministry for War and the Cabinet Office and he was now turning to the much larger Foreign Office. Bernstein explained that it would take him a few days to identify likely suspects among those with 'A' as an initial. 'I'll select those who live alone, subject each to a week's surveillance and see where that leads.'

'I know that it's like looking for a needle in a haystack, David', the Inspector offered sympathetically. 'But it's vital work. Good luck and keep me posted.'

***

Friday 23rd August 1940, Sevenoaks, Kent.

Why the hell doesn't the stupid old bitch have a telephone? This question had occupied Brandt's furious mind for several days. *And why didn't Rösel think to bring a record of his informants' addresses? By God, if the smarmy fool had used his brain, it would have saved me a lot of wasted effort.* Brandt had only Perrygo's estimated age, a general description and the information that she lived in Sevenoaks. He was beginning to doubt the accuracy of this last piece of information, however, as he was nearing the end of a day spent tramping around that wretched town, trying to pick up any trace of the woman. *It's not as if she's called Smith or Jones, for God's sake,* he fumed, as he prepared to enter yet another newsagents to buy a packet of cigarettes that he didn't want and to pretend to be her long lost nephew from the States. *People seem so stupidly trusting here*, he thought contemptuously as he pushed open the door and heard, once again, the tedious tinkling of the shop bell. *They're prepared to believe almost anything, if it's said with a smile.*

'What's that you say, dearie?' the aged woman behind the counter of the small shop in Bank Street asked self-consciously. 'You'll have to speak up. I'm a bit hard of hearing, you see.' Brandt repeated his patter much louder and more slowly. He had no expectation of any success, so was astonished when the old woman began to nod her head vigorously. 'Oh yes, dear. Yes, indeed.'

Come on, get on with it, you stupid old crone, thought Brandt irritably, simultaneously smiling affably through gritted teeth.

'You must mean Martha Perrygo... it's a funny sort of name, isn't it, love?' Brandt had to struggle against his urge to pull the old fool out from behind her counter and shake the information out of her. Indeed, the old lady had stopped talking, seemingly having forgotten what she had been asked, or perhaps believing that she had already offered a sufficient answer.

'But please, ma'am', Brandt pleaded in his most artificially pleasant way, 'could you just tell me where she lives. I've come a long way to see her.'

'Of course, lovey', she answered, much to the further irritation of Brandt. How he was coming to hate this endless supply of British pleasantries. 'She lives just around the corner on the High Street. It's a semi-detached. You can't miss it. It's the one with the black door.'

'Thank you very much ma'am,' Brandt smiled, as he touched the brim of his hat. 'Now, you won't spoil things by mentioning me, will you? And you won't tell your husband?' A look of uncertainty and sadness briefly crossed the old woman's face, as if she couldn't quite understand what this charming young American meant. Finally the penny dropped and she replied with a wink, 'Oh no, darling. I won't say anything to Martha. And my Albert, God bless him, he's been dead these past ten years. I'm quite alone here now. No, love, I wouldn't dream of it. You can trust me.'

Brandt left the shop thinking, *I'll arrange things so that trust won't come into it.* Perrygo's house had a pleasant front garden and, as he walked past, he tipped his hat at the unfeminine, middle-aged woman working there. She barely acknowledged him and returned quickly to her digging, wielding her spade more like an Irish navvy than a forty something spinster.

It was now early evening and Brandt was pleased to find a bustling inn, some three hundred metres further down the High Street, where he could have something to eat and kill some time. The Sennockian, a black and white, Tudor style building with leaded windows and a wood lined, smoke filled interior suited his purposes perfectly. It was crowded with people, but he was fortunate to find a quiet corner where he sat to consume his beer and cheese sandwich.

Sitting in the pub, he decided to observe Perrygo for a few days, *I can check if she's been turned by the British and if there's a chance she's still active in some other way.* He quickly recognised that this delay would necessitate the elimination of the gossipy old woman in the newsagents. The pub was still busy when, as dusk was falling, he left and made his way to the rear of the newsagents in Bank Street. It took him less than a minute to gain entry by the woefully insecure rear door and he quickly crossed the well organised store room to the foot of the stairs which led to the old lady's first floor flat. He could hear the radio and gave silent thanks as he remembered that the woman was hard of hearing. *This is going to be simple*, he told himself as he silently crept up the stairs. The door into the small living room was ajar and he peered in to see the old lady, sitting in an armchair in front of an unlit fire with her back to him. The sound of quiet 'put putting' having confirmed that she was asleep, he quickly moved to the rear of the chair, reached over and around her head and snapped her neck like an old twig. Working quickly, he picked up and took the body to the top of the stairs, where he stood it upright before letting it fall. Smiling broadly, he acknowledged that the broken body looked exactly as if the old woman had accidentally fallen down the stairs. Leaving everything else untouched, he quickly made his way back through the rear door, secured it as badly as it had been when he arrived and returned to the railway station, where he caught the next train back to London.

CHAPTER TWENTY SEVEN

Friday 30th August 1940, The Foreign Office, London.

Ever since mid-August, when the decisive air battle between the RAF and the Luftwaffe had begun, most British eyes had been focused anxiously on the skies over Kent and Sussex. Bernstein, however, had been wholly occupied putting under surveillance those Foreign Office employees who he suspected of being Lazarus's contact. He had eliminated two from his list of six people and was on his fifth day of observing a young woman called Abigail Stevenson. As a relatively junior member of the secretarial staff, he had had little expectation that she would prove to be anything other than a total waste of his time for a week. As was his pattern with the other suspects, he had observed her over the lunch hour and again from her time of leaving work until midnight, or even later.

The first four days of his observation had, as expected, yielded nothing of interest and the day's lunchtime surveillance had been equally insignificant. He had been waiting unenthusiastically for her to emerge from the Foreign Office building, but quickly snapped to attention as he saw her emerge in company with several other secretarial staff. The group was smiling and chatting, as it first made its way towards Trafalgar Square and then entered The Silver Cross pub on Whitehall. Around 7PM the group began to disperse and Bernstein relaxed, feeling sure that she would go home to her small flat in Maida Vale. To his surprise, however, she moved quickly to catch a bus in Trafalgar Square, a manoeuvre that forced him to dash across the road in pursuit. Ignoring the horn blasts of outraged drivers, he ran after the departing bus and leapt athletically onto its rear platform. 'Nearly missed us there, son,' said the middle-aged bus conductor with a smile. 'Anybody would think you were in some kind of a hurry. Late for a date with your girl, eh?'

'Something like that, Bernstein replied, intrigued by this unexpected development. Uncertain of where Stevenson would leave the bus and not wishing to show his warrant card to the conductor, he bought a ticket to the route's terminus and sat three rows behind his target. As the bus approached Hyde Park Corner she rose from her seat and Bernstein again waited until the last minute before he jumped off the bus as it pulled away from the stop. The bus conductor simply shook his head in confusion. 'Young 'uns these days,' he muttered as he collected fares, 'How will we ever beat the bleedin' Jerries with lads who don't even know where they're going?'

Bernstein bent, as if tying his shoelace, while Stevenson crossed the road and walked up Park Lane towards Marble Arch. It was a fine, warm evening and many Londoners, having enjoyed time in Hyde Park, were now happily strolling arm in arm in the failing daylight. None of his other suspects had behaved in this uncharacteristic manner and, for the first time in his long pursuit of the mysterious 'A', he began to feel a twitch of excitement. As Stevenson approached the Dorchester Hotel, she was met by a tall, slim man, dressed in a fashionable suit topped off by a dark-coloured hat. Bernstein whistled softly as they went into the hotel arm in arm. *Surely that's far too expensive for Abigail Stevenson?* he reasoned. *Pity I couldn't get a good look at him. I'd love to know who he is.*

***

Brandt had experienced a frustrating week. Berlin was becoming increasingly impatient for valuable information for the *'Informationsheft GB.'* However, having spent the week observing Martha Perrygo, he was convinced, both that she was still active in gathering intelligence and that she had a wide network of potentially valuable informants based in the south east of England. But whichever way he looked at it, he couldn't work out what had been happening in this network since the deportation of Rösel. *Who the hell is she working for? I need an answer and soon!*

Tonight, however, he intended to focus his attention on Abigail Stevenson. As she breathlessly approached him, his mind reflected on her increased fawning over him. *She's definitely keen to move the relationship on. And that could be very pleasurable.* He planned to wine and dine her, followed by a return to her flat, where he would have her. *Once that's done, it should be easier to get her to open up fully.*

'I've never had dinner anywhere like this,' gushed Abigail as they followed the Maitre d' towards a table, positioned in a discreet part of the dining room. 'But you should have told me so that I could have gone home to change. I'm still in my work clothes.'

'And mighty pretty you look in them, too,' replied Brandt, utilising all his charm. 'You know, Abby, we Americans don't set too much value on fuss and show. Believe me, you look great.' He squeezed her hand and she smiled happily as they strolled across the luxurious, blue patterned carpet. Once seated, the young woman gazed, wide eyed, at the panelled ceiling, the upholstered wooden furniture and the stylish, yet discreet lighting before whispering, 'Now I understand why they call this 'The Spanish Room', it's just beautiful.' Touching his hand across the table and, unusually for her, looking him squarely in the eye, she breathed, 'Thank you for this treat, Joe. It's marvellous ... and so are you.'

'You're worth it, and a whole lot more besides', he replied with a smile which didn't quite reach his eyes. 'Now, what about a cocktail while we consider what we should eat?' Abigail Stevenson asked him to order for her as she needed to 'powder her nose'. He could feel his sexual interest rise as she walked with a natural elegance out of the Grill Restaurant and into the main hotel lobby. When she returned to the table, her face still flushed with excitement, a heavy cut glass tumbler occupied each of their place settings. Both glasses contained a good measure of a pale orange liquid and were garnished beautifully with a twist of fresh orange peel.

'Whatever's this?' she asked excitedly, lifting her glass and breathing in the heady mixture of alcohol and fruit. Picking his glass up, ready to propose a toast, he answered. 'It's called 'The Bronx' and, in my opinion, it's the classiest cocktail for a very classy lady.' Brandt could see her eyes twinkle with joy and, somewhere in their deepest recesses, also with desire.

They both chose Chicken Caesar Salad, followed by Beef Tournedos from the grill and Orange Soufflé for dessert. Without consulting her, Brandt chose a crisp, dry Chablis to accompany the salad, a much fuller bodied Chateauneufdu-Pape for the main course and a rich Sauternes for the dessert. 'Goodness me!' Stevenson cried sweetly, 'How on earth will I cope with all that?'

Brandt smiled reassuringly. 'Relax, honey. The night's very young. We've lots of time to enjoy the meal, the wine and getting to know one another even better.' He noted a fleeting look of suspicion enter her eyes before it was quickly banished by a much more open and happy expression. 'Very well,' she countered. 'But I want to know much more about you first!' They both laughed, as young people often do when they find themselves on the verge of some deeper, sexual attachment and Brandt was determined to maintain the open and revelatory mood. He therefore modified her demand, suggesting, 'OK. OK. You win. But let's each of us say something in turn. That way, you won't get too bored, having to listen to a lot of dull stuff about me.'

The first part of the meal passed quickly, with Brandt offering humorous anecdotes from his fictitious back-story, while Stevenson told him of her childhood and youth in Hertfordshire and her pride in gaining employment at the Foreign Office. As soon as her workplace was mentioned, Brandt seized the opportunity by asking if she liked working there. She replied enigmatically that, 'Perhaps it's not good to be so close to those making very important decisions as one is aware that they are mere mortals, with their all too human weaknesses.' Just as they finished the entrée, Brandt leaned across the table and said earnestly, 'You know, Abby, I've been surprised that in my time here, I've come across quite a few people who aren't convinced that you guys are fighting the right enemy…' In reply to her shrug of the shoulders and non-committal 'Really?' he continued. 'Yeah, that's right. Many feel that the real enemy lies further east. In Soviet Russia.'

'But surely, they're now allied to Germany… to fight one is to fight the other,' countered the young woman firmly.

'Well, yes. But of course, that's just an alliance of convenience, isn't it?' Brandt argued persuasively. 'No one in the States thinks that will last long once Hitler knocks out Britain.'

Abigail Stevenson looked startled by this assertion. 'You really think that will happen, Joe?'

He put down his wine glass, looked her in the eye and said in his most sincere voice. 'It's inevitable, Abby. Dunkirk was a disaster, whatever your Prime Minister says, and you surely cannot hold out for long. My employers are concerned about the threat of invasion here. They want me home. And, by the way, many at home think that an invasion here would be no bad thing.'

The young woman's expression shifted from shocked to distraught. 'Oh no, Joe!' she cried, her eyes filling up with tears. 'Please don't say that. Don't say you're going back to America.'

'Hey! Sweetheart,' he said consolingly, 'no one's going anywhere just yet.' With this reassurance, Stevenson calmed down and looked at Brandt with a quizzical expression. 'You said that a lot of people in America wouldn't be worried by a German invasion of Britain?'

While she was now taking his bait, he answered cautiously. 'That's right. Don't forget that there are a great many people of German extraction in the USA. They don't see this as their fight at all and if they did, a lot of them would support Germany. I've spent some time among the members of the German American Bund. You should've seen their rally last year at Madison Square Garden. There must've been twenty thousand there, uniforms, swastikas, the lot.'

The young woman's eyes widened, as he continued, 'It's also true that most Americans see Stalin, not Hitler, as the real threat to the world. No, Abby, honestly, it's not as simple as just supporting poor, little Britain.' He knew instinctively that this was the moment to reel in his fish. 'You know, I've been speaking with some folks here who are frankly against what they see as Churchill's pointless war making. I just wish I could meet more. There's a great story there for the readers back home.' Disappointed by her blank expression, he decided to make a strategic retreat, changing the subject deftly. 'But, hey! We've talked enough about that kinda stuff for one evening… what say we have dessert and then decide what to do next?' Abigail Stevenson smiled with relief and nodded.

***

David Bernstein had had enough of waiting outside the Dorchester. No amount of famous people entering and leaving what had become one of the most stylish and popular luxury hotels in London could compensate for his discomfort and boredom. Just as he was trying to get the circulation in his left leg moving again, he saw Stevenson emerge with the tall stranger. Before he could move to get a closer look, they had leapt into an obviously pre-ordered taxi and sped off towards Marble Arch. Alone, he couldn't continue the surveillance, but he felt the hairs on the back of his neck telling him that there was at least a chance that he had finally found his 'A.'

***

Within a few minutes they were standing outside Stevenson's home. She had clearly made up her mind that she did not want the evening to end with a chaste kiss on the pavement and, having unlocked the door, she led him upstairs to her flat. Once inside, Brandt fell on her, showering her with kisses and hastily beginning to undress her. 'Come, my darling. We'll be more comfortable in here,' she whispered as she led him into her bedroom. She was self-evidently not an experienced nor, Brandt reflected ruefully afterwards, a particularly skilful lover. Though he readily conceded that she was a very pretty girl and had a firm young body. Long after they had made love, as Stevenson snoozed contentedly on his chest, Brandt lay staring at the darkness above his head. He reached carefully for his jacket, which had been thrown carelessly on the floor next to the bed, found his cigarettes and lighter and lay back, enjoying the nicotine. The evening had gone well, their relationship was developing nicely and he would very soon be in a position to get much more of the information he wanted out of her. He was more and more certain that, from the date of his expulsion, something had not been right with Rösel's networks. The British were obviously not aware of the informers, otherwise they would have already been arrested. But he couldn't rid himself of the belief that someone was still running the networks. *But who? Not a German... so who?* He burned with the desire to solve this puzzle and knew that this had to be his priority.

CHAPTER TWENTY EIGHT

Tuesday 3rd September 1940, London.

'You off to see the show in the sky?' asked the grinning ticket inspector at the entrance to the platform at Charing Cross. 'Our boys are giving Goering's lot a right bashing, you mark my words.' Brandt mumbled a quick, 'Sure am,' in response, but looked with barely disguised disdain at the eager face of the weakling in the uniform. He had deliberately planned to arrive at the station just as his train was departing and had to run to catch it as it heaved itself into motion. He immediately leaned out of the window to verify that he had been the last person to pass through ticket control and then found an empty compartment. Having selected a window seat, he carelessly threw his case onto the luggage rack above his head before making himself comfortable. There were still many commercial travellers or, more prosaically, door to door salesmen operating in Britain and a case full of junk gave him a good pretext for his trip to meet Martha Perrygo. Once the train began to steam out of the station, however, he began to review the events of the weekend and what they signified.

He had spent much of the bank holiday weekend playing the part of Stevenson's lover. While she certainly did not possess the skills of Emma de Jongh, he had found her innocence and classic Englishness something of a thrill. With a sense of superiority, he reflected that this was similar, though not as distasteful, as the way that many of the most fervent SS officers enjoyed taking their pleasure with young Jews. He had, of course, asked her about previous male friends and she had thought about this for a few seconds before replying earnestly. 'No, not really. There is no one special. There is someone who I thought I was interested in. But that was before I met you. I knew really that it could never have been. Whereas with you, I knew right away.' *Could this person still be a complication?* Brandt wondered as he gazed out of the train window. *Hopefully not. But I know what to do if necessary.*

As the train steamed away from Bromley, Brandt groaned as the door to the corridor was pulled open and four people entered, including a young, bespectacled schoolboy who was clearly excited that the train would pass fairly close to RAF Fighter Command's strategically important base at Biggin Hill. Sliding across the bench seat to sit by the window and face Brandt, he was beside himself with excitement. 'Do you think we'll see some Spitfires, mummy?' he shouted to a harassed looking woman. 'Oh, I do hope we will. And I hope they shoot all those nasty Germans down out of the sky.' Brandt offered a pained smile as, using a crudely made wooden model of a Spitfire to wave around the 'sky' in the compartment, he began to enact imaginary dogfights which, to Brandt's extreme irritation, the British pilots always won.

Thinking again about his weekend with Stevenson, he recalled his huge excitement when, as they were walking in Regents Park on the Sunday afternoon, she had suddenly said, 'Joe... You know you were talking the other day about people who are not so keen on Churchill. Well, I'm not so keen on him myself.'

'Come on, Abby,' he had replied lightly. 'You know that you don't have to say things like that to make me keen on you.' He had squeezed her hand and, releasing it suddenly, had jogged away from the path onto the grass. He was rather pleased with himself as this had seemed to be a purely spontaneous action. But of course, he had wanted some privacy for what she might have said next.

'No, no really, Joe,' she had insisted, panting to catch up with him, inhibited as she was by the flowing skirts of her bright summer frock. 'If I told you what I had been doing, you'd never believe me in a month of Sundays. No one would.' Brandt had pulled her down onto the warm lush grass, sensing that this was the moment that she would confess to having been Rösel's informant. His sweet anticipation, however, had dissolved into pure fury as she had then said quickly, 'But not now, Joe. Not now. I've said too much. Let's leave it.'

Despising himself for sinking so low, he had tried wheedling, 'Come on, Abby. You can't leave it like that. That's not fair.'

She had made up her mind, however, and closed the subject firmly for the day. 'No, Joe. I'm not ready to say anything more just yet. But I will soon, I promise.' *Idiotic bitch!* he had fumed, *I should strangle you here and now!*

The train arrived punctually in Sevenoaks and, hat pulled down over his face and dressed in an appropriately shabby suit, he reached Martha Perrygo's house after fifteen minutes of brisk walking. The street was deserted as he strode purposefully up to the front door and knocked. After what seemed like an eternity, he heard a shuffling, followed by a key turning and the door opened slightly to reveal the craggy face of Martha Perrygo. She quickly, if totally erroneously, summed up Brandt and barked, 'No hawkers here! Did you not see the sign attached to my front gate? Now be gone with you before I summon the police.'

Brandt could see that he had taken her by surprise and stood his ground, smiling sardonically. 'I'm no door to door salesman, Mrs Perrygo,' he announced confidently, 'In fact, I bring greetings to you from one of your dear friends. Parsifal. I know that you've not seen him since the early summer of last year, but I can assure you that he is in fine health back in his home town of Berlin.' Brandt was gratified to see both the shock register on Perrygo's face and her slight backward stagger. 'May I be of assistance,' he smirked as she reached out to the door frame for support. 'Perhaps you're feeling faint?'

'I… I… I don't know anyone of that name,' Perrygo gasped unconvincingly. 'Now, please, I would like you to leave before I call a constable.'

Brandt merely chuckled at this empty threat, 'Come now, Martha. We're friends here. How can I convince you of my bona fides? Let me think… yes, I know…' He then offered Martha Perrygo sufficient details of her meetings with Rösel and, more importantly, information she had given which only her controller could have known. He was not surprised to see her expression change from suspicion and hostility to incredulity.

'For heaven's sake be quiet, man,' she hissed. 'Do you want to get us both arrested? Careless talk costs lives and I don't want mine to be one of them.' With this admonishment, she hurried Brandt into the hallway and, with a final look to ensure that no one had witnessed the exchange, she firmly closed the door. As she ushered him into a rear facing room, Brandt immediately detected the unpleasant odour of cat and he made a mental note not to forget its presence. From there, he could see a doorway into the small kitchen, with a back door opening onto a small, walled garden which had a high gate at the rear.

'Who on earth are you and what are you doing here? How did you find me?' she demanded, suspicion returning to her flushed and perspiring face.

'It's quite simple, Martha,' he said, as if to reassure a frightened child. 'May I call you Martha? Good. Now, as I was saying, Parsifal and his friends in Berlin wanted to contact you. You must be aware that an invasion is imminent. We need all the help we can get from our loyal friends.'

'Of course, I understand, Mr....?' she asked pointedly.

'Just call me Joe for now', he replied smoothly.

'Very well, Joe,' she continued, 'I've been gathering all kinds of information from my informants over the last weeks and months, some of which would be very useful to our forces when they arrive. 'Here,' she went to a florid looking Gainsborough print on the wall and lifted it off its hook, revealing a small door set into the wall. She then took a key from her pocket, unlocked the door and lifted out a thick folder, whispering, 'I know it's not strictly allowed. But I saw no harm in keeping copies of all the information that I've passed on, as well as the details of those who provided it. It's been perfectly safe here and I wanted some kind of insurance for when our troops liberate Britain from Churchill and his warmongers.' Brandt's eyes lit up at this treasure trove, but he sensed there was more to come from the old hag. 'I mean, those Abwehr identity cards we got are useful. But there's nothing like a dossier of proof to demonstrate my loyalties.'

'Naturally,' purred Brandt, 'A very sensible precaution, if I may say so. I can see why Parsifal was so impressed with you.' As Perrygo preened in self- congratulation, Brandt's mind raced to make sense of what he had heard. *Could it really be that the Abwehr is still running this network? But Schellenberg had insisted that was not the case. So, what the hell's going on here? There's something fishy for sure.*

Perrygo's voice finally broke into his thoughts with a stunning revelation, 'I believe you are who you say you are Joe. But surely you must know Lazarus? After all, he was sent out to replace Parisfal. I've been giving him information for more than a year now. I've been doing the right thing, haven't I?'

'Of course you have, Martha,' he replied reassuringly. 'I should explain that I am a member of the SS, whereas Lazarus is obviously a member of the Abwehr. I know it sounds crazy, but sometimes we are so hell bent on secrecy that we each don't know what the other is doing.' Brandt attempted a philosophical laugh, before promising her, 'I'll contact Berlin as soon as possible in order to get this confusion cleared up. After all, preparing for the invasion is all that matters now.'

'Yes, you're right, Joe,' agreed Perrygo readily. 'But this has all been a bit of a shock… would you like a cup of tea?'

Brandt almost burst out laughing at her absurdly English solution for any problem or crisis … *a damned cup of tea!* He was, however, glad to accept the offer, as she would be busy for a couple of minutes, affording him time, which he desperately needed to collect his chaotic thoughts.

In many ways things could not have gone better, *I've got all the recent information gathered by Perrygo and her network as well as the names and addresses of all her informers. But who the hell is Lazarus? He can't be an Abwehr agent. But what else can he be? I'll have to check with Berlin, but I'm getting more and more suspicious of Rösel's networks.* Finally, he decided that he must take personal control of Perrygo's informers and that, apart from any more information on Lazarus, she had outlived her usefulness.

When she returned with a tray set for tea, Brandt detected a certain suspicion in her eyes. *I'd better get this over with quickly*, he resolved. 'It's really urgent that I get in touch with Lazarus as soon as possible. Of course, I can do this via Berlin, but, if you have a method of communicating with him that would save me a great deal of time. It would help us to sort this out faster.'

As she poured the tea, Perrygo did not look him in the eye but answered regretfully, 'Yes, Joe. I can see that would help. But, unfortunately, Lazarus always contacts us. We don't have a means to communicate directly with him. Security, I imagine.'

She's a tough old bird, thought Brandt, admiring the credible manner in which she had finally looked at him and smiled sadly as she reached her inevitable conclusion. He, of course, was aware that Rösel's informants could get in touch via a post office box number. *She's clearly suspicious, or she's playing a game of her own. Either way, I think I have everything I'm going to get out of her. Time to wrap things up here.*

The sense of this decision was immediately confirmed when Perrygo asked him to return her dossier. 'I must keep it in my safe as proof of my support of Germany. I do hope you understand.'

'Of course, Martha,' he replied agreeably, handing it back across the table. 'And while we're at it, you might as well have a couple of my samples which I've brought here as part of my cover.'

The middle-aged woman smiled uncertainly, 'Oh no. That's not necessary.' Brandt ignored her and carefully opened his suitcase, took out a British service issue Webley revolver and pointed it directly at her head. Perrygo simply nodded her head in quiet resignation as he took a silk scarf which he stuffed into her mouth. He then took some simple handcuffs to fasten her hands behind her back, while he used rope to tie her feet by the ankles. He then replaced the cuffs with more rope before he closed the curtains of the room. He had already noticed a wooden clothes dryer suspended from the ceiling by two strong hooks. Working silently and methodically, he took a coil of much thicker rope which he fastened around one of the hooks. Perrygo's eyes swivelled in terror and she involuntarily gagged as she realised what he had planned for her. She began to struggle madly, trying to free her hands and feet, but he had fastened the rope expertly. It neither gave an inch, nor tightened, so as to avoid leaving tell-tale marks on her ankles and wrists. Recognising the inevitable, she finally slumped back in resigned defeat. Brandt had now almost finished his preparations and, having placed the noose round her neck, he hauled her up onto a dining chair and pulled the rope tight. 'Just so you know, Martha,' he spoke almost kindly, 'I don't know what has been going on here, but I have told you the truth. I am a genuine SS agent.' With that, he expertly cut the ties on her wrists and ankles and removed the scarf from her mouth, while simultaneously kicking away the chair. 'No... I can hel....' were the last sounds uttered by Martha Perrygo as she dangled and twitched violently at the end of the rope. Brandt sat back in the armchair, poured himself another cup of tea and enjoyed watching the life drain out of her.

Once he was absolutely certain that she was dead, he washed and dried the tea cups and saucers and placed the handcuffs, rope, ties, scarf, revolver and dossier in the hidden compartment at the bottom of his case. He then locked the safe and replaced the painting and put the safe key back into her pocket, as her body swung grotesquely in death. He had previously locked the cat upstairs and, just as the light had faded completely from the day, he opened the door to allow it back into the room. He then silently sneaked out of the back door, leaving it unlocked, and made his way under cover of darkness into the alleyway and away from the scene of his handiwork.

Once seated in a second-class compartment of a train to London, he planned his next steps. *I'll have to contact Berlin to check out this Lazarus. But I wonder, could he be the man that Abigail Stevenson was talking about? The other man? If so, she may well be my best route to him.*

CHAPTER TWENTY NINE

Saturday 7th September 1940, Tower of London.

Abigail Stevenson, a hopeful expression on her pretty face, squinted into the distance towards the unmistakable shape of Tower Bridge. For one bizarre moment, she wondered whether she was looking for a sign, such as departing ravens, to help her divine the future. With a slight, almost imperceptible shake of the head, she realised how ridiculously out of character that would be, for she had never been a superstitious person. In fact, her rationality had marked her out among her female contemporaries. Whenever she had a problem to solve, she typically found the perseverance and mental capacity required to reach a solution, often when this seemed impossible. As a young girl, she had loved sitting with her father trying to solve the crossword puzzle or a brain teaser in the daily newspaper. That was long ago, however, her father having taken his own life after being held responsible for a terrible mistake at the Treasury. He had been a mid-ranking clerk and had been blamed for the leaking of market sensitive information immediately before the Budget of 1931, even though the police never found firm evidence to point to his involvement. Everyone had said after his death that a more reliable and hardworking colleague could not be found. But the most senior civil servants in the Treasury had hushed the leak up by implicitly blaming an innocent man.

It was some years after his death that Abigail, looking for a sense of purpose, had turned to fringe movements that worked against the British Government. Rightly or wrongly, she firmly held the amorphous British Establishment to be responsible for her father's suicide. It was through such involvement that she had been introduced to Parsifal and had begun her secret life as an informer for Germany. Parsifal had initially seemed so urbane and charming and what she was doing had given her a sense of repaying something for the injustice served on her father. But that had been in peacetime. Now Britain was at war with Germany, and especially since the start of the Blitz, she was having doubts about carrying on. Of course, she had also met and fallen in love with the lovely American reporter and for the first time since her father's suicide, she had begun to look forward to the future with eager anticipation.

She had been summoned to one of her regular briefings with Lazarus who she liked very much. *He has such a calm and gentle manner, especially for a German,* she had often thought, *and his face somehow looks much younger than his general appearance suggests. If only he would get rid of that hideous moustache.*

She spent a pleasant half hour strolling with him around the perimeter of the Tower of London, watching the gardeners tend the vegetable patches that had been planted in its moat. They discussed the likelihood of an invasion and what appeared to be the success of RAF Fighter Command in preventing the Luftwaffe from destroying its defensive capability. *I can't really explain it,* she recognised, *but neither of us seemed so disappointed at the failure of Goering's numerically superior air force.*

Although he was scarcely an expert in the interpretation of the moods of women, throughout their meeting King could not help but notice that her manner had once more changed... *perhaps happy is the best way to describe it*, he decided. *She's smiling a lot more and seems more open and confident. Odd, given the current situation here.* She had dressed in vibrant summer colours which accentuated the blondness of her hair and her feminine figure. 'You seem happy, Abigail… has something changed?' he asked her naturally. 'You seem full of the joys of life.'

She immediately blushed and looked away. 'It's nothing, Lazarus, really,' she said, rather too quickly and too firmly.

'Have you met someone?' enquired King, playing a hunch. He hoped that he was right, because Abigail had always seemed such a serious and lonely young woman. Needy even, and he was very taken with this new version which seemed in contrast so full of life and playfulness. Yet, at the same time he could hear Professor Pym's warning voice in his ear. 'You can't afford to react as you would normally, John. You must think how an agent would think and act accordingly.'

'That would be telling,' she replied pertly. 'Why? Isn't it allowed?'

'Of course. I can't stop you,' reasoned King with a half-smile. 'But you should be very careful, Abigail. In our line of work, relationships with the wrong person could be very dangerous.'

'Don't worry,' she reassured him, 'I'm in control. But now, I really must be going. I'll be in touch.' Having offered him a beaming farewell smile, she began to walk hastily towards the City of London, her hair streaming out behind her in the sunlight.

As he stood staring down river towards the labyrinth of docks which comprised the huge port of London, he could see formations of dark specks in the distant sky. *What on earth are they?* he wondered, only to be answered by the loud drone of the air raid sirens. The evident size of the raid surprised him as, since the fall of France, the major targets had been the airfields of Fighter Command, far to the south of the city. Transfixed, he stared at the huge formations approaching the capital, the sound of their engines increasing as they grew nearer. Within a few minutes, the first bombers were clearly visible, twin engine Heinkels with their unmistakable black cross markings. They had already started to deposit their deadly cargo over the dockland area and both the sounds of explosions and the dreaded palls of dark, heavy smoke began to fill the air. A new wave of the monstrous planes was approaching the target zone every two minutes, such was the ferocity of the attack.

By now, it was clear that the docks and the East End of the city were the principal targets and he could hear the frantic clang of fire engines, as they rushed to deal with the worst of the fires. The anti-aircraft defences had also opened up, making a ferocious counterpoint to the sounds of the aircraft engines and the all too frequent blasts caused by the bombs. He had no idea exactly how many aircraft were taking part in the raid, but estimated their number in the hundreds, rather than dozens. The spectacle was to go on for almost two hours, before an end to the incoming waves of bombers offered some brief respite to the emergency services.

Without making a conscious decision, King began walking quickly northwards away from the river, towards Whitechapel and the East End, with its densely packed working people's housing. His suspicion was soon confirmed that this area was bearing the brunt of Goering's first major daytime raid on the capital. As he walked deeper into the narrow streets, he could feel the heat of the numerous fires which were breaking out across a wide area of East London. He turned a corner into a mean and narrow street and immediately saw that a bomb had exploded, more or less in the centre of a long row of tenements. His first feeling was one of utter fury, a futile, though arguably natural reaction to the bomb's horrible violation of the residential street. He was acutely aware that while it may look desperately poor and deprived, these were people's homes and he felt outraged on their behalf. He was still brimming with anger, when he heard a woman shouting to him. 'Please, can you help? You must help... it's my baby girls. They're both still in there. They're only four and three. They're too young to die...' The woman was pointing frantically at the remaining half of one of the bombed tenements. 'I tried to get them out and to the shelter, but the planes came so quickly. I never heard the sirens and it was too late...' she shrieked. 'They're still in there, on the top floor. There's no one else. Please can you get them out?'

Without pausing to think, King crashed into the fiercely burning building, taking off his jacket which he soaked using the cold water tap in the downstairs kitchen. Holding his new shield in front of his face, he began to run up the stairs. He was hardly aware of the dreadful creaking and cracking noises as parts of the structure of the building began to take the strain and prepare to collapse. Rather, he was only conscious of the desperation he had seen in the terrified mother's eyes. As he moved further up the stairwell, he could see the doors on one side of the landings start to blister as the fire which was raging in the bombed out part of the tenement threatened to break through. One door had been blown open and, as he passed the gaping space, he could see the inferno just a few feet away. For a second he paused, remembering that in a lecture he had attended on what to do in case of bombing, the speaker had said that, on no account should people venture alone into burning buildings. The risk of asphyxiation and even gas explosion was far too great. *Too late to remember that now, old son,* he thought grimly, as he approached what he hoped was the topmost landing of the building. To his enormous relief he could hear, over the pounding of his own heart and the roaring of the fires all around him, the sound of children whimpering. He threw open a smouldering door and was immediately thrown back onto the landing by a blast of hot air. The children, who had had the good sense to hide underneath a sideboard, began to scream in terror. King clambered back to his feet and approached the girls, shouting, 'Come on, darlings. Your mummy's waiting outside for you. She sent me to fetch you. There's nothing to be afraid of, I promise.' The sisters quickly climbed out from under the furniture and rushed to King, who took one up under each of his arms. Having covered their heads as best he could with his still damp jacket, he immediately plunged back down the stairs. Just as he reached the half way point, the upper landing, totally consumed now by fire, started to rain burning wood down onto them. The girls, though terrified, had a child's trust that this man would save them and simply hugged ever closer into his chest. King, however, had been hit by a piece of wood and staggered down the next flight of stairs, almost coming to grief when he reached the landing. His lungs were bursting and the smoke and heat were making him feel increasingly light headed. *One more flight to go*, he desperately urged himself through gritted teeth. *Come on! You can't give up now!* His jacket was smouldering, and the muscles in his arms and legs were screaming as he made one last rush down to the ground floor and safety. Once he reached the narrow entrance hallway, now filled with dense black smoke, he flung off the now burning jacket and half ran, half fell through the front door. He didn't see the sudden burst of the press photographer's flash bulb freeze the three of them, covered in ash and dust, but mercifully not seriously injured, as he staggered away from the burning building. Just as he reached a safe distance, the whole front of the tenement collapsed in a cloud of dust, flames and smoke. The woman ran up to King and hugged her two daughters, neither of whom could be prised from his embrace. 'Come on, girls,' croaked King in a voice made rough and hoarse by the choking smoke. 'Here's your mummy.' The two girls finally allowed themselves to be led away from King and were taken up by their now weeping mother. Once the sisters had become calmer and the fire brigade and ambulance crew had arrived, the woman looked around for King, but he had already disappeared.

'Where's that man gone?' she asked an ARP warden desperately. 'The tall one who was covered in ash and dust?'

'He's gone,' replied the warden with distaste. 'I told him that he should have left well alone. Fool that he was going into a building like that. Alone and with no equipment. Shouldn't be allowed.'

'But he saved my girls,' the mother shouted hysterically, as if unable to grasp his attitude . 'Don't you understand? Without him, they would've been killed!'

After a respite of no more than a couple of hours, a second Luftwaffe attack was visited on the burning city. The formations of bombers had little difficulty finding their targets in the failing light, as the East End of London was a mass of flames. Unbeknownst to King, lying in the bath in his flat on Charing Cross Road, this was to be the first of fifty seven consecutive days on which the Luftwaffe would launch attacks on London – the Blitz had begun.

CHAPTER THIRTY

Monday 9th September 1940, Paddington Station, London.

Henry King was relieved finally to settle himself into the first-class compartment of the 6.15PM train to Gloucester. His wife had been concerned when the German bombing raids had begun just before her beloved husband was due to make a business trip to the capital. However, like most women of her generation, she recognised that responsibilities had to be fulfilled and she had dropped him off at Gloucester station that morning, not for one moment showing any anxiety.

Henry had completed his legal business and had rung his wife to say that he would be on the early evening train from Paddington. Having stopped only to buy that day's *Evening Standard*, he now turned to read the news of the latest casualty figures and damage suffered in the capital. As he began to leaf quickly through the inside pages which reported more local news, his attention was drawn to a small, but very clear photograph under the headline; *'Unknown Hero Saves the Day.'* He quickly scanned the story, which concerned the rescue of two young sisters from a bombed tenement by a mysterious passer-by who had then simply disappeared. While the story probably engaged most of the newspaper's readers, Henry couldn't take his eyes off the close-up photograph of the tall man, his hair lightened by dust and ash, who was carrying the two young girls out of the burning wreck of the tenement. The photographer had caught him square on as he was moving directly towards the camera and Henry's heart lurched as he frantically reached for his reading glasses to study the photograph more carefully. 'My God', he whispered, 'My God, it's him. I'll swear it's John!' Without taking a second to consider the wisdom of what he was about to do, he rapidly gathered up his possessions and jumped down off the train, just as it had started to move away from the platform.

'Now you didn't ought to be doing that kind of thing, if you forgive me for saying so, sir,' said the Platform Master.

His kindly voice and sympathetic smile disarmed Henry, 'You're absolutely right. I'm sorry. I've just realised there's something very urgent that I need to do.'

He immediately telephoned his wife to let her know that something had come up at the last minute, that he would be staying in London for at least one and possibly two nights and that she was not to worry at all. He had just finished reassuring her that he was fine, when the first wails of the air raid sirens signalled the latest stage of Hitler's attempt to bomb Britain into submission. *That damned little Austrian corporal knows nothing of the British mentality,* Henry thought as he patiently followed the orderly stream of people towards the nearest shelter. He was actually glad of the raid because it gave him time to calm himself and to decide what to do. *I always knew John didn't die on that Swiss mountain. And now I have the proof!* When the all clear sounded at just after 8.00PM, he reached into his briefcase and breathed a sigh of relief as his fingers closed around his small address book. He quickly found a vacant telephone box, looked up the number of Professor Pym and, his hands shaking with tension, phoned the St John's Wood number.

***

A pleasant, relaxing light, produced by stylish art deco standard and table lamps, suffused Pym's elegant flat. Mozart *Divertimenti* were issuing from his gramophone and the academic was sitting in his favourite armchair, pondering the unexpected telephone call that he had just received. Apart from a quick visit the previous Christmas, he had not heard from Henry King since the Summer of 1939, when he had visited him and his wife in their lovely Gloucestershire home. He had informed them that the Swiss authorities had given up the search for their son's remains. 'They say that, in such cases, it's not at all unusual that no trace is ever found,' he had said quietly, but firmly enough to dissuade any objection. He knew from Gerhardt Rösti, the local Swiss mountain guide, that both parents had made a sentimental visit to the place of their son's accident. Afterwards, the Swiss had reported his uneasy feeling that Henry seemed very sceptical about the whole episode. Indeed, Pym had left the family home with the distinct sense that the mother had accepted the loss of her son stoically, but that the father had not entirely believed in the truth of his son's unfortunate walking accident in the snows of the Bernese Oberland.

Pym welcomed his guest, to the sound of yet another bombing raid over the relatively distant East End of London. Henry King politely thanked his host for agreeing to see him at such short notice. 'Not at all, Mr King. It's my pleasure. Though I'm not sure how I can help you,' the Professor responded somewhat cagily. 'But, anyway, do come in and sit down please. Would you take a brandy with me?'

Henry King nodded, before saying brusquely, 'I'll get straight to the point, Pym. Have you seen this?' He exchanged his *Evening Standard*, opened to the page on which the photograph appeared, for a beautiful balloon glass of fine cognac. Pym looked at the newspaper in some bafflement. 'This evening's edition… no, I don't think I've seen it…'

'Just look carefully at the photograph on that page, would you? The man carrying the children.'

Pym picked up his reading glasses and studied the newspaper. Of course, he recognised John King immediately and struggled to suppress his sense of alarm. In order to give himself time to think, he moved the newspaper towards the light, as if to get a better view, before saying in his most academically eccentric way. 'I'm not sure what I'm supposed to be looking at, Mr King. Other than the man shows some similarity to your son, John.'

'Some similarity… some similarity!' Henry King thundered. 'My God, man. You must be able to see, it is John. No question about it!'

A startled Pym tried immediately to pacify his guest. 'Look, Mr King, he does look like John, I agree. But we both know that John, tragically, is dead.'

'I'm disappointed in you, Professor,' replied King scathingly. 'I really thought that you were a man of moral fibre. I understand that you needed to create this fiction of John's death, presumably because he is involved in some kind of secret war-related work. He more or less implied that to me at our last meeting just before he left for Germany. But, come on man. Face facts! The cat's out of the bag now! You might as well tell me the whole story.'

Pym inwardly cursed John King for his naïve failure to accept the rules by which he had to operate as an agent in the field. *What on earth was he thinking? Rushing into that house to rescue those children and, as a direct consequence, causing his own exposure and with it risking the whole operation? Does he still not understand that some casualties are inevitable in war?*

Henry King took advantage of the Professor's silence to interrogate his host further. 'Does it not strike you as odd that this man, injured as he probably was, simply disappeared without trace? Why would he do that, unless he had something to fear from publicity?'

'I can't explain any of this, I'm afraid,' Pym responded firmly. 'But I can assure you that this man is not your son.'

Henry King, his bitterness and fury subsiding, merely sat shaking his head sadly. 'I suppose I should've expected this kind of response from you. You have no children, have you, Pym? You're a sad excuse for a human being. Anyway, thank you at least for listening to me. I will go to the offices of the *Evening Standard* tomorrow to obtain a clear print of the photograph. I shall then run a series of advertisements in the press, asking for information on my son's whereabouts. In the meantime, sir, I will bid you good evening.'

Shocked by Henry King's determination, Pym fumed, *Damn John King! Damn the day I ever thought of him for this mission! What a blunder that was!* As his guest was preparing to leave, Pym cracked. 'All right, Mr King,' he said in a defeated tone. 'You win. I'll tell you what you want to know.'

For the next ten minutes, Pym briefly outlined the deception of his son's death and the reasons for it. 'Of course, you may not say anything of this to anyone,' Pym said firmly, 'Not even, I'm afraid, to your wife. I must insist on that.'

Henry King studied his host with disdain. 'Please do me the courtesy of withdrawing that insistence, Pym. I can assure you that I know my duty and I would do nothing to jeopardise John's safety. Even to the extent of keeping my beloved wife in ignorance.'

The Professor had the good grace to look shamefaced as he realised that he had both totally underestimated Henry King and unfairly cursed his son. *The pressure of this damned war's getting to me,* he told himself. *But I must, at all costs, retain my humanity. If that's lost, what on earth am I fighting for?* In a strange way, he had to admit that it was a relief to have been able to tell the truth to King's father. He could now acknowledge that he had dreaded having to tell him of an actual injury to his son, or even of his death whilst on active service. 'At least you're now fully aware of the risks John is running and of the vital nature of his work. This is, of course, especially the case now that Britain stands alone and in imminent danger of invasion.' Looking at his straight-backed and principled guest, Pym realised that, after the deception of the last year and more, he owed him his best attempt at rebuilding trust. 'It would give me great pleasure, if you would stay here tonight,' he said tentatively. 'I rarely go down to the air raid shelter. If my name's on one of those damned Jerry bombs, then it's on it. But I can show you to the shelter if you prefer.'

Henry King recognised his own ex-serviceman's approach to danger and, despite his lingering annoyance, smiled before replying, 'Yes, Professor, it would be good to see out this raid together.

As the two men settled down with another generous glass of cognac, Pym made a mental note to arrange for the *Evening Standard* to be instructed to destroy all copies of the photograph.

***

It had been another extremely frustrating week for Brandt. Heightened security, introduced in response to the invasion threat, made his Portuguese Embassy contact far more reluctant to meet. This had caused some delay to the response from Berlin to his query about Lazarus. Eventually, however, he was able to forget such irritations when he received definitive news that Lazarus was neither an Abwehr nor any form of German agent.

***

'*Standard*! Get your *Standard* 'ere,' cried the newspaper seller as Abigail Stevenson approached Trafalgar Square underground station on her journey home. She had been badly shaken by the daily and nightly air raids and, as if to confirm her anxiety, the moaning of air raid sirens began again just as she was entering the station. A collective groan rose from the crowds of commuters as they realised that their journey could be significantly delayed. Stevenson, fearing that it might be a long raid, paused at the station entrance to buy a newspaper, before she hurried down to track level. As she moved deeper, she saw that much of the passage and platform space had already been staked out. Blankets, rolled up lengthways, had been placed against the wall and an adult, or older child had been assigned to protect the space earmarked for the later use of the whole family. The noise of exploding bombs had not penetrated down to platform level by the time her train rattled into the station. It was full of commuting office staff, their faces tense and grey in the artificial light.

'Looks like Jerry's having another go at us tonight, eh my dear?' said a middle-aged man in a bowler hat. Gallantly, he felt that it was his duty to protect the attractive young woman from the worst of the crush behind him. She smiled in thanks at his ruddy, well- meaning face and he took this as encouragement to advise her. 'Don't worry. We're too far underground to be in any real danger. Try to think of something nice to take your mind off things. I always think about my lovely rose garden at home.'

Suddenly the lights went out, plunging the whole carriage into pitch darkness as the train screeched and swerved. Many of the standing commuters staggered, some even fell and several screamed, either in pain as they were trodden underfoot, or in terror that the train would crash. Gradually the train steadied itself and began to pick up speed towards Maida Vale. She was relieved to leave the train, only to find the platform crowded with people sheltering from the raid. Eventually, she found a tiny space on a set of stairs, where she could wait for the sound of the all clear. Squatting miserably on the cold concrete, she bemoaned how the constant bombing had reduced her chances of meeting Joe. *And I really need him much more now! Still,* she supposed, *he must be very busy reporting The Blitz. I'll just have to be patient.* In truth, however, she was rapidly tiring of her secret role as an informer. It had all seemed so clear at those first meetings of like-minded people before the war. Soviet Russia was the real enemy and Britain could surely have worked with Germany, had it not been for Churchill and his fanatical anti-Hitler stance. But since the Nazi-Soviet Pact and the stories spread by refugees about what life is like for some in Germany, she had begun to have doubts. *I even think Lazarus has concerns too. I can tell by that look he sometimes has in his eyes.* She had been planning to speak to him about stopping, but things became even more complicated with the arrival of Joe Brand, her growing feelings for him and his obviously sympathetic stance on Germany. Giving up on the conundrum of what to do for the best, she searched in her bag for cigarettes. 'Sorry, Miss,' advised a nearby policeman regretfully. 'You can't smoke here, not while there's a raid on... risk of gas explosion. Hope you understand.'

'Of course, officer, I'm sorry. Should have realised,' she replied quickly, relieved that she could hide her embarrassment behind the newspaper which she had quite forgotten about. As soon as she saw the photograph of the dust-covered man carrying the two young girls out of the bombed tenement, she gasped. Before she had even recovered herself, the all clear sounded and she patiently waited her turn to exit the station.

CHAPTER THIRTY ONE

Friday 13th September 1940, Scotland Yard, London.

David Bernstein sighed with frustration as he stared at the pile of paper covering his desk. *This isn't on. I can't deal with all of these. I'd better talk to the Inspector.* It was true that since Dunkirk and the Fall of France, fears of a German invasion of the south coast of Britain had increased enormously. And those fears had led to an exponential rise in reports of 'Fifth Column' activity in London and the South East. From bitter experience, Bernstein knew that almost all of these were misguided, or even maliciously directed at those who didn't quite fit in, who lived alone, who kept themselves to themselves or who had unusual habits. Nevertheless, every one of the reports had to be checked and, given the difficulties of travelling which the now daily bombing raids were causing, the work was taking an increasing amount of his time. Renton had tried to allow him to focus on the pursuit of Lazarus but this new pile of reports suggested that his boss was also fighting a losing battle.

On entering the Inspector's office, he could see immediately that, if anything, Renton's desk was more heavily laden than his own. 'Sit down, David and tell me what progress you're making,' said the Inspector setting aside his smoking pipe.

Bernstein knew immediately what he meant; *he doesn't want to know about all the other reports and cases, he just wants progress in the search for Lazarus.* 'I've kept the woman Stevenson under observation during this week and have identified the man at the Dorchester as Joe Brand. He's an American journalist assigned to provide reports from Britain to his news agency in the United States.'

'Does his story check out?' asked Renton sharply.

'As far as I can make out, yes it does. And, to be honest, he seems a most unlikely Lazarus. After all, would Lazarus appear so publicly with someone who may well be one of his key informers?'

Bitter disappointment clouded the Inspector's face, 'Yes, David. You've a pretty good point there. OK, then let's work on the basis that he isn't our man... what ideas do you have to progress the case?'

'Well, sir,' began Bernstein hesitantly, 'at the moment, she's still the only likely 'A'. No one else seems even a remote possibility. So, I think I should take a look around the woman's flat. Try to pick up some sort of lead.... She always goes out with colleagues after work on Friday, so I thought I'd try it next Friday. Early in the evening.'

Renton looked worried by the suggestion. 'I don't like it, David. What if it goes wrong? It could be very embarrassing.'

'I'm prepared to take that risk, sir,' countered Bernstein. 'I'm pretty good at picking locks and I'll be in and out in a few minutes.' Renton finally agreed that, if no further progress had been made in the case during the next week, he should put his plan into operation.

***

After a tiresome day, during which her colleagues had quizzed her non-stop about her love life, Abigail Stevenson took great satisfaction in being met from work and swept off by her handsome American. It somehow felt perfect that those nosey parkers were now standing in line, mouths agape and eyes flashing with jealousy, as she rushed towards him. On catching sight of Stevenson, Brandt immediately hailed a passing taxi and ordered the driver to take them to her flat. 'We're going out somewhere really special,' he drawled with a glint in his eye. 'So maybe you'd like to go home, freshen up and get changed after work? Not that I think you need it, of course,' he added, while reaching over and pecking her cheek. 'You always look sensational to me.' Stevenson looked down at her functional office wear and sensibly flattish shoes and laughed out loud. 'Though, perhaps,' he teased, 'you may be interested in this...' Brandt indicated the flat cardboard box lying on one of the empty seats and Abigail Stevenson's eyes widened at the name of the couturier emblazed on its upper side. Eagerly anticipating the box's contents, she squeezed Brandt's hand tightly before eagerly returning his kiss.

As soon as they were inside her flat, Brandt's surprise was revealed to be a stylish dress. 'I saw it in the shop window and could only see you wearing it. I hope you don't mind.'

'Don't mind?' she gasped. 'Oh Joe it's beautiful! I can't wait to try it on.' Brandt followed her into the bedroom, picked her up in his arms and carried her to the bed, where he laid her gently down. Once again, he found their lovemaking banal in comparison to his preferred style, but he recognised that this was as much business as pleasure. She, in contrast, lay back on the pillow afterwards with a dreamy, satisfied look on her face. 'You know I was saying the other day, that you wouldn't believe me if I told you some of the things that I'd done, Joe?' she asked with a mixture of excitement and anxiety. Suppressing his eagerness, Brandt merely raised his eyebrows in a quizzical expression. 'Well, now that we love one another, I don't think we should have any secrets. Do you?'

It took all Brandt's self-control not to laugh in her sadly deluded face, but to reply seriously, 'Of course not, honey. You can tell me anything.'

Stevenson settled herself for her confession, 'Well, I have a particular friend who is sympathetic to Germany and we have had lots of discussions on many themes.'

'Really?' responded Brandt in a casual manner far removed from the eager anticipation he actually felt. 'Who is he, and what do you talk about? Remember, Abby, my country is not at war with Germany and I'm interested in reporting all sides of this war to the folks back home.'

Stevenson reached for a cigarette, but he held her hand back, leaning over her so that she was looking him straight in the eye. 'It's OK honey,' he murmured softly. 'Really. It's OK. You can tell me. You know you want to tell someone. So best it's someone like me who has feelings for you.'

This seemed to destroy her final inhibitions and she tearfully explained her recruitment by the agent Parsifal, who she now knew to be a German agent called Rösel. She went on to describe passing information to him, his expulsion from Britain and then his replacement by a new German Abwehr agent known only by the codename Lazarus.

Brandt's heart was pounding now. He was so close to being able to confront this imposter that he could almost feel him trapped in the sights of his gun. 'It's OK Abby, I understand,' he said earnestly, 'I think what you've been doing is very brave.'

She laughed harshly as she replied, 'Not half as brave as him... just look at this.' She handed him the copy of the *Evening Standard* containing the photograph of King.

'What's this, Abby?' asked Brandt in genuine confusion. 'What am I looking at here?' She sat back and smiled like the cat with the cream. Finally, after what for Brandt was an excruciating pause, she explained very slowly. 'That's him, Joe. That's Lazarus. Right there. The man carrying those girls. I couldn't believe it when I saw him...'

Brandt squinted at the photograph in the subdued light, but could not see the man's face clearly. 'Would you mind switching on your bedside light? I can't really make him out.' As soon as the light had improved, he could see the man's features quite clearly and was immediately struck by a sense of familiarity. *Do I know this man? Have I seen him somewhere?*

'He's so brave and good, Joe... I think you'll like him,' said Stevenson in gushing admiration.

Her fawning attitude towards the man hit him like a thunderbolt, as bitter memories of similar reactions from young women to an Englishman who was once his best friend came flooding back. *King!* he thought savagely. *But surely, he's dead. Killed in a walking accident in Switzerland?* Suddenly, the scales fell from his eyes and he could see the whole incredible deception. *Lazarus*, he thought dismissively, *How fucking typical of him to choose such a codename.* His mind whirring wildly now, he recalled, *Wait a minute. His body was never found, was it? How damned convenient and how typical of the Swiss to help fake his death.* He could see clearly how King had replaced Rösel and had run the expelled agent's networks since mid-1939. *That's why we never got any reports after that time and why none of them tried to get in touch with us. They use him as a bogus Abwehr agent to harvest this intelligence, which the informers think is going to Germany. But all the time it's helping British Intelligence to identify risks to national security. Damned clever!*

'Joe, Joe, are you all right?'

He suddenly became aware of the woman's concerned voice, interfering with his train of thought. *Damn her!* 'What? Oh yes, Abby, I'm fine thanks,' he answered reassuringly, though cold fury filled his eyes.

'You seem disturbed by something, darling. Are you sure you're OK? Have I upset you?' she persisted, much to his irritation.

'Yes, honestly. I'm fine. I suppose I was just thinking what a heroic man Lazarus must be, to risk his life and his anonymity to save two children from the country he is fighting against.' Speaking these words almost made

Brandt retch, but he realised that he couldn't arouse any suspicions in her. *She's my only route to King!*

'You're right, he is,' said Stevenson dreamily, stoking Brandt's anger even more.

'Then I'd dearly love to meet him. Would that be possible?' asked Brandt eagerly. 'I'm sure my readers would be really interested in his story and, of course, I'd reveal nothing that could allow the British authorities to identify him. What do you say, honey?'

Stevenson looked genuinely torn; on the one hand, she would have liked Lazarus to gain some recognition for the heroic man he undoubtedly was and, of course, she would like to please Joe. But on the other hand, even to her naïve mind, it all seemed rather unlikely. An American writing a story about a German agent operating in London, saving British children. 'I'm not so sure, Joe. It's difficult.'

'OK, darling, forget it,' he responded quickly and sharply. 'If I'm not to be trusted, then that's fine. We won't mention it again.'

'No, you're right, Joe. Of course, I trust you. How could you suggest that I don't?' she said miserably. 'And it's only right that the people in America get an accurate picture of both sides in this war. It's just that, ever since meeting you I've been thinking that I want to stop giving him information.' She was speaking very quickly, as if she wanted to get all this said before she had the chance to change her mind. 'In fact, I almost told him the last time we met. But now that we've fallen in love with one another, I realise I must tell him. Since the war started and after

Dunkirk and now all this bombing, it's all so horribly real. I just don't want to go on. What do you think, Joe, darling?'

While Brandt was repulsed by such self-serving, weak drivel, especially that nonsense about them being in love, he realised that he could now get her to do whatever he wished. 'I think you're right, sweetheart,' he said, smiling in anticipation of his own imminent triumph over his old enemy. 'But I want to be there when you tell him. Just in case he tries anything on with you.' Abigail snorted with derision as she rejected that possibility out of hand, to which Brandt declared that he would never forgive himself if anything were to happen to her. Relishing the supreme irony, he emphasised, 'after all, this guy is a German spy. He could be dangerous.' Interpreting his motives as those of love and concern, Stevenson agreed to request a meeting with Lazarus and promised that he would be present.

'OK, Abby. That's a deal!' said Brandt, a gleam of triumph, rather than the love which Stevenson saw in his eyes. 'Now. Shall we stay in bed, or would you like to put on that new dress I bought and come dine at the Ritz?' He was gratified to see her eyes widen in excitement, before she replied with uncharacteristic suggestiveness. 'But, Joe. Why can't we do both?'

***

Monday 16th September 1940, London.

King was doubly surprised. First, Abigail Stevenson had requested a meeting just one week after they had last seen one another. *That's not like her at all,* he reflected. *And I wonder what she means about 'discussing a very urgent issue?* Intrigued, he decided he should discuss it first with Pym, so offered her a meeting at 8.15PM on Tuesday 24th at the Bandstand on Hampstead Heath.

CHAPTER THIRTY TWO

Friday 20th September 1940, London.

After receiving confirmation of her meeting with Lazarus, Abigail Stevenson had barely been able to contain her excitement. *Joe's bound to be delighted*, she told herself as she sat at her old dining table eating breakfast. *It's bound to make our love even stronger!* She did, however, have mixed emotions about telling Lazarus that she would provide no more information. *The problem is I like him. He's nothing like that odious Parsifal. Ugh! What a revolting man he was, with his suggestive comments and leering. But Lazarus is obviously very intelligent. He's kind and sensitive too.* Her thoughts turned briefly to some of her highly intelligent colleagues at the Foreign Office and their almost complete lack of social competence or grace. *Yes, Lazarus is different. He's handsome, but not at all aware of it. Not like those strutting, arrogant peacocks at work.* For a short time, she reflected with embarrassment, she had even had vague hopes that her relationship with Lazarus might have developed into something altogether more personal. *But,* she sighed, *he was far too professional for anything like that. No, I'll be quite sorry never to see Lazarus again, but my life is so different and so much better now with Joe.*

In a total daydream, she pondered how considerate and charming, yet at the same time how strong and assertive Joe is. She knew that it was highly likely that she did not fully satisfy him in bed. *But*, she told herself without embarrassment, *I can be a quick learner. I can't wait to see him after work and to tell him that he has his chance for a scoop with Lazarus.*

As her mind went racing on in a whirl of romance, fine dining, dancing and lovemaking, she completely lost track of the time. Finally realising that she would be late for work and have to suffer a severe telling off by her miserable manager, she left the remains of her toast and put on her lightweight coat. Carelessly, she grabbed her handbag from the sofa and, smiling broadly because today of all days not even Mrs Tripe's ill humour could affect her happy mood, she rushed towards the door. She didn't notice that her handbag was unfastened and that, as she snatched it up, a small blue book fell to the floor and skittered away under her old sideboard.

***

David Bernstein's week had been wasted, responding to preposterous reports of 'Fifth Column' activity in and around London. Neither had he made any progress in the Lazarus case and so was due to break into Stevenson's flat that evening. His deep, dark eyes focused on the set of thin metal hooks that he would use to pick the lock. One of his grandfathers, a skilful locksmith back in Heidelberg, had taught him this skill. 'You never know when it may come in handy, my boy,' he had chuckled with a mischievous glint in his eye. *Good job my mama never found out,* Bernstein thought as he remembered his happy early childhood.

He went over his plan again. He would make his entry in the early evening, when Stevenson would be enjoying an after work drink with her colleagues or a night out with the American journalist. He reasoned that most of the other tenants would either still be returning from work, or would be preparing or eating their dinner. At half past five, he left Scotland Yard in Special Branch's own 'Black Cab' which parked in a side street near the Foreign Office. 'You wait here while I have a quick look at what's going on,' he said to the paunchy young officer who was his driver. The man looked bleary eyed and not fully alert, but Inspector Renton had assured him that this man was 'the best in the business' at tailing other vehicles. Bernstein immediately recognised the tall American journalist lounging by the entrance, carrying a large bouquet of flowers and with a taxi awaiting his instructions. Since getting his first real view of the man, Bernstein had experienced a niggling doubt about him. But his identity had checked out and he'd decided that it must be his imagination. He dodged back into the side street and updated his driver. 'It looks like our girl's going to be leaving in a taxi with her American boyfriend. Keep your engine running and I'll keep an eye on things. When I see her emerge and they get in the taxi, I'll jump in and we can follow them. The job's off if they go back to her place.' The driver silently nodded and went back to reading his *Daily Mirror*. As Bernstein waited for the woman to emerge, he prayed that the Luftwaffe's daily raid would not arrive in the next hour. That would make following their taxi virtually impossible.

***

After her wretched day at work, Abigail Stevenson was more than normally delighted to see Joe Brand waiting for her with a bunch of flowers and a taxi. She had been severely told off for lateness by that old trout Mrs Tripe and had been picked on the whole day. And there was also her diary. As soon as she had got on the tube to work, she had realised that it was not in her handbag. She was not overly concerned, as she had noticed that her handbag was open just as she left her flat. She had immediately closed it, so, she reasoned, it must still be somewhere in there. A thrill of excitement sped down her spine, almost making her shiver despite the warm evening, as she left her colleagues and ran into the waiting arms of Brandt. 'Oh Joe, thanks for picking me up,' she gushed. 'I've had a beast of a day. But it already feels much better.' Brandt made sure to give her a lingering kiss for the benefit of her co-workers, before ushering her carefully into the taxi and giving the driver his instructions. 'I've got such a lot to tell you, Joe,' she gabbled. 'I think you'll be very happy. You'll never guess...'

'Let's talk about that later, honey,' said Brandt firmly, 'we've all evening and we'll be there in a minute.' Slightly deflated by her lover's manner, Stevenson gazed at the flowers, before saying happily, 'Oh, Joe, they're beautiful. Thank you. But where are we going?' Brandt leaned across to kiss her and murmured, 'I thought we'd have an early dinner and go straight back to your place.'

***

Bernstein readily admitted that Renton was correct about this driver; he had kept the American's taxi in sight all the way to the small restaurant, without ever running the risk of being spotted. It really was driving of the highest skill. Smiling, he tapped the driver on the shoulder. 'Thanks, it looks like they'll be in there a while. Can you take me to Stevenson's flat and then I won't need you any more.'

'But I'm scheduled to be on duty till 2am...' the man protested.

'Don't worry about that. You'll still get paid,' Bernstein reassured him. 'We can say you were on call for me.'

'Thanks, guv,' the man replied happily, already clear in his mind what he would do with the rest of the evening.

Bernstein had come prepared to force an entry through the front door of the building. He knew how to do this without leaving a trace and he had just arrived at the steps leading up to the front door, when a young couple, totally engrossed in one another, was emerging. He quickly reached the door before it closed and, with a muffled 'Thanks', went unchallenged into the bright and tidy hallway. From there he silently ascended the stairs until he reached her flat. He smiled to himself, as he noted the various aromas of cooking and the music, audible from the flat opposite Stevenson's. He rapidly took out his tools and, using them deftly to avoid leaving any tell-tale scratches, had gained entrance to the flat in less than a minute.

He removed his shoes, before methodically searching the flat, beginning with the small bedroom. He swiftly looked under the bed and through the wardrobe, taking out any item with pockets and rifling through them. He then turned to the chest of drawers and, having gone through the various underwear, blouses and sweaters, he carefully extracted each drawer in turn and verified that nothing was attached to the underside. Having done the same with the dressing table, he had again turned up a blank. A quick look on top of the wardrobe and behind the chest of drawers and a more thorough check for any loose floorboards and he had basically finished with the bedroom. This left the living room, kitchen and small bathroom. His first thought, as he turned to review the living room, was that Stevenson had left in a hurry that morning. The uneaten toast and half full cup of tea on the table stood in marked contrast to the neat and tidy bedroom. He felt a tingle of hope that perhaps the urgency of her exit may have caused her to make some small mistake that would give him the breakthrough he needed. He looked through the small bookcase, taking out each book for inspection and felt under the cushions of the small sofa and chair. Once again, he checked carefully for any loose floorboards which might conceal a hiding place. The kitchen also yielded nothing and he was about to move into the bathroom, when he realised that he hadn't looked under the sideboard. His heart began to race as he caught sight of the blue book pressed right up against the skirting board. He carefully picked up the book and immediately realised that it was Stevenson's diary. *What a stroke of luck! She must have accidentally dropped it this morning.* Almost laughing at the absurdity of it, he realised that, had she not been late for work, he would in all probability have been wasting his time in searching the flat.

He sat down at the table and began to leaf through the book, back to front so as to see the most recent items first. It wasn't long before he found what he was looking for. In the section for Tuesday 24th September, she had written: **' L. 20.15 H.H. B.S.'** While he was not sure what the last part of the entry meant, he was instantly certain that 'L' referred to Lazarus and that the figures represented the time of the meeting. He swiftly made an exact copy of the note in the diary and then began to review previous entries. Almost all the most recent ones referred to 'Joe', the American journalist. There were also frequent mentions of 'L', followed by a time and abbreviated location. Feverishly, he searched through the address section of the book for anything that might look like contact details for 'L', but found nothing. Satisfied he had gathered all the available information, he carefully replaced the diary in exactly the same spot he had found it, completed his search of the rest of the flat and then quietly exited. *Renton will want to know about this immediately, even if he's sitting in his favourite armchair, puffing that dreadful pipe and with his family all around him listening to the radio.* Bernstein's fresh young face grinned at the prospect of his Inspector's likely response to the catch from his 'fishing expedition'.

***

Brandt's spirits had lifted considerably as soon as the woman had told him about her arrangement to meet King on the coming Tuesday. He had chosen the restaurant well. There were very few diners and no one within earshot, as Stevenson excitedly recounted details of the planned meeting. He smiled broadly in encouragement, though, in truth, he was beginning to find the whole business of romancing this woman increasingly tiresome. *It'll all be worth it*, he reassured himself, *when I've got King in the sights of my pistol.* 'That's great, honey,' he replied, touching her hands across the small, square table. 'I really appreciate it. But you didn't mention anything about me, did you?'

Stevenson looked almost hurt. 'Of course not, Joe! I'm not completely stupid. I told him that I have something very important to discuss with him. I really don't know how he'll react, when he realises that I've brought you to meet him. I must admit that I am concerned about that.'

Her face creased into a worried frown, while Brandt almost laughed out loud. *I can easily imagine how he'll react.* 'That's no problem, Abby,' he answered sincerely, 'I understand he may not want to talk at all. That's fine. Just a chance to pitch the idea to him, that's all I want.'

'I'll be so happy when I'm out of this whole business, Joe. Then we can start our lives together properly,' she said hopefully. 'I was thinking, I may even leave the Foreign Office. Try my hand at something different. After all that's gone on, it wouldn't seem right to me, staying on there.' She looked at Brandt, for all the world like an unhappy child, craving the basic reassurance that everything would be all right.

Brandt knew exactly what she wanted to hear and earnestly replied, 'Of course. It's a big strain on you, honey. And I'm sure you'll be glad when you don't have to see this guy ever again. But let's not make too many big decisions too quickly. You can quit, if you like. But there's plenty of time for that.'

A middle aged waiter, with thinning black hair, slicked back to reveal a narrow, rodent-like face, appeared noiselessly at their table to take their orders. Brandt despatched him fairly quickly to bring a bottle of Chianti and to place the food order with the kitchen. The wine was mediocre, but he was happy enough to delight Stevenson by toasting long life and happiness. In the pause between the starter and the main course, he broached the one question, over which he still had some concerns. 'Hey, Abby,' he began lightly, 'You've told me when you're going to meet Lazarus but not where. In some crowded place, right?'

Stevenson looked pleased with herself, as she replied, 'Not at all, Joe. We'll meet at the Bandstand on Hampstead Heath. It's on Parliament Hill and at that time of the evening it should be deserted. I wouldn't say it's remote, but it's a good spot for a private meeting.'

Brandt's heart leapt at this news. It meant that this whole thing might be resolved with far fewer complications than he had expected. *Fading light, in a remote place,* he eagerly calculated, *I'll surely be able to arrange things to look like she shot King and then turned the gun on herself. I'll have plenty of time to get away and with any luck, the idiotic police will think it's a crime of passion.* However, the doubts soon began to creep into his mind, *But what about the location itself? I've got to see it before Tuesday.* Masking his face with an air of concern, he said, 'I'm not so happy with that, Abby. You being alone with him in a remote place. Do you know where it is?' She nodded, but her face betrayed mounting worry and he quickly made his suggestion. 'Let's take a cab out there, right now, after we've finished here. It'll be near the time of the meeting and we can plan how we're going to play it.' Reaching over to squeeze her hand, he managed to make himself sound extremely concerned. 'You see honey, we don't know how this guy will react when you tell him that you want out.' Emboldened by her evident agreement, he insisted, 'That's settled then. We'll finish up here and then go see how the land lies. Now, let's talk about something else. How'd you like to go away for a weekend?' He knew, of course, that this would never happen, but they were able to excitedly discuss the possibilities until the end of the meal.

The evening, Brandt reflected, was going perfectly, there was even a taxi just outside the restaurant as they came out into the pleasant evening. The driver dropped them at Dartmouth Park, from where it was a short walk onto the heath. The light was beginning to fade as they walked briskly across Parliament Hill and the famous old Bandstand came into view. In her heels, Abigail couldn't keep up with Brandt as he moved swiftly down the pathway. 'Joe! Slow down, please. I can't keep up with you,' she wailed as he forged ahead, totally caught up in the moment. He saw the paths, coming from all directions to meet at the Bandstand, which was a simple, open construction of wrought iron overlooking the sequence of Highgate Ponds. The area around it was relatively clear, only two clumps of bushes, about twice the height of a man, to the north and south west, the nearest about six metres away. Having taken in and assessed the scene, he turned to see a wretched looking Abigail hobbling towards him. 'I'm so sorry, Abby,' he said rushing to help her, 'I just wanted to work out how best we should approach this.' He put his arm around her slim back and under her arms so that he could support her weight.

'Oh, that's better, Joe,' she said with a tight grimace. 'I didn't dress this morning for hiking, you know.' Brandt grinned wolfishly at her, 'Don't worry honey. I'll make it up to you when we get back to the flat. But now, I want you to listen very carefully to me. This is how we're going to play things on Tuesday.'

CHAPTER THIRTY THREE

Saturday 21st September 1940, Scotland Yard, London.

'That was excellent work yesterday, David,' said Inspector Renton with a generous smile. 'But, blast it! Knowing when Stevenson is going to meet Lazarus does us no good, if we don't know where.' They had just spent a couple of fruitless hours trying to decipher the last part of the message and their optimism was beginning to fade.

'We could always try following her,' Bernstein suggested, more in hope than expectation

'I think I'd like to keep that as a last resort,' Renton replied. 'Too many things could go wrong too easily. We lose her in crowds or our man Lazarus runs his own check that she's not being followed, sees us and scarpers. No, we must try to work out where the hell they're meeting.' The Inspector punched his left palm with his right fist in irritation. Not even a good pipe full of his favourite tobacco was easing his growing anxiety that this may be his one chance to catch Lazarus and that the blighter may yet slip through his hands.

'Would you mind nipping down to the canteen and picking us both up a cuppa and a sandwich,' he said. 'Maybe salmon would be good, huh? We could both use a bit of brain food.'

Coming right up, sir,' replied Bernstein as he jumped to his feet and made for the door.

The canteen was a large, airless room in the basement of Scotland Yard, its long refectory style tables rapidly filling up with noisily chattering police officers. As he joined the lunchtime queue, he nodded and acknowledged several waves and friendly greetings. Predictably, salmon was once again off the menu and he settled for two rounds of egg and cheese sandwiches, accompanied by two sizeable pots of tea. His tray being heavily laden with the two lunches, he was grateful that the canteen door was held open for him and he raised his eyes to thank the officer. He immediately recognised his driver from the previous evening and called out over his shoulder as he passed out of the canteen. 'Good Morning! I hope you enjoyed your early finish.'

To his surprise, the officer replied brightly, 'Actually, I didn't finish early after all.'

There was something in the officer's tone of voice that made Bernstein pause. He stopped a police cadet on his way to lunch, thrusting the tray into his hands saying, 'Sorry, mate. Can you hold onto this for me, just for a minute or so? Thanks.' Leaving the hapless young cadet with his tray, Bernstein hurried back into the canteen to catch up with the driver. Touching him gently on the shoulder, he asked, 'Excuse me. Sorry to bother you. But what did you mean that you didn't have an early finish?'

The heavy man led Bernstein away to a relatively quiet corner of the canteen, shouting across the room, 'Sorry, lads. Be with you in a minute. There's just something I have to do first.'

Bernstein came straight to the point, 'Look, all I want to know is why you didn't finish early after you'd dropped me off at the woman's flat yesterday.'

'I know I shouldn't have,' replied the driver, 'but I decided to go and see if I could track our couple after they left that restaurant.' Seeing the look of astonishment cross Bernstein's face, he explained. 'Since being a nipper, I've always wanted to be a detective. As a uniformed plod, I don't get much chance to try myself against the job, so I thought I'd give it a go. But it was basically a waste of time.'

Eager to hear everything now, Bernstein said quickly, 'You mean you didn't see them again? Tell me everything that happened.'

'Oh no!' the driver replied with a shrug. 'As luck would have it, there were no other cabs around when they came out, so I picked them up.'

Bernstein gaped at his beaming face. 'You did what?'

'Yes. But the American simply told me to take them to Holland Park. You know, not far from the edge of Hampstead Heath and I dropped them off there.' Looking somewhat crestfallen, he added, 'I'm afraid that's all there is. As I said, bit of a waste of time.'

The young driver was astonished to see Bernstein's beaming face and hear him laugh out loud as he punched the air before declaring, 'Hampstead Heath! Of bloody course!' He then clapped the confused driver heartily on the back and cried, 'Now you come with me, my lad, and tell all this to Inspector Renton. Don't worry about your lunch. You can have mine. And the Inspector's too, I'll bet.'

Totally bemused and thinking perhaps that what everyone said about Special Branch was true – that they're all a bit mad – he allowed himself to be ushered out of the canteen. Stopping only to pick up the tray from the still bewildered cadet, Bernstein led him quickly to the Inspector's office.

Once the driver had retold his story, Renton's face creased into a huge grin. 'So, you want to get into detective work, eh my boy? Well, you'll do for me! I like such initiative. I'll have a word with your guv'nor and get you transferred over here.'

The driver almost choked on his half of Bernstein's sandwich, 'You really mean it, sir? That would be excellent!'

Renton, all thoughts of lunch now far from his mind, pulled a large map of the area of Holland Park and Hampstead Heath from a desk drawer. As he spread the map out on his desk, he said almost to himself, 'Now. Let's see, the American got you to drop them in Holland Park… so the meeting point is probably in that part of the Heath. Remind me, David. What exactly did the note say?'

Almost as soon as Bernstein had replied, 'the letter 'B', sir,' the driver's face lit up again. 'Begging your pardon, sir, but that's got to be the Bandstand.' Pointing to the map with the last part of his sandwich, he continued rapidly. 'It's just there, on Parliament Hill. I grew up in this area and it was always a favourite meeting place. You know, sir?' His face now glowed bright red as the two Special Branch officers looked at him expectantly. Swallowing his last piece of bread, he muttered, 'Meeting girls and that, sir.'

Renton sat back happily in his chair, his hands clasped behind his head, 'Well, David and?'

'Catesby, sir, Derek Catesby,' replied the driver.

'Well, David and Derek, it looks like we've cracked this message and we owe it all to you, Derek.' After further thanks and congratulations, Catesby was dismissed, with both the order that he keep to himself everything he had heard about the case and the promise from Renton that he would do all in his power to expedite his immediate transfer to Special Branch.

Renton and Bernstein immediately began discussing the implications of what they had learned. They were especially interested in why the American had been involved in reconnoitring the meeting spot. 'I just don't get it sir,' said Bernstein, running his hand through his mop of unruly black hair. 'Unless he plans to go to the meeting as well.'

'But that makes no sense at all, David,' countered Renton firmly. 'Why on earth would Lazarus agree to meet him? It'd be a terrible risk. And why would the woman want him to be there? She is committing treason, after all.'

Bernstein gazed, unseeing, out of the famous round windows of Renton's tower room office. 'Unless, sir,' he suggested, 'Lazarus doesn't know anything about the American.' The Inspector looked sharply at his subordinate who added, 'Let's just suppose that Lazarus thinks that he's meeting only Stevenson. But for some reason, she has involved the American journalist. Maybe the Yank thinks that he'll get a story, she's besotted with him and has offered this to please him. Who knows? Maybe she's scared to meet Lazarus alone in such a place at such a time? Maybe she needs her buddy there to ride shotgun for her? Whatever the reason, I think we must operate on the assumption that Lazarus doesn't know about the American.'

'I see your point, David,' said Renton thoughtfully. 'Right, let's work on that basis. But it does, of course, add a complication. There's something not quite right with all this. It doesn't smell right to me. After all, the American is also taking a great risk, consorting with a German agent and a traitor. She must have told him she's a traitor, mustn't she? Would he really do that?'

'Yes, I see that, sir,' conceded Bernstein. 'But let's not forget that America isn't at war. As a neutral, representing people in a neutral country, he might be interested in the Jerry side of things. But I agree, he's running a tremendous risk and I suspect that there's more to his motivation than we understand.'

'Agreed,' concluded Renton decisively. 'But forewarned is forearmed. And we'll find out on Tuesday what's going on. In the meantime, I suggest we visit the Bandstand this evening to plan our strategy. But we mustn't lose sight of the fact that Stevenson and the American are bit part players. It's Lazarus I want. And I won't be happy unless we get him alive.'

CHAPTER THIRTY FOUR

Monday 23rd September 1940, St James's Park, London.

Is my memory playing tricks? King wondered as he approached the park bench where he was scheduled to meet Professor Pym. *I could swear this is the very place where I agreed to participate in the operation.* Pym arrived shortly afterwards, looking decidedly older and more careworn than he had less than two weeks before, when they had last met. His usually tanned features were pale and drawn, his hair was thinning and he looked like he hadn't recently enjoyed any fresh air and had had little sleep. 'Are you feeling alright, sir?' King asked with concern. 'Only you look a little peaky, if you don't mind me saying.'

Pym sat on the bench with a heavy groan, 'I'm fine, thanks, John. I surely can't complain about a few nights' lost sleep, when one considers what some people are having to put up with. Anyway,' he continued, 'we didn't arrange to meet to talk about me and any piddling problems I may have. I'm afraid I have some bad news for you, John. You remember that you reported that you had tried unsuccessfully to contact Martha Perrygo? Well, I've seen a report from the Sevenoaks police. Apparently, she hanged herself almost three weeks ago.'

King's face drained of all colour. 'I don't believe it!' he protested. 'She was as tough as old boots. She'd never have done such a thing. She'd have seen it as a coward's way out. And Martha Perrygo was certainly no coward. Anyway, why would she do such a thing now, when she was firing on all cylinders, desperate to give us information that she hoped would assist a German invasion?' Shaking his head emphatically, he concluded, 'It just doesn't make sense. There must be another explanation.'

'Yes, John, it worries me too,' agreed Pym, a frown wrinkling his face. 'And that's not all. Apparently, the old biddy who ran the newsagent just around the corner from her house fell down the stairs and broke her neck just a week before the suicide. Coincidence, don't you think?'

King looked even more concerned, 'I should say so, sir. And both are methods of murder which could quite easily be faked as suicide or accident. But who would do such a thing and why?'

'That's exactly it, John,' replied an exasperated Pym, 'I haven't a damn clue. I just know that it's odd. And, until we know what's going on, maybe you should lie low.'

As soon as King mentioned his planned meeting with Abigail Stevenson, Pym asked with genuine concern, 'She asked for it, you say?'

'Yes, sir. She said that she had something very important to discuss with me.'

'And what might that be, do you think?'

King paused before replying, 'I'm not really sure. To be honest, the significance of what she reports has declined over the past couple of months. Obvious, I suppose, as the war develops and other types of information become a priority. The only thing I've come up with is that maybe she wants out of the relationship.'

'What on earth makes you think that?' asked Pym urgently, 'Could she have been approached by a genuine German agent who managed to slip through our net? If so, it changes everything.'

'Well, as you know,' King reminded him, 'I feel that her enthusiasm has declined significantly in recent weeks. I initially put this down to her genuine horror at the fall of France and then the Blitz. But I also wonder if something has changed in her private life. Perhaps she's met someone and that's altered things.'

'Well,' murmured Pym ominously, 'if that's the case, we shall have to consider what we do about Miss Stevenson. We'll have a much clearer idea after Tuesday, but I must say I don't like this at all. Maybe I should ask McNair to keep an eye on you?'

King immediately dismissed the suggestion, 'I've arranged to meet her in a safe place and I don't see her as dangerous. Let me get to the bottom of it all and report back, then we can decide what to do. Now, what do you make of the Luftwaffe's shift in strategy? An attempt to destroy British morale before an invasion, you think?'

'That's the odd thing, John,' Pym replied eagerly. 'Our latest intelligence tells us that the Huns have halted all invasion preparations. They seem to accept that they've achieved neither control of the air nor of the Channel and they won't risk their army in such circumstances. Of course, it's a bit early to be absolutely certain, but we believe the invasion has been postponed, if not cancelled.'

'But that's marvellous news,' King exploded, a great grin spreading across his face. 'This was obviously their big chance. Next year will be very different.' For several minutes, the two men discussed the possible implications of this for the mission, especially that King would have to work hard to maintain the morale of his informants who would face the disappointment of a postponement, or even a cancellation of the expected invasion. They eventually parted to the sound of air raid sirens and with Pym still very uneasy about King's imminent meeting on Hampstead Heath.

***

Bernstein and Renton spent much of the day disagreeing about how to handle the operation. The Inspector was firmly of the opinion that they should act alone. 'We can easily hide in that nearby shrubbery,' he reasoned, 'and the two of us could easily take the German agent by surprise and deal with him.' They discussed again the role the American journalist might play in all this, Renton insisting that he could only be after a scoop for his newspaper syndicate. 'Just think, David,' he argued persuasively, 'How big a hit would a story on 'The War in Britain from a Nazi Agent's Viewpoint' be in many areas of the USA? Don't forget a lot of Yanks are sympathetic to Hitler.' While Bernstein could see the logic of his Inspector's opinion, he sensed that they were misreading the reason for the American's presence. *Something doesn't feel quite right about the whole thing,* he worried. *But I just can't come up with a sound argument to convince the boss.* Correctly interpreting the younger man's uncertainty,

Renton reasoned, 'Look, David, just forget the American. He's a bit part player in all this. Keep your focus on Lazarus. He's the big prize.' The continued doubt on Bernstein's face eventually forced Renton to compromise, 'OK,' he suggested sympathetically, 'I understand your concern, so how about this? We deploy officers at every entrance and exit to the heath, but they move into position only ten minutes after the planned time of the meeting. We want to give Lazarus and the Yank time to show their hand. But if it all goes wrong at the Bandstand, there's a good chance that we'll still get our man. We can alert our boys to move in by police whistle.'

CHAPTER THIRTY FIVE

Tuesday 24th September 1940, London.

   After receiving the Professor's strict instruction to observe King's meeting on Hampstead Heath, McNair had decided to leave nothing to chance. He was aware of the location, but thought it safest to follow his mark all the way from the bookshop. His plan was to watch King enter Hampstead Heath and then quickly work his way around to approach the Bandstand from the opposite direction. He had identified a couple of dense bushes which would screen him while he observed the meeting at close quarters. From there, he could also intervene if necessary. The Professor had been absolutely adamant on that score, 'Take your Webley, Mac and if it looks like things might be going pear shaped, make sure he's unharmed. I don't care about the others.' Like King, McNair had felt that Pym was over reacting, *Surely the woman isn't a real threat,* he reasoned. *But there was something in the Professor's expression....*

   From his position on the opposite side of the road, McNair observed King as he left the bookshop and turned towards the nearest underground station. The Scot was just about to turn the corner out of Charing Cross Road, when a section of scaffolding, erected to enable repairs to a bomb -damaged property, fell onto his head. He was immediately rendered unconscious and King, without ever knowing he should have had one, had lost his protective shadow.

***

Having issued the final instructions to the back-up squads, Renton and Bernstein collected firearms from the official store at Scotland Yard before setting off for Hampstead Heath. A thin mist was gathering as they hid in the bushes near the deserted Bandstand, both men sensing that tingle of excitement that comes at the end of a long pursuit. Twenty-five minutes after they had taken up their stations, Renton tapped Bernstein gently on the arm and indicated the figure of a man approaching the Bandstand. Over six feet tall, dressed in a thin overcoat and wearing a hat over his black hair, the bespectacled and moustachioed man first walked past the Bandstand, before turning back and heading straight for it.

Approaching the agreed meeting point, King felt an involuntary shiver slip down his spine as he remembered turning down the offer of McNair's support. *Relax,* he encouraged himself with a grin, *a bit of mist and you get all in a funk.*

***

'OK now Abby, let's go over it one last time,' whispered Brandt with a sense of pent up urgency that she had never heard before. 'I know it's tedious, but we have to get this right. I simply can't let you walk into danger.' In fact, Brandt was inwardly cursing the woman's inability to grasp a set of simple instructions. Impatiently, he kept repeating to himself, *I can't let her mess the whole thing up now. King shouldn't be too dangerous, but it would be much better to take him totally by surprise.*

Looking pale and drawn, Stevenson recited slowly by rote, 'I will approach the Bandstand from the direction of Dartmouth Park. My main task is to get Lazarus to position his back towards Highgate Ponds because, five minutes after me, you will approach from that direction. This will allow you to remain unseen and he'll not be scared off, before you get the chance to speak with him.'

Excitedly fingering the grip of his pistol, securely hidden in a deep pocket of his trench coat, Brandt replied, 'Excellent, honey. You've got it. Now, let's go see this Lazarus guy.'

***

Thankfully, the mist had not thickened as Renton and Bernstein gazed towards the solitary figure, leaning on the wrought iron railing of the Bandstand. The younger officer could sense the tension in the posture of his superior, thinking, *it wouldn't surprise me if the old man ordered us to rush him now*. He still had the uneasy feeling that there were aspects of the meeting which were unknown and his initial sight of Lazarus had disturbed him even more. *What the hell am I missing here?* he repeatedly asked himself.

At last, Stevenson gradually emerged from the mist and made her way slowly towards the Bandstand from the eastern edge of the heath. He heard a frustrated sigh from his Inspector, whose body slumped back from its alert state and silently gave thanks for the woman's timely appearance.

As he peered through the gloom towards London, King felt a surge of feeling for the embattled city, preparing itself to be revisited by the squadrons of Luftwaffe bombers which would surely come during the night. His thoughts were interrupted as he caught sight of Abigail Stevenson walking rather hesitantly, as if being pushed towards a meeting against her will. He raised a welcoming hand to her and, as she joined him in the Bandstand, he was disappointed to note her closed, almost furtive demeanour. 'Hello, Abigail,' he began warmly. 'It's good to see you again. But I must say that I'm intrigued by what it might be that you have to tell me.' Disturbed that she would not look him in the eye, he was surprised when, rather than replying, she moved carefully around the Bandstand. In order to continue speaking with her, he had to mirror her movement and was now facing away from the Ponds below. *What's she up to?* he wondered briefly.

Finally, she spoke in a voice hoarse with emotion, 'Thank you for agreeing to see me at such short notice Lazarus. And yes,' she added with a mixture of sadness and relief, 'There is something important that I wish to discuss with you.'

Stevenson's manoeuvre in the Bandstand meant that she was now standing with her back to the bushes which concealed the two Special Branch officers. King, on the other hand, was now directly facing them. 'Damn!' muttered Renton softly. 'Why the hell did she do that? For us, it's the worst possible position for the blasted German to adopt.'

The answer to the Inspector's question was soon evident, when a third figure approached the Bandstand quickly from the direction of the ponds. He was walking on the grass, rather than the gravel of the pathway, which softened considerably the noise of his rapid footsteps. 'Looks like our American friend is putting in an appearance, David,' whispered Renton excitedly. 'Keep your eyes and ears open. Things are sure to start happening now.'

King's entire attention was focused on Stevenson, as she prepared to unburden herself to him. He looked on with an understanding smile as she at last began her explanation. 'As you know, I've been loyal to Germany for over two years now and I've offered you a great deal of information. But now, Lazarus, I hope you can understand that things are different. The Nazi-Soviet Pact, the return of the wounded from France and now this terrible bombing of London and the other cities have made what I'm doing seem unjustifiable. I had my reasons for what I did and I don't regret anything. But, frankly, I don't see them as valid any longer.' The woman was sobbing openly now and King spontaneously moved across the Bandstand to offer her comfort. Just as he was passing her a handkerchief, he was shocked to hear an oddly familiar voice behind him. A voice speaking German.

'Hello, John. It's been a couple of years, hasn't it? I do hope that you don't mind if we speak German. I'd rather this stupid woman doesn't understand everything that we're saying.' Stunned by the use of his real name, King spun round, his eyes quickly taking in the gun pointing directly at him and a smiling Joachim Brandt. 'Who'd have thought John, all those years ago in Heidelberg and more recently in Berlin, when I swore that I'd have my revenge on you, that we'd meet again here, in the heart of London? But, of course, I forget my manners. Perhaps I should call you Lazarus? That seems to be your preferred name these days. I'm sure that you can imagine how much I've been looking forward to this moment, especially when I'd thought that your 'accident' in the Alps had denied me this pleasure. I suppose to call yourself Lazarus was some kind of pathetic joke?'

Before King could offer any reply, Stevenson, her face a picture of fear and betrayal, shouted. 'What's going on here? Joe, I don't understand. Why are you speaking in German and why do you have a gun?' A dreadful realisation dawning on her, she whispered 'Oh God! What have I done?' before fainting into King's arms.

'Always the British gentleman, eh John?' scoffed Brandt. 'You should have let the love-struck fool fall. It might have knocked some sense into her.'

'What the hell's going on?' hissed Renton, his normally calm face a mask of confusion and uncertainty. 'What are they saying?'

'I can't hear every word because of the distance,' replied Bernstein urgently. 'But the American is definitely speaking in German and he has Lazarus covered with a gun. Stevenson has fainted, so presumably she didn't expect that.' *But what the blazes is the American up to?* both Special Branch officers wondered simultaneously.

Bernstein was now absolutely certain that they didn't understand what was taking place and he whispered to his superior. 'I can't hear clearly from here. I'm going to crawl to the edge of the bushes to try to get a better picture.'

'I'm very tempted to go in now, David, but I'll give you five minutes. Then we move.'

Bernstein nodded grimly, before carefully crawling his way forward to the very edge of the bushes.

King had quickly realised that he was in a hopeless situation; his decision to catch the fainting Abigail Stevenson had eliminated any opportunity he might have had to tackle Brandt. Now, as she started to regain consciousness, he was defenceless and prepared himself for the worst. Much to the Englishman's surprise, however, Brandt did not immediately shoot him, but shook his head with a wistful smile, as if he had just realised something of great importance. 'You know, John,' he began pensively, 'right from that day in Heidelberg in '33 up to this last second, I really thought I hated you. I was absolutely convinced that I did. Because you always seemed so sure of who you are, where you belong and what you stand for. Did you never realise that all I wanted was your acceptance, both of me and the path I've taken? Would that really have been so difficult for you?'

King was suddenly transported back to a far simpler time, when he and the man now facing him with a gun had been the closest of friends. A great wave of sadness for lost fellowship and innocence broke over him as he softly admitted, 'I simply couldn't do it, Joachim. Not even for your friendship. We'd become opposites you see...'

Brandt interrupted eagerly, 'But that's just it, John! That's exactly what I've just this minute understood.' King looked uncertainly at the German, as he attempted to persuade his erstwhile friend of what he now saw as a self-evident truth. 'I've just realised that you and I are actually two sides of the same coin. Mirror images of one another. You could say even brothers.'

'I'm afraid I don't understand,' said King in genuine confusion, 'what do you mean?'

'Don't you see? It's obvious really. You are an Englishman pretending to be German. And I am a German pretending to be an American. Both of us are what we have been made into by such deceptions. And neither of us really knows who or what we are any more.'

***

As soon as he heard Lazarus address the American as Joachim, Bernstein's brow furrowed in concentration. *I thought there was something off about that reporter, but everything about him checked out*, he thought as he pummelled his memory. *And now that name. It must be significant, but how?* Infuriatingly, he still couldn't imagine a satisfactory answer to his own question.

***

King responded dismissively to his former friend's conviction that they were alike, 'You can't be serious! You've come to represent everything that I hate. How can you say such a ridiculous thing?'

Brandt again wrongfooted King with his sympathetic reply, 'Of course I understand that it's hard for you to accept, John. I felt exactly the same, until I realised just now that while we may have chosen opposite sides in this war, who we are as people and what we do in the name of our values and beliefs are very much the same. It's this that makes us brothers.'

Brandt's assertions disoriented King by reawakening his grave doubts about the moral justifiability of his actions as a spy, issues with which he had been grappling since the death of Albert Shaw. *Surely*, he reasoned desperately, *it can't be true? I must be better than him. It's not possible that we are in any way alike.*

The two men stared at one another in silence. One holding a gun and smiling benevolently, as if waiting for the other to catch up with his blinding insight and the other looking crestfallen and confused. In the key turning point in their encounter however, King's thoughts shifted away from a concern to refute Brandt's argument to the more basic goal of survival. He quickly calculated that the German's desire to convince him of his newly acquired opinion was almost certainly his only weapon. Surprised and appalled by the detachment and cynicism of his new reaction, King nevertheless began to consider how he might use Brandt's unexpected reflectiveness to turn the tables on him. *I've got to prolong the conversation, but I need to change its direction. Impose myself on him. Disturb him. Irritate him so much that he loses his composure and makes a mistake.* Recognising grimly that this, his only possible tactic, offered very little chance of success, King took a deep breath and asked, 'So tell me, Joachim, what are you doing here? I never had you cut out for a spy.'

'Well, that's where you're wrong,' replied the German smugly. 'I was sent here by the SS to find out if our networks could be revived.' Smiling, as if what he was about to say confirmed the truth of his analysis, Brandt continued, 'You see, John how alike we are. We are both masters of deception.'

Continuing to direct the conversation away from Brandt's desired topic of their similarity, King again interrupted quickly. 'And how did you get here, parachute, U-Boat?'

'Oh, come now, Herr Dr King. Surely you can imagine a more innovative approach? No? Well, I suppose that now we see the truth of our brotherhood, there is no harm in telling you. As it happens, for me, that was one of the most significant parts of the operation. Witnessing at first hand the utter chaos of your army's retreat to Dunkirk and having the opportunity to serve my country fully at a place called Le Paradis. What we did there will be the stuff of legend in The Thousand Year Reich.'

***

The fog of confusion began to disperse for Bernstein as soon as the journalist referred to Lazarus as 'Dr King'. The Special Branch officer's head began to pound and he felt a little nauseous, *Can it possibly be him? I used to know a John King, but he was killed in a mountain accident in '39.* Squinting through the mist and the fading light, Bernstein focused fully on the man he had pursued for months. *The hair colour's wrong and so is the moustache. And the spectacles are definitely not right. But now they have fallen off…..* Bernstein tried desperately to imagine the man with fairer hair and clean shaven. Within seconds, he recognised with a start that Lazarus was in fact John King. The man without whom, he, his sister and his parents would never have been able to leave Nazi Germany. Almost instantaneously, it also dawned on him that the 'American' was, in fact, the SS officer Joachim Brandt who had been John's friend back in Heidelberg. The hairs on the back of his neck also suggested to him that the missing airman three months ago in Dover had in fact been Brandt. *So, I was right about that bloody RAF man*, he realised. *It was Brandt, infiltrating Britain. But why is John acting as the German agent Lazarus? And why is Brandt pointing a gun at him?* Looking quickly at his watch, he saw with a start that his five minutes were almost up.

***

Alarmed by the tightening of Brandt's grip on his pistol, King desperately kept talking, 'And how did you get on to me, Joachim, I'd really like to know.'

To King's relief, the German seemed to relax and replied matter of factly, 'It wasn't so difficult. You just couldn't resist being the hero, could you?'

'Ah,' acknowledged King with a wistful smile, 'the photograph in the newspaper? That was just bad luck.'

'Of course you would say that, John. I prefer to see it as sentimental weakness.' Suddenly Brandt's face took on a more menacing expression. 'You know, maybe I was wrong. It seems we're not so alike after all. Maybe I should show you how real men deal with things.' Brandt once again primed his revolver and steadied his hand with the barrel pointing directly at King's head.

King sought one final time to deflect him by pleading, 'But wait, please, Joachim. You still haven't explained to me how you come to be here with Abigail?'

Brandt tilted his head to one side, as if balancing the strength of an argument, before smirking and replying, 'Yes, John. I think that you deserve to know that. After all, it will be the last thing that you ever learn.' Noticing that Stevenson had regained consciousness and was struggling to her feet, Brandt effortlessly switched to his American drawl. 'In fact, I had a very interesting conversation in

Berlin with Herr Rösel, whose networks you took over for the British.' Abigail's tear-filled eyes widened in shock as she took in the implications of this revelation. 'Yes, honey,' Brandt said, looking at her with utter contempt. 'You're so stupid that you've been giving information to the British for the last eighteen months.'

'So that's how you got the contacts here in Britain?' asked King, hoping desperately that Abigail Stevenson might even distract him just long enough. 'And I suppose you killed Martha Perrygo and the harmless old newsagent in Sevenoaks?'

'And proud to have done so,' replied Brandt with a conceited smile. 'But never fear. I have the details of all Martha's contacts safely in her little black book.'

***

Bernstein, having returned to his original position, frantically tried to explain to Renton, 'I know it's incredible, but I actually know both these men, sir. But I'm still not certain what's going on because I couldn't hear it all. The American is an SS officer called Joachim Brandt. I knew him in Germany before the war. And Lazarus is in fact an Englishman called John King. Everyone thought he'd been killed in an accident. I think we should both get closer so we can hear more of what's being said.'

Recognising the grim determination of his sergeant's expression, Renton didn't argue, but simply followed the younger man to the edge of the bushes. They arrived just in time to hear King's voice, bravely challenge Brandt. 'You may have the upper hand now, Joachim. But you must be as aware as I am that it's over for you here.' Encouraged by the first signs of doubt flickering across the German's face, King continued. 'The invasion, Joachim; Germany's one and only chance to deliver a quick knock-out blow to Britain. And guess what? You've fluffed it.'

'What do you mean?' demanded Brandt, waving his pistol furiously.

Gratified that he was at last getting under the German's skin, King continued calmly, 'If you don't already know, I can tell you that your troops are being withdrawn from the French coast. The Luftwaffe has failed to win air superiority and the invasion is off. Even someone as intellectually limited as yourself must have realised that the shift from attacking RAF fighter bases to this barbaric bombing of cities means that the invasion is not going to happen.'

'For the time being, perhaps, that may be true,' Brandt conceded hesitantly and King seized the opportunity to emphasise the point.

'Come on, Joachim. You say you were at Dunkirk. You saw how much equipment the British Army left there. If Germany was going to invade Britain successfully, it would have had to be now. By next year, our army will be re-supplied and we'll throw you back into the sea, if you try it.'

King's tactic had worked. Brandt was now beside himself with frustrated anger. *How dare this beaten Englishman act with such confidence? He even rejected my generous identification with him!*

Before King could launch an attack on the furious Brandt, Abigail Stevenson looked at the German and asked, sadly, 'So, it was all a lie, Joe? Or whatever your name is. You had no interest in me at all?'

This tipped Brandt even further out of control as he shouted, 'Of course not, you fool! And now, see what will happen to you very soon.' He raised his revolver, pointed it straight at King's heart and pulled the trigger. *It's strange,* Brandt thought calmly as he fired his pistol, *I could have sworn that I heard a shot just before mine....*

***

No one knew for certain what happened in those desperate split seconds around the Bandstand. Did Abigail Stevenson deliberately stand in front of John King? As soon as he had aimed and shot at Brandt, Bernstein struggled out of the bushes and rushed towards the wrought iron enclosure shouting, 'Special Branch! Stay where you are and put down your weapons!' Renton, surprised by his subordinate's sudden action, hurried after him towards the chaotic scene. The person he had known as the American journalist, Joe Brand, was face up on the ground, his head covered in blood and his eyes gazing sightlessly into the fading light of the evening sky. His face, so often sneering, now simply wore an expression of vague bewilderment, as if he couldn't quite work out how this had happened. On the other side of the Bandstand, Renton saw Lazarus, the German agent he had been pursuing for months, kneeling on the floor and cradling the head of Abigail Stevenson. It was immediately obvious, both that she had taken the bullet intended for him and that he was struggling in vain to staunch the rapid flow of blood from her chest as her life rapidly drained away.

Confused, Renton was only vaguely aware of Bernstein's urgent voice shouting, 'Sir, sir! You must go quickly for help. Get an ambulance. She's very badly wounded.' When the Inspector didn't immediately respond, the younger man shook him roughly by the shoulder and repeated his instructions.

'What's going on here, David? I don't understand.'

'There's no time for that now, sir,' the younger man replied urgently. 'We have to try to save Miss Stevenson. For God's sake go and get help! Here's my police whistle to alert the back-up. But it's an ambulance we need.' This seemed to bring Renton to his senses and, after giving several long blasts on the whistle, he stumbled off towards the entrance to the heath at Dartmouth Park.

King's anguished, blood streaked face looked up at Bernstein as the Special Branch man crouched down next to him. A faint hint of recognition flitted across his eyes, before he turned back to gaze forlornly at the deathly pale face of Abigail Stevenson. 'What happened? Why is she dead and not me?' King asked with a dull, defeated voice.

'She's not dead, John,' replied Bernstein calmly. 'We've sent for help. There's still hope.'

King looked sharply up at Bernstein, as he registered the use of his real name, recognition now in his eyes. 'And why did Joachim wait so long to shoot? He could've killed me at any time.'

'I don't know, John,' replied Bernstein shaking his head gently. 'I honestly have no idea. But it definitely saved your life and cost him his.'

King nodded, as if he had finally understood something important about both himself and his former friend. His confused attention was drawn back to the dying woman as she stirred in his arms and attempted to speak between coughing mouthfuls of blood. 'He... he called you John,' she said, looking weakly up at King. 'Why?'

'Because that's my name, Abigail,' replied King softly. 'I work for British Intelligence. He was a German agent. I am not.'

King could almost see the woman's brain processing this information, her eyes darting right to left in their sockets until, like the sun emerging briefly from behind the darkest grey clouds, a smile spread across her face. 'Then that means....'

She was unable to continue, her mouth again filling with blood. So King did all that he could for her. He finished her thought. 'Yes, that's right, Abby. You didn't betray your country. Nothing that you said to me ever went to help the Germans.' This seemed to take a huge weight off the young woman's shoulders and she relaxed into King's arms as if she no longer saw any reason to cling on to life. 'Hold on, Abigail,' King said desperately. 'We've sent for help. Don't talk now. You'll be fine. We'll all be fine now.'

It was obvious to Bernstein that the woman's wound was fatal and he muttered a silent prayer of his old religion as she smiled at King, nodded her head slowly and mouthed the words 'Thank you'. As the first wailing sounds of the air raid sirens began, Abigail Stevenson slipped quietly away from life.

CHAPTER THIRTY SIX

Monday 7th October 1940, St John's Wood, London.

The daylight had been failing for about an hour when Professor Bernard Pym reluctantly drew the heavy blackout curtains of his mansion block flat and relied once more on electric lighting. He often did his most creative thinking as the day faded and he sat, in increasing gloom, gazing out of the window which overlooked Lord's cricket ground. Despite its necessary use, both as a local fire station and a reception centre for RAF crew, some cricket was still played at the famous old ground and Pym found it a vital backdrop to aid his concentration. *Helps me remember what we're all fighting for, I suppose,* he pondered as he awaited his guest.

In truth Pym was not looking forward to his meeting with Inspector Renton of the Special Branch. After the dust had settled on the events on Hampstead Heath, Renton had been rightly furious at the way in which his service had been kept in the dark about the Lazarus operation. And from what Pym had been told, while his raw anger had begun to subside, he was still far from happy. The appointment was intended by Pym as a kind of bridge building exercise and he was steeling himself to take whatever Renton threw at him. *After the storm has blown itself out, I'll tell him as much as I dare about the operation. Hopefully that will calm him down a bit. Oh well,* he concluded as his intercom began to buzz, *it sounds like he's here. I suppose I'm about to find out if I'm right.*

Having been instructed where to go by the mansion block concierge, Renton arrived to find Pym's door open and the Professor extending a hand in greeting. 'Glad you could come, Renton. Please, come inside and let's make ourselves comfortable.' When the Special Branch man accepted Pym's offer of a single malt, he began to entertain hopes that the meeting might not after all descend into a confrontation. Renton, however, soon disabused him of such notions. No sooner had he taken an appreciative sip of the spirit, than he launched into a tirade. 'I'm grateful that you've finally come out of hiding and recognised that you have to face the music, Pym. But that's as far as my gratitude extends. What the hell did you think you were playing at? Keeping the Branch in the dark about King? Have you any idea how many valuable man hours were wasted in pursuit of one of our own men? One of our own fucking men! You couldn't make it up! And if my sergeant hadn't been on the ball, your precious agent would have been history, wouldn't he? A bloody shambles I call it. Don't you?'

Pym had been listening quietly, nodding his head occasionally while he twirled his whisky glass in his hand. 'I don't wish to argue with any of the points you make, Renton,' he began calmly. 'You have every justification for being furious and it is entirely appropriate that your anger is directed towards me. I can only apologise and assure you that it was a necessary deception to give the operation its best chance of success.'

'What the hell do you mean? Are you implying that we're not to be trusted? If you are,' fumed Renton as he began to rise menacingly from his armchair, 'you bastard, I'll damn well...'

Pym held up a conciliatory arm, 'No, I'm not saying anything of the sort, Renton. But you should know that 'C' believes that there are worrying leaks in the security services. Not in Special Branch, I hasten to add, but in our own backyard.'

'What the hell's that got to do with the Branch?' demanded Renton 'It doesn't justify cutting us out.'

'Don't you see, man? Everybody had to be excluded. We had to take the operation completely 'off the books' right from the start. That's why we couldn't use an experienced agent and had to rely on someone unknown like John King. Do you honestly think I'd have done that, had there been an alternative? It was the very fact that Special Branch, entirely appropriately, works closely with the security services, that meant we just couldn't take the chance of letting you in on it. I'm really sorry, but surely you see that?'

Pym only realised how seriously Renton was taking his explanation when, after taking another sip of whisky, he unexpectedly changed tack. 'Can you believe it, Pym? My sergeant actually blames himself for the fiasco on Hampstead Heath. He thinks he should have recognised that Jerry when he was trying to get into the country through Dover. He's absolutely convinced that he saw him and, while he didn't recognise him, he knew there was something queer going on.'

'Well, I hope you told him that that's ridiculous,' replied Pym firmly. 'Firstly, there's no evidence, other than Brandt's absurd claim on Hampstead Heath, that he entered Britain in that manner.' Encouraged by Renton's firm nod, Pym went on to dissemble, 'It's clear the Jerry was just trying to destabilise King. I don't believe that there's a shred of truth in it. And that's what will be in the official report.'

Renton nodded in recognition of Pym's gesture towards his junior officer, 'That's generous of you, Pym,' he admitted. 'Damned generous. I'm not sure it will mean much to Sergeant Bernstein now, but he'll come round in time. And it does mean a lot to me. But, blast it all, what was so bloody special about this operation? After all, we collaborate and exchange information routinely with the other services.'

Pym was quickly coming to the conclusion that Renton was basically a good man and a sound officer and decided that he should go even further than he'd planned. 'Look, Renton,' he continued, 'I cannot disagree that there were aspects of the operation that were far from satisfactory. And I hope you will accept that we have learned valuable lessons. But,' he emphasised, 'let's not lose sight of the fact that it did achieve its principal objectives. We learned a lot which will help us develop our operations against Nazi informers here in Britain.'

'What do you mean? You're not sending King back into the field are you? The young chap looked just about done in a fortnight ago.'

'No, Renton, nothing like that. It's true that John paid a very heavy price for his involvement. And both he and I must live with that. Thankfully he is recovering well at his parents' home in Gloucestershire.'

'He doesn't still blame himself for the woman's death, does he? Because that's just as daft as my sergeant's potty idea.'

Pym shrugged his shoulders sadly, 'Unfortunately, he still bears the scars from that, yes. But his father has told me that he is getting brighter every day and has even begun to talk about getting back into action.'

'Surely it's too soon?'

'Yes, of course it is,' conceded Pym. 'But, you know, the invasion might have been postponed for now, but we shouldn't fool ourselves. We've still got our backs right up tight against the wall and we'll need every single Briton to do his or her duty in the coming months and years. Look,' he added as he refilled their glasses, 'I do want to explain why this mission was so different. It actually was always intended as a kind of test, a trial run, if you like.'

'How do you mean?'

'Once it was clear that the Lazarus mission was working well and we'd effectively prevented the informers from sending information back to Berlin, we deployed numerous operatives across the country who are now engaged in similar activities. We really think that we have these 'Fifth Columnists' well in hand now. So, you see, it wasn't just the Lazarus mission that could have been at risk from a leak. Our whole strategy to deal with these traitorous types could have been compromised, or even derailed before it got properly on track.'

'Yes,' agreed Renton, 'I can see your argument. But, if King is at least temporarily out of the picture, what will happen to his networks?'

'That's an interesting question, Renton. In point of fact, we have selected another agent, Eric Roberts. He's an interesting type, a bank clerk believe it or not, who is getting ready to pose as a German agent and infiltrate Nazi sympathising groups in Britain, including the remnants of John's informers. Now this Roberts is much more experienced than King; he did a similar job for MI5 in the thirties, first with communist and then with fascist groups. All in all we have very high hopes both for 'Agent Jack,' as he'll be known, and all our other agents.'

Author's Note

The inspiration to write Codename Lazarus came from reading several newspaper accounts of Eric Roberts, also known as Jack King. In February 2014, National Archive files on this singular character had just been released and the British press ran short accounts of his activities during the war. Extensive documentation on the so called 'Fifth Column' or 'SR' case was also accessed at the National Archive.

The incredible story of Eric Roberts really caught my imagination and I decided very quickly that it would make a great background subject for a novel. As this note makes clear, I definitely did not produce anything like a factual account of Jack King's exploits, but I hope that, in imagining a forerunner of the incredibly successful real agent, I paid some respect to his actual bravery and achievements.

What follows is some basic information both about the real Eric Roberts/Jack King, on whose exploits, those of the fictional character John King were very loosely based, and about some of the perhaps lesser known real events and people depicted in the novel.

A father of three, living an ordinary family life in Surrey and working as a clerk at the Euston Road branch of the Westminster Bank in Central London, Eric Roberts was hardly the stuff of secret agents, in the mould of James Bond. Indeed, his employers were shocked to receive an official request for his release, in order to undertake work of national importance.

Despite having no great knowledge of German, by the end of the war Eric Roberts had successfully posed as an undercover Gestapo officer and effectively neutralised literally hundreds of Nazi sympathisers in the UK.

Alarmed by the evident extent of sympathy for Nazi Germany among Britons in the early years of the war, the Security Services initially sent Roberts, posing as Jack King, to ascertain the extent of Nazi sentiment among the workers at Siemens UK. The scope and effectiveness of his mission increased beyond all expectation, however, after he met and cultivated Marita Perigoe, on whom the fictional character Martha Perrygo is very loosely based.

The files now released to the public make it absolutely clear that King was extremely successful in controlling large groups of potentially dangerous fifth columnists throughout the war. These people believed they were providing information of great significance to the Nazis, when in fact it was all going direct to MI5. For those readers who would like to know more about Eric Roberts, Robert Hutton's 'Agent Jack: the true story of MI5's secret Nazi hunter (2018), published after Codename Lazarus first appeared, is excellent.

Codename Lazarus also refers to many real events, such as Kristallnacht, the retreat to and evacuation from Dunkirk, the first daytime bombing raid over London and the so called Kindertransport arrangement. I tried to keep the dates and descriptions as accurate as possible. Also, historical characters, such as Goering, Heydrich and Canaris make brief appearances.

The book also features lesser known, real people and dramatic events.

The massacre at Le Paradis on 27th May 1940, which is described in the book, actually took place as described. Some 97 British troops, having surrendered, were disarmed, lined up against a wall and shot. The man responsible for ordering the atrocity, SS Hauptsturmführer Fritz Knöchlein, was eventually located and convicted by a war crimes court. He was executed in 1949.

Walter Schellenberg was responsible for editing a detailed analysis of how Britain functioned in preparation for Operation Sealion - the planned Nazi invasion of Britain in 1940.

Thank you for reading this book and I hope you have enjoyed it. Please take the time to leave a rating or a review, these are extremely important to self-published authors.

I am always very happy to hear directly from readers and, if you wish to contact me, this is possible via my website at apmartin.co.uk. In the meantime I would like to wish you happy and enjoyable reading!

Printed in Great Britain
by Amazon